A Bird Of Passage

by

B. M. Croker

Double9
BOOKS

A Bird of Passage
by B. M. Croker

ISBN: 978-93-64288-61-3

Published by

DOUBLE 9 BOOKS
2/13-B, Ansari Road
Daryaganj, New Delhi – 110002
info@double9books.com
www.double9books.com
Tel. 011-40042856

ABOUT THE AUTHOR

Bithia Born on November 6, 1849, Mary Croker, sometimes known as B. M. Croker, was a British author who died on October 20, 1920. During the late 19th and early 20th centuries, she was a well-known and prolific writer who was well-known for her captivating novels and short stories. Croker lived a significant portion of her life in India, where her husband was a British Army soldier. Her experiences there had a profound effect on her work. Her paintings frequently portrayed the life of British expatriates in India, providing realistic depictions of the people, customs, and natural surroundings of the area. Croker's writing was distinguished by its intricate character development, captivating narratives, and vivid descriptions.

CONTENTS

CHAPTER I
PORT BLAIR

"Droops the heavy-blossom'd bower; hangs the heavy-
fruited tree:
Summer isles of Eden lying in dark purple spheres of sea."

Locksley Hall.

Few travellers penetrate to the Andamans, unless it be an enthusiastic
astronomer to witness a rare comet, or an enterprising professor, who
happens to be fired with a desire to study the language and the skulls of
the aborigines.

These islands are as yet sacred from the foot of the globe-trotter, Cook's
tourists ignore them, and they lie in serene semi-savage seclusion, in the
midst of the Indian Ocean, dimly known to the great outer world as the
chief Indian convict settlement, and the scene of Lord Mayo's murder in
1872. The inland portions of the great and lesser Andamans have been but
cursorily explored, (those who have made the attempt, having learnt by
tragic experience that the inhabitants were addicted to cannibalism); but
outlying islets, and fringes of the coast, have been opened up by the Indian
Government, and appropriated for the benefit of thousands of convicts
(chiefly lifers), who are annually poured into Port Blair—from Galle to the
Kyber, from Aden to the borders of China, the cry is still they come!

Port Blair, the Government headquarters, is situated on Ross, a high
conical islet that lies about a mile south of the Middle Andaman, and
although of limited circumference, it boasts a stone church, barracks, a
Commandant's residence, several gaols, a pier, a bazaar, a circulating library,
and a brass band! Every foot of ground is laid out to marvellous advantage,
and the neat gravelled pathways, thick tropical hedges, flowering shrubs

and foliage plants, give the numerous brown bungalows which cover the hillsides, the effect of being situated in a large and well-kept garden.

The summit of the island commands a wide view: to the north lies the mainland with its sharply indented shores, and a wide sickle-shaped estuary, sweeping far away into the interior, where its wooded curves are lost among the hills; the southern side of Ross looks sheer out upon the boundless ocean, and receives the full force of many a terrible tropical hurricane, that has travelled unspent from the Equator.

There was not a ripple on that vast blue surface, one certain August evening, a few years ago—save where it fretted gently in and out, between the jagged black rocks that surrounded the island; the sea was like a mirror, and threw back an accurate reflection of boats, and hills, and wooded shores; distant, seldom-seen islands, now loomed in the horizon with vague, misty outlines; a delicate, soft, south wind barely touched the leaves of the big trees, among whose branches the busy green parrots had been chattering, and the gorgeous peacocks, screeching and swinging, all through the long, hot, sleepy afternoon.

Surely the setting sun was making a more lingering and, as it were, regretful adieu to these beautiful remote islands than to other parts of the world! No pen could describe, no brush convey, any idea of the vivid crimson, western clouds, and the flood of blinding golden light, that bathed the hills, the far-away islets, the tangled mangroves, and the glassy sea.

To the cool dispassionate northern eye, which may have first opened on a leaden sky, snow-capped hills, pine woods, and ploughed lands, there was a general impression of wildly gaudy, south sea scenery, of savage silence, and lawless solitude.

Soon that scarlet ball will have plunged below the horizon, a short-lived grey twilight have spread her veil over land and sea, the parrots' noisy pink bills will be tucked under their wings, and the turbulent peacocks have gone to roost.

Close to the flagstaff (which was planted on a kind of large, flat mound, at the highest point of the island), one human figure stood out in bold relief against the brilliant sunset; an elderly gentleman with grizzled hair and beard, a careworn expression, and mild, brown eyes,—eyes that were anxiously riveted on the at present sailless sea. He carried a small red telescope in his hand, and divided his time between pacing the short grass plateau, and spasmodically sweeping the horizon. For what was he looking so impatiently? He was looking for the smoke of the Calcutta steamer, that brought mails and passengers to Port Blair once in every six weeks. Think of but one mail in six weeks, ye sybarites of Pall Mall, revelling in a dozen daily posts, scores of papers, and all the latest telegrams from China to Peru! Imagine reading up forty days' arrears of your *Times* or *Post*; imagine six *Punches* simultaneously! Gladly as Colonel Denis usually hailed his letters, and especially the *Weekly Gazette*, yet it was neither news nor promotion that he was so restlessly awaiting now—his thoughts were altogether centred on a passenger, his only daughter, whom he had not seen for thirteen years, not since she was a little mite in socks and sashes, and now she was a grown-up, a finished young lady, coming out from England by this mail to be the mistress of his house! He was glad that this long anticipated day had dawned at last, and yet he scarcely dared to analyze his own feelings—he was ashamed to own, even in his inmost heart, that mingled with all his felicity, there is a secret dread—a kind of stifled misgiving. This girl who is to share his home within the next few hours, is in reality, as far as personal acquaintance goes, as much a stranger to him as if he had never seen her before, although she is his own little Nell, with whom he used to romp by the hour in the verandah at Karkipore, thirteen years ago. Those thirteen years stand between him and that familiar merry face, dancing gait, and floating yellow hair; they have taken that away, and what are they going to give him instead? Of course he and his daughter had corresponded by every mail, but what are nice affectionate letters, what are presents, yea photographs, when the individuality of the giver has long been blurred and indistinct; when the memory of a face, and the sound of a voice, have faded and faded, till nothing tangible remains but a name! Children of five years old have but short memories, and in Helen Denis's case, there was no one near her to revive her dying recollections.

"I wonder if she will know me among the crowd," her father muttered as he paced the platform, with the telescope behind his back.

"I'm sorry now, I never had my photo taken, to prepare her! How strange I shall feel with a girl in the house, after all these years. I've quite forgotten woman's ways!" From an expression that came into his eyes, one might gather that a backward glance at "woman's ways" was not altogether one of the most agreeable memories of the past. "If she should be like—" and he paused, shuddered, and looked out over the sea for some minutes, with a face that had grown suddenly stern. His thoughts were abruptly recalled to the present, by the sound of footsteps coming up the gravel pathway behind him.

"Hullo, colonel!" cried a loud, cheery voice, "why are you doing sentry here? Oh! of course, I forget; you expect Miss Denis this mail!"

"Yes. I'm looking out for the steamer," he replied, as he turned round and accosted a very handsome young man, with aquiline features, brilliant teeth, and eyes as blue as the surrounding sea. A tall young man, carefully dressed in a creaseless light suit, who wore a pale silk tie run through a ring, gloves, and carried a large white umbrella. He had an adequate appreciation of his own appearance, and with good reason, for men frequently referred to him as "the best-looking fellow of their acquaintance," and women— well—women spoiled him, they had petted him and made much of him, since he was a pretty little curly-headed cherub, with a discriminating taste in sweets, and a rooted objection to kissing old and ugly people, down to the present time, when he (although you would not think it) had passed his thirty-second birthday! He had been sent to Port Blair in connection with some new works on the mainland, and was "acting" for another man, who had gone on furlough. His name was James—variously known as "Beauty," "Apollo," or "Look and Die"—Quentin, and he was really less conceited than might have been expected under the circumstances! Mr. Quentin was not alone; his companion was a shorter, slighter, and altogether more insignificant person, dark as an Arab, through exposure to the sun; he wore a broad-leafed, weather-beaten Terai, pulled so far over his brows that one could only guess at a pair of piercing eyes, a thin visage, and a black moustache; his clothes were by no means new, his hands burnt to a rich mahogany, and innocent of gloves, ring, or umbrella.

Somehow, with his slouched hat, slender figure, and swarthy skin, he had rather a foreign air, and was a complete contrast to his broad-shouldered patron, "Look and Die" Quentin, whom he followed slowly up the hill, and muttering an indistinct greeting to Colonel Denis, he walked on a few paces, and stood with his arms folded, looking down upon the sea somewhat in the attitude of the well-known picture of Napoleon at St. Helena! This sunburnt, silent individual was known by the name of "the Photographer;" he was a mysterious stranger, who three months previously had dropped into the settlement—but *not* into society—as if from the clouds, and during these three months, the united ingenuity of the community had failed to discover anything more about him, than what they had learned the very first day he had landed on Ross; to wit, that his name was Lisle, and that he had come from Calcutta to take photographs among the islands. Immediately after his arrival, he had established himself in the Dâk Bungalow, on Aberdeen, had hired a boat, and in a very short time had made himself completely at home; his belongings consisted of a small quantity of luggage, a large camera, some fishing-tackle, and a native servant, who refused to elucidate any one on the subject of his master, and the public were very inquisitive about that gentleman,—and who shall say that their curiosity was not legitimate!

People never came to Ross, unless they were convicts, settlement officers, formed part of the garrison, or were functionaries like Mr. Quentin, who was "acting" for some one else. Mr. Lisle did not come under any of these heads; he was not an officer, Hindoo or otherwise, he did not belong to the settlement, nor was he one of the class for whose special behoof the islands had been colonized. The problem still remained unsolved, who was Mr. Lisle, what was he doing at Port Blair, where did he come from, when, and where, was he going, was he rich or poor, married or single? All these queries still remained unsolved, and opened up a fine field of speculation. Society, so isolated from the outer world, so meagrely supplied with legitimate news, were naturally thrown a good deal upon their own resources for topics of conversation and discussion. A week after mail-day, most of the papers had been read and digested, and people had to fall back upon little items of local intelligence—and such items were wont to be scarce: think, then, what a godsend for conjecture and discussion Mr. Lisle would, and did prove! this waif blown to them from beyond the sea, without address or reference! If he had been a common-looking, uneducated person, it would have been totally different; but the aggravating thing was, that shabby as were his clothes, he had the unmistakable bearing and address of a gentleman,—yet he spent all his days photographing natives, trees, islands, as if his daily bread solely depended on his industry! He lived not far from where Mr. Quentin dwelt, in a splendid bungalow, in solitary state; and the former, constantly meeting the photographer, had scraped up an acquaintance with him, had dropped in and smoked friendly cigarettes in the Rest House verandah, had thrown out feelers in vain—in vain!—had come to the conclusion that Lisle was a very gentlemanly fellow in his way,—that he was no fool, that he was a most entertaining companion, and wound up by insisting that he should come and share his roof!

A Bird Of Passage | 13

To this Lisle objected, in fact he refused the invitation point-blank, but when he learned that the Rest Bungalow was requisitioned for some missionaries, and when his would-be host became the more pressing, the more he was reluctant, he gave in, after considerable hesitation.

"You see, it's not a purely unselfish idea," said Mr. Quentin; "I'm awfully lonely at this side—not a soul to speak to, unless I go to Ross, and I'm often too lazy to stir, and now I shall have you to argue with, and to keep me company of an evening. Then, as to your photographs, there's lots of room for them. You can have a whole side of the house to yourself, and do as you please."

"I'll come on one condition," replied the other, looking straight at him; "I'll come, if you will allow me to pay my share of the butler's account, and all that sort of thing. We are speaking quite frankly—you require some one to talk to, I want a roof, since you say the missionaries are coming to the Rest House,—and I doubt if we would assimilate!"

Mr. Quentin, who had been lounging in a low cane chair, took his cigar out of his mouth, blew a cloud of smoke, and hesitated; it was all very well to have this chap up to keep him company of an evening, but to chum with him—by Jove!

The other seemed to read what was passing through his mind, for he said, with a twinkle in his eye,—

"I'm not a fellow travelling for a firm of photographers, as no doubt every one imagines. I'm"—pushing an envelope over to his companion—"that's my name."

Mr. Quentin took up the paper carelessly, cast his eye over it, became rather red, and laughed nervously. From this time forward, Mr. Lisle and Mr. Quentin chummed together on equal terms,—somewhat to the scandal of their neighbours, who were amazed that such a fastidious man as "Look and Die" Quentin should open his house, and his arms, to this unknown shabby stranger! His manners were studiously courteous and polite, but he understood how to entrench himself in a fortress of reserve, that held even Mrs. Creery, the chief lady of Port Blair, at bay, and this was saying much— driven very hard, two damaging statements had been, as it were, wrested from him! he liked the Andamans, because there was no daily post, and no telegrams, and he had no occupation *now*. Did not admission number one savour of a dread of suggestive-looking blue envelopes, and clamouring, hungry creditors—to whom he had effectively given the slip; and admission number two was worse still! no occupation now, was doubtless the result of social and financial bankruptcy. Mrs. Creery was disposed to deal hardly with him—in her opinion, he was an "outlaw." (She rather prided herself upon having fitted him neatly with a name.) If he had thrown her one sop of conciliation, or given her the least little hint about himself and his affairs, she *might* have tolerated him, but he remained perversely dumb. Mr. Quentin was dumb too—though it was shrewdly suspected that he knew more about his inmate than any one—and indeed he had gone so far as to deny that he was a professional photographer; when rigidly cross-examined by a certain lady, he only laughed, and shook his head, and said that "Lisle was a harmless lunatic—rather mad on the subject of photography and sea-fishing, but otherwise a pleasant companion;" but beyond this, he declined to enlighten his questioner. No assistance being forthcoming, society was obliged to classify the stranger for themselves, and they ticketed him as a genteel loafer, a penniless ne'er-do-well, who had come down to Port Blair in hopes (vain) of obtaining some kind of employment, and had now comfortably established himself as Mr. Quentin's hanger-on and unpaid companion!

It must be admitted that the stranger gave considerable colour to this view; he did not visit and mix with society on Ross, he wore shabby clothes and shocking hats, and spent most of his time tramping the bush with a gun on his shoulder or a camera on his back, "looking for all the world like an Italian organ-grinder or a brigand," according to that high authority, Mrs. Creery. For three months he had been without a competitor in the interest of the community, but now his day was over, his star on the wane: he was about to give place to a very rare and important new arrival, namely, an unmarried lady, who was currently reported to be "but eighteen years of age and very pretty!"

CHAPTER II
EXPECTATION

"For now sits expectation in the air,

And hides a sword."

—*Henry V.*

All this time Colonel Denis had been engaged in animated conversation with Mr. Quentin. Nature had been doubly generous to the latter gentleman, for she had not merely endowed him with unusual personal attractions, but had increased these attractions by the gift of a charming manner that fascinated every one who came in contact with him—from the General himself down to the sullen convict boatmen; it was quite natural to him, even when discussing a trivial subject, with an individual who rather bored him than otherwise, to throw such an appearance of interest into his words and looks that one would imagine all his thoughts were centred in the person before him and the topic under discussion.

To men this attitude was flattering, to women irresistible, and what though his words were writ on sand, his manner had its effect, and was an even more powerful factor in his great popularity than his stalwart figure and handsome face. At the present moment he stood leaning on his furled umbrella, listening with rapt attention to what Colonel Denis had to say on the subject of whale-boats *versus* gigs (every one at Ross kept a boat of their own, like the O'Tooles at the time of the Flood). The Colonel was enlarging on the capabilities of his new purchase—bought expressly in honour of his daughter, as he would have bought a carriage elsewhere—when he was interrupted by Mr. Lisle (who meanwhile had been keeping watch on the horizon and whistling snatches of the overture to "Mirella" under his breath), abruptly announcing, "Here she is!"

Colonel Denis was so startled that he actually dropped the telescope, which rolled to his informant's feet, who, picking it up, noticed as he returned it that Colonel Denis was looking strangely nervous, and that the hand stretched towards him was shaking visibly. He gazed at him with considerable surprise, and was about to make some remark, when Mr. Quentin exclaimed in a tone of genuine alarm, —

"By George! here is Mrs. Creery. I see the top of her topee coming up the hill, and I'm going."

But he reckoned without that good lady, who had already cut off his retreat. In another moment her round florid face appeared below the topee, followed by her ample person, clad in a sulphur-colour sateen costume, garnished with green ribbons; last, but not least, came her fat yellow-and-white dog, "Nip," an animal that she called "a darling," "a treasure," "a duck," and "a fox-terrier," but no other person in the settlement recognized him by any of these titles. Before she was within twenty yards, she called out in a thin, authoritative treble, —

"Well, what are you all doing here? what is it, eh? Any news? You need not be looking for the *Scotia*; she can't possibly be in till to-morrow, you know — I told you so, Colonel Denis. Oh," in answer to a silent gesture from Mr. Lisle, "so She *is* coming in, is she?" in a tone that gave her listeners to understand that she had no business to be there, contradicting Mrs. Creery.

"And so you have been up playing tennis at the General's," to Mr. Quentin. "I saw your peon going by with your bat and shoes; but what has brought *you* over to Ross, Mr. Lisle — I thought you rarely left the mainland?" fastening on him now for that especial reason.

"I don't often come over," he replied, parrying the question.

"You've been shopping in the bazaar," she continued; "you have been buying collars."

"Mrs. Creery is unanswerable — she is gifted with 'second sight.'" (All the same it was not collars, but cartridges, that he had purchased.)

"Not she!" returned the lady with a laugh, "but she has eyes in her head, and that's a collar-box in your hand! I can tell most things by the shape of the parcel. Still as charmed as ever with Aberdeen?"

Mr. Lisle bowed.

"I heard that you were going away?"

"So I am —" he paused, and then added, "some day."

"What do you do with all your photographs — sell them? Oh, but to be sure you can't do that here. You must find the chemicals terribly costly."

"They are rather expensive."

"I'll tell you what, I will give you a little commission! How would you like to come over some morning and take me and Nip, and then the bungalow, and then a group of our servants?"

If Mr. Lisle's face was any index of his mind, it said plainly that he would not relish the prospect at all.

"I want to send home some photos to my sister, Lady Grubb. Of course I shall pay you—that's understood."

During this conversation, Colonel Denis looked miserably uncomfortable, and Mr. Quentin as if it was with painful difficulty that he restrained his laughter; the travelling photographer alone was unmoved; he surveyed his patroness gravely, as if he were taking a mental plate of her topee with its purple puggaree, her little eager light eyes, her important nose and ruddy cheeks, and then replied in a most deferential manner,—

"Thank you very much for your kind offer, but I am not a professional photographer."

Was Mrs. Creery crushed? Not at all, she merely raised her light eyebrows and said,—

"Oh, not a professional photographer! Then what *are* you?"

"Mrs. Creery's very humble slave," bowing profoundly.

"Photographs are rather a sore subject with him just now," broke in Mr. Quentin in his loud, hearty voice. "You have not heard what happened to him yesterday when he was out shooting?"

"No; how should I?" she retorted peevishly.

"Well, I must say he bore it like a stoic. I myself, mild as I am, and sweet as you know my temper to be, would have killed the fellow."

"What fellow?"

"My new chokra. Time hung heavily on his hands, and I suppose he thought he would be doing something really useful for once in his life, so he went into the room where Lisle keeps all his precious plates—photographic plates, not even printed off—plates he has collected and treasured like so many diamonds—"

"Well, well, well?" tapping her foot.

"My dear lady, I'm coming to it if you won't hurry me. My confounded chokra took them all for so much DIRTY GLASS, and washed every man Jack of them, and was exceedingly proud of his industry!"

"And what did you do to him?" demanded Mrs. Creery, turning round and staring at the victim of ignorance.

"Nothing—what could I do? he knew no better; but I told my fellow not to let him come near me for a few days."

"Colonel Denis," said the lady, now addressing him, "is it true that you have not seen your daughter for thirteen years?"

"Yes, quite true, I am sorry to say."

"Why did you not go home on furlough?"

"I never could manage it. When I could get home I had no money, and when money was plentiful, there was no leave."

"Ah, and you told me she was a pretty girl, I believe; I hope you are not building on *that*, for pretty children are a delusion; I never yet saw one of them that did not grow up plain."

"Excepting *me*, Mrs. Creery," expostulated Mr. Quentin; "if history is to be believed, I was a most beautiful infant—so beautiful that people came to see me for miles and miles around, and (insinuatingly) I'm sure you would not call me plain now?"

Mrs. Creery (who had a secret partiality for this gentleman) laughed incredulously, and then replied, "Well, perhaps you are the exception that proves the rule. Of course," once more addressing Colonel Denis, "your daughter will bring out all the new fashions, and have no end of pretty things—that is if you have given her a liberal outfit."

She here paused for a reply, but no answer being forthcoming went on, "If you feel at all nervous about meeting her, I'll go on board with you with pleasure; I should *like* it, and you are well enough acquainted with me to know that you have only to say the word!"

At this suggestion, the eyes of the two bystanders met, and exchanged a significant glance, and whilst Colonel Denis was stammering forth his thanks and excuses, they hastily took leave of Mrs. Creery and made their escape.

"The steamer is coming in very fast, and I think I'll go home and see that everything is ready," said the Colonel after a pause.

"Well, perhaps it would be as well," acceded the lady; "but are you really certain you would not like me to meet her, or, at any rate, to be at your bungalow to receive her?"

A Bird Of Passage | 19

Once more her companion politely but firmly declined her good offices, assuring her earnestly that they were quite unnecessary, and the lady, visibly disappointed, said as she shouldered her parasol and turned away, "Perhaps you will have your journey for nothing! I should not be the least surprised if she did not come by this steamer after all! and mark my words, that ayah—that Fatima—that you would engage in spite of my advice, will give you trouble *yet!*"

Colonel Denis, nothing daunted, hurried down to his own bungalow, a large one facing the mainland, entirely surrounded by a deep verandah, and approached by a pathway hedged with yellow heliotrope. A good many preparations had been made for the expected young mistress; there were flowers everywhere in profusion, curious tropical ones, berries, and orchids, and ferns.

The lamps were lit in the sitting-rooms, and everything was extremely neat, and yet there was a want; there was a bare gaunt look about the drawing-room, although it had been lately furnished and Ram Sawmy, the butler of twenty years' standing, had disposed the chairs and tables in the most approved fashion—in his eyes—and put up coloured purdahs and white curtains, all for "Missy Baba." Nevertheless, the general effect was grim and comfortless. There were no nick-nacks, books, or chair-backs: there certainly were a few coarse white antimacassars, but these were gracefully arranged, according to Sawmy's taste, as coverings for the smaller tables! Colonel Denis looked about him discontentedly, moved a chair here, a vase there, then happening to catch a glimpse of himself in a mirror, he went up to it and anxiously confronted his own reflection. How wrinkled and grey he looked! he might be fifteen years older than his real age. After a few seconds he took up and opened a small album, and critically scanned a faded photograph of a gentleman in a long frock-coat, with corresponding whiskers, leaning over a balustrade, his hat and gloves carelessly disposed at his elbow—a portrait of himself taken many years previously.

"There is no use in my thinking that it's the least like me *now*; she could not know me again—no more than I would know her—" then closing the book with a snap, and suddenly raising his voice, he called out: "Here, Sawmy, see that dinner is ready in half an hour and have the ayah waiting. I'm going for missy."

Doubtless dinner and the ayah had a long time to wait, for it was fully an hour before the *Scotia* dropped anchor off Ross; she was immediately surrounded by a swarm of boats, including that of Colonel Denis, who boarded her, and descended among the crowd to the cabin, with his heart beating unusually fast.

The cabin lamps were lit, and somewhat dazzled the eyes of those who entered from the moonlight. There were but few passengers, and the most noticeable of these was Helen Denis, who sat alone at the end of a narrow table, with a bag on her lap, the inevitable waterproof over her arm, and her gaze fixed anxiously on the door leading from the companion ladder. Colonel Denis would not be disappointed; his daughter *had* fulfilled the promise of her youth, and was a very pretty girl. She was slight and fair, with regular features and quantities of light brown hair—hair that twenty years ago was called fair, before golden and canary-coloured locks came to put it out of fashion. Her eyes were grey—or blue—colour rather uncertain; but one thing was beyond all dispute, they were beautiful eyes! As for her complexion, it was extremely pale at present, and her very lips were white; but this was due to her agitation, to her awe and wonder and fear, to her anxiety to know *which* of the many strange faces that came crowding into the cabin was the one that would welcome her, and be familiar to her, and dear to her as long as she lived? She sat quite still, with throbbing heart, surveying each new-comer with anxious expectation. As Colonel Denis entered she half rose, and looked at him appealingly.

"You are Helen?" he said in answer to her glance.

"Oh, father," she exclaimed tremulously, now putting down the bag and stretching out her hands, "how glad I am that you are *you!*—it sounds nonsense, I know, but I was half afraid that I had forgotten your face. You know," apologetically, "I was such a very little thing, and that man over there, with the hooked nose, stared at me so hard, that I thought for a moment—I was half afraid—" and she paused and laughed a little hysterically, and looked at her father with eyes full of tears, and he rather shyly stooped down and touched her lips with his grizzly moustache—and the ice was broken.

Helen seemed to immediately recover her spirits, her colour, and her tongue—but no, she had never lost the use of that! She was a different-looking girl to what she had been ten minutes previously—her lips broke into smiles, her eyes danced; she was scarcely the same individual as the white-faced, frightened young lady whom we had first seen sitting aloof at the end of the saloon table.

"I remember you now quite well," said Miss Denis. "I knew your voice; and oh, I am so glad to come home again!"

This was delightful. Colonel Denis, a man of but few words at any time, was silent from sheer necessity now. He felt that he could not command his utterance as was befitting to his sex. If this meeting was rapturous to Helen, what was it not to him? Here was his own little girl grown into a big girl—this was all the difference.

In a short time Miss Denis and her luggage (Mrs. Creery would be pleased to know that there was a good deal of the latter) were being rowed to Ross by eight stout-armed boatmen, over a sea that reflected the bright full moon. It was almost as light as day, as Helen and her father walked along the pier and up the hill homewards. As they passed a bungalow on their left-hand, the figure of a girl (who had long been lying in wait in the shadow of the verandah) leant out as they went by and watched them stealthily; then, pushing open a door and hurrying into a lamp-lit room, she said to her mother, an enormously stout, helpless-looking woman,—

"She has come! She has a figure like a may-pole. I could not see her face plainly, but I don't believe she is anything to look at."

However, those who had already obtained a glimpse of Miss Denis in the saloon of the *Scotia* were of a very different opinion, and, according to them, the newly-arrived "spin" was an uncommonly pretty girl, likely to raise the average of ladies' looks in the settlement by about fifty per cent.!

Almost at the moment that Colonel Denis and his daughter were landing at Ross, another boat was putting her passengers ashore at Aberdeen, *i.e.* Mr. Quentin's very smart gig. A steep hill lay between him and his bungalow, but declining the elephant in waiting, he and Mr. Lisle, and another friend, to whom he had given a seat over, commenced to breast the rugged path together. This latter gentleman was a Dr. Parks, the principal medical officer in the settlement; a little man with a sharp face, grey whiskers and moustache, and keen eyes to match; he was comfortable of figure, and fluent of speech, and prided himself on having the army list of the Indian staff corps at his fingers' ends; he could tell other men's services to a week, knew to a day when Brown would drop in for his off-reckonings, and how much sick-leave Jones had had. More than this, he had an enormous circle of acquaintances in the three Presidencies, and if he did not know most old Indian residents personally, at any rate he could tell you all about them—who they married, when, and why; who were their friends, enemies, or relations; what were their prospects of promotion, their peculiarities, their favourite hill-stations; he was a sort of animated directory (with copious notes), and prided himself on knowing India as well as another man knew

London. He was unmarried, well off, and lived in the East from choice, not necessity; he was exceedingly popular in society, was reputed to have saved two lacs of rupees, and to be looking out for a wife!

After climbing the hill for some time in silence, Dr. Parks paused — ostensibly to survey the scene, in reality to take breath.

"Hold hard, you fellows," he cried, as the other two were walking on. "Hold hard, there's no hurry. Looks like a scene in a theatre, doesn't it?" waving a hand towards the prospect below them.

"With the moon for lime light?" rejoined Mr. Quentin as he paused and glanced back upon the steamer, surrounding boats, and the sea, all bathed in bright, tropical moon-shine; at the many lights twinkling up and down the island, like fire-flies in a wood.

Dr. Parks remained stationary for some seconds, contemplating Ross, with his thumbs in the arm-holes of his waistcoat. At length he said, —

"I daresay old Denis hardly knows himself to-night, with a girl sitting opposite him. I hope she will turn out well."

"You mean that you hope she will turn out good-looking," amended Mr. Quentin, turning and surveying his companion expressively. "Ah, Parks, you were always a great ladies' man!"

"Nonsense, sir, nonsense. I'm not thinking of her looks at all; but the fact of the matter is, that Denis has had an uncommonly rough time of it, and I trust he is in shallow water at last, and that this girl will turn out to be what they call 'a comfort to him.'"

"I hope she will be a comfort to us all. I'm sure we want some consolation in this vile hole; but why is Old Denis a special charity?" inquired Mr. Quentin.

"*Old* Denis — well, he is not so old, if it comes to that; in fact, he is five years my junior, and I suppose *I'm* not an old man, am I?" demanded Dr. Parks, with a spark of choler in his eye.

"Oh, you! you know that you are younger than any of us," rejoined Mr. Quentin quickly; "time never touches you; but about Denis?"

"Oh! he has had a lot of bother and worry, and you know that that plays the deuce with a fellow. The fact of the matter is, that Tom Denis came to awful grief in money matters," said Dr. Parks, now walking on abreast of Mr. Quentin, and discoursing in a fluent, confidential tone.

"His father's affairs went smash, and Tom became security to save the family name, mortgaged all his own little property that came to him through his mother, exchanged from a crack regiment at home, and came out here into the staff corps. It was a foolish, quixotic business altogether; no one was a bit obliged to him: his sisters thought he might have done more, his father was a callous old beggar, and took everything he got quite as a matter of course, and Tom was the support of his relations, and their scapegoat."

"The very last animal I'd like to be," remarked Mr. Quentin; "but don't let me interrupt you; go on."

"Well, as if Tom had not enough on his hands, he saddled himself with a wife—a wife he did not want either, a beautiful Greek! It seems that she burst into tears when he told her he was going to India, and I'm not sure that she did not faint on his breast into the bargain. However, the long and the short of it was, that Tom had a soft heart, and he offered to take her out with him as Mrs. D——.

"Mrs. Denis had a lovely face, an empty head, no heart, and no money; in fact, no interest, or connections, or anything! and she was the very worst wife for a poor man like Tom. She came out to Bombay, and carried all before her; one would have thought she had thousands at her back—her carriages, dresses and dinners! 'pon my word, they ran the Governor's wife pretty hard. There was no holding her; at least, it would have taken a stronger man than Tom Denis to do that. She flatly refused to live on the plains, or to go within five hundred miles of his native regiment; and his *rôle* was to broil in some dusty, baking station, and to supply my lady up in the hills, or spending the season at Poonah or Bombay, with almost the whole of his pay.—I believe she scarcely left him enough rupees to keep body and soul together!"

"The man must have been a fool!" said Mr. Lisle emphatically, now speaking for the first time.

"Aye, a fool about a pretty face, like many another," growled the doctor. "There was no denying her beauty! The pure Greek type; her figure a model, every movement the poetry of motion. She was Cockney born, though; her father a Greek refugee, conspirator, whatever you like, and of course, a Prince at Athens, and the descendant of Princes, according to his own tale meanwhile a fourth-rate painter in London, whose Princess kept lodgers! Well, Mrs. Denis was very clever with her pen, and made capital imitations of her husband's signature! She borrowed freely from the Soucars, she ran bills in all directions, she had a vice in common with her kinsfolk of Crete, and she was the prettiest woman in India! Luckily for Denis (I say it with all respect to her ashes), she died after a short but brilliant social career, leaving him this girl and some enormous debts. The fact of the matter was, Tom was a ruined man. And all these years, between his father's affairs and his wife's liabilities, his life has been a long battle, and poor as he was, and no doubt *is*, he never could say no to a needy friend; and I need scarcely tell you, that people soon discovered this agreeable trait in his character!"

"It's a pity he has not a little more moral courage, and that he never studied the art of saying 'no,'" remarked Mr. Lisle dryly; "it's merely a matter of nerve and practice."

"It's not that, exactly," rejoined Dr. Parks, "but that he is too much afraid of hurting people's feelings, too simple and unselfish. I hope this girl who has come out will stand between him and this greedy world!"

"*I* should have thought it ought to be the other way."

"So it ought, but you see what Denis is yourself," turning and appealing to Jim Quentin. "Go over to him to-morrow morning, and tell him that you are at your wits' ends for five hundred rupees, and he will hand it out to you like a lamb."

"I only wish lambs *were* in the habit of handing out five hundred rupee notes, I'd take to a pastoral life to-morrow!" returned Mr. Quentin fervently, casting a woeful thought to the many long bills he owed in Calcutta, London, and elsewhere.

"Let us hope Miss Denis will have some force of character," said Dr. Parks; "that's the only chance for him! A strong will, like her mother's, minus her capabilities for making the money fly, and a few other weaknesses; and here," halting and holding out his hand, "our roads part."

"No, no. Not a bit of it," replied Mr. Quentin, taking him forcibly by the arm. "You just come home and dine with us, doctor, and tell a few more family histories."

Dr. Parks was a little reluctant at first, declaring that he was due elsewhere, that it was quite impossible, &c. &c.

"It's only the Irwins, I know, and they will think you have stopped at Ross—it will be all right. Come along."

Thus Dr. Parks was led away from the path of duty, and down the road approaching Mr. Quentin's bungalow;—he was rather curious to see the *ménage*; that was the reason why he had been such an unresisting victim to Mr. Jim's invitation,—Mr. Jim rarely entertained, and much preferred sitting at other people's boards to dispensing hospitality at his own.

Dinner was excellent—well cooked, well served. Dr. Parks, who was not insensible to culinary arts, was both surprised and pleased; he had known his host for many years, had come across him on the hills and on the plains, on board ship, and in the jungle; they had a host of acquaintances in common, and after a few glasses of first-rate claret, and a brisk volley of mutual reminiscences and stories, Dr. Parks began to tell himself that "he was really very fond of Apollo Quentin, after all, and that he was one of the nicest young fellows that he knew!" And what about the man who sat at the foot of the table? Hitherto he had not been able to classify this Mr. Lisle, nor had he been so much interested in the matter as other, and idler, people. He had seen him often coming and going at Aberdeen, and had nodded him a friendly "Good-morrow," and now and then exchanged a few words with him; his clothes were shabby, his manner reserved; Dr. Parks understood that he was a broken-down gentleman, to whom Quentin had given house-room, and, believing this, he could not help feeling that he was performing a gracious and kindly action in noticing him, and "doing the civil," as he would have called it himself, to this beggarly stranger! But now, when he came to look at the fellow, his appearance was changed. What wonders can be worked by a decent coat! Seen without his slouch hat and rusty Karki jacket, he was quite another person; and query, was that reserved manner of his *humility*? Dr. Parks noticed that there was nothing subservient in his way of speaking to Quentin; quite the reverse; that far from holding a subordinate position in the establishment, servants were more prompt to attend on him than on any one else, and sprang to his very glance; that he, more than Quentin, looked after his (Dr. Parks') wants, and saw that his plate and glass were always replenished to his liking, in which duties Apollo (who was a good deal occupied with his own dinner and speculations on Miss Denis's appearance,) was rather slack. When the meal was over, and the silent, bare-footed servants had left the room, cigars and cigarettes were brought out, and conversation became general, Mr. Lisle had plenty to say for himself—when he chose—had travelled much, and had the polished manners and diction of a man who had mixed with good society. Dr. Parks scrutinized him narrowly, and summed up his age to be a year or two over thirty he looked a good deal younger without his hat; his hair was black as the traditional raven's wing, slightly touched with grey on the temples, his eyes were deep-set, piercing, and very dark, there was a humorous twinkle in them at times, that qualified their general expression—which was somewhat stern. On the whole, this Lisle was a handsome man; in quite a different style to his *vis-à-vis* Apollo (who lounged with his arm over the back of his chair, and seemed buried in thought), he was undoubtedly a gentleman, and he looked as if he had been in the service. All the same, this was but idle speculation, and Dr. Parks had not got any "forrader" than any one else.

The pause incident to "lighting up" lasted for nearly five minutes, then Mr. Quentin roused himself, filled out a bumper of claret, pushed the decanter along the table, and said,—

"Gentlemen, fill your glasses. I am about to give you a toast. Miss Denis—her very good health."

"What!" to Dr. Parks. "Are you not going to drink it? Come, come, fill up, fill up."

"Oh, yes. I'll honour your toast, I'll drink it," he replied, suiting the action to the word. "And now I'll follow it up by what you little expect, and that's a speech."

"All right, make a start, you are in the chair; but be brief, for goodness' sake. What is the text?"

"The text is, Do not flirt with Miss Denis."

"Oh, and pray why not, if she is pretty, and agreeable, and appreciative?"

"You know what I told you this very evening. She is a mere school-girl, an inexperienced child, she is Denis's one ewe lamb, she is to be his companion, the prop of his old age; if you have any sense of chivalry, spare her."

"Spare her!" ejaculated Mr. Quentin with a theatrical gesture of his hand. "One would think I was a butcher, or the public executioner!"

"I know," proceeded Dr. Parks, "your proclivities for tender whisperings, bouquet-giving, and note-writing, in short the whole gamut of your attentions, and that they never *mean* anything, but too many forlorn maidens have learnt to their cost, you most agreeable, but evasive young man," nodding towards his host with an air of pathetic expostulation.

"I say, come now, you know this is ridiculous," exclaimed Mr. Quentin, pushing his chair back as he spoke. But Dr. Parks was in the vein for expounding on his friend's foibles, and not to be silenced.

"You know as well as I do your imbecile weakness for a pretty face, and that you cannot resist making love to every good-looking girl you see, until a still better-looking drives her out of your fickle heart."

"Go on, go on," cried his victim; "you were a loss to the Church."

"Of course," continued the elder gentleman, clearing his throat, "I can readily imagine that for you—a society man before anything—these regions are a vast desert, you are thrown away here, and are figuratively a castaway, out of humanity's reach. And now fate seems induced to smile upon you once more, in sending you a possibly pretty creature to be the sharer of your many empty hours. If I thought you would be serious, I would not say anything; or if this girl was a hardened veteran of a dozen seasons, and knew the difference between jest and earnest, again I would hold my peace; but as it is, I sum up the whole subject in one word, and with regard to Helen Denis, I say, *don't.*"

"Hear hear," cried his friend, hammering loudly on the table. "Doctor, your eloquence is positively touching; but you always *were* the ladies' champion. All the same you are exaggerating the situation; I am a most innocent, inoffensive——"

"Come now, James Quentin; how about that girl at Poonah that you made the talk of the station? How about the girls you proposed to up at Matheran and Murree; what about the irate father who followed you to Lahore, and from whom you concealed yourself behind the refreshment-room counter? Eh!"

"Now, now, doctor, I'll cry peccavi. Spare me before Lisle."

Who lay back in his chair smoking a cigar—and looking both bored and indifferent.

"*You* don't go in for ladies' society on Ross?" said Dr. Parks, addressing him abruptly.

"I—no—" struggling to an erect posture, and knocking the ash off his cigar. "I only know one lady over there, and she is a host in herself."

"You mean Mrs. Creery?"

"Yes, I allude to Mrs. Creery."

And at the very mention of the name, they all three laughed aloud.

"And how about Miss Denis, Quentin? you've not given your promise," said Dr. Parks once more returning to the charge.

"I'll promise you one thing, doctor," drawled the host, who was beginning to get tired of his persistence. "I'll not marry her, now that you have let me behind the scenes about her bewitching mother, and I'll promise you, that I'll go over and call to-morrow, and see if I can discover any traces of a Grecian ancestry in Miss Denis's face and figure."

"You are incorrigible. I might as well talk to the wall; there's only one hope for the girl, and that's a poor one."

"Poor as it is, let us have it."

"A chance that she may not be taken like twenty-three out of every two dozen, with fickle Jim Quentin's handsome face!"

"Where has Lisle gone to?" he added, looking round.

"Into the verandah, or to bed, or out to *sea*! The latter is just as likely as anything; he did not approve of the conversation, he thinks that ladies should never be discussed," and he shrugged his shoulders expressively.

"Quite one of the old school, eh?" said the elder gentleman, raising his eyebrows and pursing out his under-lip.

"Quite," laconically.

"By-the-bye, Quentin, I daresay you will think I'm as bad as Mrs. Creery, but *who* is this fellow Lisle, and what in the name of all that's slow is he doing down here?—eh, who is he?" leaning over confidentially.

"Oh, he fishes, and shoots, and likes the Andamans awfully.—As to who he is—he is simply, as you see, a gentleman at large, and his name is Gilbert Lisle."

Thus Dr. Parks, in spite of his superior opportunities, was foiled; and returned to his own abode no wiser than any of his neighbours.

CHAPTER III
FIRST IMPRESSIONS

"And I am something curious, being strange."

Cymbeline.

The morning after her arrival Helen Denis found herself alone, as her father was occupied with drills and orderly-room till twelve o'clock, when they breakfasted.

She went out into the verandah, and looked about her, in order to become better acquainted with the situation of her new home. The bungalow stood a little way back from the gravel road, that encircled the whole island, and was shaded by a luxuriant crimson creeper; a hedge of yellow flowers bordered the path leading up to the door, and between the house and the sea was a clump of thick cocoa-nut palms, that stood out in bold relief against the deep cobalt background of the sky. Jays, parrots, and unfamiliar tropical birds were flitting about, and from the sea a faint breeze was wafted, bearing strange fragrant odours from the distant mainland; a light haze lay over the water, betokening a warm meridian. A few white clouds slumbered in the hot heavens overhead; and save for the hum of insects and birds, and a distant sound of oars swinging to and fro in the rowlocks, the place was as silent as a Sunday morning in the country, when every one has gone to church.—At first Helen stood, and then she sat down on the steps to contemplate this scene, which formed the prelude to a new epoch in her life—she gazed and gazed, and seemed afraid to move her eyes, lest the vision should escape her. She sat thus without moving for fully half an hour.

"Well, what do you think of it all, young woman?" from a voice behind her, caused her to spring up, and she found her father standing there in his white uniform, with his sword under his arm.

"Oh, papa! I never, never saw anything like it; I never dreamt or fancied there could be such a beautiful spot—it's like fairyland! like an enchanted country, like"—her similes running short—"like Robinson Crusoe's island."

"Rather different to Brompton, eh? I suppose you had not much of a view there?"

"View!" she exclaimed; "if there had been one, we could not see it! for in the first place we were shut in by high, dirty brick walls, and in the second, all the lower windows were muffled glass; there was one window at the end of the school-room that overlooked the road, and though it was pretty high up, it was all painted, but some one had scratched a little space in it, right in the middle, and often and often, when I've been saying my lessons, or reading translations in class, every idea has been sent right out of my head, when I've looked up at that pane and seen an *eye* watching us—it always seemed to be watching *me*! but of course that was imagination; it used to make me feel quite hysterical at times, and many a bad mark it cost me!"

"Well, you are not likely to get any bad marks here," said her father, laying his hand on her shoulder as he spoke; "and you think you will like Port Blair?"

"Like—why it seems to me to be a kind of paradise! I wonder half the world does not come and live here," she replied emphatically.

To this remark ensued a rather long silence, a silence that was at length broken by a noise as strange to Helen's ears, as the lovely scene before her was to her still admiring eyes; this noise was a loud, fierce, hoarse shout, something like an angry cheer. She glanced at her father with a somewhat heightened colour, and in answer to her startled face he said,—

"Those are the convicts! they leave off work at twelve o'clock, they are busy on the barracks just now. Stay where you are, and you will see them pass presently."

The approach of the convicts was heralded by a faint jingling of chains that gradually became louder and louder; and in a few moments the gang came in sight, escorted by four burly, armed warders. Helen drew back, pale and awe-struck, as she watched this long, silent procession file past, two and two, all clad in the same blue cotton garment, all heavily manacled, otherwise there was but little resemblance among them. There passed the squat Chinaman, chained to the tall, fiery Pathan (who flung as he went by a glance of bitter hatred and defiance at the two European spectators); they were in turn followed by a brace of tattooed Burmans, who seemed rather cheerful than otherwise; then a few mild Hindoos, then more Arabs, more Burmans, more fierce Rohillas, more mild Hindoos!

Helen stood almost breathless, as they glided by, nor did she speak till the very last sound of clanking chains had died away in the distance.

"Poor creatures! I had forgotten *them!*" she said; "this place is no paradise to 'a prisoner.'"

"Poor creatures!" echoed her father, "the very scum and sweepings of her Majesty's Indian Empire—poor murderers, poor robbers, poor dacoits!"

"And why are they in chains? such heavy cruel-looking chains?"

"Because they are either recent arrivals or desperate characters, the former probably; the worst of the 'poor creatures' are not kept in Ross, but colonized in other gaols on the mainland, or at Viper."

"And are there many here on Ross?"

"About four thousand, including women, but some of these have tickets-of-leave, and only go back to 'section'—*section* is a delicate way of putting it—at night; many of them are our servants."

"*Our* servants, papa!"

"No, I am speaking of the settlement, but our boatmen, our water-carrier, and—I may as well break it to you at once—our cook, are, each and all, people who have a past that does not bear close inquiry! And now, my dear, shall we go in to breakfast?"

It was a delightful change from his usual solitary meal to have that bright, pretty face sitting opposite to him; he watched her intently for some minutes—she was pouring out tea with all the delight of a child.

"I've never done it before, papa!" she exclaimed as she despatched his tea-cup; "be sure you don't let Sawmy know, or he will despise me.—Of course, being at school I never got a chance. Miss Twigg herself presided over the hot water, and then in the holidays I had much better tea, but I never made it."

"Ah, your holidays, Helen; that is what puzzled me so much about your Aunt Julia. I understood that you were always to spend your vacation with the Platts."

"I did once, when I was small, and I do not think they liked me; so after a lapse of five years they tried me again I suppose to see if I was improved; but these holidays were even *worse* than the others. I have a quick temper, and I got into fearful trouble."

"How?"

"Oh, it's a very old story, and I hope and trust that I have more command of my feelings now. I remember I was in the room at afternoon tea, rather by accident, for I usually took that refreshment in" —lowering her voice to a stage whisper—"the kitchen! My cousins are a good deal older than I am— they were grown up then, I perfectly recollect, though they declare they were *not — —*"

"Well, but it is not a question of your cousins' age, but of some domestic fracas that you were about to tell me."

"Yes, I'm always wandering from the point. I recollect it was a Sunday afternoon, some gentlemen were calling, and they noticed me, and talked to me, and I was flattered, and doubtless pert; they asked Cousin Clara who I was, and where I and my classic profile came from, and Aunt Julia told them that I was her poor brother's child, and added something about— about—no matter."

Helen had never heard a word with regard to her other parent, save that she was a beautiful Greek, who had died young. Her picture she had seen, and this in itself was sufficient for her to idealize her and adore her memory—for Azalie Denis had the face of an angel! "She—no, I won't tell you what she said! but I have never forgotten it; in a passion of rage, and scarcely knowing what I was doing, I snatched up a cup of scalding tea, and flung it in Aunt Julia's face. Yes! cup and all! You may imagine the commotion; you can believe that I was in disgrace. I was led solemnly from the room, and locked away in a lumber-closet upstairs, where I remained for the rest of my vacation. Each day I was asked to apologize, and each day I said 'I *won't*,' so there I stayed till I went back to school. Ere leaving I was taken down to my aunt's apartment and told that I was a wicked, bad, abominable child, and that I would come to an untimely end; and then Cousin Clara took up a pair of big scissors, and seizing my beautiful thick plait of hair, sawed and hacked it off close to the nape of my neck!"

"What! cut off your hair!" exclaimed Colonel Denis, roused to sudden animation.

"Yes; though I screamed and struggled, it was of no use. I well remember the appearance of my poor pigtail in Clara's hand! Well, after *this* you will not be surprised to hear that I was never asked to Upper Cream Street again,—and I was not sorry. I never could get on with Aunt Julia; I'm so glad that *you* are not a bit like her, papa! She used to make me shake in my shoes."

"And how do you know that I won't do the same?" he asked with a smile.

"I'm sure you won't. Have another cup of tea, do, please."

"It's strange that we have so few relations," he said, obediently passing his cup as he spoke. "Besides your Aunt Julia there's only my sister Christina; she has been an invalid for years, and never writes."

"Is not she married to a queer Irishman who lives at a place with a ridiculous name—Crow-more? And Aunt Julia won't have anything to do with her?"

"Yes, your Aunt Julia did not approve of the match. This Sheridan was a kind of professor that Christina met abroad, a most dreamy, unpractical genius, with a magnificent head, and a brogue that you could cut with a hatchet. After living for some years in a small German town, they went over to Ireland, and there they reside on a property that was left to him. I write now and then" (and he might have added, enclose a cheque), "but Christina never sends me a line—I'm afraid they are very badly off," shaking his head as he stirred his tea.

"Now tell me something about this delightful place, papa! I've been reading a good deal about it, I mean the Andamans. They were first taken possession of in 1789 by the British Government, or rather, the East India Company, were abandoned in 1796, and resumed in 1858, the year after the Mutiny; don't I know it all nicely?"

"You know a great deal more about it than *I* do."

"This is Ross, is it not?"

"Yes, the other settlements are scattered about. People come over here to church, to shop, to play tennis, and to hear the news."

"And are there many other people—I don't mean convicts and soldiers?"

"There are about fifty men, and fifteen or sixteen ladies. No doubt you will have a good many visitors to-day."

"Oh, papa! you don't mean it—not to call on *me*?"

"Yes, of course; who else would they come to see?"

"It makes me feel quite nervous, the palms of my hands are cold already; only six weeks ago I was doing French composition and German translation, and not daring to speak above my breath without leave. And now all at once I am grown up! I am to receive visitors, I may wear what I like, and," with an interrogative smile across the table, "do as I *please?*"

"As long as you don't throw cups of tea at people, my dear."

"Now, papa, I'm very sorry I mentioned that if you are going to use it against me. But do tell me something about the fifteen ladies,—and who are likely to come and call."

"Well, there is Mrs. Creery; she is the wife of the head of the Foolscap Department, and lives close to this. She—well," hesitating, "she is a very energetic woman, but her"—hesitating again—"manner is a little against her! rather arbitrary, you know; but we all have our faults. Then there is Mrs. Caggett; her husband has some trade with Burmah, and his wife lives here in preference to Moulmein. Miss Caggett is our only young lady, and"—rather dubiously—"you will see what you think of *her.* Mrs. Home is the wife of the colonel of this regiment—I'm only second fiddle, you know; you are certain to have a kind friend in her. Then there is Mrs. Durand, wife of Captain Durand of the European detachment here; she is away just now, and a great loss to the place. There are several ladies at out-stations, whom you are sure to like."

"I wish I was sure that they would like *me,*" rejoined his daughter in rather a melancholy voice. "You must bear in mind that I am not accustomed to the society of grown-up people, and I know that I have *no* conversation!"

"*No* conversation! and pray what have we been having for the last three-quarters of an hour?"

"Oh, that is quite different. I can talk away to you by the week, but with strangers what can I discuss?—not even the weather, for I don't know what happens here; it's always fine, I suppose?"

"You will find plenty to say, I'll engage," returned her father, with emphasis; "and I have no doubt"—whatever he was going to add was cut short by the imperious rapping of an umbrella on the wooden steps of the verandah, and a shrill female voice calling "Boy!"

CHAPTER IV
MISS DENIS HAS VISITORS

"What's his name and birth? I cannot delve him to the root."

Shakespeare.

"There is Mrs. Creery!" exclaimed Colonel Denis, starting up rather nervously. "She has come to call *first*. Don't keep her waiting." To Helen, who was hastily smoothing her hair and pulling out her ruffles, "You will do first-rate; go into the drawing-room, my dear."

"Yes, but not alone, papa!" taking him by the arm. "You will have to introduce us—you must come with me."

You see she had begun to say *must* already!—Colonel Denis was by no means reluctant to present his pearl of daughters to the visitor who had prognosticated that she would be plain, and he was sufficiently human to enjoy that lady's stare of stolid astonishment, as she took Helen's hand, and kept it in hers for quite a minute, whilst she leisurely studied her face.

"How do you do, Miss Denis? had you a good passage?"

"Very good, thank you," replied the young lady demurely.

"I see," sitting down as she spoke, and specially addressing Colonel Denis, "that you have had new curtains and purdahs put up, and have actually bought that white marble table that Kursandoss had so long on hand! How much did you give for it?"

"One hundred rupees," replied the purchaser in a guilty voice.

"Heavens and earth!" casting up hands and eyes, "did any one ever hear of such folly! It is not worth *thirty*. Miss Denis, it's a good thing that you have come out to look after your father—he is a most extravagant man!"

Helen thought that this was a pleasantry, and laughed immoderately. Mrs. Creery was really most amusing,—but how oddly she was dressed! She was quite old, in Helen's eyes (in truth she was not far from fifty), and yet she was attired in a white muslin polonaise trimmed with rose-coloured bows, and wore a black sailor's hat, with the letters *Bacchante* stamped in gold upon the ribbon! Meanwhile the elder lady had been taking a great deal of interest in Miss Denis's pretty morning-dress; she had come to the conclusion that the pattern was too complicated to be what is called "carried away in her eye," and was resolved to ask for it boldly,—and that before she was many days older!

"You may go up to the mess," she said, playfully dismissing her host with a wave of her plump, mittened hand. "I want to have a chat with your daughter alone. I came to see her—*you* are no novelty!"

"Now, my dear, we shall be quite comfortable," she said, as Colonel Denis meekly took his departure. "Did you find him much changed?" she continued, lowering her voice mysteriously.

"A little, but not"—smiling—"*nearly* as much changed as I seem to him!"

"How much is he going to allow you for the housekeeping?"

Helen assured her questioner that the subject had not even been considered.

Mrs. Creery, on hearing this, was visibly disappointed, and said rather tartly,—

"Well, don't listen to anything under five rupees a day—you could not do it less. The Durands spend that! The Homes *say* they manage on four, but that's nonsense, and the children could not be half fed. Maybe your father will still leave it to Ram Sawmy, but"—with sudden energy—"you must not hear of that,—the man is a robber!"

"He has been twenty years with papa," ventured Helen.

"So much the worse for your father's *pocket*," returned Mrs. Creery emphatically. "I suppose you have brought out a number of new gowns? What have you got?"

"I have a white silk, and a black silk," replied Helen, with some exultation in her own mind, for they were her first silk dresses.

"Both perfectly useless here!" snapped the matron.

"A riding-habit."

"Stark, staring madness! There's not a horse between this and Calcutta—unless a clothes-horse! What else?"

"A cashmere and plush costume."

"You may just send it back to England, or throw it away."

Helen paused aghast.

A Bird Of Passage | 37

"Well, well—go on, go on—that's not *all*, surely?"

"I have some pretty cottons and muslins, and a tennis-dress."

"Come, that's better; and when are your boxes to be opened?"

"This afternoon, if possible."

"Oh, well, I'll come down and see your things to-morrow; I may get some new ideas, and we are a little behind-hand with the fashions here," waving once more her mittened hand. "And now to turn to another subject! It's a great responsibility for a young girl like you to be placed at the head of even a *small* establishment like this! I am older than you are" (it was quite superfluous to mention this fact), "I know the world, and I wish to give you a word of caution."

Helen became crimson.

"I hope you are a steady, sensible girl."

"I hope so, Mrs. Creery," raising her chin in a manner well known to Miss Twigg,—a manner betokening insurrection.

"There now, don't be huffy! I mean to be your friend. I would have come down and stayed here for the first week or two, to set you going, if your father had asked me, as you have no lady in the house; however, I've spoken to him most seriously. All the men in the place will of course be flocking to call, and turning your head with their silly compliments. As a rule they are not a bad set of young fellows; but Mr. Quentin and Captain Rodney are the only two who *I* should say were in a position to marry,—the others are just paupers—butterflies! Oh, and yes"—here her voice became hollow and mysterious—"I must put you on your guard against a Mr. Lisle."

"A Mr. Lisle!" echoed Helen, opening her eyes very wide.

"Yes, Lisle—don't forget the name. He seldom comes over; he lives at Aberdeen with Mr. Quentin—lives *on* him, I should say," correcting herself sharply. "He came here a few months ago—goodness knows from where. It is generally believed that he is in *hiding*—that he is under a cloud; he is poor as a rat, has no visible means of livelihood, and is as close as wax about his past. However, Mr. Quentin shields him, keeps his secret, and there is nothing more to be said except this—don't *you* have anything to say to him; he may have the impudence to call, but indeed, to give him his due, he does not push. It is a most unpleasant feeling to have this black sheep living in the neighbourhood at all; I wish he was well out of the settlement!" shaking her head expressively.

Helen, amazed at Mrs. Creery's volubility, sat staring at her in speechless surprise. Why should she take such pains to warn her against a man who she admitted did not push, and whom she was not likely to see? Another knocking in the verandah, and a rather timid voice calling "Boy!" announced the arrival of a second visitor, and Mrs. Creery rose, saying,—

"You will be coming up to the General's tennis this evening, and we shall meet again, so I won't say good-bye;" then, casting one last searching glance around the apartment, she, as if seized by some afterthought, hurried across, coolly pulled back the purdah (door-curtain), and looked into the dining-room. "Nothing new *there*, I see," dropping the drapery after a long, exhaustive stare; "nothing but a filter! Well, *au revoir*," and nodding approvingly at Helen, she finally took her departure.

The new arrival was a complete contrast to the parting guest; a pale, faded, but still pretty little woman, with imploring dark eyes (like a newly-caught fawn), attired in a neat white dress, a solar topee, and respectable gloves. She was Mrs. Home, the wife of Colonel Denis's commanding officer, and the mother, as she plaintively informed Helen, of no less than nine children!

"They make me so dreadfully anxious, dear Miss Denis, especially the seven at home. I live on tenter-hooks from mail-day to mail-day. Imagine my feelings when they were *all* in measles last spring!"

But this was a feat beyond Helen.

"You have two here?" she asked politely, after a pause.

"Yes, Tom and Billy. Your father is so fond of them, and they wanted so much to come and see you. But I told them you would think them a trouble—and the first call too!"

Helen eagerly assured her visitor that they would have been most welcome, and rushing impulsively out of the room, returned with a box of chocolate-creams she had purchased for her own delectation; which she sent to the young gentlemen with her best love, requesting that they would come and call as soon as possible. This gift, and message, completely won their mother's heart. At first she had been a little doubtful, a little in awe, of this pretty, fashionable-looking girl, but now she became much warmer in manner, and said,—

"You know, my dear, I'm not a society lady, I have no time for gaiety, even if I were fitted for it; between sewing for my boys and girls at home, and my letters, and my housekeeping, not to mention Tom and Billy, I never seem to have a spare moment. I came down here early on purpose, hoping to be the *first* to welcome you, but I was late after all!" and she smiled deprecatingly. "Your father is such a very dear friend of ours, that I feel as if I had a kind of claim on you, and hope you won't stand on ceremony with us, but come to see us as often as you can. Will you?"

"I shall be very glad indeed, thank you."

"You see, you and I being the only ladies in the 'Puggarees' too,—it is a kind of bond, is it not? If I can help you in any way about your housekeeping, be sure you let me know, won't you? I am an old campaigner of fifteen years' standing, and everything, of course, is quite new to you. You and your father, I hope, will come up and dine with us quietly to-morrow night, and then you and I can have a very nice long chat."

Helen thanked Mrs. Home for her invitation, and said that if her father was not engaged, she was sure they would be most happy to accept it.

"And now, my dear," said the little lady, rising, "I must really go! the Dhoby has been waiting for me at home this half-hour, I know, and I have all the clean clothes to sort, so I will wish you good-bye. May I kiss you?" holding Helen's hand, and looking at her with timid, appealing eyes. Helen became rather red, but smiled assent, thereupon the salute was exchanged, and Mrs. Home presently took her departure.

After this visit, there was a long interval. Colonel and Miss Denis were equipped and ready to start for the General's tennis party, when Sawmy brought in another card; a small one this time, bearing the name of "Mr. James Quentin." The card was almost instantly followed by that gentleman, looking as if he had just stepped out of a band-box. Having cordially wrung his host's hand, and been presented to his daughter, he seated himself near the young lady, placed his hat on the floor, and commenced to discuss the climate, her passage, &c., surveying the new arrival critically at the same time. "She was much prettier than he expected," he said to himself as he summed her up; "her profile was not classical, but it would pass; her eyes were fine in shape and colour, though their expression was rather too merry for *his* taste; he imagined that she had plenty of spirits, and but a meagre supply of sentiment. Her complexion was perfect, but of course *that* would not last three months!" On the whole, he was most agreeably surprised, and her dainty dress, and ladylike deportment, were as refreshing to his eyes, as a spring of water to a traveller in the desert! The shape of her hat, the fit of her long gloves, her brilliant colour, and pure English accent, all mentally carried him back to the Park once more—his Mecca! Yes, the fall of Miss Denis's draperies, the very lace in her ruffles, were each a source of gratification to her visitor, who had a keen eye for such things, and was a connoisseur in toilettes. He told himself emphatically that this young lady was "no end of a find!" but, aloud, he politely inquired if Colonel and Miss

Denis were going up to the tennis. They were. Well, he was going too—a sudden resolution—and might he be permitted to accompany them?

Mr. James Quentin felt an additional sense of importance, as he strolled up the narrow path towards the General's grounds, personally conducting Miss Denis (coolly leaving her father to bring up the rear alone, as the pathway was too narrow to permit of three abreast), and he honestly believed, that the young lady beside him could not be launched into settlement society under happier, or more distinguished, auspices.

CHAPTER V
WHAT IS SHE LIKE?

"So sweet a face, such angel grace,

In all that land had never been."

Helen found her reception a most trying ordeal. She was very cordially welcomed by the General, who instantly came forward to meet her, and escorted her towards Mrs. Creery; she ran the gauntlet of two groups of men who were standing on the tennis-ground, ostensibly discussing the recent mail, but naturally watching the new arrival, who was the cynosure of every eye, as she passed by; and approached a row of seats on which the ladies—a still more formidable phalanx—were seated in state. Mrs. Creery (who occupied the social throne in the shape of a stuffed arm-chair) now rose majestically, and, like Cedric the Saxon, advanced two steps, saying in her most dulcet company voice, "Very glad you have come, Miss Denis; I am *charmed* to welcome you to Port Blair!"

Helen blushed vividly. Was this august, this almost regal, individual, the same who had questioned, exhorted, and warned her, a few hours previously? She could scarcely believe it! But this was merely her ignorance. That visit had been made in a private capacity, here Mrs. Creery was in a public and responsible position—that of chief lady of the station.

She now took Helen's hand in hers, and proceeded to present her to her immediate circle.

"Mrs. Caggett, let me introduce Miss Denis."

Mrs. Caggett rose, made a kind of plunge, intended for a curtsey, and subsided again, muttering incoherently.

"Miss Denis, Mrs. Graham. Mrs. Graham is our musician. She sings and plays most beautifully!"

Mrs. Graham, who was a pretty brunette, with lovely teeth, shook hands with Helen, and smiled significantly, as much as to say, "You must not mind Mrs. Creery."

"Miss Denis, Mrs. King.—Mrs. King has a nice little girl, and lives at Viper."

"Miss Denis, Mrs. Logan, our authoress." Poor Mrs. Logan blushed till the tears came into her eyes, and said,—

"Oh, Mrs. Creery, *please* don't."

"Nonsense, nonsense! Miss Denis, she has written the *sweetest* poetry—one really exquisite ode, called, let me see, 'The Lifer's Lament,' and numbers of charming sonnets! You must get her to read them to you, some day."

Alas for Mrs. Logan! who in a moment of foolish expansiveness had mentioned her small poems (under the seal of secrecy) to another lady, and had, to her horror, "awoke and found herself famous!"

"Mrs. Manners, Miss Denis," and she paused, as if deliberating on what she could possibly say for Mrs. Manners.

"Please don't mind about *me*, Mrs. Creery," exclaimed that lady. "You know that I neither play, nor sing, nor write poetry."

Mrs. Manners was a sprightly person, regarded by Mrs. Creery with suspicion and dislike, and she now glowered on her menacingly.

"I am very glad to see Miss Denis, and I hope she will overlook my numerous deficiencies!" quoth Mrs. Manners unabashed.

All the ladies had now been, as it were, "told off," excepting Miss Caggett, who approached and squeezed Helen's fingers, and looked up in her face, and said,—

"So *thankful*, dear, that you have come! It's so wretched for me, being the only girl in the settlement. You can't think how I have been looking forward to *this*," another squeeze.

Miss Lizzie Caggett was small in person (and mind) and had a very pretty little figure, black hair, bright, reddish-brown eyes, an ugly nose, and an almost lipless mouth, garnished with beautiful teeth. She had been born in India, had had three years at school in England, and been "out" for a considerable number of seasons. She danced like a sylph, talked Hindostani like a native (and it was whispered that she gossipped with her ayah in that language), dressed extravagantly, was as lively as a French-woman, and sufficiently nice-looking to be considered a beauty—where she was the only unmarried lady among fifty men.

She had a shrewd eye to the main chance, and never allowed her feelings to betray her, save, alas! in the case of James Quentin!

He, from sheer lack of something to do, had been wont to spend his idle hours in Miss Caggett's society. She was amusing and lively, and said such deliciously spiteful things of other women, and told capital stories, accompanied by vehement gesticulation with her tiny hands. She had also a nice little voice,—and it came to pass that they sang duets together, and walked on the pier by moonlight alone!

Mr. Quentin meant nothing, of course, and at first Lizzie quite understood this, but by degrees her strong foothold of common sense slipped away from under her feet, and she fell desperately in love with the blue-eyed gay deceiver, and naturally tried to convince herself that it was mutual! She steeled herself to see him pay a little attention to the rising sun—Miss Helen Denis—they would *all* do that, but when the novelty had worn off, things would right themselves, and fall back into their old places—meaning that Mr. Quentin would fall back into his, *i.e.*, at her side. Mrs. Creery had previously broken the news to her that "Helen Denis was nice-looking, and beautifully dressed," but she was by no means prepared for the face and figure she beheld coming up the walk; and James Quentin in attendance *already*,—actually before she was twenty-four hours on the island! However, she made a brave struggle, and bit her lips, and clenched her small hands, and broke into a smile. She had made up her mind to be the bosom friend (outwardly), and, if possible, the confidante of this tall, shy-looking Denis girl!

After all, who could expect her to be pleased, to see a young and pretty rival monopolizing every one's attention, and thrusting her into the background?

When all the introductions had been effected, a game of tennis was got up, and a number of little Andamanese boys, in white tunics and scarlet caps, came forward from some lurking-place, to field the balls, and the settlement band, which was stationed at the end of the plateau, struck up their latest waltz, and presently the entertainment was in full swing. Every one played tennis, even Mrs. Creery, who was old or young as it suited her at the moment—old enough to ask questions, to give advice, and to lay down the law, and to be treated with unquestioning deference and deep respect; sufficiently young to waltz, to wear sailor hats, and to disport herself at tennis. Helen had been the championess player at Miss Twigg's, and played well. Lizzie Caggett's sharp eyes noted this, and after a little while she challenged her to a single set there and then.

Vainly did Helen decline to pick up the gauntlet, vainly did she beg to be excused; Mrs. Creery threw the weight of her authority into the scale, and the match was to come off immediately.

"A capital idea, a match between the two girls," she remarked to the General; "there will just be time for it before tea."

Before Helen could realize her position, a ball was thrust into her hand, a crowd had gathered around, and she alone stood *vis-à-vis* to Lizzie Caggett on the tennis-ground. It was one thing to play in Miss Twigg's back-garden, with no spectators but Miss Twigg's girls, but quite another affair when one of the principals in a contest, before forty complete strangers, and pitted against a determined-looking antagonist, who knew every inch of the courts, and was firmly resolved to try conclusions with this brilliant visitor!

And so the match began, the assembled bystanders watching each game intently, and hanging expectant on the issue of each stroke. The excitement grew intense, for the ladies were well-matched, the play was brilliant, and the games hard fought. Helen served well, and had a longer reach of arm than her challenger, but the other played with an energy, a vivacity, and if one might say so, a spitefulness,—as if the issue of the contest was a matter of life and death. She scored the first game, Helen the second and third, and during a rally in the latter, the new arrival was loudly clapped. This incited Miss Caggett to extraordinary exertions. She played with redoubled fire, her teeth were set, her eyes gleamed across the net, she served as though in hopes that she would strike her opponent in the face; she flitted up and down her court, springing and bounding, like a panther in a cage! Her style was by no means graceful, but it was effectual. During the last two games she wearied out Helen, with her quick, untiring onslaught, playing the final, and conquering game, with an exuberance of force that was almost fierce! When it was over, she threw down her bat and clapped her hands, and cried,—

"Oh, I knew I could beat you." This was not, strictly speaking, polite, but her triumph was so great, she really could not refrain from this little song of victory. In her own heart, she had made a kind of test of the match, and told herself that, if she conquered the new-comer in *this*, she would be invincible in other things as well!

After this exciting struggle, tea and refreshments were served in a rustic summer-house. Mrs. Creery's dog Nip—who had occupied his mistress's chair as deputy, and eyed the cake and bread and butter with demure rascality,—was now called upon to vacate his place, whilst his owner dispensed tea and coffee, and servants carried round cakes and ices. As Helen was partaking of one of the latter, her late antagonist accosted her and said,—

"Come and take a turn with me, dear. All the men are having 'pegs,' and I do so want to have a chat with you.

"Well, now," taking her arm affectionately, "tell me what you think of the place?"

"I think it is beautiful," returned Helen with enthusiasm. "I've never seen anything like it. Of course I've seen very little of the world, and am not a good judge, but I scarcely think that any scenery could surpass it," glancing over towards Mount Harriet as she spoke, and dreamily watching the peacocks sailing homewards.

This speech was a disappointment to Miss Caggett, who was in hopes that she would have called it an "unearthly, outlandish, savage hole, a gaol!" And then she would have imparted this opinion to the settlement at large,—and such an opinion would have scored a point against Miss Helen.

"Oh," she replied, "you won't think it delightful always. It's frightful in the monsoons, that is in the rains, you know. And how do you like the people?"

"I scarcely know them yet."

"Well, at least you know Mr. Quentin," eyeing her sharply.

"Yes, I have known him an *hour*," she replied with a laugh.

"He is nice enough," speaking with assumed nonchalance, "but as you can see, awfully conceited, isn't he?"

Helen did not fall into the trap; if she had, Miss Caggett would have lost no time in giving Apollo the benefit of Miss Denis's impressions with regard to him!

She only said, "Is he?" and, leaning her elbows on the wooden railing that fenced in the edge of the cliff, looked down upon the sea.

"A great many men are here from Aberdeen and the out-stations," proceeded Miss Caggett with a backward jerk of her head, "but they did not come over altogether to see *you*."

"I should hope not indeed," returned Helen, reddening.

"No, the mail is in, so they kill two birds with one stone," continued the other, coolly. "They are not a bad set, though they may seem rough and unpolished to you, don't they?"

"Really, I am no judge; I have scarcely ever spoken to a gentleman in my life."

"Gracious!" ejaculated Miss Caggett. "You weren't in a convent?"

"No; but what amounted to the same thing, I spent all my holidays at school."

"Oh, *how* slow for you! Well, you will find this rather a change. There is Dr. Malone, an Irishman, and very amusing; he has any amount of impudence, and has thought of a lovely name for Mrs. Creery—Mrs. Query—isn't it splendid? We all call her that, for she never stops asking questions, and we all have to answer them whether we like it or not—all but one; there is one person she never gets anything out of, he is too close even for her, and clever—I grant him that,—much as I detest him!"

"And who is this clever man that baffles Mrs. Creery?"

"A Mr. Lisle, a genteel loafer, a hanger-on of Mr. Quentin's; he actually has not got the money to pay his passage back to Calcutta, and so he is obliged to stay. His manners are odious, polite to rudeness, if you know what that means? and he has eyes that seem to look down into your inmost thoughts, and laugh at what they see there! I hate him, though he is extremely anxious to be civil to me, and, in fact, I don't mind telling you in confidence that he is a great *admirer* of mine,—but it's by no means mutual. Whatever you do, have nothing to say to him. I need not tell you, that *I* never speak to him!"

"We cannot permit you two young ladies to monopolize each other in this fashion," said the General, approaching with a telescope in his hand. "Would you like to look at some of the islands through this glass, Miss Denis? I can introduce you to several this fine clear evening. Havelock looks quite close!"

"It seems to be very large," she said, after a long struggle with the focus.

"Well, yes, it is; we will take you there some day in the *Enterprise* if you like. The *Enterprise* is the station steamer."

"Thank you, I should like it very much indeed, if it is *safe*—I mean, if the people are safe," she replied rather anxiously.

"Oh! you will see very little of the natives. They are a curious set; it is almost impossible to get at them, or to tame them."

"Have you ever tried?"

"Yes; we once had a young fellow from Havelock, as it happened; we showed him every kindness, gave him the best of food, loaded him with beads and every old tall hat on the island, but it was all of *no* use; he just fretted like a bird in a cage, and regularly pined away of home sickness.— He used to sit all day long, gazing, gazing over the sea in the direction of his home, and one morning when they went to see him, they found him sitting in his usual attitude, his face turned towards Havelock—quite dead!"

"Poor, poor fellow!" said Helen, with tears in her eyes; "how *could* you be so cruel, how could you have had the heart to keep him?"

"My dear young lady, it was not a matter of heart, but of duty."

Mr. Quentin's quick ear caught the significant word *heart*. Surely the General was never going to enter the lists against him, although he was unmarried and eligible beyond dispute? Leaning his elbows on the rail at the other side of Miss Denis, he resolved to make a third—welcome or otherwise—and said,—

"You are talking of the natives, sir? They are certainly most mysterious aborigines, for they do not resemble the Hindoos on one side, nor the Malays on the other. They are more like stunted niggers—you never see a man above five feet, some not more than four."

"Niggers, yes," replied the General; "there is some idea that they are descendants of the cargo of a slaver that was wrecked among these islands; other people think that they hail from New Guinea."

"They have very odd customs, have they not?" asked Helen.

"Yes," replied the General; "their mode of sepulture, for instance, is peculiar. When a man dies, they simply put his body up a tree."

("Whence the slang term 'up a tree,' I suppose," muttered Mr. Quentin, *sotto voce*.)

"And when the fowls of the air have picked his bones, they remove the remains, and present his skull to the widow, who wears it round her neck, slung to a string."

"But will freely part with it at any time," added Dr. Malone, who had now joined the group, "aye, even in the early days of her affliction, in consideration of a bottle of rum."

"And pray what about the *men*?" inquired Helen, jealous for her sex.

"Oh, their tastes are comparatively simple," responded the doctor; "they are all a prey to a devouring passion for—you will never guess what—*tall hats*! I believe some firm in Calcutta drives a brisk trade with this place and the Nicobars, bartering old tiles for cocoa-nuts. When a chief dies, he can have no nobler monument in the eyes of his survivors than a pile of tall hats impaled above his grave. They are almost the only article they care about, and I suppose they have an idea that it endows them with dignity and height; besides the hat, a few rags, and a necklace of human finger-bones, and their costume is complete."

"They have another weakness," put in the General—"dogs. We get rid of all the barrack curs in that way."

"What! to *eat*?" almost screamed Miss Denis.

"No, no; they are very much prized—merely to look at. I wish to goodness we could export that brute of Mrs. Creery's!"

"She would far sooner be exported herself!" said Dr. Malone. "What was his last feat, sir?"

"I wish I could believe that it *was* his last," returned the General angrily. "The other day, when Mrs. Creery was dining up at my place, she unfortunately shut him up in the drawing-room, and for sheer spite at missing the meal, he tore up a valuable fur rug, gutted the seats of two chairs, and ate the best part of the last army list! Yes, you may laugh, Miss Denis, and it certainly sounds very funny—but you don't know Nip."

"No, but *I* do," cried Dr. Malone. "He lies down and feigns death if he sees a larger dog coming in the distance, and will murder any unfortunate pup of half his size; some dogs have a sense of chivalry, generosity, gratitude, but he is a *brute*!"

"Yes," chimed in Mr. Quentin, "if things are not going to his liking, he adjourns to Creery's dressing-room, and devours a couple of pairs of boots; that is to say, tears and gnaws them to pieces, just to mark his sense of injury. If they only disagreed with him!—but they don't, and Creery can't even have the poor satisfaction of licking him; for whenever Nip sees him arming himself with a stick, he at once fastens on his leg, believing the first blow to be half the battle!"

"A portrait from life!" exclaimed Dr. Malone. "I wish I might be allowed a shot at him at 100 yards!"

"I wish you might; and if you do get the chance, I'll wink at it," returned the General; "he is an insufferable nuisance—a savage, mean, mischievous, lazy, cowardly——"

"Now, now, General," cried Nip's mistress, coming across the grass in a swinging walk, her arms dangling loosely at her sides, "what is all this wonderful laughing about? and who are you abusing—man, woman, or child? It's seldom that you say a word against any one! Come, who is it? Shall I guess who is mischievous, lazy, and *mean?* Now really you might let *me* into the secret, when it's known to Miss Denis. Can it be any one in Ross? Dear me!"—with sudden animation,—"I have it!—it's——"

Of course she was just about to exclaim "Mr. Lisle," when the General hastily interrupted her, saying, "We were not talking scandal; it was merely a little joke of ours"—looking appealingly at Dr. Malone and Helen, who were choking with suppressed laughter—indeed the very railings behind the former were shaking dangerously,—"it was only a miserable jest, Mrs. Creery," reiterated the General, nervously (seeing that her mind was bent on dragging the secret from his bosom), "that was all, really, you know. And, by-the-way," lowering his voice, and speaking confidentially, "I wanted to consult you about something—about getting up a little dinner for Miss Denis."

To be consulted, and by the General, was much to Mrs. Creery's mind, so she immediately walked aside with him, prepared to give her whole attention to the discussion. It now was nearly eight o'clock, and people were leaving. Helen was escorted to her own door by Dr. Malone and Mr. Quentin, Colonel Denis once more bringing up the rear, but this time he had a companion—Miss Caggett. Mr. Quentin lingered below the steps of the verandah, and squeezed Helen's fingers as he took a very reluctant leave of her. He half hoped that he would have been earnestly requested to honour them with his company at dinner, but this hope was doomed to disappointment, he was dismissed by Colonel Denis with a careless nod! Later on, as Helen sat alone in the verandah, and looked out over the sea, recalling the scenes of this most wonderful, eventful day, and dwelling on all the new faces she had seen and the strange things she had heard, it is an extraordinary, but veracious fact, that—with the perversity common to her sex—she cast more than one thought to a man she had been twice warned against in the same afternoon, in short, Mr. Quentin's pauper-friend, Gilbert Lisle.

Meanwhile Mr. Quentin had been rowed over to Aberdeen, had climbed the hill in capital spirits, and with a healthy appetite; and had found his companion already at home, reposing in an arm-chair in front of the bungalow, smoking. He fully expected to be severely cross-examined about his visit, and on the subject of Miss Denis, and was prepared to enter into the fullest details, and to paint the lady in the richest tints, but, alas!

a disappointment awaited him. Lisle never once referred to Ross—much less to the young lady. He had had a big take of fish, and had caught three bottle-nosed sharks off the Red Buoy—bait, hooks, and nets engrossed his mind entirely.

Mr. Quentin was seriously affronted. Was ever such callousness known? could such indifference be matched? Indifference that would not even take the trouble to ask such a simple question as "What is she like?"

CHAPTER VI
QUEEN OF THE CANNIBAL ISLANDS

"An eye like mine,

A lidless watcher of the public weal."

Tennyson.

Perhaps it would be as well, before going further with this story, to dedicate a page or two to a description of that very important lady, Mrs. Creery. The gentleman who occupied a position in the background as "Mrs. Creery's husband," was a hard-working, hard-headed Scotchman, who thoroughly understood domestic politics, and the art of holding his peace. He had come to Port Blair soon after the settlement was opened up, and had subsequently gone home, and returned with a bride, a lady not, strictly speaking, in her first youth—this was twenty years ago. But let no one suppose that Mrs. Creery had spent the whole of that interval on Ross. She had made several trips to England, and had passed like a meteor through the circles in which her sister, Lady Grubb, was as the sun. Oh, how utterly weary were Mrs. Creery's intimates of those brilliant reminiscences—heard for the thousandth time. Did they not, one and all, detest the very name of "Grubb"?

How was it, people asked each other, that Mrs. Creery had reigned so long and so tyrannically at Ross? How came she to occupy a position, from which nothing could dislodge her—there had been mutinies, there had been social risings, but they all had been quelled. Even a lady who had positively refused to go in to dinner, unless she was taken in before Mrs. Creery, had been quenched! Circumstances had placed the latter on the social throne, and not election by ballot, much less the potent power of personal popularity. The General was a widower, the chaplain a bachelor, the next senior officer unmarried also, the wife of another was an invalid, and spent nearly all her time in the south of France (according to Mrs. Creery, for south of France, read lunatic asylum). She herself was a woman of robust constitution, and always ready to say "present," consequently, the position of leading lady in the settlement fell to her happy lot! She "received" at the General's parties and dances, she occupied a chief place at feasts, a front pew in church, and had a whole programme to herself on band nights. After all, there was not much in this, one would imagine; but Mrs. Creery thought otherwise. The General, an urbane and popular elderly gentleman, was governor over the Andamans, in the Queen's name; he was her Majesty's representative, and held the lives of fifteen thousand convicts in the hollow of his hand; his dominions stretched from the Cocos to Havelock, and included even the distant Nicobars. As his social coadjutor, Mrs. Andrew Creery considered that she shared all his other dignities, and had gradually come to look upon herself as a species of crowned head, ruling not merely the settlement, the Europeans, and the convicts, but even the far-away savages of the interior! These royal ideas had developed but gradually—a little germ (sown by the first strains of "God save the Queen," played as she accompanied the General to a presentation of prizes) had thrown out roots and suckers, and planted a sense of her own dignity in her bosom, that nothing but death could eradicate!

Mrs. Creery had no children and ample leisure, and with such a magnificent idea of her social status, no one will be surprised to hear that she condescended to manage the domestic concerns of all within her realms. She had come to look upon this as a sacred duty, and viewed all comings and goings with microscopic scrutiny. The position of her house favoured this self-imposed supervision; it was close to the pier, had a good back view of the bazaar, and the principal road ran by her door, and consequently it is no exaggeration to say that *nothing* escaped her. From long practice she could tell at a glance where people were going as they ran the gauntlet of her verandah; if the General wore a "regulation" helmet, he was probably *en route* to an execution at Viper (an island five miles away); if his Terai, he was bound for the new buildings on Aberdeen, or to make semi-official calls; if his old topee, he was merely going out shelling. Ross was a small island, very thickly populated. Mrs. Creery could easily make the circuit of it in twenty minutes, and did so at least thrice in the twenty-four hours.

She had no home ties, no domestic tastes; she did not care for flowers nor work; never opened a book, and looked upon shelling as childish nonsense. Her one taste was for poultry; her one passion, her dog "Nip," and when she had fed her hens, collected their eggs, given out daily stores, scolded her domestics, she had nothing to occupy her for the remainder of the day. After early breakfast she generally donned her well-known topee, and sallied forth on a tour of inspection; to quote Captain Rodney, who could not endure her, she "turned out" each family at least once daily, and never omitted "visiting rounds." She had by this time pretty well exhausted Ross—and the patience of its inhabitants; she knew every one's affairs, and what they paid their servants (and what their servants said of them in the bazaar), and what stores they got in, just as well as they did themselves.

Mr. Lisle had undoubtedly baffled her (though she had not done with him yet); however, Helen Denis was a novelty, and opened up an entirely new sphere of interest; therefore, ere nine o'clock on the day after the tennis party, Mrs. Creery's umbrella was once again heard imperiously rapping on the steps of Colonel Denis's verandah.

"You don't breakfast till twelve, I know," she called out; "for I met your cook and asked him, and it's only just nine"—this to Helen, who had come to the drawing-room door. "It's only just nine, and we shall have a nice long morning to ourselves, and be able to look at your things comfortably. Are you unpacking now?"

Helen very reluctantly acknowledged that she was—had just got all her boxes open.

"Then I shall come and help you," said her visitor, laying down her umbrella, and speaking as if she were conferring a great favour. "You go first, and I'll follow."

She was quite as good as her word. There she sat, with her hands on her knees, her topee pushed well back (so as not to interfere with her vision), in closest proximity to Helen's largest trunk, and saw every article separately taken out and unfolded. Nothing escaped her; all she saw, she priced; and all she fancied she tried on (or tried to try on), and meanwhile she kept up a running fire of comments somewhat in this style:—

"So *that's* your black silk; and trimmed with lace, I declare! most unsuitable for a girl like you quite ridiculous! I shall speak to your father, and if he likes, I don't mind taking it off his hands. I dare say there is *some* letting out, and I'm rather in want of a dress for my receptions."

"Yes," gasped Helen, who was kneeling on the floor, "but I do not wish to part with my black silk."

"What use is it? *You* can't wear it," irritably. "Every one would laugh at you if you came up to one of the 'at homes' in a gown like that, and saw *me* in a simple muslin. It's not suitable to your position—do you understand that?"

"I did not mean to wear it at tennis," stammered Helen—who was a little cowed by Mrs. Creery's eye; "but Miss Twigg said that it would be useful."

"Not a bit of it! What does she know about what would be useful?" retorted the lady rudely.

Miss Denis made no reply, but was firmly resolved that nothing short of physical force should part her and her very best dress. Mrs. Creery said no more either, but determined to have a word with the Colonel by-and-by, and also to give him *her* opinion of the absurd extravagance of his daughter's outfit!

As she sat drawn up beside Helen's trunks whilst she unpacked, her perpetual queries, "What is this? What did you give for that?" were, to say the least of it, trying. However, her victim was but recently emancipated from school, had a wholesome awe of her elders, and a remarkably sweet temper, so the whole inspection passed off quite smoothly, and entirely to Mrs. Creery's satisfaction.

"I saw you talking to Lizzie Caggett last evening," she remarked, as she arranged her topee at the mirror, and dodged her profile in a hand-glass. "What was she saying to you?"

"She was asking me what I thought of the place?"

"Well, don't tell her much—that's *my* advice to you! She is certain to come here borrowing your patterns, but don't lend her *one*! I shall be really angry with you if you do." (This came well from a lady who was carrying off the promise of half-a-dozen.) And little did Helen know the large reading a Dirzee gives to the term "taking a pattern." It means that he rips up seams, punches holes in the material with his gigantic scissors, and turns a new garment inside out and upside down, with as little ceremony as if it were an old thing that was going to the rag-bag. At present, ignorance was bliss. Mrs. Creery's convict Dirzee was coming down that very afternoon to carry away Helen's two prettiest and freshest costumes!

"Now," continued the elder lady, "mind with I say about Lizzie Caggett; she has dozens of dresses, and is head over ears in debt in Calcutta, not to speak of the bazaar here—I know myself that she owes Abdul Hamed two hundred rupees,—and do not encourage her in her wicked extravagance."

Then walking to the window, she cried out rapturously, "What a view! Why, I had no idea of this; you can see every *bit* of the road—and there's the General going up home, and Mr. Latimer with him! I suppose he has asked him to breakfast—that's the second time this week! And here comes Dr. Malone, *running*; he has something to tell him! Oh, I must go! Where's my umbrella? Don't forget the dresses," and without further adieux, Mrs. Creery was flying down the steps, brandishing her arms, and calling out in a shrill falsetto,—

"Stop, stop, Dr. Malone. I'm coming. Wait for *me!*"

CHAPTER VII
MR. QUENTIN'S PIANO

"I have assailed her with music, but she vouchsafes no
notice."

Cymbeline.

Mail-day had come round once more, and Helen could hardly believe
that she had been already six weeks on Ross, it seemed more like six days.
She had made the acquaintance of almost everybody, had visited the
mainland, and Chatham and Viper; had ridden on a settlement elephant,
had been to two picnics, and dozens of tennis parties, and was beginning to
realize that she really was the mistress of that pretty bungalow under the
palm-trees on the hill-side.

She was now great friends with Mrs. Home, and solemnly engaged
to Billy; she saw Miss Caggett daily, and Mrs. Creery almost hourly, and
other people called with complimentary frequency; notably Mr. Quentin,
who found many excuses for tarrying in Miss Denis's drawing-room, and,
remarkable to relate, Miss Caggett invariably contrived to drop in on the
same occasions. She was usually in the highest spirits, and laughed, and
smiled, and chatted as agreeably as if she had not come on purpose to mount
guard over a recreant admirer, and by her presence endeavour to modify
his attentions to her rival! Mr. Quentin found her company a bore; how
could he settle down to read poetry, or to talk vague sentimental follies,
whilst Miss Lizzie's sharp, shadeless eyes were following every look and
movement? Moreover, she seasoned her conversation with disagreeable
remarks, uncomfortable questions, and unpleasant insinuations.—
Miss Denis was musical, but at present she had no piano; her father had
promised her a new one from Calcutta after Christmas, but in the meantime
she must wait. Mr. Quentin was surprised to find that he did not make
as rapid strides in Helen's good graces as he usually did under similar
circumstances, but he accounted for this amazing fact quite readily in his
own mind, and was not one whit daunted. In the first place, she had but
little sentiment in her composition; she was a sort of a girl who, if you
invited her "to come out and look at the moon" in your company, would be

certain to burst out laughing in your face—and yet it seemed to him that her own face would make an admirable subject for a very charming romance— she was so absurdly matter-of-fact, so ready in turning off tender speeches, and so provokingly inclined to ridicule his most warranted compliments. Of *course* she liked him—the reverse never once dawned upon his arrogant brain—but why was she so hard to get on with? Doubtless, Lizzie Caggett's haunting presence handicapped him heavily; but Rome was not built in a day, and he had a grand idea—nothing less than sending Miss Denis over his piano as a loan—with a view to vocal duets. His attentions to the young lady had been very "marked" in Mrs. Creery's opinion; he was her shadow at all the "at homes," no other man had a chance of speaking to her; but *this* "attention," which Mrs. Creery beheld coming up the pier, and borne by twenty staggering coolies, threw all his previous advances entirely into the shade.

The good lady hurried on ahead, and burst into Helen's drawing-room, breathless (the umbrella-rapping stage was a ceremony of the past), saying,—

"What do you think? There is a piano coming up the pier in charge of Mr. Quentin's butler—twenty coolies carrying it, at eight annas each! Mr. Quentin is sending it over to you—and, of course, it's *all* settled? and," aggrievedly, "I really think you might have told *me*," and here she was obliged to pause for breath.

Helen stared at Mrs. Creery; never had she seen her so excited, was she going out of her mind, and about a piano?

"A piano, Mrs. Creery?—what piano?"

"A large square."

"And you say that Mr. Quentin is sending it; but it is certainly not coming *here*."

"But it *is*. I saw a note addressed to you in the butler's hand."

"Well, it shall go back at once; it is some mistake. I don't know what papa would say!"

"Your father!" scornfully, "as if *he* would meddle, and as if your wishes are not his law; besides, he knows it would be an excellent match!"

"Mrs. Creery," interrupted Helen, becoming scarlet, "please don't say such things; it's no question of—of—what you hint, but of this piano. What does it mean?"

"It's the thin end of the wedge, *that's* what it means."

"It shall go back!"

"Well, here it comes now at any rate," said the elder lady triumphantly, as the chanting, thin-legged bearers came staggering along under the heavy piece of furniture, with its wadded red cover; and a big, bearded butler presented a note with a profound salaam.

"Wait!" cried Helen, making an imperative gesture, tearing the envelope open. "Don't bring it up yet."

"What's all this?" inquired her father, appearing upon the scene at this juncture.

"A piano for your daughter from Mr. Quentin," volunteered Mrs. Creery with infinite gusto.

"Here, papa," handing him the note, "what am I to say?"

"You will have to keep it for the present, I suppose," he answered rather reluctantly, as he glanced over the missive; "you will have one of your own soon."

Mr. Quentin's note ran as follows:—

> "Dear Miss Denis,—Please do not be alarmed at the size of the accompanying package, nor angry with me for my temerity in sending it; the piano is going to pieces over here, with no one to play on or look after it, and the hot winds on Aberdeen are ruination to an instrument. You will be conferring a great favour on me, if you will give it room, and honour me by making use of it, until the arrival of your own. I will crave permission to bring over *a few* songs, and we might have a little practice occasionally. If possible, I shall come across this afternoon.
>
> "Yours very sincerely,
> "JAMES QUENTIN."

Of course, when the matter was put in the light of a favour to be conferred, there was nothing for it but to allow the instrument to be brought in, and lodged in the drawing-room.

Helen received the open note somewhat mechanically from her father, and will it be believed, that Mrs. Creery actually held out her hand for the missive—just as if it were quite a matter of course, that she should peruse it also?

Peruse it she did, and so slowly, that one would imagine that she was committing it to memory; then she folded it up and returned it to Helen, saying rather tartly, "So you *are* going to keep it, after all?"

"Yes! I suppose so."

"It's only an excuse, of course. You will have him here singing, day and night, mark my words! However, I must allow that he has a sweet tenor, and I shall often drop in for an hour," with which dire threat, Mrs. Creery took her departure, and hastened away to spread the last piece of news, viz., "that it was all *quite* settled between Helen Denis and Mr. Quentin; he had sent her over his piano, and written such a sweet note!"

To Miss Caggett this intelligence was a painful shock; she never believed half of what Mrs. Creery said, but the arrival of the piano had been witnessed. What wrath and anguish filled her mind, as she thought of swains she had snubbed, and chances she had thrown away, for that agreeable shadow, that fickle, faithless, heartless, handsome Jim Quentin! But Lizzie was not easily suppressed; in some respects she was as dauntless as the Bruce!

She put on her best hat, and went up and listened to some solos and duets that very same afternoon; and Mr. Quentin, whose patience was almost threadbare, remarked to her very significantly,—

"I like duets, Miss Caggett, as well as any one, but I don't much care for trios; they are never so harmonious. I'm sure you agree with me."

Lizzie turned pale. She understood, though Helen did not—indeed, *she* was exceedingly glad of Miss Caggett's society on these occasions; it took the too personal edge off her visitor's remarks, and acted as a wet blanket to his compliments. She (Helen) was not quite sure whether he was in jest or earnest at times, but she sincerely *hoped* that it was the former. Strange as it may appear, she was utterly indifferent to the almost invincible Jim Quentin. Why, she could not have told. She knew that he was handsome, agreeable, and showed a flattering penchant for her society. More than this, he had informed her, hundreds of times (indirectly), that he admired her beyond words. And yet, and yet——

Miss Caggett was firmly resolved to punish her recreant lover, and to humble him in the eyes of his new Dulcinea; so she smiled, and showed all her teeth, and put her head on one side, and tried to look playful, and said,—

"Mr. Quentin, you are a *naughty* man! What will Mr. Baines say when he hears you have sent his new Collard and Collard travelling about the settlement?"

Mr. Baines was the gentleman for whom Mr. Quentin was acting.

"*He* say?" colouring. "What is it to him?"

"Only his property," laughing rather boisterously.

Helen felt extremely uncomfortable. There was an undercurrent of hostility in Miss Caggett's laugh, that now struck her for the first time.

Mr. Quentin was not easily cowed, and never had any hesitation about telling what Mark Twain calls a "stretcher," and answered quite promptly,—

"I bought it from Baines; he was hard up. So you are not as wise as you imagined, Miss Caggett."

Miss Caggett did not believe a word of this. Men who come to "act" for six months, and have the use of a furnished house as a matter of course, are not likely to purchase the piano—especially when they can't *play*. But what was the use of speaking out her mind? For once she was prudent, and held her peace; however, she cast a glance at Mr. Quentin that said volumes, and presently she got up and went away; and, when she had departed, Mr. Quentin exclaimed,—

"How I wish that odious young woman—or middle-aged woman—would not favour us with so much of her society; her presence has a most irritating effect on my nerves."

"I thought you and she were great friends," said Helen calmly. "I am sure she told me that, at one time, you were with them every day, and dined, and boated, and sang duets with her."

"I suppose I was three times in their house—I don't know what she will say next! However," anxious to turn to another subject, "do not let us waste our time, or rather *my* precious time over here, on such an insignificant subject. Will you try over the accompaniment of the Wanderer?"

Mr. Quentin found himself so much out of practice that he went across to Ross for an hour's vocal exercise about four times a week. Latterly Mr. Lisle had listened with a gleam of mockery in his eye, as his companion made excuses for these frequent visits, and one day Mr. Quentin up and spake boldly, —

"You are right to laugh at my talk about books and music and new songs, when I say that they are the errands that take me over so often — of course, it's the girl herself."

"Oh, of course," sarcastically.

"I tell you what it is, Lisle — I'm really serious this time; and the queer part of it is, that it's her cool airs and sharp little speeches that have carried the citadel."

"What citadel?" raising his eyes, and searching the other's face.

"My heart, to be sure!"

"Pooh! your heart! Why that has been taken as often as there are days in the year."

"Merely a temporary occupation, my dear sir, but this time it's a complete surrender. 'Pon my word, if she had any money, I'd marry her to-morrow!"

In answer to this remark, Mr. Lisle blew a cloud of smoke into the air, and calmly ejaculated the word, —

"Bosh!"

"I never knew such a fellow as you are," cried Apollo indignantly. "You have no appreciation of sentiment; you are as tough and matter-of-fact as an old boot! All you care for are rough field sports, such as a long day's shooting, hunting, or fishing, and then to come home to your dinner, and sleep like a dog."

"I only wish I *could* sleep like a dog," rejoined the other with a laugh. "What with the gun and bugles, and those confounded peacocks, there is no such thing as getting a wink of sleep after four o'clock."

"Now," continued Mr. Quentin querulously, "I hate your style of life. You don't care what clothes you wear, you tramp the bush and over hill and dale with a gun on your shoulder, on the off chance of a wild pig, or a paltry brace of snipe! Or you grill by the hour in a boat, fishing for sharks and sword-fish. Now give me instead — —"

"Yes, I know exactly what I'm to give you instead; the refining charms of ladies' society, vocal duets and afternoon tea. Far, far pleasanter, is it not, to sit in a cool, shady verandah, whispering soft nothings to a pretty girl—I believe you said she *was* pretty—than to be out in a boat blistering in the sun, or tramping the woods, gun on shoulder, with a good average chance of being winged oneself by an Andamanese arrow? But let me tell you, James Quentin, that your amusement is in reality the most dangerous of the two, and, if Dr. Parks is to be believed, you have already burnt your fingers badly."

"Hang Dr. Parks! I don't want to hear about him, or any one else, except Helen Denis."

"Helen Denis! And does she not wish to hear about any one but James Quentin?"

Mr. Quentin smiled a seraphic smile that inferred much; his companion was not surprised. Quentin was exactly the sort of fellow to please a young lady's fancy; naturally he would seem to her the very beau ideal of a hero, with his low voice, heavenly blue eyes, and handsome face; but then she was not aware that he did not stand the test of close intimacy. *She* had never heard him cursing his chokra or his creditors—she never saw him in ragged moral deshabille!

"Of course she does not know that this is by no means your first tender effort at gallantry?—However, that is of no moment, Miss Caggett will undeceive her," tranquilly remarked his companion.

"What a beastly ironical fellow you are, Lisle! First you rake up old Parks, and then Lizzie Caggett. I wish she were in a sack at the bottom of Ross harbour!" blustered Mr. Quentin.

"Because she represents a kind of conscience in her own person? Take care that Miss Denis does not do the same some day."

"No fear," stoutly. "She is now a mere child in many ways, full of delight with everything about her, and with no more idea of flirting than——" pausing.

"I have," suggested his listener, innocently.

"I would be sorry to name her in the same breath with you; and that reminds me, that more than once she has asked me questions about Mr. Lisle."

"Oh, of course, they all do *that*!"

"She has heard of you."

"From my good, kind friend, Mrs. Creery, I'll bet a fiver, and I'll bet another that she has painted me as black as an Andamanese,—and the devil himself would not be blacker."

"Well, come over with me to-morrow, and let Miss D. see that you are not as bad as you are painted."

"What would be the use? If she is all you *say*, I might fall in love with her also! and that would be a very uncomfortable state of affairs."

Mr. Quentin looked at him for a second with a cool stare, and then burst out laughing.

"Well, upon my word! you are the queerest fellow I ever met, and that's saying a good deal; you can never be in earnest for five minutes. Now look here, I want to talk to you seriously about my money affairs.—You see my governor is an old man, and when he is laid in the family vault, I'll have a decent little competence, but until *then* I cannot keep myself, much less a wife. I'm certain he won't give me a halfpenny more allowance than I have already. I've an uncontrollable knack of spending coin, and running into debt; but with the family acres, I think I might manage to rub along pretty well."

"So you might," agreed his listener.

"But then the governor may live till he is a hundred."

"So he may," again admitted the other gentleman.

"For goodness' sake, Lisle, don't sit there with your eyes half shut, driving me mad with your 'so you might' and 'so he may.' Make a suggestion."

"My dear sir, I cannot think of any to offer. If you were an Earth Indian, you would be all right; you know they tie up their aged as bait for wild beasts. Being a mere Englishman——"

Mr. Lisle never finished what he was about to say; for his companion sprang to his feet, towered above him, glared at him for a second, opened his mouth and endeavoured to speak,—but failed; and then flung out of the apartment in a terrible passion.

CHAPTER VIII
"I WAS HIS DEAREST LIZZIE!"

"Alas! for pleasure on the sea,

And sorrow on the shore."

Hood.

Mrs. Home's entertainments to her friends generally took the form of a picnic or gipsy tea, partly, we suspect, because these outings were in great favour with Tom and Billy, and partly because she had a knack of making these "camp affairs," as Mrs. Creery contemptuously dubbed them, go off to every one's satisfaction. She had now issued invitations for a tea at North Bay, where her guests were to ramble about, and stroll on the beach, or botanize in the jungle; and two large boats left the pier carrying the company, which comprised the host, hostess, and family, Col. and Miss Denis, Miss Caggett, Mr. Latimer, Dr. Parks, Dr. Malone, the Grahams from Chatham, and the Greens from Viper. Mr. Quentin did not patronize these rustic *réunions*, and he was rather annoyed to find that the Denises were bent on going, and leant over the pier as they were rowed away, looking unutterable reproaches at Helen—looks not lost on Miss Caggett, who was sitting beside her. It was an oppressive afternoon; even at four o'clock the sky was molten and the sea like oil, and Mr. Quentin shouted after the pleasure party,—

"I would not be a bit surprised if you people were in for a storm coming back—better not stay late."

"Storm! what nonsense! Why, the water is like glass!" exclaimed Mrs. Home. "He merely says that because he is not coming himself—though I asked him, and told him he might bring Mr. Lisle, for I really do not see why he should be debarred from everything."

"If he is debarred, it's his own fault," rejoined Lizzie Caggett, accepting the challenge in the absence of Mrs. Creery in the other boat. "If he would only be open about himself, no one would mind his poverty."

Mrs. Home looked sweetly incredulous, and Miss Caggett continued,—

"At any rate the chances are that he would not come if he was asked. I don't suppose he has any decent clothes, and he is more in his element in the bush, or out in that white boat of Mr. Quentin's, sailing among the islands; he half lives on the water, but," with a peculiar laugh, "there is no fear of his being drowned!"

Miss Lizzie was merciless to this mysterious pauper, chiefly because she had an idea that he had talked his host out of certain matrimonial designs that were very near to her heart. Jim Quentin's visits had been less frequent, ever since he had given lodging to this odious adventurer!

Now Mrs. Home considered Mr. Lisle inoffensive and gentlemanly-looking, and quite entitled to keep his affairs to himself if he chose, and she took up the cudgels at once, and the argument was waxing hot, when, luckily, some one commenced to sing, and politeness enforced silence. It was a long row to North Bay, fully eight miles, and it was past five o'clock when the party landed, and began to walk about and stretch their rather cramped legs, and to stroll along the beach with a careless eye to shells.—But this was not a *bonâ fide* shelling trip.—Presently, in answer to a whistle, with various degrees of alacrity they flocked round Mrs. Home's well-spread table-cloth, which was laid out on the moss under a big Pedouk tree, and in a position, that commanded a fine view of the open sea. Here every one ate and drank, and were merry; and afterwards they sang songs and gave riddles and exchanged stories, well-known or otherwise, and then by degrees they scattered once more, and went up into the woods close by, in couples or in small parties, and commenced (the ladies especially) to tear down orchids that would be priceless in grey-skyed England; to fill their hands and their baskets with enormous bunches of Eucharis lilies that carpeted the jungle. Helen was somewhat surprised to find herself alone with Lizzie Caggett, but this was a mere passing thought, her whole attention was given to the flowers; she felt quite bewildered among such an *embarras de richesse*, and she paused every now and then to exclaim, and to gather handfuls. She was also in ecstasies at the love-birds, honey-suckers, blue-jays and golden orioles that flew "with a shocking tameness" across their path.

Miss Caggett was accustomed to these sights; her enthusiasm—if she had any—she kept bottled up for the benefit of a male companion, and did not trouble herself to respond to Helen's raptures; she had dogged her, and purposely kept off Dr. Malone, and singled her out as her own special associate, in order that she, as she said to herself, "might have it out with her here in the jungle," where she could be as shrill as she pleased,—yea, as one of the island peacocks! where she could give reins to her wrath, and no one but her unsuspicious rival would be any the wiser!—Now on Ross the very walls had ears.

The two girls wandered along, one empty-handed, and the other laden with spoils, till they came to an opening in the forest, where there was a very beautiful shallow pool, apparently a spring. It was an unusual sight, and Lizzie halted, and looked down into it, and beheld the reflection of her own figure, and of her, at present, very cross, discontented little face as seen in a mirror set in a lovely frame of ferns, and mossy stones, and graceful grasses.

As she pondered over her own appearance, and felt an agonizing thrill, at the patent fact that she was now beginning to look *old*! a bright young face came into view over her shoulder—a bright young face that she hated from the bottom of her heart! No wonder she was a prey to envy, as she gazed at Helen's reflection; never had she looked better, than in that soft white gown, with a wreath of Eucharis lilies twined round her sailor hat. Lizzie stared, and noted every item of that pretty vision, and felt a conviction of her own powerlessness to crush the horrible truth, that one of those two faces was lovely, and smiling, and young, and that the other was pinched, ill-tempered, and *passée*—and that other her own! Her day was on the wane, the summer of her life—oh, that it would come again! she would sell her soul to recall it!—was gone. And in Helen Denis's case, she had all her golden youth before her. These bitter thoughts were too much for her self-control, her face worked convulsively, the corners of her mouth went down, and all of a sudden she burst into tears! Helen was dismayed; she led her gently to a fallen log of ebony, and implored of her to tell her if she was ill, or what was the matter?

The tears were but a summer shower, and quickly spent, and Miss Caggett came to herself, dried her eyes, and said that it was merely a slight nervous seizure, the result of a racking headache, and meant nothing. "But," she added, "I'm tired, and we may as well rest here awhile, there is no hurry."

"Very well," agreed Helen, "I want to settle these flowers, they are in a most dreadful state," proceeding to arrange her much-crowded basket.

"Then, whilst you arrange your flowers, dear, I will tell you a story," said Lizzie, now completely composed.

"Oh, do! how nice of you! I like stories, and this"—looking round—"is the very place for one. A ghost story?"

"But mine is going to be a love-tale," said Miss Caggett briefly.

"I don't care for them so much," rejoined Helen, sorting out orchids as she spoke. "However, anything *you* like."

"Once upon a time there was a girl, and she lived in the East Indies with her mother; her name was Lizzie Caggett," she commenced. Helen, who was kneeling at the log, using it as a table for her flowers, looked up as if she did not believe her ears. "Her name, as I tell you, was Lizzie Caggett. She was not a great beauty like *some* people, but she was not bad-looking. A young man came to Port Blair, paid her marked attention, fell in love with her, and she with him; he gave her songs and presents, he wrote her heaps of letters, he told her that he could not *live* without her. His name was James Quentin!" She paused, and Helen got up slowly from her knees and stood in front of her—her heart was beating rather fast, and her colour was considerably brighter than usual. "A girl arrived at Port Blair named Helen Denis, and he, man-like, paid her attention at first because she was *new*,— he half lives at her house, he is always at her side, and" (viciously) "he has made her the talk of the whole place. He," also rising and suddenly dropping the narrative form for plainer speaking, "is a hypocrite, he told you a *lie* about that piano!—it belongs to Mr. Baines—he has pretended to you that he scarcely knew *me*. Scarcely ever was out of our house, is nearer the truth! One thing he can't deny, and that is his own hand-writing. Look here," dragging out a thick packet of letters tied with blue ribbon, "you can read them if you like. You won't!" in answer to a scornful gesture. "Then there," tossing them violently on the ground, where they fell with a heavy thud, and the ribbon coming undone, lay scattered about like a pack of cards.

Miss Caggett after this outbreak paused, and folded her arms akimbo, but her eyes were gleaming, and her lips working convulsively.

Helen was thunderstruck, never had it dawned upon her till now, that she had come and seen, and conquered, this furious lady's lover; the sudden announcement gave her a shock and for some seconds she was speechless.

"There," proceeded Miss Caggett, pointing to a letter at her feet, "three months ago I was his dearest Lizzie, and now you are his dearest Helen," and she laughed like a hyena.

"You are altogether mistaken, and quite wrong," cried her companion, speaking at last; "I am nothing to him but an ordinary acquaintance, and I don't think you should repeat these terrible things about him to me! You can't care very *much* for him, or you would not say that he is a hypocrite and does not speak the truth. As to his making me the talk of the place, I am quite distressed to hear that Port Blair is so hard up for a topic." Helen was very angry, and her face was an open book, in which every emotion that swayed her was eloquently expressed. Mr. Quentin was utterly indifferent to her, and this fact gave her a considerable advantage over Miss Caggett. Besides being angry she was disgusted, and looked down upon her opponent with a glance of unmistakable scorn.

"Of course you will *tell* him all I have said," exclaimed Lizzie, with a hysterical smile.

"Oh, of course," ironically.

Miss Caggett was filled with a horrible fear that she had overshot her mark (which had been merely to blacken Mr. Quentin to Helen, to arouse her ire, and take advantage of the ensuing quarrel and coolness, and once more ingratiate herself with her late adorer). But who would have expected Miss Denis to be supremely ironical and scornful, and to have taken the news in this very strange way, for Lizzie believed that no girl living could be indifferent to James Quentin? Instead of tearing her hair and weeping and denouncing him, she was quite unmoved. She had even spurned his letters! hateful, cold-blooded thing!

"Shall you tell him all I have said about him?" she reiterated defiantly.

"Your suggestion is of course prompted by what you would do *yourself* under similar circumstances," returned her companion in a cutting tone.

"Do you pretend that you don't *like* him?" demanded Miss Caggett; "that you never told me you thought him handsome? Do you pretend that you are not in love with him and have lured him away from *me*?"

"*I* pretend nothing; I do not even pretend to be his friend before his face, and then abuse him unmercifully behind his back! And now," pointing with the tip of her shoe, "there are your letters. I advise you not to leave them here for the amusement of some picnic party. And I *request* that you will never speak to me in such a way again, nor mention the name of your friend Mr. Quentin."

So saying, Helen picked up her basket, turned her back on Lizzie, and walked off into the jungle in a rather stately fashion, never once looking back at the little figure on the log. If she had done so, she would have seen that little figure shaking a tiny menacing fist in her direction; but ignorance was bliss, and she rambled on mechanically, her mind not a little disturbed by the recent "scene." Lizzie Caggett was *not* a nice girl—not a lady—and as to Mr. Quentin, she had never quite trusted his dreamy blue eyes. Now she came to ponder over the subject, his stories were often a bad fit—one tale did not exactly match another—he forgot what he had said previously, and although he had angrily disowned Miss Caggett, yet she had noticed one mezzo soprano song among his music, on which was scribbled in pencil, "Lizzie, with J.'s love." Deeply occupied in unravelling various new ideas, the young lady strayed further and further into the wood, occasionally stopping to cull some too tempting flower or fern—and pondering as she plucked. She was extremely reluctant to go back to the company and to face Miss Caggett after their late conversation, but a sudden cessation of birds' notes, a duskiness, and a little chill wind, warned her that it was really time to retrace her steps. She had come further than she imagined, and it was fully half an hour ere she had extricated herself from among the trees and once more gained the open space looking down upon the shore. But what was this? To her astonishment the beach was deserted. There was no sign of living creature to be seen (save the dying embers of the gipsy fire), and, did her eyes deceive her, or did she really behold two heavily laden boats steadily rowing back to Ross? Indeed, one was already a mere speck on the water, and she had been left behind! At first she could not realize her position; she, the chief guest—in whose honour the party had been given—she forgotten and abandoned to pass the night on that terrible, desolate mainland alone! She ran to a rock jutting out far into the water and waved her parasol, and screamed, and called, but the boats were far beyond earshot, and the awnings were up.

She stood looking after them like a modern Dido, with strange, fixed, despairing eyes, then turned and gazed behind her at the thick, black, and now forbidding-looking forest, that loomed all round her, and encompassed the shore. She sat down on the rock, locked her arms round her knees, and watched the two heartless boats till they were quite out of sight. This operation lasted for some time, and when there was nothing further to be seen in the direction of Ross, she turned her face towards the open sea, and beheld, to her horror, a large canoe coming rapidly in her direction! It was still at some distance, but she knew that the build of the boat was not European, nor did Europeans go out boating in *tall hats*. She did not wait for a closer inspection; she fled—fled for dear life—right up into the much-dreaded forest, and dashed among the underwood like a mad creature; in a certain thick covert she threw herself down, and there she lay panting like a hunted hare. From her hiding-place, she could see the savages; they paddled close into the shore, attracted by the smoke of the fire that had boiled Mrs. Home's mild domestic kettle! They came in a big red war canoe, and were about fifty in number; one or two remained in the canoe, the rest sprang over the side, and waded to land—followed by a whole legion of dogs. They swarmed round the fire, and found but little to repay their visit, beyond a box of matches, which was evidently a great prize. There were several monster fish caught by Mrs. Creery's boatmen,— and left behind as worthless—these they tore to pieces, and devoured raw. A tin of Swiss milk and half a loaf of bread were also discovered and shared. Whilst they sat round the embers in a circle, and greedily discussed these rarities and the fish, Helen, with every nerve in her body throbbing, and her heart nearly bounding out of her bosom, was presented by her own vivid memory with that scene in Robinson Crusoe, where he sees the savages sitting round a fire, and feasting on their human victims! Supposing they were to discover her, and kill her, and eat her? At this moment she nearly shrieked aloud, for a large red dog, a kind of pariah (who, unknown to her, had been sniffing among the underwood), now suddenly thrust up his head close to hers, and gazed at her in amazement for some seconds; luckily for Helen, instead of breaking at once into a loud "bay," and triumphantly announcing his "find," he was evidently one of the barrack curs whom the General had colonized; he had seen a European before,—and probably understood English! At first, when she whispered in a faltering voice, "Oh, Toby, Toby, like a dear, good dog, go away, and don't betray me," he took no notice, but merely stood staring with his round yellow eyes. However, when emboldened by desperation, she said, "Hoosh! be off!" and made a movement as though to pick up a stone—he fled!

But what if a less educated animal were to discover her? If he did, she was lost. She lay in her hiding-place scarcely daring to breathe, the very sound of her own heart seemed appalling; indeed, it stood quite still for some seconds, when—the fish being despatched—the aborigines stood up and sauntered back to their canoe, and several of them pointing at the jungle, seemingly suggested a ramble in that direction! But these enterprising spirits had no weight, and Helen, although fainting with terror, noticed that a fat old man, in a huge cocked hat (evidently a person of much authority), waved his hands with decision towards the horizon; and making gestures at the big bank of clouds that were gathering there, peremptorily collected all his party, who immediately swarmed out into the canoe, followed by their pack of dogs, and paddled away as swiftly and as suddenly as they had come—and Helen breathed a deep sigh of relief, when she was once more left upon the mainland, entirely alone!

CHAPTER IX
A DAMSEL IN DISTRESS

"The storm is up, and all is on the hazard."

Julius Caesar.

Mr. Lisle had been out boating far beyond North Bay; but a sombre sultry afternoon, and the ominous silence that precedes a tropical storm, had warned him to steer homewards. He had heard of the awful tornadoes that occasionally churned these seas into white mountains, that dashed wrecks around the islands; that the storm god in torrid regions was a terrible sight when aroused, and that a sunny, sleepy afternoon had been known to develop into a howling hurricane in less than an hour. Moreover, that tragic tales of boats blown out to sea, or capsized with all hands, were but too well known at Port Blair.

The sky was now so inky black that it could scarcely look blacker, low muttering thunder was heard from behind the clouds, and an occasional red flash shot along the horizon. The breeze was rising steadily, and a quick cool ripple was on the water. On the whole, Mr. Lisle said to himself that there was every prospect of a very dirty night, and the sooner that he was under the lee of Ross the better. Passing a kind of cove in North Bay, he happened to notice a long white object in the now gathering dusk: it seemed to be near the shore, and was probably a blighted tree. Luckily, he looked again, and observed that it moved. Could it be a human figure, at that hour?—quite impossible! But although moments were precious, he resolved to give the thing, whatever it was, a chance; and to take a nearer view and to accomplish this, he was obliged to steer in closer to the land, which he did—to his boatmen's unconcealed uneasiness. Vainly did they scowl, and point expressively to the storm that was coming up so rapidly: he assured them that this delay would be but momentary; a few vigorous strokes, and they were sufficiently near to make out that the seemingly blighted tree was the figure of a European woman, in a white dress! In two or three seconds they had touched the beach, and Mr. Lisle sprang out of the boat, waded through the water, and another instant brought him to the side of a trembling, distracted girl, whom he had never seen before, but who nevertheless accorded him a half-frenzied, though silent welcome.

Helen, after she had seen the last of the war canoe, had once more ventured down to the shore. The dark thick tropical jungle seemed to stifle her, and, for all she knew, might be swarming with wild beasts! The solitude was something appalling, and the silence!—save for queer outlandish sounds in the forest every now and then, which caused her to tremble violently. Her position may not seem so very terrible to some people,—who will say, "She knew she was sure to be fetched in the morning;" but a night alone upon that savage coast, was enough to make even a stout-hearted man feel nervous, much less a girl like Helen, and by this time she was completely unhinged. As she sat staring into the gloom, she suddenly made out a boat, positively a European boat, with three people in it,—and for the first time her hopes rose. She waved her arms frantically, and she ran up and down the beach like a demented creature. She was seen, and they were coming. Oh, the relief of that moment! For the first time during these dreadful hours, tears rolled down her cheeks.

The boat came in as close as it could, and a man jumped out of it, and approached her rapidly. Stranger as she was, she rushed to him, seized his arm, and tried vainly to speak, but her whole frame was shaken with convulsive sobs.

"What is it? What does it mean?" he asked, as she clung to him, like a drowning person.

"It's a—pleasure party," she stammered out. "I was gathering flowers, and was left behind. Oh, take me with you! Take me home!"

"Come on, then,"—an Englishman's usual formula; "I'll take you back to Ross. But we must look sharp," speaking rather brusquely. What if this tearful, frightened young lady were to go into hysterics, or to faint in his arms? that would be a nice business!

Without a single word, but with obedient alacrity, she followed him to the edge of the sea,—and something told her that she was walking in the wake of the notorious *Mr. Lisle.*

"I'd better carry you through the surf," he said, turning at the water's edge; and coolly putting his arm round her, he was just about to lift her on the spot, but, with flaming cheeks, she thrust him aside, saying, "Thanks, no; I'll manage it myself."

A Bird Of Passage | 73

"Oh, all right," he returned indifferently, "but I think you are foolish! What's the good of two people getting wet, when *one* will do?" now wading out to the boat through surf, which took the young lady up to her knees. He got in first, helped her in afterwards, and, making a sign to the impatient boatmen to raise the sail, he said to his dripping companion, "There is going to be a bit of a blow" (a mild way of putting it), "but we shall have it with us, we shall be home in no time," he added, in a tone of assumed cheerfulness.

In a few seconds they were gliding along over the water, before a nice stiff breeze, and Helen found time to collect her senses, and to relate her adventures—at first in rather a broken, husky voice, but latterly with more composure.

And lest the reader should all this time be angrily blaming Colonel Denis and Mrs. Home, I here beg to state that each believed Helen to be in the other's boat—a thought for which they were indebted to Miss Caggett.

The rising wind and threatening sky made prudent Mrs. Home collect her party, and start; being under the impression that Helen would return with her father. When the people belonging to number two boat were mustered, and inquiries were made for Miss Denis, Miss Caggett assured them that she had long since departed with Mrs. Home, and had been quite animated in declaring that "there was no mistake about the matter, as she and Miss Denis had been walking in the woods together." She also displayed quite a feverish eagerness to be off!—for reasons which we can easily understand. (Miss Lizzie had picked up her letters and pocketed them, and sauntered down to the beach, and there had joined the company, and come to the conclusion that a night's solitary reflection among the tall Gurgeon and Pedouk trees would do her rival a world of good! "How easy," she said to herself, "to say afterwards, that I must have made a mistake—every one is liable to make mistakes!") Thus reassured, the picnic party took their places in the second boat, and no search or calling acquainted Helen of their departure; and consequently, she was left behind, thanks to Miss Lizzie Caggett.

The small white gig which had picked off the young lady, now flew before the wind, and Helen's new acquaintance sat with the tiller-ropes in his hands, and his gaze bent apprehensively on the south.

"I suppose I may as well introduce myself," he said presently. "My name is Lisle. Perhaps you have heard of me?" he added expressively—at least to his listener, his words seemed to have an ironical, significant tone!

Helen muttered a faint affirmative.

"And you, I think, must be Miss Denis?"

"Yes."

"And were you really afraid of the savages?"

"I never was so much frightened in all my life, I thought I should have *died*."

"I see a good deal of them knocking about the islands. They are not such bad fellows, and I doubt their cannibalism."

"I should be sorry to trust them," returned Helen, shuddering.

"You are cold, I see, and wet, of course, but that was your own fault. Here," suddenly removing it, "you must take my coat," throwing it over her knees, where it remained all the time, in spite of her anxious disclaiming. After this there was a long gap in the conversation.

Mr. Lisle undoubtedly possessed what the French call, "a talent for silence." "How grave he looked!" thought Helen. How fast they were going! How frightfully down on one side! The wind was getting louder and louder, till it reached a kind of hoarse scream: the dusk had suddenly given place to Egyptian gloom, and Helen felt sure (as she sat with her hands tightly locked in her lap, and her heart beating very quickly) that they were having more than a mere "blow" as they tore through the water! All at once, the first splash of a cold, salt wave dashed over the boat, and drenched her so unexpectedly that she could not refrain from a stifled exclamation; but this was the only time that she lost her self-control. She sat motionless as an image, and neither moved nor spake, not even when a shrieking gust carried her hat away, and whirled it into the outer darkness; and the storm loosened her long hair, and flung it to the wind to play with. How they flew up the water mountains, and were hurled down like a stone into the corresponding valleys! If they were to be drowned, she hoped that it might be soon; this present suspense was torture. All was so black—an awful opaque blackness—the roar of the tempest the only sound; it came in furious gusts, then died away, whilst wave after wave swept over the boat; and now the low rumble of thunder burst suddenly into one frightful peal, that seemed to shake the very sea itself: a blinding flash lit up the gloom, for a moment it was as daylight. Helen involuntarily turned her eyes towards her companion, and met his point blank. In that second, their two souls seemed to recognize one another; in his glance she read intrepidity, coolness and encouragement. She at least was with a brave man, and might die in worse company! He, on his side, noted the rigid figure of his passenger, her locked hands and firmly-set lips; she was no longer the timid, shrinking creature he had dragged on board the gig less than an hour previously; she was a heroine, capable of looking death in the face, and Death's grim visage was never closer to her than *now*. Another would have been shrieking and clinging to him; but this girl was nerved to meet her fate alone, and he honestly respected her fortitude. It was certainly just touch and go, if they ever weathered Ross Point, but the boat was a stout one, and the sails were new. The twinkling lights on the island now came in view; how scornfully they seemed to mock these four people, who were struggling for life and death in the surrounding howling darkness!

Another awful plunge into the hollows, and a hissing of boiling waves, and a feeling as of water closing all round them. It seemed to Helen as if *this* was the end—they had shipped a heavy sea, the boat reeled, staggered, and made another effort—she was not going to founder just yet.

The stricken boatmen shouted hoarsely to one another, and baled in the dark; Helen crept unconsciously closer to the steersman, and during a lull in the blast, she said,—

"You can swim, Mr. Lisle, of course, and if *you* escape, will you take a message from me to,"—with a sob—"poor papa?"

"No, I won't," he answered roughly.

"But I shall be drowned, I know," and she caught her breath at the chilling thought.

"If you are, I shall be drowned *too*, you may be sure of that. If I am saved, you may rely upon it that you will be saved also. We will sink or swim together. If she *does* capsize, don't lose your head, and don't cling to me, whatever you do; trust me, and I'll take care of you; but I hope it's not going to come to that," he added; then, after a long silence and another blinding sea, he exclaimed, "Thank God, we are over the worst, and under the lea of Ross!"

It was still quite bad enough, but they were no longer exposed to the full fury of the hurricane; in another ten minutes they were being violently washed up and down against the soaking pier, in the presence of a crowd of anxious faces, who were peering over, amidst the glare of torches and general excitement. The first person to greet them was Colonel Denis, looking like a man of seventy, and scarcely able to articulate.

"Oh, Helen," he cried, as he seized his tottering, dripping daughter, "this has nearly killed me! Only an hour ago we missed you, and you were sighted from the lookout just before dark, and I never believed that any boat could live in that," pointing his hand at the black, hissing sea.

As Helen and her father stood thus together on the steps, she trying to realize that she was safe, and he most thankfully doing the same—the white boat showed signs of shoving off.

"You are not going over to Aberdeen now!" shouted Colonel Denis, descending, and making a futile grab at the gunwale. "Are you a madman?"

"It's not so bad inside, between the islands," roared the other in reply. "Good-night."

"Papa, stop him! Mr. Lisle," shrieked Helen, "come back—come back, Mr. Lisle."

The idea of any one putting out again among those tumbling waves, seemed to her nothing less than suicidal; but the white boat was already gone,—lost almost instantaneously in the surrounding darkness.

"It's not so risky between this and Aberdeen, Miss Denis," said Dr. Malone; "and Lisle is a capital sailor. But what a grand fright you have given us all, and what a terrible trip you must have had!"

Miss Denis made no reply; she staggered up to the top of the steps and stood upon the pier in the light of half-a -dozen torches—a strange figure, in a dripping dress, with her long hair covering her as a kind of mantle, and hanging far below her waist in thick dark masses.

"Take her home, and put her to bed at once," said Dr. Malone, "and give her a warm drink, and don't let any one worry her with questions" (doubtless he was thinking of Mrs. Creery); "to-morrow morning I will call, and she will be all right, and will tell us how it happened that she let us go off without her."

But how that came to pass was never clearly explained up to the present day; people had their suspicions, but suspicions go for very little.

Miss Denis carried out Dr. Malone's instructions to the letter. She went home and went to bed and fell sound asleep. One thing she did which he had not prescribed,—

She dreamt of Mr. Lisle!

CHAPTER X
MR. LISLE FORGETS HIS DINNER

"A little fire is quickly trodden out,

Which, being suffered, rivers cannot quench."

Henry VI.

Miss Denis was none the worse for her adventure the next morning, and was called upon to give a full, true, and particular account of herself to Mrs. Creery and Mrs. Home, also Mrs. Graham and Mrs. Green (who had prudently stayed all night on Ross). No one could imagine how the mistake had occurred, and all these ladies talked volubly together on the subject, and it afforded the island a nine days' wonder, though that was not saying much! Mrs. Creery was certainly most thankful that Helen (she now called her by her Christian name) had been brought back in safety, but she was by no means as well pleased at the means to which they owed her restoration.

"Of course, my dear Helen, you need not notice him," she said, *apropos* of Mr. Lisle; "just let your father thank him, or send a message by Mr. Quentin; that will be ample!"

Mr. Lisle having made Aberdeen with some difficulty, had toiled up hill, closely followed by the shivering boatmen, in quest of glasses of rum. He was cold, and stiff, and exhausted; both mind and body had been strung to their utmost tension for the last three hours, and he sank into a Bombay chair in the verandah, and threw off his soaking hat with a sense of thankfulness and relief. There he remained for a long time in his wet clothes, staring out on the black, ragged-looking clouds, through which a very watery moon was vainly trying to assert herself. Mr. Quentin was dining elsewhere, and Mr. Lisle kept dinner waiting till it was his good pleasure to partake of that meal. (Eastern cooks are accustomed to a meal being put back or forward an hour or so according to their masters' whims. These sudden orders never ruffle their composure, whilst in England such proceedings would cause domestic revolutions.) For more than an hour Mr. Lisle lay back in the comfortable chair which he had first occupied as a mere momentary resting-place; evidently he had something out of the common to occupy his thoughts. How long was it since he had spoken to a lady? (Apparently Mrs. Creery went for nought.) His mind reviewed but cursorily his morning's sport, dwelt a short time on the various incidents of that terrible sail, and rested finally for a considerable period on the contemplation of his lady passenger; he could see her before his mental vision quite distinctly *now*, as she stood on the pier steps, with her soaking, clinging dress, her streaming hair and colourless face, on which the torches threw a blinding light; see her stretching out her hands, and calling after him in a tone of agonized appeal,—

"Mr. Lisle, come back! Come back, Mr. Lisle!"

It was a curious fact, he said to himself with a rather cynical grin, that this was positively the very first invitation he had ever received to Ross; and the circumstance seemed to amuse him not a little.

After a while he began to think that he was rather a fool, sitting there mooning in his wet clothes, and he rose and stretched himself and went into the house, and having changed his garments, sat down to his solitary meal. He and Jim Quentin met at breakfast as usual; the latter was generally too much engrossed with his own proceedings to take any vivid interest in his companion's pursuits—to do as little work as possible, to get as much novel-reading, cigarette-smoking, and physical and mental ease, was the bent of his mind, and his thoughts were solely centred in himself and his own arrangements.

He never troubled his head about Lisle's "manias;" fishing, and boating, and shooting were all bores to him, involving far too much bodily exertion and discomfort. He took all his partner's adventures for granted, and never expected that these were of a more thrilling description than the capture of a big shark or the slaughter of a wild hog.

"What a gale that was last night!" he said, as he languidly helped himself to devilled kidneys. "By George! the picnic party must have found it pretty lively coming back. It blew a hurricane! But I suppose they were in before that?"

"They were," assented Mr. Lisle—and whatever else he was going to add was interrupted by the appearance of one of the boatmen in his blue cotton suit, salaaming profoundly at the foot of the verandah steps. He had something in his hand. What? It was the miserable wreck of a lady's smart, cream-coloured parasol! A jaunty article, that had tempted Helen's fancy in a London shop window, and was now a mere limp rag, cockled and shrunken with sea-water—having been thrown into the bottom of the boat and there forgotten.

"Halloa!" exclaimed Mr. Quentin. "What is that?"

"Miss Denis's parasol, which was left in the gig. I brought her back from North Bay last night," replied his companion, with as much composure as if it were a part of his daily programme.

The other made no immediate reply, but turning half round in his chair, surveyed him steadily for some seconds.

"*You* brought her back?" he repeated incredulously. "And why, in the name of all that's extraordinary?"

"For the very excellent reason that she wished to be my passenger," returned Mr. Lisle, coolly.

"I hate riddles"—irritably. "What the deuce do you mean?"

"I mean that Miss Denis was left behind by her party owing to some very queer mistake, that I happened to be sailing by, like Canute the king, and that she hailed the boat, and we took her off."

"Quite romantic, upon my word"—with a rather forced laugh. "Well," after a pause, "now that you have seen her, what do you think of her?"

"How can I tell you? It was as dark as pitch; I only had a glimpse of her now and then by lightning."

"Yes; and that glimpse?"

"Showed me that she had heaps of hair. She did not scream or make a fuss, but kept quiet, for which I was really grateful."

"And did you have any talk?"

"Talk! My good sir, are you aware that we were out in that hurricane between seven and eight o'clock last night, and that it was by God's mercy we escaped with our lives?"

"I dare say you would like to improve the acquaintance now you have seen her—eh? Come, tell the truth."

Mr. Lisle made no reply; this question had hit the goal—he certainly *did* feel a curious and unusual interest in this girl. All the same, he made up his mind that this novel sensation would wear off within the next twenty-four hours, and whether or no, he did not mean to yield to it.

Mr. Quentin crossed to Ross alone, somewhat to his own surprise; and Helen, as she listened to his condolences, felt rather an odd little twinge of disappointment, for she had half expected that for once he would have been accompanied by his mysterious companion. To-day her smiles were not as responsive, nor her laughter as ready as usual. Her keen-witted visitor did not fail to notice this,—also a curious abstraction in her manner. She was partly thinking of Mr. Lisle (with an interest that surprised herself), and partly recalling to her mental eye that little pink figure seated on the log, with a face convulsed with passion, and dozens of love-letters scattered round her on the moss!

About a week later Colonel Denis met Mr. Lisle in the Bazaar and insisted on his accompanying him home, and being there and then presented to his daughter.

"She wants to thank you herself; only for you she believes that she would have lost her wits; only for you she would have had to pass a whole night on that coast alone."

Vainly did his captive mutter "that it was nothing; that he was only too glad to have had the opportunity," &c., Colonel Denis was not to be denied, and he led him off, *nolens volens*, to make formal acquaintance with the island beauty at last.

Miss Denis was sitting on the steps of the bungalow feeding a tame peacock, but as she saw her father approaching with a visitor in tow, she stood up, rather shyly, to receive them. She looked quite different to-day (naturally). Her dress was soft, cream-white muslin, a heavy Indian silver belt encircled her slender waist, her hair was bound round her head in thick plaits, her countenance was serene—and marvellously pretty. It struck Mr. Lisle's artist eye that she and her pet peacock would make a very effective picture, with that glimpse of blue sea and palms as their background.

Of course she had a conviction that this spare, sunburnt man following her father was the redoubtable *bête-noire*, who, although she had been two months in the settlement, she had never yet met with face to face, save in the gloom on that eventful evening.

After a little talk about the storm and the picnic, they adjourned indoors and sat in the shady drawing-room, whilst Sawmy brought in afternoon tea.

"How do you like this part of the world, Miss Denis?" asked her visitor. "No doubt you are tired of the question by this time?"

"I like it extremely; so much that I believe I could live here all my life."

Mr. Lisle smiled incredulously and slightly raised his brows.

"Yes," in reply to his expression. "Where could you find a more lovely spot—a kind of earthly Paradise?"

"And a land where it is always afternoon," quoted her companion; "but you will probably get tired of it in six months, and be glad enough to stretch your wings."

"No, indeed"—indignantly—"why should I? I have everything I want here, and every wish fulfilled." She paused, became exceedingly red, as if she were afraid she had been too gushing to this stranger.

"I am filled with amazement and respect, Miss Denis; you are the only person I have ever come across who admitted that they were now, in the actual present, absolutely contented, and had no unsatisfied cravings. But perhaps yours is a contented mind?"

"No, I have not been contented elsewhere; but here it is different; here I have my home, and papa——"

She hesitated, and her listener mentally added—"And Jim Quentin!"

"And I think perpetually fine weather, and beautiful surroundings, and liberty, go a long way towards making one feel as I do. Every morning when I wake, I have an impression that something delightful is going to happen during the day."

"Jim's visit of course," thought her companion. A sure sign that she is in love, but he merely said aloud,—

"It's well you mentioned liberty, for I fancy that scenery and sunshine go a short way with those beggars," pointing to a group of brown convicts, who were now wending silently down the road. "Do you not find everything very different out here to what it is at home?"

"Yes; but I had no home, I was always at school. Papa and I have so few belongings—but I am quite forgetting all this time that I have not offered you a cup of tea."

Mr. Lisle watched her as she busied herself among the spoons and saucers, and thought what a nice child she was, and what a shame it would be to let Jim Quentin break her heart!

"You see a good deal of Quentin," he remarked rather suddenly; but her colour did not rise as she handed him his tea, nor did the cup rattle in the saucer at the mention of that potent name. She met Mr. Lisle's keen interrogative glance with the utmost composure. How different he seemed without his hat, and how strange it was that it had never occurred to any one to mention that Mr. Lisle was handsome! The circumstance came home to her quite unexpected, as she now noticed his well-shaped head and profile; true his skin was tanned brown by the sun, his hair was touched with grey upon the temples, but in her heart she there and then discovered that he had a far more striking face than irresistible "Apollo" Quentin.

"I am taking this to papa," she said, rising; "he sits in the verandah, you see."

"Yes, I see"—receiving the cup from her hand and carrying it out to his host who was absorbed in a blue document. (Mr. Quentin had trained him to efface himself in this fashion, for to be quite frank, he could not stand that gentleman's society, much less his songs and sentimental speeches.)

"I suppose," said Mr. Lisle, as he passed the piano—Helen's own property,—"that that is Quentin's last new ditty," indicating a piece on the music stand. "I know it's just in his line, 'Told in the Twilight.'"

"Yes."

"I'm sure it gives him great pleasure coming over here, and listening to your music?"

"I believe he derives some enjoyment from his own singing also," she replied, demurely,—remembering the hours that she had toiled over his accompaniments. "Are you musical?"

"In theory only, not in practice. I am very fond of listening to a string band, or to good instrumental performers, but as far as I'm concerned myself, I cannot play on a comb, much less a Jew's-harp! I see"—glancing at some books—"that you read, Miss Denis. May I ask where you get your literature?"

"Some from the library at Calcutta,—some from Mr. Quentin." This latter announcement was a shock.

"Ah!—I daresay his contributions are more entertaining than instructive! So you read French novels?"

"Oh, no!"—becoming scarlet—"I have never read any except a few French stories, Miss Twigg picked out. Mr. Quentin merely lends me books of poetry and magazines, more solid reading I get elsewhere."

"Why do you read solid books?"

"Chiefly to discover my own deplorable ignorance, I live and unlearn," and she laughed.

"Really"—also smiling—"and how?"

"Well, for instance, until last week I was under the impression that America had been discovered by Christopher Columbus, in the year 1492."

"I fancy that most people are still labouring under the same delusion."

"But it is quite wrong"—shrugging her shoulders—"it was found by Buddhist priests in the fourth century, at least so says a book that I have just finished, and there does not seem to be the smallest doubt upon the question in the author's mind."

"Miss Denis," said her listener, gravely, "your reading is too deep for me, and I shall be quite afraid of you. The next time I see you, you will be telling me that it is all a mistake about the battle of Waterloo, that there was no such person as Queen Elizabeth, and that Ireland was first discovered by the Japanese."

Helen laughed immoderately, and then said,—

"Why Ireland of all places?"

"I don't know, unless because it is generally the unexpected that happens with regard to that country."

"Have you ever been there?"

"Yes, frequently; I've an uncle in the Emerald Isle, who has carried on an ink feud for years with my father,—but is gracious enough to me."

"And I've an aunt there, who is the very reverse, for she never answers papa's letters!"

"Then supposing we make an exchange of relatives?" suggested Mr. Lisle.

Colonel Denis was quite astonished to hear so much animated conversation and laughter in his neighbourhood, and could not see why he should not have a share in whatever was going on; but shortly after he made his appearance Mr. Lisle took his leave; and Helen was really amazed, when she saw by the little clock that his visit had lasted almost an hour!

"A very gentlemanly, agreeable man, no matter *who* he is," said her father, after he had sped the parting guest; "eh, Nell?"

"Yes, papa."

"And *I* don't believe with Mrs. Creery, that he is one of our fellow-countrymen who are obliged to roam the world over,—owing to their invincible ignorance of the number of kings which go to a pack of cards," added Colonel Denis as he picked up a newspaper, and subsided into an arm-chair.

Mr. Lisle imparted the history of his visit to his host that same evening after dinner.

"And what do you think of her now you have seen her in daylight?" asked Mr. Jim, who seemed anxious to have his friend's verdict.

"Oh, that she is a pretty girl, of course, unspoiled as yet, and charmed with her surroundings, and immensely delighted at finding herself grown up, and mistress of that bungalow,—which is her doll's house so far."

"And do you think she likes *me*?"

"Yes; of course I did not put the delicate question point-blank as your deputy, but I daresay she does; for her own sake I hope she won't get any further than liking!"

"You are frankness itself, my dear fellow, and *why*?"

"Because she is much too good for you, and you know it! You have been in love about fifty times already, and for pure lack of something to do, are thinking of offering the shell of your heart to this pretty penniless child. She would accept it—if she cared for you—*au grand sérieux*, and give hers in return, for always; but you, once your little *entr'acte* was played out here—say in three months—would sail away, leave her, and forget her! You have done it to dozens according to your own confession;—why not again?"

The expression of tolerant amusement on his hearer's face rapidly gave way to indignation, and he said with much asperity,—

"This is vastly fine! You are uncommonly eloquent on behalf of Miss Helen's maiden affections; you beat old Parks in a common walk! One would imagine that I was some giant Blunderbore who was going to eat her! Or that——" and he paused, and blew a cloud of smoke into the air.

"Or what?" asked the other quietly.

"That you meant to enter the lists yourself, since you *will* have it."

Mr. Lisle picked a crumb off the cloth, and made no reply, and his companion proceeded,—

"But of course you know as well as I do myself, that such an idea for *you* would be all the same as if you went and hanged yourself out on the big tree in Chatham!"

To this Mr. Lisle said nothing, but smoked on for a long time in dead silence. At last he got up, threw his napkin over the back of his chair, and said, gravely,—

"If you are really in earnest for once, and hope to win the girl, and marry her,—well and good. I believe you will have all the luck on your side; if on the other hand, you merely intend to seize such a rich opportunity for amusing yourself, and playing your old game——"

"What then?" demanded Jim with a lazy challenge in his eye.

"You will see what then!" rejoined the other, standing up and looking at him fixedly, with his hands grasping the back of his chair. He remained in this attitude for fully a minute, and neither of them spoke; then he turned abruptly, walked out into the back verandah, and down the steps, and away in the direction of the sea-shore.

Mr. Quentin took his cigar out of his mouth, leant his head on one side, and listened intently to his fast receding footsteps. When their final echo had died away, he resumed his cheroot with a careless shrug of his shoulders.

"Did Lisle mean to threaten him?"

It certainly looked uncommonly like it.

CHAPTER XI
THE FINGER OF FATE!

"Gigantic shapes and shadows gleam,

Portentous through the night."

Longfellow.

From this time forward, Mr. Lisle occasionally accompanied his companion to Ross, and listened to the band, and was even to be met with at tennis parties, in brave defiance of Mrs. Creery's frowns and Miss Caggett's snubs. Helen noticed that he was tabooed, and lost no opportunity of speaking to him or smiling on him—but such opportunities were rare. Mr. Quentin had a way, acquired by long practice,—of elbowing away all intruders from the vicinity of those whom he delighted to honour; and effectually introduced his own large person between Helen and any other swains that might seek her society;—in short, he monopolized her completely. Mr. Lisle had entirely abandoned photography, shooting, and sailing, for the very poor exchange of the *rôle* of a dispassionate spectator. Why did he come to Ross to see what he did not like? his friend's handsome face bent over the beautiful Miss Denis, eliciting her smiles and merry laughter. Naturally, like most lookers-on, he saw a good deal—the envious outer circle of young men, and Miss Caggett, who had long ago made a truce with Helen, but who loved her as little as of yore, and was about as fond of her as any lady could be who beheld her rival appropriating her own special property! Still, she figuratively folded her enemy to her bosom, and smothered her feelings wonderfully,—but Mr. Lisle fathomed them. Perhaps he had a fellow-feeling for her, who knows? It appeared to him, that the citadel of Miss Denis's heart was carried at last; and who could wonder, that an inexperienced school-girl would long hold out against the artillery of Mr. Quentin's attractions; attractions that had proved irresistible to so many of her sex! No, he noticed that she coloured, and looked conscious whenever he appeared, and was not that a sure symptom that the outer fosse was taken? Little did he imagine, that the unfortunate young lady felt exactly as if she were helplessly entangled in the web of a huge spider, that she would have given worlds to rid herself from this ever-hovering, ever-overshadowing presence,—that so effectually kept any one she wished to speak to aloof and out of reach. Her natural good nature, and politeness, prevented her from actually dismissing him, and she had not the wit, or the experience to get rid of him otherwise. She had indeed ventured on one or two timid hints, but with regard to anything touching another person's wishes, Mr. Jim had no very keen perceptions; and with respect to his own company being anything but ever welcome, he would not have believed Miss Denis, even if she had told him so in the plainest terms! Why should *she* be different to the rest of her sex? they all liked him! So Mr. Quentin kept his station by her side, by his own wish, and by public concurrence. He immediately joined her whenever she appeared, carried her bat, her shawl, or her band programme, held her tea-cup, walked home with her, and visited her three or four times a week. It was too tiresome, that he should be her invariable companion, and vainly had she endeavoured to break her chains, but he was older, and more experienced, than she was,— and thoroughly understood the art of making *her* conspicuous, and himself immovable! Little did Mr. Lisle guess that Miss Denis would have much preferred him as a companion. Alas! the world is full of contrariness.

Mr. Quentin appreciated Helen because she was difficult to fascinate, Helen appreciated Mr. Lisle because he held himself aloof, and never gave any one the chance of acquiring that familiarity, which notably breeds contempt! and Mr. Lisle was greatly surprised to find, that he was exceedingly envious of his friend, that he admired Helen Denis more than any girl he had ever seen! But he admired, and stood afar off; no thought of disloyalty to James Quentin. No *arrière pensée* of that motto, "All's fair in love and war," ever entered his mind, he was only sorry, as he said to himself, that he was too late!

The Settlement band played twice a week in the little public gardens on Ross, and their strains were an irresistible summons to all the (free) inhabitants. One special afternoon, we notice Mrs. Home holding animated converse with Mr. Latimer, in his cool, black alpaca coat; we see Mrs. Creery enthroned on a sofa (which she always provided) alone, clad in a gorgeous combination of colours, that could only have been achieved by a daring soul! We observe Helen and Miss Caggett in company—the latter had apologized for her outbreak. "It would not *do*," she said to herself, "to be on bad terms with the Denis girl, she was too popular, all the men would be on her side, Captain Rodney, Mr. Green, and that ugly Irishman, Dr. Malone; wretches who were always praising her rival in her hearing!" A day or two after the storm, she had gone to Helen, and begged and implored her to forget a certain scene between them in the forest above North Bay; declared that she would be miserable for life if Helen was not her friend, that she would rather have her little finger than Mr. Quentin's whole person, that she would sooner marry the typical crossing-sweeper than him, and that she had been very cross and bad-tempered, and hoped that Helen would forget an occasion that it would make her blush to recall! This was very fine, but *who* had ever seen Miss Caggett blush? However, Helen was quite ready to accept the olive-branch, and, like the school-boys, to say "Pax."

There was a considerable gathering at the band, including "Mr. Quentin and Co.," as Mrs. Creery humorously called them. On band nights, the former usually reclined on the sward, literally and figuratively at Helen's feet, but to-night this butterfly was occupied (in quite a temporary manner) with a nice-looking widow, who had come over from Rangoon to pay a visit to her sister, Mrs. King, at Viper. People were walking about in couples, standing in groups, and sitting down in rows. Mrs. Creery (who did not appreciate the solitude of greatness) nodded to Helen to approach, and take a place beside her, saying, rather patronizingly, as she accepted the invitation, "So I hear that your little bachelor's dinner went off quite nicely, and that everything was eatable except the ice pudding!"

Helen felt annoyed, "quite nicely" was indeed but faint praise, after all the trouble she had taken, and the success that she flattered herself she had achieved.

She made no reply, but became rather red.

"And you had Mr. Quentin, of course, and the General, and Mr. Latimer, and Dr. Parks. What champagne did you give them; from the mess, or the bazaar?"

"Bazaar champagne! Oh, Mrs. Creery" —indignantly—"there is no such thing, is there?"

"Yes, and why not? I believe no one can tell the difference between it and that expensive stuff at the mess. I declare—" her attention suddenly distracted to another quarter—"look at Mr. Lisle, in a respectable suit of clothes"—glancing over to where that gentleman was talking to three men.

"Billy!" she screamed to one of Mrs. Home's little boys, "go over to Mr. Lisle, and tell him that I want him at once. Fancy"—turning to Helen and speaking in a tone of pious horror—"those men are European convicts, tickets-of-leave, and allowed to use the garden and library—a very unwise indulgence. I quite set *my* face against it, and so I've told the General. Of course no decent person would speak to the wretches; no one but a man like Lisle!"

"What have they been sent here for?" asked her companion.

"One for forgery, one for stabbing a man in a sailor's row in Calcutta, and one was, *he* says, sent here by mistake; but most of them say *that*! Well," raising her voice, "Mr. Lisle, permit me to congratulate you on your choice of companions."

"Poor creatures! They never have the chance of exchanging a word with any one but each other, it pleases them, and does *me* no harm. Lots of worse fellows are at large,—and prospering!"

"Oh, pray don't excuse yourself, Mr. Lisle. Birds of a feather—you know the adage."

"Yes, thank you, Mrs. Creery," making an inclination of such exaggerated deference, that Helen now understood what Miss Caggett meant, when she said that he was polite to rudeness. "You sent for me, Mrs. Creery?"—interrogatively.

"Yes, because I did not choose to see you talking to those jail birds! You can talk to *me* instead."

Here was alluring invitation!

"Of course you know Miss Denis—but only recently. You were late in welcoming her to Port Blair!"

"I have the pleasure of knowing Miss Denis, but as to welcoming her to Port Blair, such a proceeding would be altogether presumptuous on my part, and no doubt she received a welcome, from the proper quarter." And he once more bowed himself before Mrs. Creery.

Helen could scarcely keep her countenance when she met his eyes, and hastily turned off her smiles by saying,—

"I am sorry you could not dine with us last night."

"Mr. Lisle *never* dines out," replied the elder lady, speaking precisely as if she was Mr. Lisle's interpreter.

"Quentin is talking of getting up a dinner," he said, "in fact he is rather full of it."

"Dinner! Well, don't let him give it till full moon. I hate crossing in the dark, and be sure it is on a mutton-day!" said the elder lady authoritatively. (N.B. Mutton was only procurable once a week.)

"I will remember your suggestions, but a good deal depends on the butler, and *his* inclination. He is rather an imperious person, we have but little voice in the domestic arrangements."

"*You!*" — scornfully — "of course not; but I should hope that Mr. Quentin is master of his own house."

"He leaves all to Abraham, and generally everything has turned out well — except perhaps the writing of the *menu*! Last time, people were a little startled on glancing over it, to see that they were going to partake of 'Roast lion and jam pupps.'"

Helen laughed delightedly, but the elder lady gravely said, "Oh, roast loin and jam puffs. Well, that's the worst of not having a lady in the house. Such mistakes never happen in *my* establishment!"

"Would you like to take a turn now, Miss Denis?" said Mr. Lisle, glancing at her as he spoke.

"I daresay she would, and so would I," returned Mrs. Creery briskly, rising and walking at the other side of him, an honour for which he was by no means prepared.

"What is that unearthly noise?" inquired Helen; "*what* are those sounds that nearly drown the band?"

"Yes; reminds me of a pig being killed," rejoined Mr. Lisle; "but it is merely the Andamanese school-children on the beach. This is the day that their *wild* parents come to see them; they arrived this morning in a big canoe, and doubtless brought all kinds of nice, wholesome, dainty edibles for their young people. They are sitting in a circle, whooping and yelling, real *bonâ fide* savages! Would you like to come out and see them?"

"Certainly not," exclaimed Mrs. Creery, indignantly.

At this moment they were joined by the General and Captain Rodney, who had just entered the gardens.

"Have you heard anything more about that fellow, sir?" inquired Mr. Lisle.

"No; nothing as yet, but Adams and King are doing their best. I fancy he has taken to the bush."

"Oh! then in that case, the Andamanese will soon bring him in," observed Mr. Latimer. "That, or starvation; roots and berries won't keep soul and body together, though many have tried the experiment."

A Bird Of Passage | 91

"What! *what* is all this about? What do you mean?" inquired Mrs. Creery, excitedly.

"Oh! rather a bad business at Hadow last night. One of the convicts killed a warder, and has got away," replied the General.

"How did it happen?"

"It seems that this fellow, Aboo Sait, a Mahomedan, has always been an unusually bad lot. A few months ago, he nearly beat out the brains of another convict with his hoe, merely excusing himself on the plea that he was tired of life, and wanted to be hanged. However, as his victim recovered, we were unable to oblige him, and he was heard to say that he would do for a white man next time! Last night, just before they went to section, he was missed, and one of the warders was sent to look for him; but as he did not return, a general search was made, and the warder was found on his face among the reeds, stabbed through the heart, and Aboo was still missing."

"I'm glad he is on the mainland!" ejaculated Mrs. Creery, with a shudder. "I would not change places with Mrs. Manners for a trifle!"

"Then he is not so desirous of being executed as you imagined," said Mr. Lisle. "He did not give himself up."

"Not he!" rejoined the General. "Life is sweet; his threats meant nothing."

"Perhaps he has gone off to sea," suggested Colonel Denis. "I know they have all a foolish notion that those far-away islands are India, and that the steamboat that brings them here, merely goes round and round for a few days to deceive them—they being below under hatches."

"No fear of his taking to the water, Colonel," replied the General. "I have put a stop to that little game with the boats, and no convict crew can now take out a boat, unless the owner, or some European, is with them. The rascals went off with no end of boats, and got picked up at sea as shipwrecked lascars, &c. Two even got so far north as London, in the affecting character of 'castaways.'"

"And how did they fare there?" inquired Helen.

"In princely style, by their own account, they would like to repeat the visit; they were fed and clothed and fêted and supplied with money; they actually went to the theatre, and had their photographs taken—the last a fatal snare—but they were vain! The moment they landed in Bombay, thanks to their photos, the police wanted them, sent them back to us—and here they are!"

"Yes, the boats were a great temptation; but now they go off on logs," said Mr. Latimer, "and even take to the sea in chains; the Malays, especially, can swim like fish. However, their fellow-convicts are getting too sharp for them; the reward of five rupees puts them on their mettle."

"Too much on their mettle, sometimes!" protested Mrs. Graham, who had joined the group. "Last monsoon, my boatmen nearly capsized the boat one evening I was returning from church. What between the runaway's struggles to escape, and their determination to land him, once or twice we were all within a point of going over. My screams and expostulations were quite useless!"

"The natives are very sharp after convicts, too," said the General; "and I'll double the reward this time; it's not pleasant to leave such a scoundrel as Aboo Sait loafing round the settlements,—especially as he is *armed*!

"Miss Denis," turning to Helen, "there is a very singular object in the sky to-night, which I'm sure you have never seen; we call it Moses' Horn. Lisle, you should take her up the hill, and let her see it before it fades. I've a lot of work to do, and I'm going home," (to Helen) "or I would not depute any one to exhibit this rather rare sight."

In compliance with the General's suggestion, Helen and Mr. Lisle left the little gardens together (despite Mrs. Creery's angry signals to the former), and walked up to the flagstaff, and surveyed the sea and sky, and beheld a long purple streak extending from the south, and pointing as it were directly to the island. It was very sharply defined, and gigantic in size, and had to Helen rather an awful, and supernatural appearance.

"It is shaped like a finger," she said at last. "I never saw anything so strange!"

"Yes, the finger of fate," agreed her companion, "and if I were superstitious, I would say that it was pointing straight at us. Perhaps there may be some remote connection between our planets; perhaps they are identical."

As they stood gazing, the phenomenon gradually melted away before their eyes, and was replaced by the moon, which now rose out of the sea like a huge fire balloon!

"The moon is irrepressible out here," remarked Mr. Lisle, "she seems always to the fore."

"So much the better," replied Helen, "these Eastern nights are splendid. I wonder, by-the-way, why the moon has always been spoken of by the feminine gender."

"As the Lady Moon? Oh! that question is easily answered:—Because she is never the same two days running."

"Now, Mr. Lisle, I call that rude—a base reflection on my sex. I don't believe we are half as changeable as yours.

" 'One foot on sea and one on shore,

To one thing constant never.'

Pray, to whom does that refer?" and she looked at him interrogatively.

"I could give you a dozen quotations on the other side, but I will spare you; it is my opinion that women are as changeable as weathercocks."

"An opinion founded on your own experience?"

"Well, no, I am wise; *I* profit by the experience of my friends."

"Oh!" rather scornfully, "second-hand things are never valuable!"

Mr. Lisle laughed and said, "Well, don't let us quarrel. What did we start with? Oh! the moon;" and gazing over at that orb, he added, "I, too, can repeat poetry, Miss Denis, and this seems just a fitting place to quote:

" 'Larger constellations burning—mellow moons and
happy skies;

Breadths of tropic shade, and palms in clusters—knots of
paradise.' "

This was an apt quotation, and exactly illustrated the scene before them. The loud striking of a clock aroused these two people from a rather reflective silence; it recalled them sharply from day dreams, to the dinner-hour! And, after a little desultory conversation, they retraced their steps, and rejoined the crowd in the gardens just as the band was playing "God Save the Queen."

CHAPTER XII
THE WRECK

"The direful spectacle of the wreck."

Tempest

It may be among the facts not generally known, that the Andaman seas and shores are wealthy in shells; and people who grumble at being despatched to do duty at the settlement are usually consoled by their friends (who are not accompanying them), saying, "Oh, it's a charming place! if you have a taste for conchology, you will have any quantity of shelling."

In most cases, the shelling is angrily repudiated, and yet the chances are, that once arrived upon the scene of action, and stimulated by general example and keen emulation, the new-comers will develop into the most unwearying, rabid, and greedy of shellers!

When I say a greedy sheller, I refer to an individual who, when tide, wind and moon favour, will secretly take boat, and steal away to the most likely parts of Corvyn's Cove, or some favourite reef at Navy Bay, and there reaping a rich and solitary harvest, return with bare-faced triumph, and swagger, dripping up the pier, between two lines of outraged acquaintances, with a shameless air of, —

"Ah, ha! see what *I* have got!"

From the General, down to Billy Home, every one went shelling at Port Blair, and some of these "shell maniacs" (as Mrs. Creery dubbed them) had superb and valuable collections. There was as much excitement and competition over a day's quest as would be expended on covert shooting or salmon fishing at home. It was not merely a frivolous picking up of pretty objects; it was a very serious business. The finder of the rarest shells was the hero of the hour: the owner of "ring" cowries was a person of repute!

Behold, then, one afternoon, a few days after the band, two large rowing-boats waiting at the pier for shellers! and kindly notice the party coming down to embark. An inexperienced eye would naturally assume that they were all going to bathe, for each individual carries a bag and a couple of bath towels—to put round the back of their heads as they stoop in the sun. Their garments are whole, indeed, and quite good enough for the occasion, but how faded, and shrunken, and cockled with sea-water! Their boots—but no, we will draw a veil over these. To be brief the appearance of the company is the reverse of distinguished. In a few short happy hours they will return: they will be all soaking in water from the waist downwards. (Luckily, wading about in the nice, warm sea is rather pleasant after the first plunge, and people in the excitement of shelling are insidiously drawn in deeper and deeper still.) Yes, by six o'clock, if all goes well, we shall see the company of shellers, returning like a party of half-drowned rats; but there will be no shyness, no reluctance, in their progress up the pier; without the least diffidence, they will run the gauntlet of all the idlers, with an air of lofty pride, born of the noble spoils they usually carry. Have they not in their bags such treasures as "woodcocks," "staircases," "tigers," and "poached eggs"! We spare the reader the Latin names of these rarities.

To-day, the General (a keen sheller,) is going, also Mr. Latimer, Captain Rodney, Dr. Parks, Miss Caggett, Dr. Malone, Colonel Home, Colonel and Miss Denis, and last, but by no means least, Mrs. Creery (and Nip). She does not condescend to shell, but she goes on principle, as she rarely suffers an expedition to leave Ross without her patronage.

Colonel Denis and his daughter came hurrying down, just as the party were about to descend the steps.

"Good gracious, Helen!" cried Mrs. Creery, "you are never going to shell in *that* dress!" speaking exactly as if it were her own property.

"No, no," shaking her head, and exhibiting a small block and paint-box. "Have you forgotten that you are to leave me on the wreck to sketch?"

"Oh, true, so we are. Well, get in, *do*! My dear, you are keeping us all waiting."

In another two minutes the boats were full, and rowing away across the water with long, steady strokes; then up the estuary, between the wooded hills of Mount Harriet on one hand, and Hadow—where the lepers were kept—at the other, past the little isle of Chatham, where, according to a legend (for which I will not vouch), eighty convicts were hanged on yon old tree, one May morning, and round the bend, till they were in sight of the wreck, a large three-masted ship, stranded on the muddy shallows, cast away there by some terrible cyclone as it tore its way up the Bay of Bengal. Her history was unknown, for she was already there when the Andamans were opened up, where she came from, and what had been the fate of her crew and passengers—would never now be learned. From her rigging, it was guessed that she was of American build,—but that was all.

Even in the brilliant afternoon light, she appeared grey and weird, with her skeleton gear aloft, and her dark, wide-open ports, looking like so many hollow eyes, as she lay among the tall bulrushes, sheathed in sea-weed. Her cabins and deck were intact, and she had been used as a hulk in former years, till, being the scene of a ghastly tragedy, and other prisons having been built, she was once more abandoned to the barnacles and the rats. She seemed much larger, and more awe-inspiring at close quarters; and as they rowed under her stern, Helen, in her secret heart, was rather sorry that she had been so determined to spend two hours upon the wreck alone; that all the way down she had jeered and laughed at Dr. Malone's warnings of cockroaches and ghosts. However, there was no possibility of changing her mind *now*, especially with Lizzie Caggett's inquiring eyes bent upon her—Lizzie, who was mentally revelling in the prospect of the undivided attentions of all Miss Denis' admirers, for the next two hours!

"Now that it has come to the pinch, I believe you are afraid," she remarked, with a malicious smile.

The only reply that Helen vouchsafed to this taunt was by immediately standing up. Greatly to her surprise, Mrs. Creery also rose, saying,—

"I think I'll go with you! Nip is fond of sniffing among old timber, and he hates shelling, like his mistress."

No one clamoured against *their* departure, and Helen was for once in her life glad of Mrs. Creery's society, and grateful to Nip. The two ladies were presently helped over the side (Nip being cautiously carried up by the scruff of his neck), and the party were left by themselves. To the last, Dr. Malone pressed Helen to "think better of it, a quarter of an hour will be more than ample, you will see."

At this prophecy, she merely shook her head, and showed her sketch-book.

"I should not wonder if we find you both in the rigging when we come back!" he shouted, as the boat rowed off, and making a speaking-trumpet of his hands, he added, "she's full of rats!"

As the sound of the oars grew fainter and fainter, Helen went to the bows, from whence she hoped to make her sketch, and stood silently looking at the view—at the wooded hills casting deep shadows into the glassy water, at the arm of the sea they had just come up, and out in the open ocean like a green gem in a silver setting—the distant island of Ross. It was undoubtedly, as Mr. Latimer had suggested, a capital place for a sketch, and she must lose no time, and make the most of the light whilst it lasted. So she got out her paint-box and immediately set to work; but,—and here I appeal specially to artists,—is it easy to draw, with a large solar topee thrust over your right shoulder, and a voice perpetually in your ear, saying,—

"Oh, you are not making Ross nearly high enough! Surely that point is never meant for Hopetown? those trees are too far apart; and Chatham is crooked!"

Helen was almost beside herself, every stroke was rudely criticized, and Mrs. Creery emphasized her remarks with her chin, which was nearly as sharp as that of the Duchess in *Wonderland*. At length she turned her attention elsewhere, much to her victim's relief, and began to investigate, and poke about among old spars and rubbish.

After a delightful respite, Helen heard her calling out,—

"I see a little boat coming this way, with two men in it—no, one man is a dog; it's from Navy Bay, and is sure to be Mr. Manners. I'll wave and beckon him here, for it's very dull for me!"

Accordingly Mrs. Creery's handkerchief (which was the size of an ordinary towel) was seen being violently agitated over the side, and met with an immediate response, for the little boat rowed by one man, with one dog passenger, was soon within easy hail.

"I do declare," cried Mrs. Creery peevishly, "if it is not that odious Mr. Lisle! I never wanted *him*." However, wanted or not, he was already alongside, looking up at the bulwarks expectantly.

"Oh! it's you, Mrs. Creery! can I be of any service to you?"

"I thought it was Mr. Manners," she called down in an aggrieved tone. "I never dreamt of its being *you*! However, you may come up," speaking precisely as if she were in her own verandah.

Mr. Lisle did not look as if he was going to seize this niggardly invitation; on the contrary, he took a firmer hold of the sculls, glanced over his shoulder, and was evidently about to depart, when Mrs. Creery casually remarked, as if it were a mere afterthought,—

"Oh! by-the-way, Miss Denis is here too, sketching."

Apparently this intelligence altered the case, for the gentleman paused, rested on his oars, and said rather nonchalantly,—

"Very well, I shall come aboard—since you wish it so particularly!" and, rowing round, made fast his boat, and was soon on deck, closely followed by a big brown retriever.

"Oh, dear me!" cried Mrs. Creery, lifting up her hands. "So you have brought that nasty dog! he is sure to fight with Nip."

"Not he, I will be security for his good conduct. And how are you getting on, Miss Denis?" to Helen, who was shyly hiding her drawing with her arm.

"Not at all well; I am not accustomed to sketching, and my attempt here is such a libel on the view, that I am quite ashamed to let you see it, but it" (apologetically) "seems a pity not to try and take away some recollections of these lovely islands."

"Yes, you are quite right; and I shall be very glad to give you some photographs, that is if you would care for them—they don't give the colours, of course."

(At this offer Mrs. Creery became rigid and gave a little warning cough.)

"But," taking up Helen's sketch, "this is not at all bad! Your perspective is a bit out here, and you have not got the right shade in the sea!"

"I know it is all frightful; sea, and land, and sky," returned Helen, colouring; "I am sure you can draw, Mr. Lisle: please have the charity to do something to it for me, and make it look less like a thing on a tea-tray," holding her box and brushes towards him as she spoke.

Mr. Lisle, without another word, laid the block upon the bulwarks, gazed for a moment at the scene, and then dashed in two or three effective strokes, with what even Mrs. Creery (who had, of course, followed up the sketch) could see was a master's hand.

Helen's pale, meek, school-girl attempt received in three minutes another complexion; with a few rapid touches, a glow of the setting-sun lit up the sky, and threw out in bold relief the dark promontory of Mount Harriet; a touch to the sea, and it became sea (no longer mere green paper); palms and gurgeon trees appeared as if by magic; Helen had never seen anything like the transformation. She almost held her breath as she gazed— not quite so closely as the elder lady, whose topee was in its old place;—

why, the drawing-master at Miss Twigg's could not paint a quarter as well as Mr. Lisle; who now looked at the view, with his head on one side, and then glanced at Helen, amused at the awe and admiration depicted on her countenance.

"Yes, *that's* more like it," cried Mrs. Creery, encouragingly. "I told you, you know," to Helen, "that your sea was too green and flat, and your perspective all wrong! I know a good deal about drawing myself." (May she be forgiven for this fable!) "My sister, Lady Grubb is a beautiful artist, and has done some lovely Decalcomanie vases; but *you* paint very nicely, too, Mr. Lisle, really quite as well as most drawing-masters!" Then, looking suddenly round, "But all this time where is Nip? I do believe that he has followed that horrible brute of yours down into the cabins!"

"Not at all likely, Mrs. Creery, you know that they are not affinities; Nip has followed his own inquisitive impulses, for Hero," moving aside, "is here."

"Well, where can he be? Nip, Nip, Nip!" walking away in search of her treasure.

"He is not *lost*, at any rate," muttered Mr. Lisle, "no such luck." Then, in a louder tone, "Is not this a strange, out-of-the-world place?" to Helen, who was watching his busy brush with childlike interest. "If I had been suddenly asked about the Andamans, a couple of years ago, I should have been puzzled to say whether they were a place, a family of that name, or something to *eat*—wouldn't you?"

"Not quite so bad as that," smiling.

"Oh, of course, pardon me—I forgot that you are a young lady of most unusual information."

"No, no, no, I knew nothing about them, I candidly confess, till papa came here."

"They certainly well repay a visit," continued her companion, painting away steadily as he spoke, "there is a sort of Arcadian simplicity, a kind of savage solitude, an absence of worry, and not the slightest hurry about anything, that has wonderful charms for me."

"Then I suppose you are naturally lazy, and would like to bask in the sun all day, and have one person to brush away the flies, and another to do your thinking."

"Miss Denis," suddenly looking up at her, with mock indignation, "you speak as if you were alluding to one of the animals of the lower creation;— what have I done to deserve this? I deny the impeachment of laziness. 'Coming, sir,' my servant, will testify that I am out every morning at half-past five; neither am I idle, but I like to spend my time in my own way, not to be driven hither and thither by dinner gongs, and railway bells, and telegrams. I like to pull my neck out from under the social yoke,—to carry out your uncomplimentary simile,—and figuratively, to graze a bit!"

Helen made no reply, but leant her chin on her hand, and looked down abstractedly at the water for some time; twice her companion glanced up, and saw that she was still buried in reflection. At last he said, "I would not presume to purchase your thoughts, Miss Denis, but perhaps you will be so generous as to share them with me?"

"You might not like them! Some of them were about myself," and she laughed rather confusedly.

"And may I not ascertain whether I approve of them or not?"

"You may, if you will promise not to be offended."

"I promise in the most solemn manner; I swear by bell, book, and candle; and I am very much honoured that you should think of me *at all!*"

"You are laughing at me, Mr. Lisle," she said, colouring vividly, divining a lurking sarcasm in this speech. "I am dumb, and indeed I have no business to criticize you even in my thoughts, much less to your face——"

"Speak out plainly, Miss Denis," he interrupted eagerly; "let me have your views, good and bad, or bad alone."

"It is very presumptuous in me I know—I am only a girl, and you are a great deal older than I am—but it seems to me that every one has some place of their own in the world allotted to them—some special duty to fulfil—" here her listener glanced at her sharply, but her eyes were bent unconsciously on the water, and she did not note his gaze—"surely it is scarcely right to shirk one's share of all the toil and the struggling in the outer world, and the chances of helping one's fellow-creatures, in ways however small,—just for the selfish pleasure of being securely moored from all annoyances among these sleepy islands!"

She stopped, and looked up at him rather timidly, with considerably heightened colour, and added, in answer to his unusually grave face, and stare of steadfast surprise,—

A Bird Of Passage | 101

"I can see that you think me a very impertinent girl, and will never speak to me again; but you *would* have my thoughts, and there they are, just as they entered my head!"

"I think you are a brave and noble young lady, Miss Denis, and you have taught me a lesson that I shall certainly take to heart. I came here for six weeks, and have stayed nearly six months, enjoying this lotus-eating existence, oblivious of my place in the world, and my duty—and I *have* duties elsewhere; thank you for reminding me of them, and indeed, my relations are beginning to think that I am lost, or have fallen a prey to cannibals!"

Here was Mr. Lisle speaking of his belongings and his plans for once,—oh, why was not Mrs. Creery on the spot?

However, she was not far off, and her shrill cry of "Nip, Nip, Nip! where are you, Nip?" was coming nearer and nearer.

CHAPTER XIII
"BLUE BEARD'S CHAMBER"

"I doubt some danger does approach you nearly."

Macbeth.

"He must be in the saloon!" cried Mrs. Creery. "I've hunted the whole ship, and I'm sure he has gone down. You," to Mr. Lisle, "will have to go after him; I dare not, it looks so dark."

To explore the rat-haunted cabins of this old hulk in search of "Nip," was by no means an errand to Mr. Lisle's taste; he would infinitely have preferred to remain sketching on the bulwarks, and conversing with Helen Denis. However, of course he had no alternative. Go he must! Somewhat to his surprise, the young lady said,—

"I shall go too; the ports are open, there will be plenty of light, and I want to investigate the cabins downstairs."

"You had much better not, mind! you will only dirty your dress," urged Mrs. Creery dissuasively, but Helen's slim white figure had already vanished down the companion-ladder, in the wake of Mr. Lisle.

At first it was as dark as Erebus—after coming out of the glare above—but as their eyes became accustomed to the gloom, there was sufficient light from the open stern windows to show that they were standing in a long narrow saloon, with numerous cabins at either side.

"It looks quite like the steamer I came out in!" exclaimed the young lady. (Anything but a compliment to a first-class P. and O.) "That is to say, the length and shape. There are tables, too!" (These had not been worth removing, and were fastened to the floor.)

"It was used as a prison long ago, I believe," said Mr. Lisle.

"Yes, and——"

Helen was about to add that murder had been done there, but something froze the sentence on her lips; it seemed scarcely the time and place to speak of *that*.

"Nip, Nip, Nip!" cried his infatuated mistress, who had cautiously descended to the foot of the stairs, holding her petticoats tightly swathed round her. "Where are you, you naughty dog? Ah!" shrieking, and skipping surprisingly high, "I'm *sure* that was a rat!"

"Not at all unlikely," rejoined Mr. Lisle, rattling noisily along the wainscot with a bit of stick, whilst Mrs. Creery hurriedly withdrew up half-a-dozen steps, where she remained plaintively calling "Nip, Nip, Nip!"

Miss Denis had meanwhile been looking out of the stern windows on the now moonlit water, the tall bulrushes, and the wooded shores; and here in a few moments she was joined by her fellow-explorer, who was examining something in his hand.

"See what I have found!" he said. "When I was hammering the old boarding just now, a plank fell away, and this thing rolled out. I believe," wiping it in his handkerchief as he spoke, and tendering it for her inspection, "that it is a woman's ring."

"A ring! so it is," returned Helen; "and it looks like gold."

"Oh, yes! it's gold right enough, I fancy, and must have belonged to one of the passengers of this ship."

"I wonder who wore it last," turning it over. "I wish it could speak and tell us its history, and how many years it is since it was lost."

"It was a woman's ring; you see it would only just fit my little finger," observed Mr. Lisle, putting it on as he spoke; "now try it on yours." Helen slipped it on—it fitted perfectly.

"It is an old posy or betrothal ring,—at any rate it resembles one that my mother used to wear!"

"Helen and Mr. Lisle! what are you doing?" screamed Mrs. Creery. "You are chattering away there, and not helping me one bit." She was standing on the ladder exactly as they had left her. "You have never searched in the cabins! He may be shut up in one of them; try those opposite, Helen! Do you hear me?"

Thus recalled to their duty, Mr. Lisle now undertook to inspect one side of the saloon, and his companion the other. All the compartments that Helen had examined were empty so far, but she came at last to one—with a closed door!

"Take care! it may be Blue Beard's closet," suggested Mr. Lisle facetiously, as he looked in and out of cabins in his own neighbourhood.

Helen laughed, turned the handle and entered; the moon shone clear through the paneless port, and showed her a cabin exactly similar to the others—just two wooden worm-eaten bunks, and that was all. Behind the door—ah! a little song she was humming died away upon her lips, and she uttered a stifled exclamation, as her startled eyes fell upon a tall, powerful man in convict's dress, in short, no less a person than Aboo Sait! In a twinkling his grasp was on her throat, crushing her savagely against the wall. Vain indeed were her struggles, he was strangling her with iron hands; his fierce turbaned face was within an inch of hers, she felt his hot breath upon her cheek! She could not scream or move, her hands fell nerveless at her sides, her sight was failing, hearing seemed to be the only sense that had not deserted her! she could distinctly catch the faint, irregular lapping of the water against the old ship's sides, and Mrs. Creery's querulous voice calling "Nip, Nip, Nip!" whilst *she* was dying!

"Well, have you found Blue Beard or Nip?" demanded Mr. Lisle, pushing back the door as he spoke. "Good God!"

In another instant she was released—she breathed again. That awful grip was off her throat, for with one well-delivered blow Aboo's prey was wrenched from his grasp, and he himself sent staggering across the cabin; but his repulse was merely momentary; the convict was armed with a knife, — *the* knife; in a second it shone in his hand, and with a tigerish bound he flung himself on the new-comer.

And now within the narrow space of that cabin commenced such a struggle for life and death as has seldom been witnessed. Mr. Lisle was a middle-sized, well-made, athletic Englishman, endowed with iron muscles and indomitable pluck—but he was over-matched by the convict in bone and weight. Aboo was six foot two, as wiry as a panther, as lithe as a serpent, and all his efforts were edged by the fatal fact that *he* had everything to gain and everything to lose!

The issue of this conflict meant to him, liberty and his very existence on one hand, and Viper Island and the gibbet, on the other.—Win he must, since the stake was his LIFE!

They wrestle silently to and fro, finally out of the cabin, locked in a deadly embrace. The Englishman, though stabbed in the arm, had succeeded in clutching the convict's right wrist, so that for the moment that sharp gleaming weapon is powerless! Aboo, on his side, holds his antagonist in a wolfish grip by the throat—they sway, they struggle, they slide and stagger on the oozy floor of the saloon. At the moment, the advantage is with Aboo

Sait—if he gets the chance he will strangle this Feringhee devil, and cut the throat of that white-faced girl, who is still leaning against the cabin wall, faint and breathless.

But he has not reckoned on another female—a female who has ceased to call "Nip, Nip, Nip, Nip," and has now rushed up on deck with outstretched arms, shrieking, "Murder! murder! murder!"

"Fly, save yourself!" gasped Mr. Lisle to Helen, at the expense of an ugly wound in the neck. She cannot fly; a kind of hideous spell holds her to the spot, gazing on the scene before her with eyes glazed with horror. Her very hair seems rising from her head, for she is perfectly certain that murder will be done; the convict will kill Mr. Lisle, and *she* will be an involuntary witness of the awful deed! And yet she cannot move, nor shake off this frightful nightmare; she is, as it were, chained to her place. But hark! her ears catch distant singing, and the rise and fall of oars. This familiar noise is the signal of her release—the spell is broken.

"They are coming! they are coming!" she screamed, and rushed upstairs, calling "Help! help! help!" She sees the boats approaching steadily in the moonlight, but, alas! their occupants are so entirely engrossed in chaunting "Three Blind Mice," that her agonized signals, and Mrs. Creery's piercing cries, are apparently unnoticed. And whilst they are singing, *what* is being done in that dark cabin down below? She thought with sickening horror of those two struggling figures, of that gleaming, merciless knife, and hurried once more to the head of the stairs. As she did so, she heard the sound of a heavy fall, and in another moment, fear thrown to the wind, she was in the saloon.

Mr. Lisle had slipped upon the slimy boards, made a valiant effort to recover himself, but, overborne by the convict's superior weight, he fell, still locked in that iron embrace. In the fall, the weapon had flown out of Aboo's hand,—but only a short way, it was within easy reach; and now, Gilbert Lisle, your hour has come! He sees it in the criminal's face, he knows that his life is to be reckoned by seconds, and yet his eye, as it meets that malignant gaze, never quails, though it seems a hard fate to perish thus, in this old hulk, and at the hands of such a ruffian! With his knee pressed down upon his victim's chest, a murderous smile upon his face, Aboo stretched out a long, hairy, cruel arm, to seize the knife, just as Helen reached the foot of the ladder. Like lightning she sprang forward, pounced on it, snatched at it, secured it—and running down the cabin, flung it far into the sea, which it clave with one silvered flash, and then sank.

Miss Denis was not nearly so much frightened now,—nay, she felt comparatively brave since *that* was gone. She heard the near sound of voices, and a noise of many steps hurrying downstairs. There was a desperate struggle. In three minutes Aboo, once more a prisoner, with his arms bound in his turban, was led up on deck, cursing and howling and spitting like a wild cat. Here we behold Mrs. Creery, the centre of an anxious circle, volubly narrating a story in which the personal pronoun "I" is frequently repeated; and Helen, quite broken-down, and trembling from head to foot, clinging to her father, looking the picture of cowardice, as at the same moment Mrs. Creery might have sat for the portrait of "Bellona" herself.

Miss Caggett (who had had a most satisfactory afternoon) approached the former and examined her curiously.—She was scarcely able to speak, and was shaking like a leaf, and at this instant the General and Dr. Malone came up from the saloon, followed by Mr. Lisle, minus his hat, his coat in rags, and his arm in a sling. Every one looked at him for a moment in silence, and then a torrent of words broke forth—words conveying wonder, sympathy, and praise.

But he, scarcely noticing the crowd, went straight up to Colonel Denis and said, "Sir, I suppose you know that your daughter has just saved my life?"

"I—I—did not," he replied, astounded at this rather abrupt address; "I thought it was the other way—that you saved hers!"

"That fellow nearly strangled her; I'm afraid she got a fearful shock."

"Miss Denis," addressing her in a lower voice, "words seem but feeble things after such a deed as yours; but believe me, that I shall never forget what your courage and presence of mind have done for me to-day."

"No, no," she answered in a choked voice, shaking her head, "it was you—*you*." More she could not utter, as the recollection of her recent ordeal flashed before her, when Aboo had his deadly clutch upon her throat. She turned away, and hiding her face against her father's arm, burst into tears.

"What a queer, hysterical creature!" remarked Miss Caggett *sotto voce* to Dr. Malone. "All this fuss, just because Mr. Lisle caught a convict, and the convict tore his coat!"

"I think there was more in it than that," objected her listener. "The man nearly strangled her, and he was armed; somehow she got hold of the knife and threw it away. The story is all rather confused as yet—but she is an uncommonly plucky girl!"

A Bird Of Passage | 107

"She *looks* it," returned Lizzie, with a malicious giggle.

"And," continued Dr. Malone, not noticing her interruption, "as for Lisle, I always knew that he was a splendid chap."

This speech was not palatable to Miss Caggett; she tossed her head and replied,—

"*I* see nothing splendid about him; and for that matter, Mrs. Creery says that she saved everybody——"

"Oh, of course," ironically. "I can tell you this much, that it's well for Mrs. Creery that it was not an elegant, indolent fop that happened to be aboard, like her friend, Mr. James Quentin; if *he* had fallen foul of Aboo, Aboo would have made short work of him with his flaccid muscles and portly figure; it was ten to one on the convict, an exceptionally powerful man—he was desperate, like a wolf in a cage, and he was armed. However, Lisle is as hard as nails, and a very determined fellow, and whatever Mrs. Creery may choose to say, we owe her valuable life to *him.*"

"He managed to save his own too," snapped Lizzie, as if she rather regretted the circumstance.

"Yes, but he has got a couple of very ugly deep cuts—one of them dangerously near the jugular!"

"It strikes me as a very curious fact, that within the last two months Mr. Lisle and Miss Denis have been concerned in two most thrilling adventures: they were nearly drowned coming from North Bay—at least, so *she* says— and now they have been all but murdered; a remarkable coincidence, and really very funny."

"Funny! Miss Caggett. I think it would scarcely strike any one else in a humorous light. It was a mere chance, and a lucky one for Miss Denis, that she had Lisle to stand by her on both occasions."

"She is welcome to him, as far as I'm concerned," retorted the young lady waspishly.

Dr. Malone grinned and thought of "sour grapes," and wondered if Miss Denis was equally welcome to Apollo Quentin.

All the shelling party were now assembled about the deck awaiting a boat, which had been signalled for from Viper, to take charge of the criminal. Mrs. Creery was still volubly expounding to one or two listeners; Helen was sitting down with her face well averted from the direction of Aboo, who, guarded by brother-prisoners (boatmen), stood near the bulwarks, looking the very incarnation of impotent fury and sullen despair. His late opponent remained somewhat aloof from the crowd, talking to Mr. Latimer; he bore evident traces of the recent deadly struggle, and leant against the weather-beaten wheel-house, as if he was glad of its support. It was many a year since the deck of the old wreck had carried such a crowd of passengers. After a considerable delay the expected boat and warders arrived, and the writhing, gibbering criminal was despatched in chains to Viper, having previously made several frantic efforts to throw himself into the sea. Mr. Lisle departed in his own little skiff, accompanied by Dr. Malone and the brown dog, and the remainder of the company re-embarked and rowed back to Ross in unwonted silence; there was no more singing, and even Mrs. Creery was unusually piano. Nip, the immediate cause of the search and the strife, and who had appeared in quite a casual manner at the last moment, now sat in his mistress's lap, the picture of dignified satisfaction— undoubtedly *he* considered himself the hero of the hour.

CHAPTER XIV
"MR. LISLE HAS GIVEN ME A RING"

"Vouchsafe to wear this ring."

Richard III.

For several days after this startling occurrence, Miss Denis did not appear in public. She would gladly have denied herself to all visitors save Mrs. Home; but who could shut out Mrs. Creery? She penetrated to Helen's room, and from thence issued daily bulletins to the whole station in this style,—

"The girl was knocked up; her nerves were unstrung. She was in a very weak state. She required rousing!"

Miss Caggett also forced her way in, and imparted to her friends and acquaintances "that, from what she saw of the invalid, it would never surprise *her* to hear that there was insanity in the Denis family, and SHE would not be astonished if she was going off her head!"

This affair had given Mrs. Creery something fresh to talk about, and she related the whole story at least thrice separately to every one in Ross, and as often as she had the opportunity to the people from the out-stations. On each occasion she added a little touch here, and detail there, till by the end of a week it was as thrilling a narrative as any one would wish to hear. Mrs. Creery flattered herself that she told a story uncommonly well; so also said public opinion—but then their reading of the word *story* was not exactly the same as hers. She had brought herself to believe that she had been the only person on the wreck who had evinced any presence of mind, and it would take very little to persuade her that she herself had been in personal conflict with Aboo—Aboo who had been duly hanged at Viper on the succeeding Monday morning! She now commenced all conversations with,—

"Of course you have heard of my terrible adventure on the wreck? and the marvellous escape we all had?" and then, before she could be interrupted, the rehearsal was in full swing. This intrepid, loquacious lady entirely ignored Mr. Lisle, of whom Dr. Malone reported that he was nearly convalescent, the cuts from Aboo's knife were healing rapidly, and that he was going about as usual at Aberdeen.

Mr. Lisle was among Helen's first visitors; and he came alone. He wore his arm in a sling—this gave him quite an interesting aspect,—and carried a small parcel in his hand. He was struck, as he entered the drawing-room, with Miss Denis's altered appearance; her face was thin and white, and her eyes had a startled, sunken look. They shook hands in silence, and for quite a moment neither of them spoke. At last he said,—

"I hope you are all right again?"

"Yes, thank you. And your arm?"

"Is well; this sling is only Malone's humbug. I have heard of you daily from him—our mutual medical attendant, you know—and would have been over before, only he said you saw no one. I have brought you this."

"What is it? Oh, my sketch!"

"Yes, I fetched it from the wreck. I thought you might not like to lose it."

"Oh, I don't care! I had forgotten it. But how *could* you go back to that horrible place?" and she shuddered visibly.

"Why not?"

She did not answer this question, but said in a rather husky voice,—

"Mr. Lisle, you remember what you said to papa. That was absurd. Only for you I would not be sitting here now. No," raising her hand with a deprecatory gesture as she saw that he was about to speak, "if you had not come that time, I know in another moment I would have been dead."

"Was it so bad as all that? Well, but Miss Denis, that I should drag that fellow off was a matter of course—that's understood. Do you think any man would stand by and see that brute throttle a girl before his face? But that you should interfere in my behalf was quite a different affair—you know that. My life hung on a thread—I believe I was within ten seconds of eternity. If you had not made that dash when you did, I should have been a dead man. I owe my life to your courage."

"Courage! Oh, if you only knew how little I deserve the word! You would not believe what a miserable coward I am. I actually tremble in the dark; I dread to open a door—much less to look round a corner; in every shadow I seem to see *Aboo's face*. I never, never could have believed that in so short a time I should have sunk to such an abject condition."

"You will get over it all right. It is the reaction. You will soon forget it all," he answered reassuringly.

"I wish I could—all but your share in it. I shall never forget that!"

"Miss Denis," he answered gravely, "I am not good at making speeches, like—" he was going to add Quentin, but substituted—"other people; but whatever I say, I mean. I shall always remember that you stood by me at a great crisis, just as a man might have done. If you were a man, I would ask you to be my friend for life—and I am not a fellow of many friends—but as it is—" and he hesitated.

"But as it is," she was the only girl he had ever cared two straws about, and she was in love with James Quentin.

As it was, she repeated, surprised at this sudden pause, "I shall be very glad to be your friend all the same." Then, with a sudden pang of apprehension lest she had been over-bold, she blushed crimson, and came to a full stop.

"Agreed, Miss Denis. If you ever want a friend—I speak in the fullest sense of the word—remember our bargain, and that you have one in me."

The conversation had become so extremely personal that Helen was glad to change it rather abruptly by saying,—

"I have something here belonging to you," opening her work-basket as she spoke, and carefully unfolding from some tissue-paper the ring from the wreck.

He received it from her in silence, turned it over several times in the palm of his hand, and seemed to waver about something. At last he said with an evident effort,—

"Would you think me very presumptuous if I asked you to keep it?"

The young lady looked at him with startled eyes and vivid colour.

What did he mean?

Observing her bewilderment, he added quickly,—

"Only as a memento of last Thursday—not to recall the whole hateful business, but just to remind you," and he stammered—"of—a friend."

"I should like to have it, thank you; and I shall always keep it," she replied, "and value it very much. Papa!" to her father, who had just entered the room, "look here—Mr. Lisle has given me a ring!"

Colonel Denis started visibly, and was not unnaturally a good deal amazed at this somewhat suggestive announcement. He liked Lisle far better than Quentin. Despite of the latter's fascinating manners to most, he scarcely noticed Colonel Denis during his constant visits; he considered him a slow old buffer, left him to walk behind, elbowed him out of the conversations, and altogether folded him up, and put him by. Helen's parent was an easy-going gentleman, but he had his feelings, and he did not care for Apollo, and he liked his pauper-friend Lisle; nevertheless he was not prepared to give him Helen—indeed, he had never dreamt of him as being one of her cloud of admirers, and he looked very blank indeed to hear his daughter say, "Mr. Lisle has given me a ring!" and saying it with such supreme *sang-froid*, as if it were a matter of course!

Mr. Lisle read his host's face like a book, and saw that, for once in his life, he was quite capable of uttering the word "No."

"It is only a queer old ring that I found on the wreck," he hastened to explain. "It fell out from behind the wainscoting in the cabin, and your daughter was looking at it, and in the subsequent confusion carried it away. She wished to restore it to me now, but I have been asking her to do me the honour of keeping it, as——"

"Certainly, certainly," interrupted the elder gentleman, greatly relieved; "and so she shall, so she shall."

"It just fits me, papa," she said, slipping it on her third finger, and holding it up for approval.

The two men gazed at it in silence, and made no verbal remark, but the same thought occurred to both—assuredly that strange old ring had never graced a prettier hand!

When Mr. Lisle had taken his departure, Colonel Denis said to his daughter, as he picked up the *Pioneer*,—

"I like that fellow—uncommonly; there is no nonsense about *him*."

"So you should, papa, if you put any value on me."

"That is a thing apart, my dear. But I had always a fancy for Lisle, for he reminds me of a very old friend of mine, who was killed in the Mutiny. His name was not Lisle, but Redmond; but, all the same, the likeness is something extraordinary, especially about the eyes—and Lisle has his very laugh!"

"Which you do not often hear," remarked his daughter. "I'm sure Mr. Lisle is a gentleman by birth,—no matter what Mrs. Creery says."

"What does she say?"

"That she is sure his mother was a Portuguese half-caste from Chittagong."

"She be blessed!" angrily. "Lisle may have empty pockets, but he has good blood in his veins."

"Mrs. Creery also says she notices — —"

"She notices everything! If any one has a button off their glove, she proclaims it on the house-top," rattling his paper irritably.

"I declare, papa!" pausing in the act of rubbing up the ring with her handkerchief, "What do you think is in this ring?"

"A finger, of course," without lifting his head.

"No, you dear, silly old gentleman, but a motto, and I believe I can make it out. Listen to this."

Colonel Denis looked over his paper, now all attention.

"It is rather faint, but," holding it close to her eye, "the first is a big L. Love—me—Love me—and leave—"

"Love me and leave!" cried her father. "A pretty motto, truly! I could do better than that myself!"

"Wait, here's another word. Now I have it; here it is, 'Love me and leave me not.'"

"Show it!" holding out his hand. "It's one of those old posy rings. Yes, there is a motto, but it was not intended for you, my young lady— —"

"Of course not, papa," colouring. "Mr. Lisle did not even see it." (We would not be so sure of that.)

"I could not make out what you meant, Nell, when you told me so suddenly that he had given you a ring—I declare, I fancied for a second that—that—but of course it was utter nonsense,—and, of all people, LISLE!"

CHAPTER XV
"WHY NOT?"

"Friendship is constant in all things, save in the office and affairs of love."

Shakespeare.

Things went on much as usual after this at Port Blair; there were no more tragedies, nothing startling to record, and people had quietly settled themselves down to wonder if Lizzie Caggett would catch Dr. Malone, and when the Quentin and Denis engagement would be given out?

There had been the ordinary settlement amusements, including a grand picnic to Mount Harriet (the last place Lord Mayo visited before he was stabbed on the pier below). Mount Harriet was a very high hill, covered with trees and dense jungle, and on the top of it was situated the general's country bungalow. He did not often live there himself, but it was in constant demand by people who "wanted a change," also for honeymoons and picnics. From the summit of the hill, there was a magnificent view of inland winding water, islands, mountains, and sea; but this view was only to be obtained by a steady two-mile climb from the pier, and an elephant, Jampanees (men carrying chairs), and two ponies, awaited the picnic party.

The elephant at Mount Harriet was a character; he was fifty years of age, and his name was "Chootie;" once upon a time he had got tired of drawing timber, and slaving for the Indian Government, and had coolly taken a holiday and gone off into the bush, where he had remained for three whole years. However, here he was, caught and once more in harness, waiting very discontentedly at the foot of the hill, with a structure on his back resembling an Irish jarvey, minus wheels, which was destined to carry six passengers.

Helen and Lizzie Caggett, with happy Dr. Malone between them, went on one side; Mrs. Creery, Mr. Quentin and Mrs. Home on the other, and presently they started off at quite a brisk pace; but the day was hot, the hill-road was rugged, and "Chootie" paused, like a human being, and seemed to express a wish to contemplate the landscape. His mahout expostulated in the strongest language (Hindustani). "What did he want?—water? Then he was not going to get water—pig that he was!" Nevertheless he exhausted his vocabulary in vain. Vainly did he revile Chootie's ancestors in libellous terms; Chootie remained inflexible, until two policemen armed with very stout sticks arrived, and whacked him with might and main, and once more he started off again, and kept up a promising walk for nearly half a mile; and now the praises lavished on him by his doating driver were even sweeter than new honey, but alas! he was praised too soon. Without the slightest warning, he suddenly plunged off the road down a place as steep as the side of, not a house—but a church; deaf to Mrs. Creery's screams and the mahout's imprecations! He had happened to notice a banana tree—he was extremely partial to bananas!—and he made his way up to it, tore off all the branches within his reach, and devoured them with as much deliberation and satisfaction, as if there were not seven furious, frightened, howling, screaming human beings seated on his back. He flatly refused to stir until he chose! The policemen were not within sight, and he seemed to be tossing a halfpenny in his own mind, as to whether he would go for a ramble through the jungle or return to the path of duty which led to Mount Harriet and his afternoon rice. The afternoon rice had it, and he accordingly strolled back, nearly tearing his load off the howdah as he passed under big branches—but that he evidently considered was entirely their affair—and then climbed in a leisurely manner up the steep bank he had recently descended, and resumed the public road,—merely stopping now and then, to snatch some tempting morsel, or to turn round and round in a very disagreeable fashion. The fact was he was not accustomed to society, nor to carrying a load of pleasure-seekers, and he did not like it. Dragging timber and conveying stores was far more to his taste, and, besides this, Mrs. Creery's squeals, and her lively green umbrella, annoyed him excessively; he had taken a special dislike to her;—Chootie was not an amiable elephant, and would have thoroughly enjoyed tossing the lady with his trunk—and stamping on her subsequently. At last the party found themselves in front of the Mount Harriet bungalow, to their great relief and delight, and scrambled down a ladder, for of course, their late conveyance would not condescend to kneel. Mrs. Creery, once safe on *terra firma*, was both bold and furious; and, standing on the steps, harangued the mahout in Hindustani on the enormity of the elephant's behaviour. She called him all the epithets she could immediately bring to mind, said she would complain to the General, and have him shipped to the Nicobars—that he was an ugly, unruly, untamed brute!

Naturally the elephant understood every word of this! (Hindustani is to them, as it were, their native language.) He calmly waited till the irate lady had said her say and furled (oh, foolish dame!) her umbrella; and then he slowly turned his trunk in her direction like a hose; there was a "whish," and instantly she and her elegant costume were drenched from head to foot in dirty water. What a spectacle she was! What a scene ensued! Vainly she fled; the wetting was an accomplished fact; it had been very sudden, and disastrously complete. Dr. Malone actually lay down and rolled in the grass, like the rude uncivilized Irish savage that he was; Miss Caggett was absolutely hysterical, and screamed like a peacock. Helen and Mrs. Home, with difficulty restraining themselves, endeavoured to ameliorate the condition of the unhappy lady. They escorted her inside the bungalow, helped her to remove her gown, gloves, and hat; she was for once in her life actually too angry to *speak*—she wept. Her dress had to be dispatched to the cook-house to be washed and dried, and she, of course, was in consequence prevented from taking the head of the table, and had to have her meal sent out to her in the retirement of the bedroom, where she discussed it *alone*. And the worst of it was, that she met with but little real sympathy. When she reappeared once more in public, she was met with wreathed smiles and broad grins. Such is friendship! The company wandered about the hill after dinner, and Helen, thinking to checkmate James Quentin for once, offered her society to Dr. Parkes, who was only too pleased to accompany her—as long as she did not go too far, and there was no climbing. To punish Miss Denis for her want of taste, Apollo once more devoted himself to Lizzie,—being under the foolish impression that, in so doing, he was searing Helen's very soul. It was soon tea-time; there was no moon, for a wonder; people had to depend on the stars and the fire-flies, and Mrs. Creery,—who had had a most disagreeable day,—gave the signal for an early departure. They all descended by a long, steep, winding pathway through the jungle, instead of by the more public road, as their boats were awaiting them at Hopetown pier; Mrs. Creery led the van, in a jampan carried by four coolies—and, indeed, all the ladies preferred this hum-drum mode of transport to trusting themselves again to "Chootie," who was the bearer of some half-dozen adventurous spirits, whom he took right through the jungle, thereby reducing their garments to rags, and covering their faces with quite a pretty pattern of scratches! Mr. Quentin travelled per jampan, but Mr. Lisle walked, and considered that he had much the best of it; so he had—for he walked at Helen Denis' right hand, and they both found this by far the most delightful part of the day!—whether this was due to the surrounding influences, or to each other's society, I will leave an open question. About a dozen ticket-of-leave men accompanied the procession with flaring lights, as it wound down and down the rugged pathway through the forest, and gave the whole scene a fantastic and picturesque appearance. It was a lovely night, though moonless; millions of silent stars spangled the heavens, millions of fire-flies twinkled in the jungle. Helen never forgot that balmy tropical evening, with the glow of torches illuminating the dark, luxuriant underwood, the scent of the flowers, and the faint sound of the sea.

Mr. Lisle realized as he descended that steep hill-path, that he was deeply in for it at last, and in love with this Helen Denis, helplessly in love—hopelessly in love—for he might not speak, nor ever "tell his love;" he could only play the part of confidant to James Quentin, and, perchance, the thankless *rôle* of best man!

Little did he guess that the young lady at his side was not wholly indifferent to him; that her blushes, when he appeared with Jim, were to be put down to his own, not to his companion's credit; that his mere presence had the curious effect of abstracting the interest from every one else, as far as she was concerned—though, to be candid, she never admitted this tell-tale fact to herself. A gleam of the truth, a ray of rapture, came to Gilbert Lisle by the flash of one of those flaming torches,—was it imaginary? or was it not? She smiled on him, as, he believed, a girl only smiles on a man she cares for—and yet Jim was absent—Jim was yards behind, a leaden burden to his lagging bearers.

A wild, ecstatic idea flashed through his mind, that she might—might not care for Quentin, after all! But this notion was speedily extinguished by his friend, who had noticed Lisle in attendance on Miss Denis on the way down the hill,—noticed that they stood a little apart on the pier before embarking, and neither "liked nor loved the thing he saw!" Lisle the invulnerable was proof no longer. Lisle was a good-looking fellow, despite his shabby clothes and sunburnt skin. Yes, he had somewhat overlooked that fact. But Lisle was not a ladies' man, and he was a man of honour, and Mr. Quentin fully determined to give him to understand that he must not trespass on *his* preserves. Miss Denis belonged exclusively to him. And now let us privately examine Mr. Quentin's mind. Briefly stated, he did not "mean anything," in other words, he did not wish to marry her now— *that* fevered dream was past. He was not an atom in love with her either; she was too irresponsive, and, in fact, too—as he expressed it to himself— "stupid." Between ourselves, if any wandering damsel had appeared upon the scene, he was ready to whistle Miss Denis down the wind at once! But damsels were rare at Ross—and he still admired her greatly; he did not mean to "drop" her, till he went away, and he intended to take precious good care that no one should have it in their power to say that *she* had dropped him— much less, abandoned him for another. His character as a lady-killer was at stake; he could not, and would not, lose what was as precious to him as the very breath of his nostrils.

He accordingly took an early opportunity of giving Lisle what he called "a bit of a hint."

"I saw you making yourself very agreeable to the fair Helen yesterday," he remarked with affected *bonhomie.* "You mustn't make yourself too agreeable, you know!"

"Why not?" demanded his companion with exasperating composure.

"Why, not? My dear fellow, the idea of your asking *me* such a question! You know very well why not."

"Am I to understand that she is engaged to you?"

Mr. Quentin hated these direct questions, and why should Lisle look at him as if he were a witness that he was examining on his oath?

"What is it to you?" he returned evasively. "Come now, Lisle," leaning on his elbow, and smiling into the other's face with one of his most insinuating expressions.

"Answer my question first," roughly.

"Well, I will."

Word fencing was easy to him, and he never thought it any harm to dissemble with a woman, and juggle his sentences so that one almost neutralized another; *they* were fair game, but a man was different. With men he could be frank enough—firstly, because he had more respect for his own sex; and secondly, because their eyes were not likely to be blinded by love, admiration, or vanity. Meanwhile, here was Lisle, an obstinate, downright fellow, sternly waiting for his reply. An answer he must have, so he made a bold plunge, and said, with lowered eyelids and in a confidential voice,—

"What I tell you is strictly masonic, mind—but I know you are to be depended on. There is no actual engagement as yet between Helen and me—but there is an understanding!"

"I confess, the distinction is too subtle for me. Pray explain it!"

"How can I go to her father whilst my money affairs are in such a confounded muddle? Until I can do that, we cannot be what you call engaged. Do you see?"

"I see. But there is one thing I fail to see—that Miss Denis treats you differently to any one else, or as if she were attached to you—in fact, latterly, it has struck me that she rather avoids you than otherwise!"

This was a facer, but his companion was equal to the occasion. "That is easily explained," he replied. "She is the very shyest girl that you ever saw—in public."

Mr. Quentin thoroughly understood the art of innuendo, and the management of the various inflections of the human voice. He was a matchless amateur "star," and could "act" off, as well as on the stage.

After receiving this confidence, Mr. Lisle was silent; he leant back in his chair, and nearly bit his cigar in two. That last speech of Jim's had made him feel what the Americans call "*real* bad." A very long gap in the conversation ensued, and then he, as it were, roused himself once more,—

"Then she *is* engaged to you!"

"No, not quite, not altogether—but our position is such, that no man of honour, knowing it, would take advantage of the situation,—would he?"

"No—of course not."

And with this admission the subject dropped.

Mr. Quentin had succeeded brilliantly. He had assured Lisle that he was not engaged; and yet he had impressed him with the fact that an engagement existed—indeed, he had almost persuaded *himself*, that there was an understanding between him and Helen! "Understanding" was a good, useful, elastic word; it might mean an understanding to play tennis, to sit next each other at an afternoon tea, or to share the same umbrella!

"No, no, Mr. Gilbert Lisle," he said to himself exultantly, as he watched the other's gloomy face, "I'm not just going to let you cut me out—not if I *know* it. 'Paws off, Pompey.'"

CHAPTER XVI
"STOLEN FROM THE SEA!"

"Love, whose month is ever May,

Spied a blossom passing fair."

Much Ado About Nothing.

"Another fine, sunshiny day," is naturally of common recurrence in the East, and it was yet another magnificent afternoon at Ross—very bright, very warm, and very still. Underneath the long wooden pier vast shoals of little silver sardines were hurrying through the water, pursued by a greedy dolphin, and leaping now and then in a glittering shower into the air to escape his voracious jaws. Coal-black, stunted Andamanese were here and there squatting on the rocks, patiently angling with the most primitive of tackle, and two or three policemen, in roomy blue tunics and portentous turbans, were gossiping together about rupees and rice. Some half-dozen soldiers, with open coats and pipe in mouth, sat, with their legs dangling over the pier, fishing. Further on, with folded arms, and wistful eyes, a tall gaunt Bengalee stood, aloof and alone. He was a zemindar from Oude, and had been in the settlement since 1858 (an ominous date); now he was the holder of a ticket, was free to open a shop in the bazaar, and make a rapid fortune; free to accept a plot of the most fertile ground on the face of the globe, free to marry a convict woman, free within the settlement, but there his liberty ended. His body is imprisoned, but who can chain the mind? His is far away beyond those dim, blue islands, and the shining "Kala Panee!" In imagination he now stands, not upon Ross pier, but on wide-stretching plains far north; his horizon is bounded by magnificent forest trees, and topes of fragrant mangoes: once more he sees his native village, and the familiar well, his plot of land, his home; just as he saw it twenty years ago. But too well does he remember every inmate of those small, white-washed hovels; their faces are before him now—for, alas! what has been left to *him* but memory? Bitterly has he expiated those few frenzied weeks, when for a brief space, he and his neighbours felt that they had broken the accursed yoke, and trampled it beneath their feet—bitterer, ten times, is it to know that he was sold and betrayed by his own familiar friend!

At this maddening recollection, a kind of convulsive spasm contracts his features, and he mutters fiercely in his beard. He would gladly—nay, gratefully—give all that remains to him of life, just to have "Ram Sing" at his mercy for one short moment—ay, but one! These are some of the thoughts that flit through his mind, as he stands apart with folded arms, and his dark, hawk-like countenance immovably bent on the sea, deaf to the hoarse, loud laughter of Tommy Atkins, who has had a good "take"—to the screeching home-bound peacocks, and the discordant yells of the Andamanese at play.

They have no tragic memories, this group of young men coming down the pier in tennis garb; or, if they have, their faces much belie them—Mr. Quentin, Captain Rodney, Mr. Reid, and Dr. Malone (whose smooth, fair skin, and sandy hair disavow his thirty summers).

"I told you so!" he exclaimed, as he hitched himself up on the edge of the pier. "They are all gone out, every man Jack of them—the Creerys, the Homes, Dr. Parkes, and Mr. Latimer, not to speak of our two young ladies. They have gone down to Chatham to take tea with Mrs. Graham, and the island is a desert!"

"Fancy going three miles by water for a cup of hot water," said Mr. Quentin derisively; "but women will go *anywhere* for tea. Where are Jones and Lea?" he inquired.

"Where you ought to be, my boy: up decorating the mess for the dance this evening."

"Oh!" rather grandly, "I sent my butler over, and lots of flowers."

"If we were all to do that, I wonder 'what like it would be,' as they say in your native land, Reid?" remarked Dr. Malone. "And where is Green?"

"Out fishing with Lisle," replied Captain Rodney. "And, ahem! talk of angels, here they come," as at this moment a sailing-boat suddenly shot round a point and made for the pier.

"I've not seen Lisle for weeks!" remarked Dr. Malone; "not since the picnic on Mount Harriet. What has he been up to?"—to Mr. Quentin.

"Oh! he only enjoys society by fits and starts, and a little of it goes a long way with him."

"Hullo, you fellows!" hailed the doctor, leaning half his long body over the railings, "any luck?"

"Luck? I should just think so!" returned Lisle, standing up. "Two bottle-nosed sharks, a conger-eel, a sword-fish, and any quantity of sea-monsters, name and tribe unknown."

"Is that all?"

"No, not all. Green caught about a dozen crabs going out."

"Oh! now I say," expostulated Mr. Green, a fair young subaltern about six months from Sandhurst, "it was those beastly oars."

"There was an animal like a sea-cow that nearly towed us over to Burmah," said Mr. Lisle, as he came up the steps, "and finally went off with all the tackle."

"The sea serpent, of course!" ejaculated Dr. Malone. "And, by-the-way, how is it that we have not seen you for a month of Sundays, eh? Coming to the ball to-night?"

"Ball! what ball? How can there be one without ladies?"

"Nonsense, man alive! what are you talking about? Haven't we seventeen?" putting his hat under his arm and commencing to count on his fingers. "There is Mrs. King, Mrs. Graham, Mrs. Manners—the widow from Viper—Mrs. Creery——"

"Mrs. Creery! You may as well say Mrs. Caggett while you are about it."

"I may *not*. Mrs. Creery is a grand woman to dance, and you will see her and your humble servant taking the floor in style before you are many hours older! If all the ladies put in an appearance, and do their duty, we shall have an A1 dance. Of course you are coming?"

"No," put in Mr. Quentin, rather quickly. "How could you ask him? Does he look like a dancing man? Here are the fish coming up. What whoppers!" turning towards the steps.

"And here comes something else!" exclaimed the doctor, pointing to a white sail approaching the island. "It's easy to see what *you* have come down for, my boy!" to Apollo, who smiled significantly, and accepted the soft impeachment without demur.

"Quentin is a lucky fellow, isn't he?" said Mr. Green, addressing himself to Mr. Lisle with all the enthusiasm of ignorance. "He has had it all his own way from the first; none of us were in it! And although our circle of ladies *is* small, I'll venture to say we could show a beauty against Madras or Rangoon; yes, and I'll throw in Calcutta, too! I'll back 'La Belle Hélène' against anything they like to enter, for pace, shape and looks!"

Here Mr. Lisle turned upon his heel and walked away.

"What's up? What's the matter, eh?" demanded the youth of Mr. Quentin, who was now gazing abstractedly at the approaching boat, with a cigarette between his teeth.

"Oh, he did not approve of your conversation; he does not think ladies should be talked about, and all that sort of rubbish."

"Pooh; why not?—and was I not praising her up to the skies? What more could I have said? And I'm sure if you don't mind, *he* need not!"

"No, but he did," remarked Dr. Malone. "He looked capable just now of tossing you out as a sort of light supper to the sharks, my little C. Green!"

"And a very light meal it would be," said Mr. Green with a broad grin. "Nothing but clothes and bones. Here comes Miss Caggett and a whole lot of people, and won't she just walk into *us* for not decorating the mess!"

At this instant Miss Caggett and some half-dozen satellites appeared in view, and behind her, walking with Dr. Parkes, came a lady we have never seen before, Mrs. Durand, who had only that morning returned to the settlement.

"Well," cried the sprightly Lizzie, surveying the guilty group with great dignity, "I call this *pretty* behaviour! What a lazy, selfish, good-for-nothing set!" beginning piano, and ending crescendo.

Dr. Malone nodded his head like a mandarin at each of these adjectives, and declared,—

"So they *are*, Miss Caggett, so they are. I quite agree with you."

The young lady merely darted a scornful glance in his direction, and proceeded,—

"Mr. Quentin, well, I've given you up long ago. Mr. Green, I cannot say much to *you*, when grown-up people set you such an example" (a backhanded slap at Mr. C. Green's tender years). "Mr. Lisle, you here? and pray what have you got to say for yourself? What is your excuse?"

"My excuse," coming forward and doffing his hat, "is, that I have no more idea of decorating a room than one of the settlement elephants—in fact, my genius is of a destructive, rather than of a constructive order. But I am always prepared to appreciate other people's handiwork."

"Well, you *are* cool," staring at him for a second in scornful silence.

"Now, Dr. Malone," pointing at him with her parasol, "let us hear what you have got to say for yourself."

Dr. Malone rested his chin on the top of his tennis-bat, and calmly contemplated his fair questioner in a somewhat dreamy fashion, and then was understood to say,—

"That as long as Miss Caggett was in a ball-room, any other decoration was quite superfluous!"

To which Miss Caggett responded by rapping him on the knuckles with the handle of her sunshade, and saying,—

"Blarney!"

Meanwhile Mrs. Durand had joined the group, and now received a very warm welcome. It was easy to see that she was a popular person at Port Blair. She was upwards of thirty, with a full but very erect figure, smiling dark eyes, good features, and white teeth, the upper row of which she showed very much as she talked. She wore a hat with a dark blue veil, a pretty cambric dress, and carried a red parasol over her arm (a grand landmark, that same parasol, for Mrs. Creery).

"Great events never happen alone!" quoth Dr. Malone, bowing over his bat. "Here, in one day, we have the mail in, the full moon, the ball, and Mrs. Durand! It is quite needless to inquire after Mrs. Durand's health?"

Mr. Quentin moved forward to accost the lady, his large person having hitherto entirely concealed his friend, and as he moved, Mrs. Durand's eyes fell upon Gilbert Lisle. She opened them very wide, shut them, and opened them once more, and said in a slow, staccato voice,—

"I believe I am not dreaming, and that I see Mr. Lisle. Mr. Lisle," holding out a plump and eager hand, "what on *earth* brings *you* here?"

Precisely what every one wanted to know.

Mrs. Durand had a habit of laying great stress on some of her words, and she uttered the word earth with extraordinary emphasis.

Her acquaintance, upon whom all eyes were now riveted, smiled, shook hands, muttered incoherently, and contrived, by some skilful manœuvre, to draw the lady from the centre of the crowd.

"I never was so amazed in my life!" she reiterated. "What put it into your head to come here, of all places?"

"Oh, I wanted to see something out of the common, and to enlarge my ideas."

"Indeed, I did not know that they required extension! One could understand our being here—we are sent, like the convicts; but outsiders—and, of all people, you!"

"There is first-class fishing to be had, and boating, and all that sort of thing; and the scenery is perfect," he answered.

"Granted—and pray how long have you been at Port Blair?"

"I came in July," he replied, rather apologetically.

"July!" she echoed, "and this is November!—*five* months! And may I ask what is the attraction, besides sailing and sharks?"

"The unconventional life, the temporary escape from politics and post cards, express trains, telegrams, and the bores of one's acquaintance."

"Well, every one to their taste, of course! You like Port Blair, give *me* park Lane. As to politics, we have our politics here. Have you not discovered that we are an absolute monarchy?"

"Yes," smiling; "but, alas! I am not in favour at court."

"No? neither am I. I'm in the Opposition. I'm one of the reds," laughing, and displaying all her teeth. "Here are all these people coming back, and I must go; I have a great deal to do at home. Remember, that I shall expect to see you very often—*sans cérémonie*. Oh, I suppose that tall girl is Miss Denis? Charlie says she is uncommonly pretty, and not spoiled *yet*. By the way," pausing, and looking at him significantly, "I wonder if you have been losing your heart, as well as enlarging your ideas?"

"Do I ever lose my heart?" he asked. "Am I an inflammable person?"

"No, indeed—quite the reverse; warranted not to ignite, I should say," shaking her head. "And now I really must be going, or Mrs. Creery will catch me, and cross-examine me. Of course, we shall meet this evening?" Mr. Lisle walked with her to the end of the pier, bending towards her, and apparently speaking with unusual earnestness, as Miss Caggett remarked. At the gate, he and the lady parted, he taking off his hat, she waving her hand towards him twice, as if to enforce some special injunction.

The gig was now alongside the steps, and its late passengers had ascended to the pier. Miss Denis was the last to leave the boat, and was at once surrounded by Mr. Quentin, Dr. Malone, Captain Rodney, and Mr. Green, a faithless quartette, who all quitted Miss Caggett in a body.

"Well, Miss Denis," said Mr. Green, "I am glad to see that you have not forgotten the button-hole I asked you to bring me," pointing to a flower in the front of her dress.

"Oh, this!" taking it out and twirling it carelessly in her fingers. "I certainly did not gather it for your adornment, but still, if you like," half tendering it; but becoming conscious of Mr. Quentin's greedy, outstretched hand, she paused.

"You surely would not?" he began pathetically.

"No, I would *not*, certainly not. I will give it to the sea," and suiting the action to the word, she tossed it over the railings into the water.

"Oh, Miss Denis," exclaimed Mr. Green with a groan, "how could you trifle with my feelings in such a manner? How could you raise me to a pinnacle of happiness, and cast me down to the depths of despair? Have you no conscience?"

"It would have been a precedent," she answered gaily. "I know you only too well—you would have demanded a bouquet every time I returned to the island."

Here, for the first time, her eyes fell upon Mr. Lisle, who had now joined the outer circle—Mr. Lisle, whom she had not seen for six weeks. She coloured with astonishment, and accorded him rather a stiff little bow. He did not come forward, but contented himself with merely raising his hat, and remaining in the background.

Helen had once rather timidly asked after him, from Mr. Quentin (it seemed so strange, that he had never been over to Ross, since the day of the picnic, when they had made that never-to-be-forgotten expedition down the mountain, escorted by torches and fire-flies).

To Miss Denis's somewhat faltering question, Mr. Quentin had brusquely replied "that Lisle had on one of his sulky fits, and the chances were, he would not come over to Ross again—he was an odd, unsociable, surly sort of beggar!"

Apparently he had now recovered from the sulks; for there he stood, looking as sunburnt, as shabby, and as self-possessed as ever!

"We had a pleasant sail," remarked Mrs. Creery, "but I could not go in at Chatham on account of Nip! Mrs. Graham makes such a fuss about that hideous puppy of hers—and, after all, it's only Nip's play! Of course, I could not leave the poor darling in the boat by himself, so we had our tea sent out to us, and were very happy all the same," hugging him as she spoke with sudden rapture.

But Nip (whose *play* was death to other dogs) stiffened his spine, and threw back his head; he evidently considered public endearments inconsistent with personal dignity. He weighed fully twenty-four pounds, and why Mrs. Creery carried an animal who had the excellent use of his four legs, was best known to herself.

As she proceeded up the pier, with his head hanging over her shoulder, he surveyed Dr. Malone and Lisle, who walked behind him, with unconcealed contempt.

"What a fool she makes of herself about that beast!" muttered the former. "He despises *us* for not being carried too. I see it in his eye! Brute! I'd like to vivisect him."

"Only imagine!" exclaimed Miss Caggett suddenly, "Miss Denis has never been to a dance in her life!—and," giggling affectedly, "never danced with any but *girls*."

"And remember," said Jim Quentin, impressively turning and speaking to Helen in a tender undertone (for the benefit of his friend), "that you have given *me* the promise of the first waltz."

The party had now reached a little square, from whence their various paths diverged.

"You wait for me on the pier like a good fellow," he said to his companion. "I am just going to walk home with Miss Denis."

Every one now departed in different directions, excepting Mrs. Creery, who remained behind at the cross-roads, for a moment, and waving her green umbrella, called after them authoritatively,—

"Now mind that none of you are *late* this evening!—especially you men!"

Mr. Lisle went slowly back to the pier; it was almost deserted now. Tommy Atkins had adjourned to his well-earned supper, the jailer to his rice, the Andamanese to unknown horrors. The zemindar is alone—alone he stands, and sees what is to him another wasted sun sink into the sea like a ball of crimson fire! Apparently he is unconscious of a figure, who comes and leans over the railings, with his eyes fixed abstractedly on the sea, till with a sudden flash they become riveted on something, scarcely deserving such eager inspection—merely a floating flower! As Gilbert Lisle gazed, he was the prey of sore temptation. Surely, he argued with himself, there would be no harm in picking up a castaway lily, even Quentin would hardly grudge him that, and *he* might as well have it as the sea! Then he turned half away, as if thrusting the impulse from him (the convict now noticed him for the first time); but the flower was potent, and drew him back; he leant his arms on the railings, and stared at it steadily. The zemindar watched him narrowly out of his long, black eyes. The Sahib was debating some important question in his own mind! he looked at his watch, he glanced nervously up and down the pier, apparently his companion was as nought. Then he hurried to the foot of the steps and unmoored a punt, and rowed out several lengths, in quest of *what*? A white flower that the tall English girl had thrown away.

The native followed his quest with scornful interest. He has it now;— no, it has evaded him, and still floats on. Ah, he has reached it this time, he has lifted it out of the water, as reverently as if it were one of the sacred hairs of Buddha! He has dried it; he has concealed it in his coat!

Bah! the Feringhee is a fool!

CHAPTER XVII
THE BALL

"There was a sound of revelry by night."

Night had fallen, and the full moon to which Dr. Malone had alluded was sailing overhead, and flooding Ross with a light that was almost fierce in its intensity; the island seemed to be set in a silver sea, over which various heavily laden boats were rowing from the mainland, conveying company to the ball! Jampans bearing ladies were to be seen going up towards the mess-house in single file, the guests kept pouring in, and, despite the paucity of the fair sex, made a goodly show! We notice Mrs. Creery (as who would not?) in a crimson satin, with low body, short sleeves, and a black velvet coronet on her head. Helen Denis in white muslin, with natural flowers; she had been forbidden by the former lady to even so much as *think* of her white silk, but had, nevertheless, cast many yearnings in that direction. All the same, she looks as well as her best friends could wish, and a certain nervousness and anticipation gives unwonted brilliancy to her colour (indeed Miss Caggett has already whispered "paint!"), and unusual brightness to her eyes.

The world seems a very good place to her this evening. She is little more than eighteen, and it is her first dance; if she has an *arrière pensée*, it has to do with Mr. Lisle, who after being so—well, shall we say "interesting?" and behaving so heroically, has calmly subsided into his normal state, viz. obscurity. What is the reason of it? Why will he not even speak to her? Little does she guess at the real motive of his absence. As little as that, during his long daily excursions by land and sea, a face, *hers*, forms a constant background to all his thoughts—try and forget it as he will.

The mess-room looked like a fairy bower, with festoons of trailing creepers and orchids twined along the walls, with big palms and ferns, in lavish profusion, in every available nook. It was lit up by dozens of wall-lamps, the floor was as smooth as glass, and all the most comfortable chairs in Ross were disposed about the ante-room and verandahs.

The five-and-forty men were struggling into their gloves, and hanging round the door, as is their usual behaviour, preliminary to a dance; and the seventeen ladies were scattered about, as though resolved to make as much show as possible. Mrs. Creery occupied a conspicuous position; she stood exactly in the middle of the ball-room, holding converse with the General, who bowed his head acquiescently from time to time, but was never so mad as to try and get in a word edgeways. "Nip" was seated on a sofa, alert and wide awake, plainly looking upon the whole affair as tomfoolery and nonsense; but he had been to previous entertainments, and knew that there was such a thing as *supper*!

Near the door, stood Miss Caggett, the centre of a noisy circle, dangling her programme, and almost drowning the bass and tenor voices by which she was encompassed, with her shrill treble, and shrieks of discordant laughter at Dr. Malone's muttered witticisms. Her dress was pink tarletan, made with very full skirts, and it fitted her neat little figure to perfection. Altogether, Miss Caggett was looking her best, and was serenely confident of herself, and severely critical of others.

Every one had now arrived, save Mr. Quentin, but he thoroughly understood the importance of a tardy and solitary *entrée*. At last his tall figure loomed in the doorway, and he lounged in, with an air of supreme nonchalance, just as the preliminary bars of the opening Lancers were being played.

He was not alone, to every one's amazement he was supplemented by Mr. Lisle—Mr. Lisle in evening dress! There had been grave doubts as to his possessing that garb; and his absence from one or two dinners, had been leniently attributed to this deficiency in his wardrobe! People who looked once at James Quentin, looked twice at Gilbert Lisle; they could hardly credit the evidence of their senses. Mr. Lisle in unimpeachable clothes, with a matchless tie, a wide expanse of shirt-front, and skin-fitting gloves, was a totally different person to the individual they were accustomed to see, in a rusty old coat, a flannel shirt, and disreputable wide-awake! How much depends on a man's tailor! Here was the loafer, transformed into a handsome (if rather bronzed), distinguished-looking gentleman. He received the fire of many eyes with the utmost equanimity, as he leant lazily against the wall, like his neighbours. Miss Caggett, having breathed the words "Borrowed plumes," and giggled at her own wit, presently beckoned him to approach, and said pertly,—

"This is, indeed, an unexpected pleasure. I thought you said you were not coming, Mr. Lisle?"

"Did I?" pausing before her. "Very likely; but, unfortunately, I am the victim of constitutional vacillation."

"In plain English, you often change your mind?"

"*Never* about Miss Caggett," bowing deeply, and presently retiring to the doorway.

Lookers-on chuckled, and considered that "Lizzie," as they called her among themselves, had got the worst of *that!* Mrs. Creery, who had been gazing at this late arrival with haughty amazement, now no longer able to restrain herself, advanced upon him, as if marching to slow music, and said,—

"I've just had a letter about *you*, Mr. Lisle."

Mr. Lisle coloured—that is to say, his tan became of a still deeper shade of brown, and his dark eyes, as they met hers, had an anxious, uneasy expression.

"Oh, yes!" triumphantly, "I know *all* about you, and who you are, and I shall certainly make it my business to inform every one, and——"

"Do not for goodness' sake, Mrs. Creery!" he interrupted eagerly. "Do me the greatest of favours, and keep what you know to yourself."

Mrs. Creery reared back her diademed head, like a cobra about to strike, and was on the point of making some withering reply, when the General accosted her with his elbow crooked in her direction, and said, "I believe this is our dance," and thus with a nod to her companion, implying that she had by no means done with him, she was led away to open the ball.

Meanwhile Helen had overheard Mrs. Graham whisper across her to Mrs. Home,—

"What do you think? When Mrs. Creery came back from us, she found her letters at home, and she has heard something *dreadful* about Mr. Lisle!"

Helen was conscious of a thrill of dismay as she listened. She was so perplexed, and so preoccupied, that she scarcely knew what she was saying, when Mr. Quentin came and led her away to dance. During the Lancers she was visibly *distrait*, and her attention was wandering from the figures and her partner, but she was soon brought to her senses by Mr. Quentin saying rather abruptly,—

"I've just heard a most awful piece of news!"—her heart bounded. "Only fancy their sending *me* to the Nicobars!"

Helen breathed more freely as she stammered out,—

"The Nicobars?"

"Yes, the order came this evening by the *Scotia*—sharp work—and I sail in her for Camorta to-morrow at cock-crow."

"And must you go really?"

"Yes, of course I must. Isn't it hard lines? Some bother about the new barracks. The Nicobars are a ghastly hole, a poisonous place. I shall be away two months—that is, if I ever come *back*," he added in a lachrymose voice.

"And what about Mr. Lisle?"

"Oh, he is such a beggar for seeing new regions—he is coming too."

"I'm sorry you are going to the Nicobars, they have such a bad name for fever and malaria."

"I believe you! I hear the malaria there rises like pea-soup!"

"Mr. Lisle is foolish to go; you should not let him."

"Oh! he may as well be there as here! He is as hard as nails, and it would be deadly for me without a companion. He promised to come, and I shan't let him off, though I must confess, what he *says*, he sticks to."

Miss Denis thought Mr. Quentin's arrangement savoured of abominable selfishness, and between this news, and the sword of Damocles that was swinging over Mr. Lisle's head, her brain was busy. Dancing went on merrily, but she did not enjoy herself nearly as much as she anticipated. After all, this apple of delight, her first ball, had turned to dust and ashes in her mouth. And why?

Mr. Lisle leant against a doorway, and looked on very gravely: doubtless he knew the fate that was in store for him. He remained at his post for the best part of an hour, and had any one taken the trouble to watch him, they would have noticed that his eyes followed Helen and Jim Quentin more closely than any other couple. As they stopped beside him once, she said,—

"I did not know that you were coming to-night, Mr. Lisle."

"Neither did I, till quite late in the afternoon. I suppose there is not the slightest use in my asking for a dance?"

Now if the young lady had been an experienced campaigner, and had wished to dance with the gentleman (which she did), she would have artlessly replied,—

"Oh, yes! I think I can give you number so and so," mentally throwing over some less popular partner; but Helen looked straight into his face with grave, truthful eyes, displayed a crowded programme, and shook her head.

Jim Quentin, who was evidently impatient at this delay, placed his arm round his partner's waist, and danced her away to the melting strains of the old "Kate Kearney" waltz.

None gave themselves more thoroughly up to the pleasures of the moment, or with more *abandon* than Dr. Malone and Mrs. Creery. They floated round and round, and to and fro, with cork-like buoyancy, for Mrs. Creery, though elderly and stout, was light of foot, and a capital dancer; and her partner whirled her hither and thither like a big red feather! Every one danced, and the seventeen revolving couples made quite a respectable appearance in the narrow room. And what a sight to behold the twenty-eight partnerless men, languishing in doorways, and clamouring for halves and quarters of dances! Men who, from the wicked perversity of their nature, were they as one man to ten girls, would certainly decline to dance at *all!* Mr. Lisle had abandoned his station at last, and waltzed repeatedly with Mrs. Durand; they seemed to know each other intimately, and were by far the best waltzers in the room. There was a finish and ease about their performance that spoke of balls in the Great Babylon, and though others might pause for breath, and pant, and puff, these two, like the brook, seemed to "go on for ever!"

They also put a very liberal interpretation upon the term "sitting out!" They walked up the hill in the moonlight, and surveyed the view— undoubtedly other dancers did the same—but not *always* with the same companion; to be brief, people were beginning to talk of the "marked" attention that Mr. Lisle was paying Mrs. Durand—attentions not lost on Helen, who noticed them, as it were, against her will, and tried to keep down a storm of angry thoughts in her heart by asking herself, as she paced the verandah with Dr. Parkes, and dropped haphazard sentences, "Was it possible that she was jealous, bitterly jealous, because Mr. Lisle spoke to another woman?—Mr. Lisle, who avoided her; Mr. Lisle, who had a history; Mr. Lisle, who was going away?"

She held her head rather higher than usual, pressed her lips very firmly together, and told herself, "No, she had not *yet* fallen quite so low. Mr. Lisle and his friends were nothing to her."

Supper was served early. Mrs. Creery was the hostess, and we know that she had "Nip" in her mind, when she suggested that at twelve o'clock they should adjourn for refreshment, and sailed in at the head of the procession on the General's arm. "Nip," who had been the first to enter the supper-room, sat close to his doating mistress, devouring tit-bits of cold roast peacock, and *pâté de foie gras*, with evident relish; *this* was a part of the entertainment that he could comprehend. His mistress was also pleased with the refection, and condescended to pass a handsome encomium upon the mess-cook, and priced several of the dishes set before her (with an eye to future entertainments of her own). She was in capital spirits, and imparted to Dr. Malone, who sat upon her left, that she had never seen a better ball in Ross in all her experience; also, amongst many other remarks, that Miss Caggett's dress was like a dancer's.

"But is not that as it ought to be?" he inquired, with assumed innocence.

"I mean a columbine!" she replied sternly; "and her face is an inch deep in powder—she is a *show*! As to Helen Denis——"

"Yes, Mrs. Creery. As to Miss Denis?"

"I'm greatly disappointed in her. She is no candle-light beauty, after all."

"Ah, well, maybe she will come to *that* by-and-by. So long as she can stand the daylight, there is hope for her—eh?"

Mrs. Creery told Dr. Malone that "she believed he was in love with the girl, or he would not talk such nonsense!" and finally wound up the conversation by darkly insinuating something terrible about Mr. Lisle, adding that he had craved for her forbearance, and implored her to hold her tongue!

"But I won't," she concluded, rising as she spoke, and dusting the crumbs off her ample lap. "It is my *duty* to expose him! We don't want any wolves in sheep's clothing prowling about the settlement," and with a nod weighty with warning, she moved away in the direction of the ball-room.

Miss Caggett had torn her dress badly—her columbine skirts— and Helen was not sorry to be called aside to render assistance. She was unutterably weary of Mr. Quentin and his monotonous compliments. His manner of protecting, and appropriating her, as if she belonged to him, and they had some secret bond of union, was simply maddening! As she tacked up Lizzie's rents, in a corner of the ante-room, Lizzie said suddenly,—

"I suppose you have heard all the fuss about Mr. Lisle? Mrs. Creery is bubbling over with the news. Don't pretend *I* told you, but she has heard all about him at last; very *much* at last," giggling.

"Yes?" interrogated her companion.

"He was in the army—I always suspected that; he looked as if he had been drilled. He was turned out, cashiered for something disgraceful about racing; and as to his flirtations, we can imagine *them*, from the way he is behaving himself to-night! He has danced every dance with Mrs. Durand, though I will say this, she asked him; and, of course, it was because *she* came back, that he changed his mind about the ball."

"Now your dress will do, I think," said Helen, rising from her knees with rather a choking sensation in her throat.

"Oh, thanks awfully, you dear girl!" pirouetting as she spoke. "I'll do as much for you another time; there's a dance beginning, and I must go!" and she hurried off.

In the doorway Helen came face to face with Mr. Lisle, who was apparently searching for some one—for her!

She held up her chin, and, with one cool glance, was about to pass by, when he said, rather eagerly,—

"Miss Denis, I was looking for you. Malone has been sent for to barracks, and he said that I might ask you to give me his dance—the next—the last."

Helen fully intended to decline the pleasure, but something in Mr. Lisle's face compelled her to say "*Yes*," and without a word more, she placed her hand upon his arm; they walked into the ball-room, and immediately commenced to waltz; this waltz was "Soldate Lieder." Her present partner was very superior to Jim Quentin, and she found that she could go on much longer with him without stopping, keeping up one even, delightful pace; but at last she was obliged to lean against the wall—completely out of breath. Her eyes, as she did so, followed Mrs. Durand enviously, and she exclaimed,—

"I wish I could dance like her." Now, had she breathed this aspiration to Mr. Quentin or Dr. Malone, they would have assured her that her dancing was already perfection, but Mr. Lisle frankly replied,—

"Oh, all you want is practice; you must remember that she has been at it for years. We used to dance together at children's parties,—I won't say *how* long ago."

"I know I dance badly," said Helen, colouring; "but the reason of that is that, although I danced a great deal at school, it was always as gentleman, because I was tall."

"Ah! I see," and he laughed. "Now I understand why you were so bent on steering me about just now. Well, you are not likely to dance gentleman again, I fancy. There!" regretfully, "it's over; shall we go outside?"

Helen nodded her head, and accordingly they went down the steps arm in arm. She meant to seize this opportunity of giving him a hint of the mine on which he was standing,—one word of warning with regard to Mrs. Creery. She had accepted his friendship, and surely this would be the act of a friend.

Mr. Quentin—sitting in the dusky shades of a secluded corner, whispering to Lizzie Caggett—saw the pair descending from the ball-room, pass down the steps, and out into the moonlight, and looked after them with an expression of annoyance that was quite a revelation to his sprightly companion.

CHAPTER XVIII
"BUT WHAT WILL PAPA SAY?"

"Joy so seldom weaves a chain
Like this to-night, that, oh! 'tis pain
To break its links so soon."

Moore.

Helen and her partner ascended the steep gravel pathway, lined with palms, gold mohur, and orange-trees, and turning a sharp corner, came suddenly upon a full view of the sea, with the moon on her bosom. It was a soft, still, tropical night; not a sound broke the silence, save a distant murmur of human voices, or the dip of an oar in the water.

That moon overhead seldom looked down upon fairer scene, or a more well-favoured couple, than the pair who were now leaning over the rustic railings, and gazing at the prospect beneath them—or rather, the man was looking at the girl, and the girl was looking at the sea. Doubtless moon-shine idealizes the human form, just as it casts a glamour over the landscape; but at the present moment Helen appears almost as beautiful as her world-renowned namesake. Her lovely eyes have a fathomless, far-away expression, her pure, clear-cut profile is thrown into admirable relief by the glossy dark leaves of a neighbouring orange-tree. In her simple muslin dress, with its soft lace ruffles, and a row of pearls round her throat, she seemed the very type of a modest English maiden (no painted columbine this!), and, perhaps, a little out of place amid her Eastern surroundings. She continued to gaze straight before her, with her hands crossed on the top of the railing, and her eyes fixed on the sea. As she gazed, a boat shot out of the dim shadows, and across the white moonlit track, then passed into obscurity again.

"Thinking as usual, Miss Denis?" said her companion.

"Yes," she answered rather reluctantly, "thinking of something that I must say to *you*, and wondering how I am to say it."

"Is it much worse than last time?" he inquired with a smile (but there was an inflection of eagerness in his voice).

"Oh! quite different."

"Ah, she is going to announce that she is engaged to Quentin," he said to himself with a sharp twinge.

"Do you find it so very hard to tell me?" he inquired in a studiously indifferent tone.

"Yes, very hard; but I must. I owe you much, Mr. Lisle—and—I am your—friend—I wish to warn you." Suddenly sinking her voice to a whisper, she added,—"Mrs. Creery has had a letter about YOU!"

"Containing any startling revelations, any bad news?"

"Yes," she returned faintly. "Bad news. Oh, Mr. Lisle,—I am so sorry!"

"Is the news too terrible to be repeated?" he asked with marked deliberation.

Helen fidgeted with her fan, picked a bit of bark off the railing in front of her, and, after a long silence, and without raising her eyes, she said,—

"Must I tell you?"

"If you please," rather stiffly.

"She—she—hears that you have been in the army."

"Yes, so I was—I was not aware that it was criminal to hold her Majesty's commission; but, of course, Mrs. Creery knows best."

"She says you were—were obliged to—to leave disgraced," continued his companion in a rapid, broken whisper.

"Cashiered, you mean, of course!"

"Yes," glancing at him nervously. To her amazement, he was smiling.

"Do you believe this, Miss Denis?" he asked, raising himself suddenly from a leaning posture and looking at her steadily.

"No," she faltered. "I think not. No," more audibly, "I do not," blushing deeply as she spoke.

"Why?" he asked rather anxiously.

"I cannot give you any reason," she stammered, somewhat abashed by the steadfastness of his gaze, "except a woman's reason, that it is so——"

"I am sincerely grateful to you, Miss Denis; your confidence is not misplaced.—I am *not* the man in question. Mrs. Creery has got hold of the wrong end of the stick for once. I know of whom she is thinking," his face darkened as he spoke, "a namesake and, I am ashamed to say, a relation of mine. It is extremely good-natured of the old lady, to make me the subject of her correspondence." Then in quite another tone he said, "I suppose you have heard of our start to-morrow?"

"Yes," she replied, scarcely above a whisper.

"I'm a regular bird of passage, and ought to have been away weeks ago; and you yourself will probably be on the wing before long." (He was thinking of her marriage with Jim Quentin, but how could she know that?)

"Oh, not for a year at any rate! Papa does not expect that we shall be moved before then," she answered quite composedly. "I am sorry you are going to the Nicobars—I mean, you and Mr. Quentin," hastily correcting herself. "It's a horribly unhealthy place—soldiers and convicts die there by dozens from—fever," her lip quivered a little as she spoke.

"Not quite so bad as you think," returned her companion, moving his elbow an inch closer to her. "I'm an old traveller, you know,—and I will look after him for you."

"Look after who?" she asked in amazement.

"Why, Quentin, to be sure. I know all about it. I," lowering his voice, "am in the *secret*."

"Mr. Lisle, will you kindly tell me at once what you mean?"

"Certainly, Miss Denis. I mean that Quentin is the happiest of men."

"I am extremely pleased to hear it, but why?" she interrogated firmly.

"What is the use of fencing with me in this way?" he exclaimed with a gesture of impatience. "You may trust me.—I know all about it. Quentin has told me himself, that he is engaged to you."

"Engaged to *me*!" she echoed with glowing eyes. "Mr. Lisle, you are joking."

"Do I look as if I was joking?" he demanded rather bitterly.

"It is not the case. It is the first that I have heard of it," exclaimed the young lady in a voice trembling with agitation and indignation. "How dared he say so?"

Mr. Lisle felt bewildered; a rapturous possibility made his brain reel. Yet who was he to believe? Quentin had been very positive; he had never known him to utter a deliberate lie. And here, on the other hand, stood this girl, saying "No;" and if ever the truth was traced upon proud, indignant lips, it was written on hers.

"Do you believe me, Mr. Lisle?" she asked impatiently.

For fully a moment he did not speak; and was it the moonlight, or some sudden emotion, that made him look so white?

"I do believe you, of course," he answered in a low voice. "And now," he continued in the same low tone, urged to speak by an irresistible impulse, "perhaps you can guess *why* i have stayed away? How, from a sense of mistaken loyalty, my lips have been locked?"

Her eyes, which up to this, had been fixed intently on his, now sank. Suddenly a suspicion of the truth now dawned upon her mind, and she turned aside her face.

"Miss Denis," he said, "I see you have guessed my secret—I love you."

These three magic words were almost inaudible; barely louder than the orange leaves which whispered in the scented air. Nevertheless a busy little zephyr caught them up, carried them away, and murmured them to the sleepy flowers and the drowsy waves, that washed the invulnerable rocks beneath them.

Helen made no reply. This was the first love-tale to which she had ever listened, and those three syllables stirred every fibre of her heart.

"Do you remember that time on the wreck," he continued, "when you told me that I was leading a lazy, useless life, and that I ought to go back to the outer world? You little guessed that it was you, yourself, who were keeping me a prisoner here!"

Still the young lady said nothing, but kept her face steadily turned towards the sea.

He waited a moment, as if expecting some reply, but none came. At last he said, in quite a different tone,—

"I see how it is.—I have been a presumptuous idiot! And, after all, I had no right to expect that you would care a straw about me. I am years older than you are; I am—"

"Mr. Lisle," she interrupted, turning towards him at last, and speaking with apparent effort, "you are quite wrong.—I—I——" she stopped, and a little half-frightened smile played round her mouth, as she added, almost under her breath, "But what will papa say?"

"Then *you* mean to say 'Yes'!" he exclaimed, coming nearer to her, and grasping the railing firmly in his hand, to conceal how it shook.

Again she made no reply, but this time Mr. Lisle undoubtedly took silence for consent.

Mrs. Creery and Dr. Parkes were standing on the very summit of the hill, overlooking everything and everybody, and the former had not failed to notice a couple at some distance below them, leaning over the rails, and contemplating the sea, a tall girl in white, Helen Denis, of course; and who was the man? It looked like Captain Durand. There, Captain Durand had just bent over her, and kissed her hand! Pretty doings, certainly, for a married man.

"There!" she exclaimed, suddenly nudging Dr. Parkes, "did you see *that*?"

"See what, my dear madam?"

"That man down there with Helen Denis. I believe it's Captain Durand; he has just kissed her hand. Oh! WAIT till I see his wife!"

"Pooh!" returned her companion contemptuously, "the moonlight must have deceived you, it was his own hand; he was stroking his moustache."

"Oh, well, I'm not so sure of that!—but I suppose I must take your word for it, doctor."

Meanwhile, to return to Mr. Lisle, who *had* kissed Helen's hand. (Mrs. Creery's eyes seldom deceived her.) "Won't you say something to me, Helen?" he pleaded anxiously.

"Yes," turning round and drawing her fingers away, "I will.—I say— don't go to the Nicobars."

"But I must; I have promised Quentin and Hall, and I cannot break my word. I would gladly give half I possess to get out of it; but I little guessed this afternoon, when Quentin asked me to go and I said 'Yes,' that I would so soon have such very strong reasons for saying 'No.'"

"I wish they would let you off; I have a presentiment about the Nicobars."

"Presentiment of what?"

"I cannot say, but of something bad. Do *you* believe in presentiments?" looking at him wistfully.

"No, and yet I should not say so! That night of the storm, when you ran down the pier steps and called me back, your voice and your face haunted me afterwards for days. I had a kind of conviction that I had met my fate, and so I *had*, you see! By the way, I wonder why you like me, Helen? or what you see in me?"

The young lady smiled, but said nothing.

"All the world can understand my caring for you, but I am, in one way, an utter stranger; you could not answer a single question about me, if you were asked! As far as appearances go, I am an idler, a mere time-killer, without friends, station, or money."

"If you are idle you will have to amend your ways— —"

"And work for you as well as myself," he interrupted with a laugh.

"As to friends, I would say you could share mine, but then I have so few. Still— —"

"Still, for better or worse you will be Mrs. Gilbert Lisle?"

"Yes—some day," faltered the young lady.

"I know I am not half as fascinating, nor a quarter as good-looking as Quentin; honestly, what do you see in me, Helen?"

"Do you expect me to pander to your conceit, and to make you pretty speeches?" she asked with rather a saucy smile.

"Indeed I do not; all the pretty speeches, of course, should come from *me*. I only want to hear the truth," he returned, looking at her with his steady dark eyes.

"Well, then, since you must know, and you seem generally to have your own way, I will try and tell you. Somehow, from the first—yes, the very *first*—I was sure that you were a person that I could trust; and ever since that time on the wreck— —" she paused.

"Yes," he repeated, "ever since that time on the wreck?—go on, Helen."

"I have felt that—that—I would not be afraid to go through anything with you, to—to spend my life with you. *There!*" becoming crimson, she added, "I know I have said too much, *far* too much," clasping her hands together nervously.

A look more eloquent than words illumined Lisle's face.

"And you would give yourself to me in this blind confidence? Helen, I little dreamt when I came down here rather aimlessly, that in these unknown islands, I should find such a pearl beyond price. You cannot understand what it is to me, to feel that I am valued for myself, simply as Gilbert Lisle, poor, obscure, and—" he paused, his voice sounded rather husky, and then he went on, "I must see your father to-night. But how? I left him at billiards. I wonder what he will say to me?"

"Perhaps, perhaps," began Helen rather nervously, "*I* had better speak to him first. I know he likes you but— —"

"Yes, there would seem to be a very considerable *but*," smiling significantly. "Nevertheless, I hope he will listen to me. No, Helen, I would rather talk to him myself."

"At any rate, you will not ask me to leave him for ages,—not for a long time?"

"What do you call a long time?"

"Two or three years; he will be so lonely."

"Two or three years!—and pray what is to become of me?"

"Have you no relations?"

"Yes, some. Chiefly a father, who is pining for the day when I shall introduce him to a daughter-in-law."

"Now you are joking, surely," looking at him with a bewildered face. "I have heard of mothers being anxious to get their daughters married—but a father his sons, never!"

"Ah," repressing a smile, "well, you see, you live and learn."

"And what is your father like?"

"He is old, of course; he has white hair and a red face, and is short in stature and in temper."

"You do not speak of him very respectfully."

"You are always hauling me up, Helen. First I am lazy, now I am unfilial."

"I beg your pardon. I forget, I am too ready to say the first thing that comes into my head."

"Never mind begging my pardon. I like to be lectured by *you*," taking her hand in his.

"Do not—supposing Mrs. Creery were to see you?" trying to withdraw hers,—and vainly.

"What if she did?" he returned boldly; "it is my own property."

Thus silenced, Helen submitted to have her arm drawn within her lover's, and her hand clasped tightly in his.

"Where does your father live, and what does he do, and like?" she asked presently.

"He lives in London. What does he do? Nothing particular. What does he like? He likes a rubber of whist, he likes politics, he likes his own way. He is certain to like *you*."

"Oh, I always get on well with old gentlemen," she rejoined with some complacency.

Her companion looked at her with an odd twinkle in his eye, and said,—

"As, for instance?"

"As, for instance, the General, Colonel Home, Dr. Parkes."

"And you call *them* old gentlemen! Why, they are men in the prime of life! Perhaps you consider me an old gentleman also!"

"Nonsense," she returned with a smile. "Now tell me something about your mother."

"Ah! my mother," he answered with a sudden change in his expression. "My mother died five years ago."

"I am sorry," began Helen.

"And *I* am sorry, that she did not live to know you. She was the most beautiful woman I ever saw—and the best."

"You were better off than I was. I do not remember my mother; she was lovely, too," returned Helen, jealous for a certain painted miniature that was the most precious of her treasures.

Mr. Lisle looked at Helen thoughtfully. His mind suddenly travelled back to the night that she had landed on Ross—and a certain scathing sketch of the late Mrs. Denis. Of course this child beside him was totally ignorant of her mother's foibles. "The prettiest woman in India" had, at any rate, bequeathed her face to her daughter. Yes, he noted the low brow, straight nose, short upper lip, and rounded chin. But what if Helen had also inherited the disposition of the false, fair, unscrupulous Greek?

That was impossible; he was bitterly ashamed of the thought, and mentally hurled it from him with scorn. His lady-love was rather surprised at his long silence. Of what was he thinking?

"It is a well-known fact," he said at length, "that the value people place upon themselves is largely discounted by the world; but when I came down here, merely to see what the place was like, and to shoot and fish, I never guessed that I should be taken for counterfeit coin by the head of the society for the propagation of scandal."

"Meaning Mrs. Creery," said Helen with a smile.

"Yes. Because I declined to unbosom myself to her, and tell her where I came from, where I was going, what was my age, my religion, etc., etc., she made up her mind that I was a kind of social outcast, and was not to be tolerated in decent company. This, as you may have remarked, sat very lightly on my mind; I did not come here for society, but it amused me to see how Mrs. Creery set me down as a loafer and a pauper. It does not always follow that, because a fellow wears a shabby coat, his pockets must be empty. I am not a poor man; far from it. Do you think, if I were, I would have the effrontery to go to your father, and say, 'Here I am. I have no profession, no prospects, no money. Hand me over your treasure, your only child, and let us see if what is not enough for one to live on will suffice for two?' Were a man to come to *me* with such a suggestion, I should hand him over to the police."

Helen looked at him in awe-struck astonishment.

"Then you are rich,—and no one guesses it here!"

"Oh, the General knows all about me; so does Quentin; so shall *you!* How I wish," he exclaimed with sudden vehemence, "that these miserable Nicobars had never been discovered! Six weeks will seem a century, especially in the company of Quentin. I shall be obliged to have it out with Master James," he added, with a rather stern curve of his lips. "I had thought that lying was an obsolete vice! Only that Hall is going, and is entirely depending on me as a kind of buffer between him and Quentin,—whom he detests,—I would not consider my promise binding. I never knowingly associate with——" he stopped short, and apparently finished the sentence to himself. "Anyway, it will seem years till I come back!"

"And you *will* come back?" she said, looking at him with a strangely wistful face.

For a moment he returned her gaze in reproachful amazement. Then, stretching his hand out towards the east, replied,—

"As sure as the sun will rise there to-morrow, so surely will I return. What have I said or done that you should doubt me now—you who have trusted me so generously?"

"I cannot tell. I have a strange feeling that I cannot get out of my head; and yet I'm sure you would laugh were you to hear it, Mr. Lisle."

"Gilbert," he corrected.

"Yes, Gilbert," she repeated softly.

"I must tell you, Helen, what I have more than once been tempted to confide to you. I am not what I seem. I——"

"It was *not* captain Durand, after all," interrupted a harsh female voice close by, and at this critical moment Mrs. Creery and Dr. Parkes came swooping down from the hill-top.

"Helen and Mr. Lisle! Well, I declare! Pray do you know that every one is going home? What can you have been thinking of? The band played 'God save the Queen' half an hour ago."

Mr. Lisle drew himself up to his full height (which was five feet ten), and looked as if he wished the good lady—say, at Jericho; and Helen fumbled with her fan, and murmured some incoherent excuse. They both hung back, evidently expecting and hoping that the elder couple would lead the way down the hill; but, alas! for their expectations, Mrs. Creery suddenly put out a plump hand and drew Helen's reluctant one under her own arm, saying, as she shouldered herself between her and her cavalier,—

"Come along with me; it's high time little girls like you were at home," and without another word Helen was, as it were, marched off under a strong escort in the direction of the ball-room.

Good-bye to those few transcendental moments, good-bye to the moonlight on the water, the scent of orange-flowers, and all the appropriate surroundings to a love-tale! Say good-bye to Gilbert Lisle and love's young dream, Helen Denis, and go quietly down the hill with Mrs. Creery's heavy arm firmly locked in yours.

The two gentlemen followed in dead silence. Dr. Parkes was infinitely diverted with this little scene; he had been young himself, and it did not need the light of his own past experience to tell him, that this good-looking, impecunious fellow beside him had been trying his hand at making love to the island belle; but Mrs. Creery was a deal too sharp for him, and on the whole, "though he was evidently a gentleman," casting a glance at his companion's aristocratic profile and erect, rather soldierly figure, he considered that it was a deuced piece of cheek for *him* to think of making up to Helen Denis! Alas! little did Dr. Parkes and the careful matron in his van, guess that they were merely carrying away the key of the stable, the steed (meaning the young lady's heart) had been stolen long ago.

As to Mr. Lisle's thoughts, the reader can easily imagine them—disgust, impatience, rage were the least of them. How was he to get another word with Helen? How was he to have a chance of seeing Colonel Denis? Oh! rash and fatal promise that he had made that afternoon. When the ladies all emerged, shawled and cloaked from the mess-room verandah, he made one bold effort to walk home with his *fiancée*; but every one was leaving simultaneously, and they all descended in one compact body, Dr. Malone escorting Miss Denis on one side, and Captain Rodney on the other; while her accepted lover walked alone behind, and angrily gnawed his moustache. However, he was the last to bid her good-bye, he even went a few paces down the little walk; meanwhile from the high road a crowd looked on— and waited! This was a trying ordeal, and Dr. Parkes' voice was heard shouting impatiently,—

"Now then, Lisle! if you are coming in my boat, look sharp, will you, there's a good fellow?"

He felt a fierce desire to throttle the little doctor! Moments to *him* were more precious than diamonds, and what was half an hour more or less to a dried-up old fogey like that?

He stopped for a second under the palm-trees, and whispered,—

"I'll come over to-morrow early; I mean this morning, if I may, and if I can possibly manage it, if not, good-bye, darling—our first and last good-bye. I shall be back in six weeks," and then he wrung her hand and went. (A more tender leave-taking was out of the question, in the searching glare of the moonlight, and under the batteries of forty pairs of eyes.)

Poor, ignorant Colonel Denis! who was standing within three yards, little guessed what Gilbert Lisle was whispering to his daughter; indeed, he was not aware that he had been whispering at *all*! nor that here was a robber who wished to carry off his treasure—his all—his one ewe lamb.

No, this guileless, unsuspicious gentleman, nodded a friendly "good night" to the thief, and went slowly yawning up the steps, then, turning round, said sleepily,—

"Well, and how did my little girl enjoy herself?"

His little girl looked very lovely in his fond eyes, as she stood below him in her simple white gown, with her face still turned towards the roadway."

"Oh! very, very much, papa!" she replied most truthfully, now entering the dim verandah, and thereby hiding the treacherous blushes that mounted to her very temples.

"That's right!" kissing her as he spoke. "There, be off to bed; it's nearly two o'clock! dreadful hours for an old gentleman like me!"

But Miss Denis did not obey her parent's injunction; on the contrary, she went into the drawing-room, laid down her candle, removed her gloves, and rested her hot face in her hands, and tried to collect her thoughts, and realize her bliss. She was so happy, she could not bear to go to bed, for fear she might go to sleep. She wanted to make the most of the delicious present, to think over every moment, every word, every look, that she had exchanged with Mr. Lisle this most wonderful evening. And to think that all along he had stayed away because he had thought that she was engaged to Jim Quentin—he had said so. Jim Quentin! And she curled her lip scornfully, as she recollected a recent little scene between that gentleman and herself.

For a whole hour she sat in the dimly-lighted drawing-room, looking out on the stars, listening to the sea, and tasting a happiness that comes but once in most people's lifetime. She was rudely aroused from her mental ecstacy, by a tall figure appearing in the doorway, clothed in white; no ghost this—merely her ayah, with her cloth wrapped round her, saying in a drowsy voice,—

"Missy never coming to bed to-night?"

CHAPTER XIX
PROOF POSITIVE

"About a hoop of gold—a paltry ring that she did give me."

Merchant of Venice.

"Is this a prologue—or the poesy of a ring?

'Tis brief, my lord—as woman's love."

Hamlet.

It will not surprise any one to hear, that there was rather a stormy meeting between Mr. Lisle and his fellow inmate. Mr. Quentin did not return home till nearly four o'clock, and when he did, he found his friend sitting up for him, and this of itself constitutes an injury, especially when the last-comer has had rather too much champagne! Apollo arrived tired and sleepy, with tumbled locks and tie, and in a quarrelsome, captious mood, swearing roundly as he came up the steps, at his unhappy servants—who had spent the night in packing.

"Hullo!" he cried, seeing the other writing at the table, "not gone to roost yet, my early bird?"

"No," looking at him gravely, "I wanted to speak to you first," rising as he spoke and shutting the door.

"I say!" with a forced laugh, "you are not going to shoot me, eh?"

"No, I merely want to ask you why you told me that you were engaged to Miss Denis?"

"Who says I'm not?" throwing himself into a chair, and extending his long legs.

"She does," replied his companion laconically.

"And how dare *you* ask her or meddle in my affairs?" blustered Mr. Quentin in a loud voice.

"'Dare' is a foolish word to use to me, Quentin. I do not want to quarrel with you," feeling that his adversary was not quite himself. "But I wish to know why you deceived me in this way. What was your motive?"

Mr. Quentin was as much sobered by the stern eyes of his *vis-à-vis*, as if he had had his head immersed in a bucket of iced water. He reviewed the circumstances with lightning speed; to tide over to-morrow, nay, this very day, was all he wanted. In a few hours they would be off; the *Scotia* sailed at nine, and the chances were ten to one that Lisle and Helen Denis would never meet in this world again. Lisle would probably go home from the Nicobars. He could not afford to get into his black books (for various reasons, chiefly connected with cheque books), and he would brazen it out now. As well be hanged for a sheep as a lamb!

"I *am* engaged to her," he said at last.

"She says you are not; it's merely your word against hers."

"And which do you believe?"

"Well, this is no time for mincing matters. I believe Miss Denis," said the other bluntly.

"Believe her against me? A girl you have not spoken to ten times in your life; and you and I have lived here under the same roof like *brothers* for months. Oh, Gilbert Lisle!" and his beautiful blue eyes looked quite misty, as he apostrophized his companion in a tone as mournful as the renowned "*Et tu, Brute.*" —But, as I have already stated, Jim Quentin was a consummate actor.

Mr. Lisle was rather staggered for a moment, and the other went on, —

"Don't you know—but how should you? for you don't know woman's ways," with a melancholy shake of the head, "that they *all*, even the youngest and simplest of them, think it no harm to tell fibs about their sweethearts? I give you my solemn word of honour that I've heard an engaged girl swear she was not going to be married to a fellow up to a week before the wedding-day. They think that being known to be engaged, spoils their fun with other men; the more proposals they can boast of the better. If you have been such a fool, as to believe Helen Denis's little joke, all I can say is, that I am sorry for you!"

This was hard swearing, certainly, but it was in for a penny, in for a pound, and the *Scotia* sailed at nine o'clock.

Still Mr. Lisle was not convinced, and he saw it and added, —

"You think very little of my bare word, I see. No doubt you would like to see some tangible proof of what I say. There is no time now ('thank goodness,' to himself) to bring us face to face, but if I promise to show you some token before we sail, will that content you?"

Mr. Lisle made no reply.

"And," he continued, "I'm going to turn in now, for it's four o'clock, and I'm dead beat. Don't let us fall out, old fellow—no woman is worth it. They are all the same, they can't help their nature," and with this parting declaration, Mr. Quentin, finished actor and finished flirt, sorrowfully nodded his head and took his departure.

Once in his own apartment he tore off his coat, called his body-servant to pull off his boots, threw himself into an arm-chair, and composed himself with a cheroot, yea, at four o'clock in the morning! He had shown a bold front, and had impressed Lisle—that he could see plainly. But how about this little token? He did not possess a glove, a ribbon, a flower, much less a photograph or a lock of hair. What was he to do? For fully a quarter of an hour the query found no answer in his brain, till his sleepy servant, asking some trivial question, gave him a clue; he saw it all, as it were, in a lightning flash.

Abdul was married to Miss Denis's ayah (a handsome, good-for-nothing virago, who, it was rumoured, occasionally inflicted corporal punishment upon her lord and master, and was avaricious to the last degree).

Abdul was a dark, oily-looking, sly person, who was generally to be trusted—when his own interests did not clash with his employer's.

"Abdul, look here," said Mr. Quentin suddenly, "I want you to do something for me at once."

"Yes, saar," said Abdul in a drowsy voice.

"Go off, now, this moment, and get the boat, go across to Ross"—here Abdul's face became very blank indeed,—"go to Colonel Denis's bungalow, and speak to Fatima, and tell her." Mr. Quentin was, for once in his life, a little ashamed of what he was about to do; but do it he would, all the same—he *must*—he had burnt his boats. "Tell her to give you that queer gold ring Missy wears—no stones, a pattern like this," talking the jargon of the East, and showing an ancient seal. "I want it as 'muster' for another, just to look at; for a present for Missy, and will give it back to-day. Mind you, Abdul, never letting Missy know: if you do, or if Fatima says one word, you get nothing; if you and she manage the job well, you shall have twenty rupees!"

Abdul stared, and then salaamed and stolidly replied,—

"I never telling master's business, master knows."

"Then be off at once, and let me see you back by seven o'clock; and don't attempt to show your face without *that*, or no rupees—you understand?"

"Master pleases," ejaculated Abdul, and vanished on his errand, an errand that was much to his taste. A little mystery or intrigue, and the prospects of a good many rupees, appeals to the native mind in a very direct fashion.

At seven o'clock he had returned, having accomplished his mission. Breathless and radiant he appeared, and roused his sleeping master, saying,—

"I've come back, saar, and here"—unfolding a bit of his turban, and holding out his hand—"I've brought the pattern master wanted."

"By Jove!" leaning up on his elbow, and now wide awake, "so you have," taking Helen's ring, and surveying it critically. Yes! nothing could be better; she always wore it on the third finger of her right hand, and there was surely some history about it, or he was much mistaken. "We will see what Lisle will say to *this*," he muttered to himself as he squeezed it on his own somewhat plump little finger. Then to Abdul,—

"Very well. All right; I'll give it back, you know. Meanwhile go to my box over there, and bring the money-bag, and count yourself out the dibs I promised you."

Abdul obeyed this order with great alacrity, salaamed, and then waited for his next instructions.

"You can go now; call me in half an hour," said his master, dismissing him with a wave of his newly-decorated hand.

"A first-class idea! and, by Jove, Miss Helen, I owed you this. The idea of a little chit like you, the penniless daughter of an old Hindoo colonel, giving yourself such airs as you did last night," alluding to a scene when Helen, wearied by his compliment, and indignant at his presumption, had plucked up courage to rebuke him in a manner that penetrated even the triple armour of his self-conceit. Such a thing was a novel experience, the recollection of it stung him still, and to such a man as Jim Quentin, the affront was unpardonable. It awoke a slumbering flame of resentment in his rather stolid breast, and a burning desire to pay her out! And he would take right good care that she did not catch Lisle—Lisle, who was certainly inclined to make an ass of himself about her. With this determination in his mind, he rose, dressed, and languidly lounged into their mutual sitting-room, where his companion had been impatiently awaiting him for an hour, intending subsequently to sail across to Ross, and take one more parting with his fair lady-love, and, if possible, obtain a word with her father.

A Bird Of Passage | 153

"So you have appeared at last?" he exclaimed; "I've been expecting you for ages."

"Have you? but we need not leave this till half-past eight," looking at his watch. "They know we are going, — and Hall is never in time."

"I'm not thinking of the *Scotia*," returned the other, scarcely able to restrain his impatience; "but of what you promised to show me last night — that proof you spoke of, you know."

"Oh! yes; by-the-bye, so I did," as if it were a matter of the most complete indifference. "I daresay I have something that will convince you. Will this do?" tendering his hand as he spoke, in quite an airy, nonchalant fashion.

Mr. Lisle glanced at it, and beheld his ring, the wreck ring, adorning Jim Quentin's little finger! He started as if he had been struck — his own gift, that she declared she would never part with! And she had bestowed it already, — given it to Quentin: this was enough, was too much — he asked no more.

"Well, will that do?" demanded Apollo, removing and tendering the token. "Are you satisfied *now*?"

"Yes," replied Mr. Lisle, who had regained his self-command. But the other had noted the sudden pallor of his face, the almost incredulous expression of his eyes, and felt that this borrowed bit of jewellery was indeed a trump card, boldly played.

Jim was immensely relieved as this one syllable fell from his companion's lips. The whole matter was now settled. Lisle was choked off: his own credit was unimpeached, but it had had a narrow squeak, and last night he had undoubtedly spent a very unpleasant quarter of an hour.

Of course Mr. Lisle did not return to Ross, although the white boat lay waiting for him for an hour, by the landing steps. Helen had more than half expected him, with trembling, delightful anticipations; how many times did she run to look in the glass? how many times re-arrange the flowers in her dress? how many times did she dart to the verandah as a manly step came up the road? But, alas! after an hour's expectation, her hopes were dashed to the ground by Miss Lizzie Caggett.

"The *Scotia* has sailed!" she screamed out from the pathway. "Come up to the flagstaff, and see the last of her."

It was the custom for the ladies on Ross to take constitutionals before breakfast, and Helen, on her way to the top of the hill with Miss Lizzie, was joined by Mrs. Creery, Mrs. Home, and Mrs. Durand, all discussing the previous evening's dissipation. Helen was (they all remarked) unusually silent: generally she was full of fun and spirits. She stood aloof, looking after the receding steamer, and said to herself, "What if he should never come back!"

But this was a merely passing thought that she silenced immediately. Mr. Lisle was, as every one knew, a man of his word, and never broke a promise.

The little group of ladies stood watching the smoke of the steamer become smaller and smaller till it vanished altogether, and Helen, as she turned her face away from the sea at last, had a suspicion of tears in her eyes,—tears which her companions attributed to Mr. Quentin. As she walked down the hill with Mrs. Home, that warm-hearted little lady, who was leaning on her, pressed her arm in token of sympathy, and whispered in a significant tone,—

"He will come back, dear."

"So he will," agreed Helen, also in a whisper, blushing scarlet as she spoke. But she and Mrs. Home were not thinking of the same person!

CHAPTER XX
"A GREAT BATTLE"

"But 'twas a famous victory."

Southey.

It is perhaps needless to mention that Mrs. Creery made it her business, and considered it her duty, to circulate the intelligence that she had received about Mr. Lisle without unnecessary delay. She read portions of the letter referring to him, in "strict confidence," to every one she could get hold of, and the missive was nearly worn out from constant folding and unfolding. If any one ventured to impugn her testimony, she would lay her hand upon her pocket with a dramatic gesture, and say,—

"That's nonsense! I've got it all here in black and white. I always knew that there was a screw loose about that man. Perhaps you will all be guided by *me* another time! I'm an excellent judge of character, as my sister, Lady Grubb, declares. She always says, 'You cannot go far wrong if you listen to Eliza'—that's me," pointing to her breast bone with a plump forefinger. Then she would produce the billet and, after much clearing of throat, commence to read what she already knew by heart.

"'You ask me if I can tell you anything about a Mr. Lisle, a mysterious person who has lately come to the Andamans; very dark, age over thirty, slight in figure, shabby and idle, close about himself, and with a curious, deliberate way of speaking; supposed to have been in the army, and to have come from Bengal. Christian name unknown, initial letter G.'"

(It sounded exactly like a description in a police notice.)

"'My dear Mrs. Creery, I know him well, and he may well be close about himself and his affairs'"—here it was Mrs. Creery's cue to pause and smack her lips with unction. "'If he is the person you so accurately describe, he is a Captain Lisle, a black sheep who was turned out of a regiment in Bengal on account of some very shady transactions on the turf.'"—"He told me himself he was fond of riding," Mrs. Creery would supplement, as if this fact clenched the business. "'He was bankrupt, and had a fearful notoriety in every way. No woman who respected herself would be seen speaking to him! The Andamans, no doubt, suit him very well at present, and offer him a new field for his energies, and a harbour of refuge at the same time. Do not let any one cash a cheque for him, and warn all the young ladies in the settlement that he is a *married* man!'"

"There," Mrs. Creery would conclude, with a toss of her topee, "what do you think of that?"

"Mr. Lisle is not here to speak for himself," ventured Helen on one occasion. "*Les absents ont toujours tort.*"

It was new to see Helen adopt an insurrectionary attitude. Mrs. Creery stared.

"Nonsense—stuff and nonsense," angrily. "And let me tell you, Helen Denis, that it is not at all maidenly or modest for a young girl like you to be taking up the cudgels for a notorious reprobate like this Lisle."

"I'm sure he is not a reprobate, and I'm certain you are mistaken," rejoined Helen bravely.

Here the elder lady flamed out, and thumped her umbrella violently on the ground, and cried in her highest key,—

"Then why did he go away? He knew that I had heard about him, for I told him so to his face. I never say behind a person's back what I won't say to their face." (Oh! Mrs. Creery, Mrs. Creery!) "And it is a very remarkable coincidence, that in less than twelve hours, he was out of the place! How do you account for that, eh?"

She paused for breath, and once more proceeded triumphantly,—

"He will never show here again, believe me; and, after all, I am thankful to say he has done no great harm! As far as *I* know he ran no bills in the bazaar, and certainly neither you nor Lizzie Caggett lost your hearts to him!"

Helen became very pale, her lips quivered, and she was unable to reply for a moment. Then she said,—

"At any rate, I believe in him, Mrs. Creery,—and always will; deeds are better than words. Have you forgotten the wreck?"

"Forgotten it?" she screamed. "Am I ever likely to get it out of my head? Only for my calling myself hoarse, you and Mr. Lisle would both have been murdered in that hole of a cabin! You know I told you not to go down, and you would, and see what you got by it."

There was not the slightest use in arguing with this lady, who not only imposed upon others, but also upon herself: she had a distorted mind, that idealized everything connected with her own actions, and deprecated, and belittled, the deeds of other people! The only persons who had *not* heard the horrible tale about Mr. Lisle were the Durands and the general; the latter was a singularly astute gentleman, and never lost a certain habit of cool military promptitude, even when in retreat. Each time Mrs. Creery had exhibited symptoms of extracting a letter from her pocket, he had escaped! The Durands were Mr. Lisle's friends,—a fact that lowered them many fathoms in Mrs. Creery's estimation, and were consequently the very last to hear of the scandal!

About a fortnight after the departure of the *Scotia*, the general gave one of his usual large dinner-parties; every one in Ross was invited, and about twenty-four sat down to the table. When the meal was over, and the ladies had pulled a few crackers, and sipped their glass of claret, they all filed off into the drawing-room in answer to Mrs. Creery's rather dramatic signal, and there they looked over photographs, noted the alterations in each other's dresses, drank coffee, and conversed in groups. In due time the conversation turned upon that ever fertile topic, "Mr. Lisle," and Mrs. Graham, who was seated beside Mrs. Durand, little knowing what she was doing, fired the first shot, by regretting very much "that Mr. Lisle had turned out to be such a dreadful character, so utterly different from what he seemed." Encouraged by one or two cleverly-put questions from her neighbour, she unfolded the whole story. Meantime, Mrs. Durand sat and listened, in rigid silence, her lips pressed firmly together, her hands tightly locked in her pale-blue satin lap. When the recital had come to an end, she turned her grave eyes on her companion, and said in her most impressive manner,—

"*How* do you know this?"

"Oh, it's well known, it's all over the place. Mrs. Creery had a letter," glancing over to where that lady reclined in a comfortable chair, with a serene expression on her face, and a gently-nodding diadem.

"Mrs. Creery," said Mrs. Durand, raising her voice, which was singularly clear and penetrating, "pray what is this story that you have been telling every one about Mr. Lisle?"

This warlike invocation awoke the good lady from her doze, and, like a battle-steed, she lifted her head, and, as it were, sniffed the conflict from afar!

"I've been telling nothing but the truth, Mrs. Durand"—rousing herself at once to an upright position—"and you are most welcome to *hear* it, though he *is* a friend of yours," and she tossed her diadem as much as to say "Come on!"

"Thank you! Then will you be so very kind as to repeat what you have heard," returned Mrs. Durand with a freezing politeness that made the other ladies look at each other significantly. There was going to be a fight, and they felt a thrill of mingled delight and apprehension at the prospect.

Bold Mrs. Durand was the only woman in the island who had never veiled her crest to Mrs. Creery. She was now about to challenge her to single combat—yes, they all saw it in her face!

"I always knew that there was something very wrong about that man," began the elder lady in her usual formula, and figuratively placing her lance in rest. "People who have nothing to hide, are never ashamed to speak of their concerns, but no one ever got a word out of Mr. Lisle, and I am sure he received every encouragement to be open! He was in the army, he admitted *that* against his will, and that was all. He never deceived *me*;—I knew he was without any resources, I—knew he was out at elbows, I knew——"

"Pray spare us your opinion, and tell us what *facts* you have to go upon," interrupted Mrs. Durand, calmly cutting short this flow of denunciation.

"I have a letter from a friend at Simla," unconsciously seeking her pocket, "a letter," she retorted proudly, "which you can *read*, saying that he was cashiered for conduct unbecoming an officer and a gentleman, that he is a bankrupt, and a swindler, and a married man," as if this last enormity crowned all.

"It is not true—not a word of it!" replied Mrs. Durand, as coolly as if she were merely saying, "How do you do?"

"Not true! nonsense; is he not dark, aged over thirty, name Lisle? did he not hang about the settlement for six months living on his wits? Of course it is true," rejoined the elder lady, with an air that proclaimed that she had not merely crushed, but pulverized, her foe!

"Lisle is not an uncommon name, and I know that my friend is not the original of your flattering little sketch."

"But I tell you that he *is*! I can prove it; I have it all in black and white!" cried Mrs. Creery furiously—her temper had now gone by the board. Who was this Mrs. Durand that she should dare to contradict her? She saw that they were face to face in the lists, and that the other ladies were eager spectators of the tourney; it was not merely a dispute over Mr. Lisle, it was a struggle for the social throne, whoever conquered now would be mistress of the realm. This woman must be browbeaten, silenced, and figuratively slain!

"I have it all in writing, and pray what can *you* bring against that?" she demanded imperiously.

"Simply my word, which I hope will stand good," returned the other firmly.

Mrs. Creery laughed derisively, and tossed her head and then replied,—

"Words go for nothing!"

This was rude—it was more than rude, it was insulting!

"Am I to understand that you do not believe mine?" said Mrs. Durand, making a noble effort to keep her temper.

"Oh," ignoring the question, "I have never doubted that *you* could tell us more about Mr. Lisle than most people, and a woman will say anything for a man—a man who is a friend," returned the other lady with terrible significance.

This was hard-hitting with a vengeance, still Mrs. Durand never quailed.

"Shall I tell you who Mr. Lisle really is? I did not intend to mention it, as he begged me to be silent."

(Here Mrs. Creery's smile was really worth going a quarter of a mile to see.)

"I have known him for many years; he is an old friend of mine, and of my brothers."

"Oh, of your brothers!" interrupted her antagonist, looking up at the ceiling with a derisive laugh and an adequate expression of incredulity.

"I am not specially addressing myself to *you*, Mrs. Creery," exclaimed Mrs. Durand at white heat, but still retaining wonderful command of her temper. "My brothers were at Eton with him," she continued, looking towards her other listeners. "He is the second son of Lord Lingard and the Honourable Gilbert Lisle."

A silence ensued, during which you might have heard a pin drop; Mrs. Creery's face became of a dull beetroot colour, and her eyes looked as if they were about to take leave of their sockets.

"And what brought him masquerading here?" she panted forth at last.

"He was not masquerading, he came in his own name," returned Mrs. Durand with calm decision. "He left the service on coming in for a large property, and spends most of his time travelling about; he is fond" — addressing herself specially to the other ladies, and rather wondering at Helen Denis's scarlet cheeks — "of exploring out-of-the-way places. I believe he has been to Siberia and Central America. The Andamans were a novelty; he came for a few weeks and stayed for a few months because he liked the fishing and boating and the unconventional life."

"And who is the other Lisle?"

"Some distant connection, I believe; every family has its black sheep."

"Why did he not let us know his position?" gasped Mrs. Creery.

"Because he thinks it of so little importance; he wished, I conclude, to stand on his own merits, and to be valued for himself alone. He found his proper level here, did he not, Mrs. Creery? He lived in the palace of truth for once!" and she laughed significantly — undoubtedly turn-about is fair play, it was her turn now.

"I must say that I wonder what he saw in the Andamans," exclaimed Mrs. Graham at last.

"One attraction, no doubt, was, because he could go away whenever he liked; another, that he was left to himself — no one ran after him!" and Mrs. Durand laughed again. "In London he is made so much of, as every one knows he is wealthy and a bachelor, and that his eldest brother has only one lung! Besides all these advantages, he is extremely popular, and is beset by invitations to shoot, to dance, to dine, to yacht, from year's end to year's end. Well, he got a complete holiday from all that kind of thing *here*!"

Then she recollected that in castigating Mrs. Creery and Miss Caggett she was including totally innocent people — people who had always been civil to the Honourable Gilbert Lisle, such as Mrs. Graham, Mrs. Home, Miss Denis, and others, and she added, —

"All the same, I should tell you that he enjoyed his stay here immensely, he told me so, and that he would always have a kindly recollection of Port Blair, and of the friends he had made in the settlement."

(Mrs. Durand, thought Helen, does not know everything; she evidently is not aware that he is coming back.) The speaker paused at the word settlement, for she had made the discovery that most of the gentlemen had entered and were standing in the background while she had been, as it were, addressing the house. A general impression had been gathered about Mr. Lisle also, as Captain Rodney whispered to Dr. Malone, that "Mrs. Creery had evidently had what she would be all the better for, viz., a rare good setting down."

Infatuated Mrs. Creery! deposed, and humbled potentate, if there was one thing that was even nearer to her heart than Nip, it was the owner of a *title*.

She could hardly grasp any tangible idea just at present, she was so completely dazed. It was as if Mrs. Durand had let off a catherine-wheel in her face.

Mr. Lisle an Honourable! Mr. Lisle immensely rich! Mr. Lisle, whom she had offered to pay for his photographs, whom she had never met without severely snubbing. And all the time he was the son of a lord, and she had unconsciously lost a matchless opportunity of cementing a lifelong friendship with one of the aristocracy. Alas, for poor Mrs. Creery, her mind was chaos!

After the storm there ensued the proverbial calm; the piano was opened, and people tried to look at ease, and to pretend, forsooth, that they were not thinking of the recent grand engagement, but it was all a hollow sham.

Helen, if it had been in her power, would have endowed that brave woman, Mrs. Durand, with a Victoria Cross for valour, and, indeed, every lady present secretly offered her a personal meed of admiration and gratitude. She had slain their dragon, who would never more dare to rear her head and tyrannize over the present or vilify the absent. Surely there should be some kind of domestic decoration accorded to those who arm themselves with moral courage, and go forth and rescue the reputation of their friends.

Miss Caggett sat in the background, looking unusually grave and gloomy, no doubt thinking with remorseful stings of *her* lost opportunities. Dr. Malone grinned and nodded, and rubbed his rather large bony hands ecstatically, and whispered to Captain Rodney that "*he* had always had a notion that Lisle the photographer was a prince in disguise!"

As for Mrs. Creery, as before mentioned, that truculent lady was absolutely shattered; she resembled an ill constructed automaton who had been knocked down and then set up limply in a chair, or a woman in a dream—and that a bad one. After a while she spoke in a strangely subdued voice, and said,—

"General, I don't feel very well; that coffee of yours has given me a terrible headache. If you will send for my jampan, I'll just go quietly home."

Thus she withdrew, with a pitiable remnant of her former dignity, her host escorting her politely to the entrance, and placing her in her chair with faint regrets. Every one knew perfectly well, that it was *not* the General's coffee that had routed Mrs. Creery, it was she whose beautiful contralto was now filling the drawing-room as her late antagonist tottered down the steps—it was that valiant lady, Mrs. Durand!

CHAPTER XXI
THE NICOBARS

"Once I loved a maiden fair,

But she did deceive me."

When last we saw Mr. Quentin, he had just succeeded in convincing his companion that he was Miss Denis's favoured suitor. This was well—this was satisfactory. But it was neither well, nor yet satisfactory, to behold Lisle calmly appropriate the posy ring, and put it in his waistcoat pocket.

"Hullo! I say, you know," expostulated Apollo, "give me back my property."

"No," returned the other very coolly; "it was originally mine, and as it has once more come into my hands, I will keep it."

Mr. Quentin became crimson with anger and dismay.

"I found it on the wreck, and gave it to Miss Denis, who said she valued it greatly, but as she has passed it on to you, I see that her words were a mere *façon de parler*, and if she asks you what you have done with it, you can tell her that you showed it to me, and that *I* retained it."

There was a high-handed air about this bare-faced robbery that simply took Mr. Quentin's breath away, and the whole proceeding put him in, as he expressed it himself, "such an awful hat;" for he had never meant to steal the ring—he only wanted the loan of it for half an hour, and now that it had served his purpose, it was to be restored to its mistress; but here was Lisle actually compelling him to be a *thief*! Vainly he stammered, blustered, and figuratively flapped his wings! he might as well have stammered and blustered to the wall. Lisle was impassive—moreover, the boat was waiting; and Abdul returned to Ross and Fatima, plus twenty rupees, but minus the ring. And what a search there was for that article when Helen Denis missed it; rooms were turned out, matting was taken up, every hole and corner was searched, but all to no purpose—considering that the ring was, as we know, on its way to the Nicobars.

Fatima, the Cleopatra-like, was touched when she saw her Missy actually weeping for her lost property; but all the same, she positively assured her that she had never seen it since she had had it on her finger last—indeed, if it had been in her power to return it she would have done so, for Helen offered a considerable reward to whoever would restore her the most precious of her possessions. Days and weeks went by, but no ring was found.

The *Scotia* left Calcutta once every six weeks, calling firstly at Port Blair, then at the Nicobars, then Rangoon, and so back to Calcutta; and the reason of Mr. Quentin's hurried departure was that the order to start for the Nicobars came in the steamer that was to take him there, otherwise there would have been the usual delay of six weeks. Once on board, he went straight below to his cabin, turned in, and recouped himself for his sleepless night. He slept soundly all day long, having immense capacities in that line. Mr. Hall, the settlement officer, walked the deck with Mr. Lisle, and subsequently they descended to the saloon and played chess. The group near the flagstaff had not been unnoticed by the passengers of the *Scotia* as she steamed by under the hill; there had been some waving of handkerchiefs, but Mr. Lisle's had never left his pocket. He had something else in that selfsame pocket that forbade such demonstration—the fatal ring, and a ring that bore for motto, as he had now discovered, "Love me and leave me not"—a motto that implied a bitter mockery of the present occasion. This wreck ring was assuredly an unlucky token! Only last night, and Helen had seemed to him the very incarnation of simplicity, truth, and faith—what a contrast to those many lovely London sirens who smiled on him—and his *rent roll*! Never again would he be deceived by nineteen summers, and sweet grey eyes; no, never again. This was the determination he came to, as he paced the deck that night beneath the stars.

The next morning the *Scotia* was off the low, long coast of the Nicobars; so low was it, that it resembled a forest standing in the water. In the midst of this seeming forest there was a narrow passage that a casual eye might easily overlook; a passage just barely wide enough to admit the steamer, with a natural arch of rock on one side; the water was clear, emerald green, and very deep, and along the wooded shores of the entrance to Camorta were many white native huts, built on wooden piles, scattered up and down the high banks clothed in jungle. Soon the passage widened into a large inland bay, lined with mangroves and poison-breathing jungles, save for a clearing on the left-hand side, where there was a rude pier, a bazaar of native houses, and some larger wooden buildings on the overhanging hill. This was Camorta, the capital of the Nicobars, to which Port Blair was as London to some small provincial town.

The natives were totally different to the Andamanese; they were Malays, with brown skins, flat heads, and wide mouths, and came swarming round the three Europeans as they landed, and commenced to climb the hill. One, who was very sprucely dressed in a blue frock-coat, grey trousers, white tie, and tall hat, and flourished a gold watch, was bare-footed, and had it made known to Mr. Lisle, before he was five minutes on *terra firma*, that he was prepared to give him one thousand cocoa-nuts in exchange for his boots.

The buildings on the hill included a big, gaunt-looking bungalow, in which the three new arrivals took up their quarters. It was rather destitute of furniture, but commanded a matchless view of this great inland bay and far-away hills; it also overlooked a rather suggestive object, an old white ship, that lay off Camorta, the crew of which had been killed and eaten, many years previously, by the inhospitable Nicobarese! Gilbert Lisle had never in all his wanderings been in any place he detested as cordially as his present residence. Days seemed endless, the nights hot and stifling, the sun scorching, the sport bad. And other things, such probably as his own frame of mind, did not tend to enhance the charms of Camorta. Mr. Hall had ample occupation; Jim Quentin an unlimited capacity for sleep. He had also a box full of literature, a good brand of cigars, and, moreover, was at peace with himself and all mankind. He could do a number of doubtful actions, and yet he always managed to retain himself in his own good graces. He had squared Lisle, who was going away direct from the Nicobars to Rangoon, thence to Singapore and Japan. This was a most desirable move, and there would be no more raking up of awkward subjects, and *he* would never be found out. His period of expatriation was nearly at an end, he was financially the better for his exile at Port Blair, and then, hurrah for a hill-station, fresh fields, and pretty faces, or, better still, Piccadilly and the Park! Meanwhile, he was at the Nicobars, and there he had to stay, so he accepted the present philosophically, and slept as much as possible, and grumbled when awake at the food, the climate, and the heads of his department, and was not nearly as much to be pitied as he imagined, not half as much as Lisle, who neither read novels nor slept many hours at a stretch, or had agreeable anticipations of future flirtations in hill-stations. He was remarkably silent, and smoked many of the drowsy hours away. When he *did* join in the conversation, his remarks were so cynical, and his words so sharply edged, that Mr. Quentin was positively in awe of him, and was more than usually wary in the choice of his topics. Out of doors, he shot the ugly, greedy caymen, caught turtle, and sketched, or explored the country recklessly; making his way through the rank, dank jungle, where matted creepers hung from tree to tree, and snakes and spotted vipers darted up their hideous heads as he brushed past their moist, dark hiding-places.

A good deal of Mr. Lisle's time was spent in absolute idleness, and though the name of Helen Denis never crossed his lips, he had by no means cast her out of his mind. Hourly he fought with his thoughts: hourly he weighed all the *pros* and *cons*. Her acceptance of Quentin's attentions went to balance against her coolness to him subsequently; her blushes when he appeared were a set-off against her solemn denial of any understanding between them; her evident agitation when he himself had wooed her was neutralized by the bestowal of his ring upon Quentin—the ring kicked the beam; the ring was the verdict. After all, Quentin was ten times more likely to engage a girl's fancy than himself. Apollo was handsome, gay, and fascinating—when he chose; *he* was sunburnt, shabby, rather morose, and seemingly a pauper; that part of it was his own fault, he had no one but himself to blame for that. Query, would it have been better if he had permitted the truth to leak out, and allowed the community to know that they had the Honourable Gilbert Lisle, the owner of ten thousand a year, dwelling among them? In some ways things would have been pleasanter, but he had not come down to the Andamans for society, but for sea-fishing, and sailing, and an unfettered, out-door life. And when he was accidentally thrown into the company of a pretty girl, who was as pleasant to him as if he were a millionaire, who smiled on him as brightly as on others, in far more flourishing circumstances, who could ask him to resist the temptation that had thrust itself into his way—the triumph of winning her in the guise of a poor and un-pretending suitor?

The temptation led him on, and dazzled him, and for a moment he seemed to have the prize in his hands; and what a prize! especially to him, who was accustomed to being flattered, deferred to, and courted in a manner that accounted for his rather cynical views of society. But, alas! his treasure-trove (his simple-minded island maiden), had been rudely wrested from him ere he had realized its possession; and yet, after all, it was no loss, the apparently priceless jewel was imitation, was paste!

Why had she told him a deliberate lie? He might forgive a little coquetry (perhaps); he might forgive the unpleasant fact of her having "made a fool of him," as his friend had so delicately suggested, but a falsehood, uttered without a falter or a blush, *never!*

Week succeeded week, and each day seemed as long as seven—each week a month. Lisle, the ardent admirer of strange scenes, and strange countries, was callous and indifferent to the natural beauties of the place. He had actually come to *hate* the magnificent foliage, golden mid-day hazes, and the gorgeous, blinding sunsets, of these sleepy southern islands. All he craved for, was to get away from such sights, and never, never, see them more! Latterly, he found ample occupation in nursing Mr. Hall to the best of his ability—Mr. Hall, who had fallen a victim to the deadly Nicobar fever, and tossed and moaned and raved all through the scorching days and suffocating nights, and was under the delusion that the hand that smoothed his pillow, and held the cup to his parched lips, and bathed his burning temples, was his mother's! Jim Quentin (the selfish) merely contented himself with languidly inquiring after the patient once a day, and shutting himself up in his own side of the bungalow, as it were in a fastness, partaking of his meals alone, totally ignoring his companions, since one of them was sick, and the other was stupid.

The thin veneer of Mr. Jim's charm of manner, could not stand much knocking about; a good deal of it had worn off, and Mr. Lisle beheld him as he really was; selfish to the core, vain and arrogant,—yet not proud, not very sensitive on the subject of borrowing money, and with rather hazy ideas with regard to the interpretation of the word "honour."

Lisle, in his heart, secretly despised his fascinating inmate; but, needless to say, he endeavoured to keep this sentiment entirely in the background, though, now and then, a winged word like a straw, might have shown a looker-on which way the wind blew.

At length, the long-desired *Scotia* came steaming up Camorta Bay, like a goaler to set free her prisoners; she remained off the pier for a few hours, and Mr. Lisle was unfeignedly delighted to see her once more, for she was to carry him away to Rangoon, to civilization, occupation and oblivion. His traps were ready, but ere he took leave of his companions and went on board, he sat for a while reading the newly-arrived letters in the verandah, along with Jim Quentin

"Hullo!" exclaimed the latter, suddenly looking up. "I say, what do you think! here is a letter from Parkes, and poor old Denis is dead!"

"Dead?" ejaculated his companion.

"Yes, listen to this,"—reading aloud,—"he was on the ranges one morning, and in trying to save a native child who ran across the line of fire, he was shot through the heart. We are all very much cut up, and as to Miss Denis, the poor girl is so utterly broken-down you would scarcely know her."

"It must have been a fearful shock," said Mr. Lisle. "I'm very sorry for Denis, very. Of course you will go back at once—now!"

"How?" thrown completely off his guard, "why?"

"How? by the *Enterprise*, which will be here in three days with stores, and why? really, I scarcely expected you to ask *me* such a question. She——"

"Oh," interrupting quickly, "oh, yes! I quite understand what you mean. Oh, of course, of course!"

After this ensued a rather long silence, and then Mr. Lisle spoke,—

"I now remember rather a strange thing," he said reflectively. "Denis and I were looking over the wall of the new cemetery together one evening, and I recollect his saying, that he wondered how long it would be till the first grave was dug.—Strange that it should be his own!"

"Strange indeed!" acquiesced his companion tranquilly, "but, of course, everything must have a beginning. Here's a Lascar coming up from the pier," he added, rising hastily, and collecting his letters as he spoke, "and we had better be making a start."

In another hour Mr. James Quentin was walking back to the bungalow alone. As he stood on the hill above the pier, and watched the smoke of the departing steamer above the jungle, he felt a curious and unusual sensation, he actually felt,—his almost fossilized conscience told him,—that he had not behaved altogether well to Lisle! Lisle, who had been his friend by deeds, not words; Lisle, who had borne the blow he had dealt him like a man; had never once allowed a word, or allusion that might reflect on Helen, to pass his lips, and had accepted the ring with unquestioning faith. Yes, Lisle, though rather silent and unusually dull (for generally he was such an amusing fellow), had taken his disappointment well. Mr. Quentin, however, rated such disappointments very lightly. Judging others by himself, they were mere pin-pricks at the time, and as such consigned to the limbo of complete oblivion within a week.

"After all," he said aloud, as he slowly strolled back with his hands in his pockets, "I am in reality his *best* friend! It would never have done for him, to entangle himself with a girl without connections, a girl without a penny, a girl he picked up at the Andamans! Haw! haw! by Jove! how people would laugh! No, no, Gilbert Lisle, you must do better than that; you will have to look a little higher for the future Lady Lingard. I don't suppose she has a brass farthing, and she certainly would not suit my book at all."

Needless to add, that this mirror of chivalry did not return to Port Blair an hour sooner than was his original intention.

CHAPTER XXII
THE FIRST GRAVE

"They laid him by the pleasant shore,

And in the hearing of the wave."

Tennyson.

The news about Colonel Denis was only too true! He had started for the ranges on Aberdeen one morning about nine o'clock, as his regiment was going through their annual course of musketry, and as he stood in a marker's butt, close to the targets, a native child from the Sepoy lines suddenly emerged from some unsuspected hiding-place, where she had been lying *perdue*, and ran right into the open, across the line of fire. Colonel Denis rushed out to drag her into shelter, but just as he seized her, a bullet from a Martini-Henry struck him between the shoulders, and without a groan, he fell forward on his face dead. Yes, he was quite dead when they hurried up to him. The shock to every one was stupefying; they were speechless with horror; but five minutes previously he had been talking to them so cheerfully, and had to all appearances as good a life as any one present,—and now here he lay motionless on his face in the sand, a dark stain widening on his white coat, and a frightened little native child whimpering beside him.

"Instantaneous," said Dr. Malone, with an unprofessional huskiness in his voice, when they brought him running to the spot. "What an awful thing, and no one to blame, unless that little beggar's mother," glancing at the imp, who stared back at the Sahib with all the power of her frightened black eyes. "Poor Denis; but it was just like him,—he never thought of himself." This was his epitaph, the manner in which he met his death, "was just like him."

And who was to break the terrible tidings to his daughter? People asked one another the question with bated breath and anxious eyes, as they stood around. Who was to go and tell her, that her father, to whom she had bidden a playful good-bye an hour ago, was dead, that that smiling wave of his hand had been, Farewell for ever!

It was about eleven o'clock, and Helen was sitting at the piano, playing snatches of different things, unable to settle down to any special song or piece. She had felt curiously restless all the morning, and was thinking that she would run over and have a chat with Mrs. Home,—for she was too idle to do anything else,—when a sudden loud sob made her start up from the music-stool and turn round somewhat nervously.

There she beheld her ayah, Fatima, staring at her through the purdah, but the instant she was discovered, she quickly dropped it, and vanished. It never occurred to Helen to connect Fatima's tears with herself, or her affairs; it was more than probable that she had been having a quarrel with her husband, and that they had been beating one another, as was their wont,—when words were exhausted. She was thinking of following her handmaiden, but she believed it would only be the old story, "Abdul, plenty bad man, very wicked rascal," when her ear caught the sound of footsteps coming up the front pathway. They halted, then it was *not* Mrs. Creery; she never did that, and peeping over the blind, she beheld to her amazement, Mr. Latimer and Mrs. Home. And Mrs. Home was crying, what could it be? And they were both coming to her.

A pang of apprehension seemed to seize her heart with a clutch of ice, some unknown, some dreadful trouble was on its way to *her.* She sprang down the steps and met them, saying,—

"What is the matter? Oh! Mr. Latimer, you have come to tell me something—something," growing very white, "about papa?"

Mr. Latimer himself was deadly pale, and seemed to find considerable difficulty in speaking. At last he said,—

"Yes; he has been hurt on the ranges."

"Then let me go to him at once—at once."

"Oh, my dear, my dear," cried Mrs. Home, bursting into tears, "you must prepare yourself for trouble."

"I am prepared; please let me go to him. Oh, I am losing time; where is he? Why, they are bringing him home," as her quick ear caught the heavy tramp of measured feet, bearing some burden,—an hospital dhoolie.

Before either of her visitors had guessed at her intention, she had flown down the pathway, and met the procession. She hastily pulled aside the curtain, and took her father's hand in hers. But what was this? this motionless form, with closed eyes? She had never seen it before in all her life, but who does not recognize Death, even at their first meeting?

"Oh! he is dead," she shrieked, and fell insensible on the pathway.

For a long time she remained unconscious, and "it was best so" people whispered. There were so many sad arrangements to be made. The General himself superintended everything with regard to the funeral, which was to take place at sundown, as was the invariable custom in the East. There, there is no gradual parting as in England, where white-covered dead lies amid the living for days. In India such hospitality is never shown to death, he is thrust forth the very day he comes. The wrench is agonizing, and, as in a case like the present, where death was sudden, the shock overwhelming.

To think that you may be laughing and talking with a relative, friend, or neighbour, one evening, that they have been in the very best of health, as little anticipating the one great change as yourself, and that by the very next night, they may be dead and *buried*! In Eastern countries, there seems to be almost a cruel promptness about the funerals, but it is inevitable. By five o'clock everything was ready in the bungalow on the hill; the bier and bearers, the mourners, the wreaths of flowers, and the Union Jack for pall. Colonel Denis had that morning been given a huge bunch of white flowers for Helen; lovely lilies, ferns and orchids, that did not grow on Ross; he had brought home and presented the offering with pride, and she, being unusually lazy, had left the flowers in a big china bowl, intending to arrange them after breakfast.

How little are we able to see into the future! Happily for ourselves. Would Colonel Denis have carried home that big bunch of lilies with such alacrity had he known that they were destined to decorate his own coffin!

In deference to Helen, who was now alive to every sound, the large *cortège* almost stole from the door, and the band was mute. The cemetery was on Aberdeen, not far from the fatal ranges, and the funeral went by boat. Once on the sea, that profoundly melancholy strain, "The Dead March in Saul," was heard, after three preliminary muffled beats of the drum; and it sounded, if possible, more weird and sad than usual. As its strains were wafted across the water, and reached the bungalow on the hill, Helen sat up on the sofa, and looked wildly at Mrs. Home and Mrs. Durand.

"I—I—hear—the 'Dead March' in the distance! Who—who is it for? It is not playing for papa.—It is impossible, *impossible*. See, here are some of the flowers he brought me this morning—there are his gloves, that he left to have mended! I know," wringing her hands as she spoke, "that people do die, but never—never like this! This is some fearful dream; or I am going mad; or I have had a long illness, and I have been off my head. Oh, that band—" now putting her fingers in her ears, and burying her face in the cushions, "it is a dream-band—a nightmare!"

After a very long silence, there was another sound from across the water—the distant rattle of musketry repeated thrice, and now Mrs. Home, and Mrs. Durand, were aware that the last honours had been paid to Colonel Denis,—who had been alive and as well as they were that very morning,—and was now both dead and buried.

Nothing short of the very *plainest* speaking had been able to keep Mrs. Creery from forcing herself into Helen's presence. But Mrs. Home, Mr. Latimer, and Dr. Malone, were as the three hundred heroic Greeks who kept the pass at Thermopylæ. They formed a body-guard she could not pass.

Every one, even the last-mentioned matron, desired to have Helen under their roof. Mrs. King came up from Viper, all the way in the mid-day sun, to say that, "Of course, every one *must* see, that the farther Miss Denis was from old associations, the better, and that her room was ready." Mrs. Graham arrived from Chatham with the same story; but in the end, Helen went to Mrs. Home, going across with her after dark, like a girl walking in a trance. Sleep, kind sleep, did come to her, thanks to a strong opiate, and thus, for a time, she and her new acquaintance, grief, were parted. The pretty bungalow on the side of the hill, so bright and full of life only last night, was dark and silent now. One inmate slept a sleep to deaden sorrow, the other lay alone upon the distant mainland, under the silent stars, within sound of the sea—and the new cemetery contained its first grave.

CHAPTER XXIII
"WAS IT POSSIBLE!"

"Joy comes and goes, hope ebbs and flows,

Like the wave.

Change doth unknit the tranquil strength of man;

Love lends life a little grace,

A few sad smiles; and then,

Both are laid in one cold place,

In the grave."

M. Arnold.

Days crawled by, and Helen gradually and painfully began to realize her lot. Hers was a silent, stony grief (now that the first torrent of tears had been shed) of that undemonstrative, reserved nature, that it is so difficult to alleviate, and that shrinks from outward sympathy. People (ladies) came to her, and sat with her, and held her hand, and wept, but she did not; this grief that had come upon her unawares, seemed almost to have turned her to stone. She opened her heart to Mrs. Home only; and in answer to affectionate attempts at consolation, she said,—

"I sometimes sit and wonder, wonder if it is *true*! You see, Mrs. Home, my case is so different to others. Now, if you were to lose one child—which heaven forbid—you have still eight remaining; if Colonel Home was taken from you, you have your children; but *I* have no one left. Papa was all I had, and I am alone in the world; I can scarcely believe it!"

"My dear, you must not say so! you have many friends, and friends are sometimes far better than one's own kin. Then there is your aunt. I wrote to her myself last mail."

"Aunt Julia! She is worse than nobody. She is an utter stranger, in reality, a complete woman of the world. She and I never got on; she was always saying hard things about *him*!"

"Well, you won't be with her long, you know! and you cannot say that you are alone in the world; you know very well that you will not be alone for long, you understand," squeezing her fingers significantly as she spoke.

Helen did understand, and coloured vividly. It seemed to her almost a sin to think of Gilbert Lisle now, when every thought was dedicated to her father, when all ideas of love or a lover had been, as it were, swept out of her mind by the blast of her recent and terrible calamity.

Mrs. Home noticed the blush, but again attributed its cause to the wrong person.

Colonel Denis' effects were sold off in the usual manner; his furniture, boat, and guns, were disposed of, his servants dismissed, and his papers examined. And what discoveries were not made in that battered old despatch-box! Not of money owing, or startling unpaid bills, but of large sums due to him; borrowed and forgotten by impecunious acquaintances—one thousand rupees here, three thousand rupees there, merely acknowledged by careless, long-forgotten I. O. U.'s. Then there were receipts for money paid,—drained away yearly by his father's and wife's creditors—his very pension was mortgaged. How little he appeared to have spent upon himself. All his life long he had been toiling hard for other people, who gaily squandered in a week, what he had accumulated in a year; a thankless task! a leaden burden!

Apparently he had begun to save of late, presumably for Helen; but, including the auction, all that could be placed to his daughter's credit in the bank was only four hundred odd pounds!

"Say fifteen pounds a year," said Colonel Home, looking blankly at Mr. Creery.

"I know he intended to insure his life, he told me so last week."

"Ah! if he only had. What is to become of the poor girl?" continued Colonel Home; "fifteen pounds a year won't even keep her in clothes, let alone in food and house-room. I believe he had very few relations in England, and see how some of his friends out here have fleeced him!"

"They ought to be made pay up," returned Mr. Creery. "I'll see to *that*," he added with stern, determined face.

"How can they pay up? The fellows who signed those," touching some I. O. U.'s, "are dead. Here's another, for whom Denis backed a bill; he went off to Australia years ago. I wonder Tom Denis had not a worse opinion of his fellow-creatures."

"In many ways, Tom was a fool; his heart was too soft, his eyes were always blind to his own interests: some people soon found that out."

"Well! what is to become of his daughter? That is what puzzles me," said his listener anxiously. "She is a good girl, and uncommonly pretty!"

"Yes; her face is her fortune, and I hope it will stand to her," rejoined Mr. Creery, dubiously. "But, to set herself off, she should go into fine society and wear fine clothes, and she has no means to start her in company where she would meet a likely match. As they say in my country, 'Ye canna whistle without an upper lip.'"

"She might not have *far* to go for a husband," returned Colonel Home significantly.

"Ah, well! I believe I *know* what you mean, but that man will be needing a fortune. He is too cannie to marry 'a penniless lass without a lang pedigree!'"

"My wife has her fancies," said Colonel Home, "and thinks a good deal of him."

"So does mine," returned the other, "and has *her* fancies too; but all the same—between you and me, Home—I never liked the fellow; you know who I mean. He is just a gay popinjay, taking his turn out of everybody that comes in his way."

(Observe, cannie Scotchman as he was, that all this time, he had never mentioned any *name*.)

Several doors were opened to Helen, offering her a home, but she steadily resisted all invitations. She felt that she would be occupying an anomalous position by remaining on at Port Blair, without having any real claim on any one in the settlement. If there had been some small children to teach,—save those in the native school,—or if there were any means by which she could have earned her livelihood, it would have been different; but, of course, in a place like the Andamans, there was no such opening. The community were extremely anxious to keep her among them, and were kinder to her than words could express. Mrs. Graham besought her most earnestly to remain with her as a sister, and urged her petition repeatedly.

"The favour will be conferred by *you*, my dear, and you know it," she said. "Think of the long, lonely days I spend at Chatham, cut off from all society in bad weather, and in the monsoon, I sometimes don't see another white woman for weeks. Imagine the boon your company would be to me.

Remember that your father was an old friend of Dick's, and say that you will try us for at least a year. We will do our very best to make you happy."

And other suggestions were delicately placed before Helen. Would she remain, not as Miss Denis, but as *Mrs.* somebody? To one and all, she made the same reply, she must go home, at least, she must go back to England; her aunt had written, and desired her to return at the first opportunity, and her aunt was her nearest relation now, and all her future plans were in her hands. Mrs. Home was returning in March, they would sail together.

"If I were not obliged to place Tom and Billy at school, and see after my big boys, I would not *allow* you to leave at all, Helen," said her friend and hostess decidedly, "but would insist on your remaining with us as one of our family, a kind of eldest daughter."

Nevertheless, Mrs. Home cherished strong but secret hopes that her young *protégée* would stay at Port Blair, in spite of her own departure. Was not Mr. Quentin expected from Camorta by the very next mail?

Mrs. Creery would have liked Helen to remain with some one (not herself, for she was not given to hospitality). She considered that she would be a serious loss to the community, and was quite fond of her in her own way. Why should she not marry Jim Quentin? was a question she often asked herself in idle, empty moments. It would be a grand match for a penniless girl; a wedding would be a pleasant novelty, no matter how quiet, and she herself was prepared to give the affair her countenance, and to endow the young couple with a set of plated nut-crackers that had scarcely ever been used! One day, roaming rather aimlessly through the bazaar, she came across "Ibrahim," Mr. Quentin's butler, and was not the woman to lose a rich opportunity of cross-examining such an important functionary. She beckoned him aside with an imperious wave of the hand, and commenced the conversation by asking a very foolish question, "When did you hear from your master?" seeing that there had been no mail in, since she had seen Ibrahim last, "when is he expected?"

"Mr. Quentin not my master any more," he returned, with dignity, "I take leave that time Sahib going Nicobars."

"Having made your fortune?" drawing down the corner of her mouth as she spoke.

"I plenty poor man, where fortune getting?" he replied, with an air of surprised and injured innocence.

"Stuff and nonsense! you know you butlers make heaps out of bachelors like Mr. Quentin, who never look at their accounts, but just pay down piles of rupees, like the idiots they are; and what about Mr. Lisle?"

Ibrahim grinned and displayed an ample row of ivory teeth.

"Ah," with animation, "that very good gentleman, never making no bobbery! Plenty money got!"

"Plenty money! How do you know?"

"First time coming paying half—after two weeks paying *all*;" in answer to the lady's gesture of astonishment. "Truth I telling! wages, boats, bazaar, and *all*!"

"And what did Mr. Quentin say?"

"Oh," laughing, "telling Lisle, Sahib plenty rupees got, I poor devil! Mr. Quentin very funny gentleman, making too much bobbery, swearing too much, throwing boots and bottles, no money giving; I plenty fraiding, and so I taking leave," concluded Ibrahim majestically.

This little side-light on Mr. Quentin's manners was a revelation to Mrs. Creery. And so Lisle was *really* rich! the dinner she had graced at Aberdeen (on a mutton day), had been given at *his* expense, and all the establishment of servants, coolies, and boatmen had been maintained by him. She pondered much over this discovery—and, marvellous to relate, kept it to herself.

Colonel Denis had now been dead about two months, and his daughter was once more to be seen out of doors, and walking about the island; but how different she looked, what a change a few weeks had made in her appearance. She was clad in a plain black dress, her eyes were dim and sunken, her face was thin and haggard, her figure had lost its nice rounded outlines. She was trying to accustom herself to her new lot in life; to that empty bungalow on the hill-side, that she never passed without a shudder, for did it not represent the wreck of her home?

Something else had also been scattered to the winds, blown away into space like gossamer-web in a gale, I mean that airy fabric known as "Love's Young Dream."

She had been dwelling on four words, more than she herself imagined; on the promise, "I shall come back," breathed under the palm-trees that night, that saw "flying between the cold moon and the earth, Cupid all armed!"

Helen occasionally spent a day with Mrs. Graham or Mrs. Durand; they liked to have her with them, and endeavoured by every means in their power, to distract her mind from dwelling, as it did incessantly, on her recent loss. One morning, as she sat working in Mrs. Durand's cool, shady drawing-room, doing her best to seem interested in her hostess' remarks, they heard some one coming rapidly up the walk, and Captain Durand sprang up the steps, and entered, holding a bundle of letters in his hand.

"The mail is in from Rangoon," he said; "Rangoon and the Nicobars."

If he and his wife had not been wholly engrossed in sorting their correspondence, they would doubtless have noticed, that their young lady guest had suddenly become very red, and then very white, but they were examining their letters, with the gusto of people to whom such things are both precious and rare.

"By the way," exclaimed Captain Durand, looking up at last, "Quentin is back; I met him on the pier."

Helen almost held her breath, her heart stood still, whilst her hostess put into words a question she could not have articulated to save her life.

"And Gilbert Lisle, did you see him?"

"Oh, no! he has gone on to Japan," responded her husband, as he carelessly tore open a note. "He is a regular bird of passage!"

"Ah, I *thought* we should not see him again," rejoined Mrs. Durand, with a tinge of regret in her voice.

Helen listened as if she were listening to something about a stranger, she bent her eyes steadily on her work, and endeavoured to compose her trembling lips. Mrs. Durand, happening to glance at her, as, opening an envelope, she said, "Why, here's a note from him!" was struck by the strange, dead pallor of her face, and by the look of almost desperate expectation in her eyes—eyes now raised, and bent greedily on the letter in her own hand. This change of colour, this eager look, was a complete revelation to that lady, who paused, drew in her breath, and asked herself, with a thrill of apprehension, "Could it be possible that Helen had lost her heart to Gilbert Lisle? Was *she* the attraction that had held him so fast at Port Blair?"

As she stared in a dazed, stupid sort of way, her young friend dropped her eyes, bent her head, and resumed her work with feverish industry; but, in truth, her shaking fingers were pricking themselves with the needle, instead of putting in a single stitch!

"A note from Lisle? And pray what has he to say?" inquired Captain Durand, ignorant of this by-play. "Here," holding out his hand, "give it to me, and I'll read it."

"Camorta, March 2nd.

"DEAR MRS. DURAND,—As I have changed my plans, and am not returning to Port Blair, I send you a line to bid you good-bye, and to beg you to be good enough to accept my small sailing-boat which lies over at Aberdeen. You will find her much more handy for getting about in, than the detachment gig. My nets and fishing-gear I bequeath to Durand. I am going on to Japan, *viâ* rangoon and Singapore, and shall make my way home by San Francisco. Hoping that we shall meet in England ere long, and with kind regards to all friends at Ross,

"I remain,

"Yours sincerely,

"GILBERT LISLE."

"By Jove!" exclaimed Captain Durand, "that smart cutter of his is the very thing for you, Em, and the fishing-tackle will suit me down to the ground. I like Lisle uncommonly, but," grinning significantly as he spoke, "this note of his, consoles me wonderfully for his departure."

Yes, so it might—but who was to console Helen? She felt like some drowning wretch, from whom their only plank has just been torn, or as a shipwrecked sailor, who had painfully clambered out of reach of the waves and been once more cruelly tossed back among them.

It was only now at this moment of piercing anguish that she thoroughly realized how much she had been clinging to Gilbert Lisle's promise, how steadfastly she had believed in his words, "I shall come back."

With a feeling of utter desolation in her heart, with her ideal and her hopes alike shattered, what a task was hers to maintain an outward appearance of indifference and composure!

After a time Captain Durand went off to the mess, to hear the news, and to look over the papers, leaving the two ladies *tête-à-tête*; his wife affected to peruse her letters, reading such little scraps of them aloud from time to time as she thought might amuse her companion, but she was not enjoying them as usual. That look she had surprised in the girl's eyes, haunted her painfully. She longed to go over to her, and put her arm round her neck and whisper in her ear, —

"What is it? Tell me all about it, confide in *me*."

But somehow she dared not, bold as she was. — Recent grief had aged Helen, and given her a gravity far beyond her years, and as she looked across at that marble face, those downcast eyes, and busy fingers, she found her kind, warm heart fail her. Whatever the hurt was, ay, were it mortal, that girl meant to bear it alone.

She was more affectionate and sympathetic to her young friend than usual, smoothed her hot forehead, kissed her, caressed her, and whilst they sat together in the twilight in the verandah, looking out on the dusky sky, found courage to murmur, —

"Dearest Helen, remember that I am your friend, not merely in name only. Should you ever have any — any little trouble such as girls have sometimes, you will come and share it with me, won't you? I am older, more experienced by years and years, and I will always keep your secrets, exactly as if they were my own!"

This was undoubtedly a strong hint; nevertheless, her listener merely smiled and nodded her head, but made no other sign. "*Little* trouble!" She was on the rack all day long. She bore the torture of her hostess's soft whispers and tender, sympathetic looks, which told her that she guessed *all*. She bore the brightly-lit dinner-table, and Captain Durand's cheerful recounting of the most thrilling news. She even endured his eloquent praises of Gilbert Lisle without flinching. Little did her gallant host guess the effort that those smiles and answers cost her. Good, commonplace man! he had got over his brief love affair fifteen years previously, and had forgotten it as completely as a tale that is told. Mrs. Durand had a more vivid recollection of her own experiences, — and a share of that fellow-feeling that makes us all akin. She was amazed at Helen's fortitude, especially when she glanced back over the past and remembered (and I hope this will not be put down to her discredit) that when *she* had seen the announcement of the marriage of her first fancy in the paper, she had spent the remainder of the day in hysterics and the subsequent week in tears. She walked back with Helen, and left her herself at Colonel Home's door, and bade her good-night with unusual tenderness. Then she retraced her steps, arm-in-arm with her husband, whose mind was abruptly recalled from planning a long day's sea-fishing, by her saying rather suddenly, —

"I know *now* why Helen refused Dr. Parkes!"

"Oh!" contemptuously, "I could have told you the reason long ago, if you had asked me. Because he was the same age as her father!"

"No, you dear, stupid man—but this is quite private. I am sure," lowering her voice, "that she likes Gilbert Lisle."

A long whistle was the only reply to his information for some seconds, and then he said,—

"Now what has put *that* into your head?"

"Her face when you came in and told us that he was not coming back. I cannot get it out of my mind, it was only a momentary expression, she rallied again at once; but that moment told me a tale that she has hitherto guarded as a secret."

"You are as full of fancies and ridiculous, romantic ideas as if you were seventeen instead of——"

"Don't name it!" she interrupted hastily, "the very leaves here have ears!"

Her husband laughed explosively, and presently said,—

"I never knew such a woman as you are for jumping at conclusions. She had a twinge of face-ache, that was all."

"A twinge of heart-ache, you mean. But what is the use of talking to *you?*—you are as matter-of-fact as a Monday morning. And now, pray tell me, though I suppose I might just as well ask Billy Home, did Gilbert Lisle ever show her any attention?"

"Ha—hum—well, do you think that saving her life could be called an attention?"

"Yes," eagerly; "yes, of course! I'd forgotten about that!"

"And another time he picked her off the mainland and brought her home in what is now your boat, through a series of white squalls."

"Did he really?" the really, as it were, in large capitals.

"And he was there a few times. But you need not get any ideas into your head about *him*, it was always Quentin, he was always hanging about her in that heavy persistent way of his—it was Quentin, I tell you!"

"And *I* tell you," responded his wife emphatically, "that it was, and is, Gilbert Lisle. I recollect his saying, the night of the ball, what a nice girl she was; or *I* said it, and he agreed, which is the same thing. And I remember perfectly, now that I think of it, noticing them leaning over a gate, and looking just like a pair of lovers."

A loud and rudely incredulous haw-haw from Captain Durand was his only reply.

"You may laugh as much as you like, but Mr. Lisle told me that he would gladly give a thousand pounds to get out of the Nicobars trip, and the last thing he said to me, as he bade me good-bye, was, 'I shall see you again soon.' I remember all these things now, and put two and two together, but I cannot make it out—I am utterly puzzled. Perhaps Mr. Quentin will be able to throw some light on the subject!"

"Quentin wants to marry her himself."

"Not he! He only wished to be a dog in the manger, to engross the only pretty girl in the place, that was all. I know him *well*. And now that she has been left an orphan, without a fraction, he has as much idea of making her Mrs. Quentin, as he has of flying over the moon!"

"All right, Em, time will tell.—I bet you a new bonnet that this time next year, she will be Mrs. Q."

"No more than she will be Queen of England," returned his wife with emphasis. This was positively the last word, and Mrs. Durand's property, for they had now reached the steps of their own bungalow, and consequently the end of their journey.

CHAPTER XXIV
"FAREWELL, PORT BLAIR"

"Farewell at once—for once, for all—and ever."

Richard II.

Mrs. Durand's surmises were correct.

A few days after James Quentin's return, without any marked haste he went over and called on Mrs. Home and Miss Denis. The former was an arrant little match-maker, and was delighted to see that *débonnaire* face once more. He was handsome, rich (?), and agreeable, he had been devoted to her young friend previous to his departure for the Nicobars, and, *of course,* it would be all settled now. With this idea in her head, she presently effaced herself so as to give the gentleman ample opportunity for a *tête-à-tête.* She even kept Tom and Billy out of the way, and this was no mean feat.

Mr. Quentin murmured some polite stereotyped regrets, then he alluded in rather strong language to "that vile hole Camorta." As he talked he stared, stared hard at Helen, and wondered at the change he saw in her appearance. She was haggard and thin; of her lovely colour not a vestige remained, and the outlines of her face were sharp, and had lost their pretty contour. She looked like a flower that had been beaten down by the storm. Never in all his experience had he beheld such a complete and sudden alteration in any one; he was glad he had never thought of her seriously, and as to Lisle, he was well out of it (thanks to his friend James Quentin); *he* took everything so seriously he would have been sure to have got the halter over his head, and to have blundered into an imprudent match. His yes meant yes; his no, no. Now he himself had a lightness of method, a nebulous vagueness surrounded his most tender speeches; at a moment's notice, he could slip off his chains, and run his head out of the noose, and always without any outward unpleasantness—that was the best of the affair. Gilbert Lisle was different, he was not used to playing with such brittle toys as girls' hearts. Well, this girl had entirely lost her beauty, so thought her visitor, as he contemplated her critically and conversed of malaria and Malays. She had not a penny, and no connections; he supposed, when she went back to England, she would go out as a governess, or a companion, or music-teacher. He entirely approved of young women being independent and earning their own bread. If there was a subscription got up for her passage money, he meant to do the handsome thing, and give fifty rupees (5*l.*).

"I suppose you were surprised to hear about Lisle?" he said at last.

"Yes," looking at her questioner with complete composure.

"He left me at Camorta, you know. He is a queer, eccentric beggar, and you would never suppose, to see him in his old fishing-kit, and with his hands as brown and horny as a common boatman's, that he had been in the Coldstreams, and was a regular London swell."

Helen made no reply, and he continued glibly,—

"He is considered a tremendous catch; they say his elder brother is dying at Algiers—consumption—but he is not easy to please!"

"Is he not?" she echoed with studied indifference.

"No.—By Jove! Mrs. Creery did not think much of him; she was awfully rough on him. How all you people did snub him! Many a good laugh I had in my sleeve!" and he smiled at the recollection.

"I do not think that many people snubbed him," returned Helen with a flushed cheek and flashing eye.

"Well, perhaps *you* did not," returned Mr. Quentin, somewhat abashed. "You know, you never snubbed any one but me," with a mental note that she should live to be sorry for that same. "Lisle made me promise to keep his secret. He wished to be accepted for himself for once, without any *arrière pensée* of money or title; and by George, he got what he wanted with a vengeance—eh? I don't think he will try it again in a hurry. He found his level,—the very bottom of the ladder, something quite new!" and again he laughed heartily at the recollection.

"I suppose it was," with elaborate indifference.

"He had been having a big shoot in the Terai before he came here. He was awfully taken with this place, the queer, unconventional life, and stayed on and on greatly to my surprise. Many a time I wondered what he saw in the place, though, of course, I was delighted to have him. My luck was dead in." (So it was, *vide* Ibrahim's domestic accounts!)

"Yes, of course it was pleasant for *you*," admitted Helen.

"He should have been a poor man; he had so much energy and resource, and such Spartan tastes. Ten times a day I wished that we could change places."

"I daresay," returned the young lady rather drily.

There was something—was it a tone of lurking scorn?—in this "I daresay!" that irritated her listener, who instantly resolved to administer a rap on the knuckles in return.

"His father is wild with him for roving about the world; he wants him to marry and settle."

"Yes?"

"I believe he has an heiress in cotton-wool for him at home. I wish my governor was as thoughtful!"

"No doubt he knows that *you* are quite equal to finding such a treasure for yourself," returned Miss Denis, with a very perceptible touch of sarcasm.

Mr. Quentin laughed rather boisterously. It was new to him to hear sharp speeches from ladies' lips, and now, looking at his watch and rising with a sudden start, he said,—

"I declare I must be going. I had no idea it was so late. I've an appointment (imaginary) at four o'clock, and I've only two minutes. Well," now taking her hand, "and so you are off on Wednesday? I may see you before that, if not, good-bye," holding her fingers with a lingering pressure, and looking down into her eyes as if he felt unutterable regret, quite beyond the reach of words; but in truth he was conscious of nothing, beyond a keen desire to make a happy exit, and to get away respectably (perhaps he had also a lurking craving for a "peg"!). "Good-bye, I hope we shall meet again some day in England. Perhaps you would drop me a line?" a query he had often found to have an excellent and soothing effect at similar partings.

Helen took no notice of the suggestion, but merely bowed her head and said very quietly,—

"Good-bye, Mr. Quentin, good-bye."

And then the gentleman took himself away in exaggerated haste, muttering as he hurried down to the pier,—

"How white she looked, and how stiff she was. I'm hanged if I don't believe she had a weakness for Lisle, after all. If *that's* the case, this humble, insignificant individual has put a pretty big spoke in her wheel."

It is almost needless to mention that Helen was now accustomed to daily interviews with Mrs. Creery, and to being cross-examined as to how she had been left, whether Mr. Quentin had said "anything," and what she "was going to do with all her coloured dresses?"

Eliza Creery was a pertinacious woman, and had not lost sight of her designs upon the black silk gown (neither had Helen).

"My dear," she said, "if you ask my advice," the last thing that was likely to occur to her listener, "you will sell all your things. They will be a perfect boon here, and it is not unusual in cases of sudden mourning, and utter destitution, such as yours." Helen winced and grew very pale. "I really think that you might have had this made with a little more style," touching her black dress. "But now," seriously, "*what* about your others?"

"Lizzie Caggett was asking about my cottons."

"Yes?" stiffening with apprehension.

"I told her that I would be only too glad to let her have them. There are one or two that I cannot bear to look at. *He* liked them," she added under her breath.

"And for how much? What did you ask for them?"

"Why, nothing, of course!" returned Helen in amazement.

"Then she shan't have them. I shall not stand by and see you fleeced. I shall certainly speak to her mother. What a horrible, grasping, greedy girl; taking advantage of your innocence—she would not get round *me* like that!" (Mrs. Creery never spoke a truer word).

"But they are useless, quite useless to me," exclaimed Helen.

"Rubbish! nonsense! is *money* useless to any one? Did you give her anything else?" demanded the matron sharply.

"Only my best hat, and a few new pairs of *gants de Suède*."

"This must be stopped *at once*. She has no conscience, no principle. You will be giving her your white silk next, you foolish girl. You must think of yourself, you have hardly a penny to live on, and are as lavish as a princess, and utterly indifferent to your own interests. Now, if you had spoken to *me*, I could have disposed of your cottons and muslins for ready money. As it is, I shall take your black silk, your white silk, your blue surah," running over these items with infinite unction, "and give you a good price for them, considering that they are second-hand. Your white satin low body would be too small, I'm afraid; and your gloves are not my size (Mrs. Creery took sevens, and Helen sixes); but I'll have your pinafore and brown hat."

"But indeed, thanking you very much for thinking of me, I do not wish to sell anything. Some day I may want these things, and have no money to replace them, don't you see?"

Mrs. Creery failed to see the matter in that light at all, and argued and stormed; nevertheless, Helen was adamant.

"Aunt Julia would not be pleased, I'm sure," she said firmly. "And I really could not do it, really I would not, Mrs. Creery."

"And I had such a fancy for your little black lace and jet shoulder-cape!" whimpered that lady, on the verge of tears.

Helen paused, looked at her hesitatingly, and said,—

"I wonder if you would be very much offended if—if I——" here she broke down.

But Mrs. Creery knew exactly what she wished to say, and rushed to her rescue.

"Yes, that's it exactly," she cried eagerly, "a *capital* idea, we will exchange! I'll take your cape, which would be brown next year, and give you something you will like far better, something that won't wear out, and will serve to remind you of the six months you spent at Port Blair." (As if Helen needed anything to remind her of that.) "Something that, I'm sure, you will be delighted to have."

On these conditions the barter was agreed to, and the elder lady folded up and carried away the cape. Doubtless she feared that Miss Denis might yet change her mind.

The same afternoon Mrs. Creery's ayah sauntered down with a small paper parcel in her hand, and when it was opened, Helen discovered an exceedingly trumpery pair of shell bracelets, tied with grass-green ribbon— total value of these ornaments, one Government rupee, in other words, eighteen-pence!

Mrs. Home, who had heard of the fate of the little shoulder-cape, became quite red with indignation, and was loud (for her) in her denunciation of Mrs. Creery's meanness. But Helen was no party to her anger and scorn, nay, for the first time for many weeks, she laughed as merrily and as heartily as she had been wont to do in the days that were no more.

The eventful Wednesday came that brought the English letters, and took away Mrs. Home and Helen. The whole community rowed out to the *Scotia* to see them off, laden with books and flowers, and eau de Cologne and fruit. When I say the whole community, Mr. Quentin was the exception that proved the rule. Jim Quentin was conspicuous by his absence, and neither note nor bouquet arrived as his deputy. Mrs. Home was keenly alive to his defection and extremely put out, though her anger smouldered as fire within her, and she never breathed a word to Helen, and thought that she had never seen a girl bear a disappointment so beautifully.

There was maiden dignity! There was fortitude! There was self-control! Mrs. Durand hung about her friend with little gifts and stolen caresses, — she had not failed to notice that Apollo was not among the crowd, and had whispered to her husband as they stood together, "*He* is not here, you see, and the bonnet is *mine*."

To Helen she said, —

"Mind you write to me often; be sure you do not drift away from me, my dear. When I go home, you have promised to come and see me, and, you know, you would be going to my people now only they are in Italy at present. Be sure you don't forget me, Helen."

"Is it likely?" she returned. "Have I so many friends? Do not be afraid that I shall not write to you often, perhaps too often. I shall look out for your letters far more anxiously than you will for mine, and is it likely that I can ever forget you? You know I never could."

Mrs. Creery was present of course, and when time was up, and the bell rang for visitors to descend to their boats, she actually secured the last embrace, saying as she kissed Helen on either cheek, —

"So sorry you are going, dear. Of course you will write? I have your address — 15, Upper Cream Street. It has all been very sad for you, but life is uncertain;" then — as a *bonne bouche* reserved for the last, a kind of stimulant for the voyage — she added impressively, "My sister, Lady Grubb, will call on you in London — and now, really, good-bye." One more final whisper yet in her ear, positively the last word, "Quentin has treated you disgracefully."

A pressure of the hand and she was gone.

The steamer's paddles began to churn, to grind the water, the boats rowed on alongside, their occupants waving handkerchiefs, till the *Scotia* gradually forged ahead and left them all behind.

Helen leant over the bulwarks, watching them and waving to the last. How much she liked them all, how good they had been to her! As they gradually fell far behind, even the final view of Mrs. Creery's broad back and mushroom topee caused her a pang of unexpected regret.

The surrounding hills, woods, and water looked lovelier than she had ever seen them, as if they were saying, "How can you bid us good-bye? Why do you leave us?"

She gazed with straining vision towards the graveyard on the hill, now fading so fast from eyes that would never see it more. Presently Mount Harriet became sensibly diminished, then Ross itself dwindled to a mere shadowy speck; Helen stood alone at the taffrail, taking an eternal farewell of these sunny islands, which had once been to her as an earthly paradise, where the happiest hours of her life had been spent, and the darkest— where she had first made acquaintance with love and death and grief! The little-known Andamans were gradually fading—fading—fading. As she stood with her eyes earnestly fixed upon the last faint blue outline, they were gone, merged in the horizon, and lost to sight. She would never more behold them, save in her dreams!

With this thought painfully before her mind she turned slowly away, and went below to her own cabin, and shutting fast the door, she threw herself down on her berth and wept bitterly.

CHAPTER XXV
THE STEERAGE PASSENGER

"Pray you sit by us, and tell's a tale."

Twelfth Night.

"Mrs. Home and party" were to be seen in the list of names of those who sailed from Calcutta in the steamer *Palestine* on the 20th of March. There were not many other passengers, but those on board were sociable and friendly; and the old days, when Bengal and Madras did not speak, paraded different sides of the deck, and only met in the saloon at the point of the knife (and fork), are gone to return no more. The weather was at first exceedingly rough, the water "plenty jumping," in the phraseology of Mrs. Home's ayah. She, like her mistress, became a captive to Neptune almost as soon as the engines were in motion. Once out on the open sea she lay for days on the floor, rolled up in her sarée like a bolster or a mummy, uttering pitiful moans and invocations to her relations. Helen was a capital sailor and took entire charge of Tom and Billy, and was invaluable to her sick friend, upon whom she waited with devoted attention, tempting her with beef-tea and toast and other warranted sea-refreshments.

Not a few of her fellow-passengers would have been pleased to while away the empty hours, in dalliance with the tall girl in black, but she showed no desire for society, and as it was whispered that she had recently lost some near relation, and was *really* in deep grief, she was left to herself, and to the company of Tom and Billy.—It seemed quite marvellous to the community, that such a pretty girl should be returning to England *unmarried.* They shrugged their shoulders, lifted their eyebrows, and wondered to one another whether it was because *she* was too hard to please, or whether the community at Port Blair were stolid semi-savages?

The first little piece of excitement that broke the monotony of the voyage, was the discovery of a stowaway in one of the boats, who was not starved out till they had passed Galle. He proved to be a deserter from a regiment in Calcutta, and was promptly sent below to stoke, as extra fireman, and doubtless he found that employment (especially in the Red Sea) even less to his taste than drilling in the cool of the morning on the Midan near

Fort William. The Red Sea was as calm as the proverbial mill-pond, and the motion of the steamer almost imperceptible. The ayah recovered from her state of torpor, and Mrs. Home actually made her appearance at meals, and joined the social circle on deck. Every evening there was singing, the songs being chiefly contributed by the ladies and one or two German gentlemen *en route* from Burmah to the Fatherland. Passengers who could not, or would not, perform vocally, were called upon to tell stories, and those hot April nights, as they throbbed past the dark Arabian coast, were long remembered by many on board. Chief among the entertainers was the captain of the *Palestine*. He related more than one yarn of thrilling adventures by sea. The German merchants told weird legends, and episodes of the late great war, a grizzled colonel gave his experiences of the Mutiny, a subaltern his first exploit out after tigers, but the most popular *raconteur* of them all was the first officer, Mr. Waters. When he appeared, and took his seat among the company after tea, there was an immediate and clamorous call for a story—a story.

"Now, Mr. Waters, we have been waiting for you!"

Apropos of the stowaway, he recounted the following tale, to which Billy Home, who was seated on Helen's knee, with his arm encircling her neck, listened with very mixed sensations:—

"When I was second officer of the *Black Swan*, from Melbourne to London," he began promptly—yes, he liked telling yarns,—"we had one uncommonly queer trip, a trip that I shall not forget in a hurry, no, and I don't fancy that many of those who were on board will forget it either! It was the year of the Paris Exhibition, and all the world and his wife were crowding home. We had every berth full, and people doubled up anywhere, even sleeping on the floor of the saloon. We left port with three hundred cabin, and seventy-five steerage passengers. At first the weather was as if it were made to order, and all went well till about the third night out, when the disturbance began, at least, it began, as far as *I* was concerned. I was knocked up about an hour after I had come off watch, and out of my first sleep, by some one thundering at my door. I, thinking it was a mistake, swore a bit, and roared out that they were to go to the third officer, and the devil! But, instead of this, the door was gently opened, and the purser put in a very long white face, and said,—

"'Look here, Waters, I want you in my cabin; there is the mischief to pay, and I can't make it out! I can't get a wink of sleep, for the most awful groans you ever heard!'

"I sat up and looked at him hard. He was always a sober man, he was sober now, and he was not walking in his sleep. After a moment's very natural hesitation, I threw on some clothes, and followed him to his cabin, which was forward. The light was still burning, and his bunk turned back just as he had leapt out of it; but there was nothing to be seen.

"'Wait a bit,' he said eagerly, 'hold on a minute and listen.'

"I did, I waited, and listened with all my ears, and I heard nothing but the thumping of the engines, and the tramping of the officer on watch overhead. I was about to turn on my heel with rather an angry remark, when he arrested me with a livid face, and said,—

"'There it is!' and sure enough there it *was*—a low, deep, hollow groan, and no mistake about it, a groan as if wrung from some one in mortal agony, some one suffering lingering and excruciating torture.—I looked at the purser, big beads of perspiration were standing on his forehead, and he looked hard at me. 'I heard it all last night,' he said in a husky whisper, 'but I was afraid to speak. I hunted to-day high and low, and sounded every hole and corner, but there is nothing to be found!' Then he ceased speaking, there it was *again*, louder, more painful than ever; it certainly came from some place below the floor, and on the starboard side. We both knelt down, and hammered, and knocked, and called, and laid our ears to the boards, but it was of no use,—there was silence.

"'Perhaps it was some one snoring,' I suggested, 'or it might be a dog?'

"'No,' returned the purser, who was still on his knees, 'it's a human voice, and the groans of a dying man, as sure as I'm a live one!'

"I remained in the cabin for half an hour, and though we overhauled the whole concern, we heard nothing more, so I fetched up for my own bunk, and turned in and went to sleep.

"The next day the purser said he heard the moans very faintly, as if they were now getting weaker and weaker, and after this entirely ceased. For a good spell everything went along without a hitch, we had A 1 weather, and made first-class runs. But one evening, in the twilight, I noticed a great commotion in the saloon, I heard high talking—a woman's voice! One of the lady passengers was the centre of a crowd, and was making some angry complaint to the captain.

"'It's the young man in the boots again!' she said. 'And it's really too bad. Why is he allowed in this part of the ship, what are the stewards about? It is insufferable to be persecuted in this manner! Every evening, at this hour, he comes to the door of the saloon and beckons to *me*, or to any one who is near, but he never seems to catch any one's eyes but *mine*! It's really disgraceful that the steerage passengers should be allowed among us in this way.'

"The saloon stewards were all called up and rigidly cross-examined by the captain, but they all most positively declared that no stranger had been seen by them, nor was there any steerage passenger on board that at all answered the lady's description.

"'Of course, that's nonsense!' she exclaimed indignantly. 'He comes to the bar for spirits on the sly—and very sly he is—for I've gone to the door to see what he wanted, and he has always contrived to slip away.'

"An extra sharp lookout was accordingly kept by the captain's orders, but the head steward privately informed me with a grin 'that there was no such person as a tall young man in a blue jumper, with long boots, on the ship's books,' and we both came to the conclusion that the lady was decidedly wanting in her top gear.

"However, after a while other people began to see the steerage passenger. Not merely ladies only, but hard-headed, practical, elderly men; and very disagreeable whispers began to get afloat that 'the ship was haunted!' The apparition in long butcher boots, could never be caught or traced, but he was visible repeatedly; and did not merely confine himself to hanging about and beckoning at the saloon door—he was now to be met in passages, at the dark turns on the stairs behind the wheel-house, and even on the bridge,—but always after dusk. Things now began to be extremely unpleasant, discipline was scorned, at the very *idea* of taking away the lights at eleven o'clock, there was uproar, and an open mutiny among the ladies. Passengers were completely unmanageable, the women going about in gangs, and the very crew in couples. The captain endeavoured to make a bold stand against the ghost, but he was silenced by a clamour of voices, and by a cloud of witnesses who had all *seen* it, and, to make matters better, we came in for the most awful weather I ever experienced, our hatches were stove in, our decks swept, and I never was more thankful in all my life than when we took up our pilot in the Downs. What between the ghost and the gales, even our most seasoned salts were shaky, and grumbled among themselves, that one would almost imagine that we had a dead body on board! However, we managed to dock without any misadventure, beyond being five days over our time, having lost three boats, and gained the agreeable reputation of being a haunted ship! When we were getting out the cargo, and having the usual overhaul below, I happened to be on duty one day when I was accosted by the boatswain, who came aft to where I was standing, with an uncommonly grave face. 'Please, sir,' said he, 'we've found something we did not bargain for; it was in the place where the anchor-chain is, and now, the chain being all paid out, it's empty, you see—' he paused a moment,— 'all but for a dead man.'

"Of course I hurried forward at once, and looked down into a dark hole, when, by the light of a bit of candle held by one of the crew, I saw, sure enough, crushed up against one side the skeleton of a man—a skeleton, for the rats had picked his bones clean; his coat still hung on him, he wore long digger's boots, and a digger's hat covered his bare skull.

"I started back, and fell foul of the candle, though I'm not a particularly nervous person, for I now remembered the groans I had heard in the purser's cabin.

"'You see, sir, how it was,' said the boatswain, 'he was a stowaway, in course. When we were in dock, this place was empty. Cause why? The anchor-chain is out, and it seemed to this poor ignorant wretch, who was no seaman anyway, to be just the very spot—as it were, made for him! I've a kind of recollection of him, too, hanging about when we were taking in cargo. He was young, and looked like a half-starved, broken-down gentleman, such as you see every day in the colony, who come out—bless their innocence!—a-thinking the nuggets is growing on the trees, and sink down to beggary, or to working their way home before the mast. Ay, he thought to get a cast back,' said the bo'sun, 'and he just walked straight into the jaws of death. The moment we began to weigh anchor, and the chain came reeling, and reeling, into his hiding-place, it had no outlet but the hole at the top, and the rattle of it and the noise of the donkey-engine drowned his cries: he was just walled in, poor chap, and buried up alive!'

"Of course, we all knew, that this was the mysterious apparition in long boots, who had created such an unparalleled disturbance on the passage home. Presently the remains were decently carried away, and there was an inquest, but nothing could be discovered about the body. We subscribed for the funeral among us, and he was buried in the nearest church-yard. We sailors are a superstitious lot, and though we got out of it (I mean, bringing home a corpse) better than could be expected, so we gave him a respectable funeral, but there is no name on the stone cross above his head, for the only one, we knew him by, was that of the 'Steerage Passenger!'"

The chief officer brought his story to an end in the midst of a dead, nay, an awe-struck silence. People shuddered and looked nervously behind them. They were on board ship, too! Why should not the *Palestine* have a ghost of her own, as well as the *Black Swan*?

The utter stillness, was suddenly broken by a loud howl from Billy Home, who had been listening with all the power of his unusually capacious ears, and seemed to have but just wakened up from a sort of trance of horror. He shrieked and clung to Helen, who had whispered a hint with regard to bed-time.

"No, no, no," he would not come. "No, not alone," he added with a yell, hanging to her with the tenacity of a limpet; "not unless you stay with me.—I'm afraid of the man downstairs,—I *know* he is downstairs."

"I declare," said the bearded story-teller, "I quite forgot that little beggar was there. I never noticed him till now, or I would not have told you that yarn."

Needless to remark, his apology came rather too late. At every turn of the companion-ladder, at every open door, Billy lived in whining anticipation of meeting what he called "the man in the boots," and for the remainder of the voyage he was figuratively a mill-stone, round Helen's neck.

They had an uneventful passage down the Mediterranean, halting at Malta for lace, oranges, and canaries; they passed Cape Bon, then the coast of Spain, and the snow-capped Sierra Nevada. The Home boys had never beheld snow till now, and were easily induced to believe, that what they beheld was pounded sugar, and languished at the mountains with greedy eyes, as long as they remained in sight. On a certain Sunday afternoon in April the *Palestine* arrived in the Victoria Docks, London. Numerous expectant friends came swarming on board, all eagerness and expectation, but there was no one to welcome Helen,—no face among that friendly crowd was seeking hers. Being a Sunday, there was, of course, some difficulty about cabs and trains, and the docks were very remote from the fashionable quarter where her aunt Julia resided: so she swallowed her disappointment and made excuses to herself. However, Mrs. Home, who had been met by her brother, insisted upon personally conducting her to her journey's end. First they went by rail above ground, then by rail under ground, finally by cab, and after a long drive, the travellers drew up at Mrs. Platt's rather pinched-looking mansion in Upper Cream Street. A man-servant answered the bell, flung wide the door with a jerk, and stood upon the threshold in dignified amazement on beholding *two* cabs, heavily laden with baggage.

Was Mrs. Platt at home?

"No, ma'am. She and the young ladies have gone to afternoon church; but Miss Denis is *expected*."

Rather a tepid reception, Mrs. Home thought, with a secret thrill of indignation. Much, much, she wished that she could have taken Helen with her there and then. She hugged her vigorously, as did also Tom and Billy; and telling her, that she would come and see her very soon, she re-entered her cab, and with her brother, children, and luggage, was presently rattled away. Helen felt as she stood on the steps, and watched those familiar trunks, turning a corner, — that her last link with the Andamans, and all her recent life, was now broken.

CHAPTER XXVI
A POOR RELATION

"Oh, she is rich in beauty, only poor!"

Romeo and Juliet.

"You had better have your big box kept in the back hall—it will scarcely be worth while to take it upstairs, and it might only rub the paper off the wall."

This was almost the first greeting that Helen received from her aunt Julia.

"And, dear me, how thin you have grown! I would have passed you in the street," was her eldest cousin's welcome.

Mrs. Platt and her two daughters, Clara and Caroline, had returned from church, and found their expected guest awaiting them alone, in the drawing-room! "Surely one of them might have stayed at home," she said to herself with a lump in her throat and a mist before her eyes. She had latterly been made so much of at Port Blair that her present reception was indeed a bitter contrast. It undoubtedly *is* rather chilling to arrive punctually from a long journey (say, half across the world), and to find that your visit is a matter of such little moment to your relations, that they have not even thought it necessary to remain indoors to await, much less to send to meet you! Helen felt strangely neglected and depressed, as she sat in the drawing-room in solitary state, still wearing her hat and jacket, and feeling more like a dependant, who had come to seek for a situation, than a near relation to the lady of the house. She had fully an hour in which to contemplate the situation, ere her aunt and cousins returned. They were three very tall women, and made an imposing appearance, as they filed in one after another in their best bonnets, with their prayer-books in their hands. They kissed her coolly, inquired when, and how, she had arrived, and then sat down and looked at her attentively.

Mrs. Platt was a thin, fair lady, with handsome profile, who had married well; and contrived to keep herself aloof from the general wreckage, when her maiden home was broken up; ambition was her distinctive characteristic; she had married well, and got up in the world, and now she hoped to see her daughters do the same.

To effect a lodgment in an upper strata of society, to mix with what she called the "best people," was her idea of unalloyed happiness.

In her grander, loftier style she was every bit as fond of a title as our dear friend Mrs. Creery.

Besides all this she was a respectable British matron, who paid her bills weekly, went twice to church on Sunday, never darkened the door of an omnibus, or condescended to use a postcard. Still, in her own genteel fashion, she was a capital manager, and generally made eighteen pence contrive to do duty for two shillings. She was honest, scheming, hard to every one, even to herself, making all those with whom she came into contact useful to her in some way; either they were utilized as social stepping-stones, or givers of entertainment, concert, and opera tickets, flowers, or better still, invitations to country houses; all her friends were expected to put their shoulder to her wheel in some respect—either that,—or she dropped their acquaintance under these circumstances.

It will be easily imagined, how very unwelcome to such a lady as Mrs. Platt was the unlooked-for return of this handsome, penniless niece!

The Misses Platt were tall young women, of from six, to eight and twenty years of age; they had unusually long necks, and carried their noses in the air; they were slight, and had light eyes and eyebrows, which gave them an indefinite, unfinished appearance; their hair was of a dull ashen shade, and they wore large fluffy fringes, were considered "plain" by people who did not like them, and "elegant-looking girls" by those who were their friends.

They were unemotional, critical, and selfish, firmly resolved to get the best of whatever was going; for the Miss Platts influenced their mother as they pleased, and had the greatest repugnance to having their cousin Helen thus billeted upon them.

They called everything, and every person, that did not meet with their approval "bad style," and worshipped coronets, as devoutly as their parent herself.

By-and-by the new arrival had some tea, was assured that she would be "all the better for a night's rest," and was escorted to the very top of the house, by an exhausted cousin, to what her aunt called "her old room."

This was true,—it was not the guest-chamber, but a very sparsely-furnished apartment, on the same floor with the maids. And here her relative deposited her candlestick, nodded a condescending good-night, and left her to her repose. This was her home-coming! However, she was very tired, and soon fell asleep, and forgot her sorrows; but very early the next morning, she was awoke by the roar of the London streets, for you could call it nothing else. Mrs. Platt, though occupying a most fashionable and expensive nutshell, was close to one of the great arteries of traffic. Helen lay and listened. What a contrast to the last place where she had slept on shore, where the bugle awoke the echoes at five o'clock in the morning, where wheels and horses were absolutely unknown, and the stillness was almost solemn, only broken by the dip of an oar or the scream of a peacock! She turned her eyes to a picture pinned to the wall, facing the foot of her bed, the picture of a merry-looking milkmaid, with a pail under her arm; the milkmaid was smiling at her now, precisely as she had done less than a year ago,—when she had slept in that very room previous to starting for Port Blair. *Then* she had seemed to her imagination, to wish her good speed. Surely that gay expression seemed to augur the future smiles of fortune! Ten months ago she had stared at that picture, ere she had set out for her voyage, full of hope and happy anticipations; and now, ere the year had gone round, she was back again, her day was over, her happy home in those sunny islands among tropical seas, had vanished like a dream! She had visited, as it were, an enchanted land, where she had found father, home, friends—ay, and lover, and had returned desolate and empty-handed (save for that "sorrow's crown of sorrow"), to face the stern realities of life,—and to earn her daily bread. She gazed at the mocking milkmaid, and closed her eyes. Oh! if she could but wake and find that the last four months had been but a horrible dream.

The Platts were late people, they scorned the typical first worm. Helen, accustomed to early (Eastern) hours, had a very long morning, entirely alone. She dared not unpack, she had no work to do, and could find no books to read; for her aunt, who was most economical in regard to things that did not make a show, did not subscribe to a library, merely took in a daily paper, and preyed, on her friends, for her other literature.

Breakfast was at eleven o'clock, and during that meal letters were read, the daily programme arranged, and people and places discussed, whose names were totally unknown to Helen. Now and then, her cousins threw her a word or two, but there was no cordiality or friendship in their tone; it did not need that, to tell her she was not welcome, and she sat aloof in silence, feeling as if she were an utter alien, and as if her very heart was frozen. And yet these were her own flesh and blood—her father's sister and nieces—her nearest, if not her dearest! How different to Mrs. Home, Mrs. Graham, and Mrs. Durand!—ay, even Mrs. Creery had shown her more affection than her own aunt.

Helen soon fell into her proper niche in the family. After breakfast she went out and did all the little household messages to the tradespeople, and made herself useful, *i.e.*, mended her aunt's gloves, and hose, wrote her notes, and copied music for her cousins.

She dined early, when her relatives lunched, as they frequently had people in the evening.

There was a kind of back room or den upon the second landing, where the Platt family sat in *déshabillé*, partook of refreshments, wrote letters, ripped old dresses, and held family conclaves. Here Helen spent most of her time, and being very clever with her needle, did many "odd jobs" for her relatives. Better this, than sitting with idle hands, staring out on a back green the size of a table-cloth, surrounded by grimy walls, with no more interesting spectacle to enliven the scene, than the duels, or duets, of the neighbouring cats. So it was, "Helen, I want you to run up this," or "to tack that together," or "just to unpick the other thing," and she became a valuable auxiliary to Plunket the lady's-maid, not merely with her needle alone,—she soon learned to be very handy with a box-iron!

Of course she was never expected to accompany the family, when they went out in the brougham, her aunt saying to her in her suavest tone, "You see, dear, your mourning is so recent" (her father was five months dead), "I am sure you would rather stay at home." Accordingly the three ladies packed themselves into the carriage most afternoons, and went for an airing, leaving their poor relation, with strict injunctions to "keep up the drawing-room fire," and "to see that tea was ready to the moment of five." Sometimes they gave "at homes," the preparations for which were left to Helen, who worked like a slavey. These "at homes" were chiefly remarkable for a profusion of flowers, weak tea, weaker music, and a crush.

Next to the cook, Helen was decidedly the most useful member of the household, she was kept fully occupied all day long, and in constant employment, was her only escape from her own thoughts. She was not happy; nay, many a night she cried herself to sleep; her aunt was cool and distant, as though she had displeased her in some way; but to Helen's knowledge, she had given her no cause of offence since the terrible incident of the tea-cup, years and years previously.

Her cousins were sharp, critical, and patronizing, and evidently considered that she occupied a very much lower social status than themselves.

She was unwelcome, an interloper, and felt it keenly. More than once she tried to screw up her courage, and ask her aunt what was to be her future. Undoubtedly, she was not to remain on permanently as an inmate of No. 15, Cream Street.—Her big box still stood in the back hall. Somehow, she rarely had a chance of a few words with her aunt alone, her affairs were never once touched upon in her hearing, and yet she had reason to believe, that certain animated and rather shrill conversations, that she frequently interrupted,—and that fell away into an awkward silence as she entered a room,—were about her, and her future destination!

Visitors came rapping at No. 15, Cream Street every afternoon, and two, out of the dozens who had called, asked for "Miss Denis." A few days after her arrival, she had been in the drawing-room with her cousins Carrie and Clara, when her first caller made her appearance.

The drawing-room was an apartment that seemed to be all mirrors, low chairs, small tables, and plush photo frames—a pretty room, entirely got up for show, not use. Several of the chairs, were not to be trusted, and one or two tables were decidedly dangerous, but the *tout ensemble* through coloured blinds, was everything that was smart and fashionable, and "good style"—the fetish the Miss Platts worshipped.

On this particular afternoon Carrie was yawning over the fire, Clara was looking out of the window, commenting on a coroneted carriage and superb pair of steppers, with what is called extravagant action, which had just stopped opposite. Mentally she was thinking, how much she would like to see this equipage in waiting at their own door, when a very curious turn-out came lumbering along, and actually drew up at No. 15. A shapeless, weather-beaten, yellow brougham, drawn by a fat plough-horse, and driven by a coachman in keeping with his steed—a man with a long beard, a rusty hat (that an Andamanese would have scorned), and a horse-sheet round his knees.

Little did Helen Denis dream that she was gazing at that oft-vaunted vehicle—Lady Grubb's carriage.

"Good gracious, Carrie, who on earth is this?" cried Clara, turning to her sister, who was now staring exhaustingly at her own reflection in the chimney-glass. "And coming to call here! Oh, for mercy's sake, do come and look!"

The door of the brougham was slowly opened, and a very stout old lady, attired in a long black satin cloak, and gorgeous bonnet with nodding plumes, descended, and waddled up the steps.

In the vacant carriage there still remained two fat pugs, a worked cushion, a pile of books, and what certainly looked like a basket of vegetables!

"It's no one *we* know," said Clara contemptuously.

"It may be a friend of Plunket's, or a mistake."

Apparently it was neither, for at this moment the door was flung open, and,—

"Lady Grubb!" was announced.

Very eagerly she advanced to Clara, with round, smiling face, and outstretched hands, saying,—

"So glad to find you at home! My sister told me to be sure and call, and as I was at the stores,"—here she paused and faltered, literally cowed by the expression of Miss Platt's eyes—Miss Platt, who drew back, elongated her neck, and looked insolent interrogation.

"I think you have been so good as to come and see me," murmured Helen, hastily advancing to the rescue. "You are Mrs. Creery's sister?"

"Yes, and of course you are Miss Denis," seizing her outstretched hand as if it were a life-belt, for poor Lady Grubb was completely thrown off her balance, by the stern demeanour of the other damsel.

Helen led her to a sofa, and tried to engage her in friendly conversation, but it was not easy to converse, with her two cousins sitting rigidly by, as if they were on a board of examination, and not suffering a word or look to escape them. They sat and gazed at Lady Grubb in quite a combined and systematic manner; to them she was such a unique object, and such utterly "awful style."

She, like her sister, was endowed with a copious flow of language, but the very fountain of her speech was frozen by these two ice maidens. The first few words she did manage to utter, were hurried and incoherent, but presently she found courage to inquire after Maria, and Nip, and Creery (horrible to relate, she called him "Creery"), and also after many people, she had heard about at Port Blair.

It was very plain to Helen, that Maria had painted her island home, with an unsparing supply of gorgeous colours, and Lady Grubb looked upon her absent relative's position, as something between that of the Queen of Sheba, and the Princess Badoura without doubt. She then murmured a few words of really kind condolence to Helen, and if she had taken her departure at this point, all would have been well; but she was now becoming habituated to the stony stare of the Misses Platt, and felt more emboldened to converse, — and some malicious elf put it into her head to say, with a meaning smile, —

"I am quite up in all the Port Blair news and Port Blair secrets, you know. I've heard a great deal about a certain gentleman."

Helen became what is known as "all colours," and her two cousins "all ears;" to them she had positively denied that she had left the ghost of an admirer to lament her departure from the Andaman Islands.

"Oh, you know who I *mean*, I can see," continued the old lady playfully. "She had any number of offers," addressing herself rather triumphantly to the Miss Platts, "but Mr. Quentin is to be the happy man," and here the wretched old woman, actually winked at Clara and Caroline.

"Indeed, indeed, Lady Grubb, you are quite mistaken!" cried Helen hastily. "Mr. Quentin is nothing to me but a mere acquaintance, and as to anything else, Mrs. Creery—was—was joking!"

"Oh, well, well, we won't say a word about it now, but you must come and spend a long day with me soon and tell me *everything*! I feel as if I know you quite well, having heard of you so often from Maria. I'll just leave my card for your aunt, and now I must really be going," standing up as she spoke. "I suppose Scully is waiting" (presumably the uncouth coachman).

The Miss Platts did not ring the bell, neither did they deign to rise from their chairs, but merely closed their eyes at their visitor, as she made a kind of "shy," intended for a curtsey, and wishing them "good afternoon," departed with considerable precipitation.

Helen went downstairs, and conducted Lady Grubb to the hall-door, and presently saw her bowled away in her yellow chariot, with a brace of pugs in her lap.

She was not a very distinguished person certainly, but she meant to be friendly, to be kind, and a little of these commodities went a long way with her now. She blushed, when she recalled her cousins' deportment. Surely an Andamanese female, in her own premises (were they hole or tree), would have shown more civility to a stranger. As she entered the drawing-room, the Miss Platts exclaimed in one breath,—

"What a creature! Who is she?"

"She looks like an old cook!" supplemented Carrie. "I was *trembling* lest any of our friends should come in."

"Her name is Grubb, she is sister to Mrs. Creery, the—" (how could she give any approximate idea of that lady's pomp?) "the principal lady at the Andamans!" she added rather faintly.

"Principal lady! What rubbish!" cried Clara. "If she resembles her distinguished sister, I make you my compliments, as the French say, on the class of society you enjoyed out there."

"Let us see where she lives. Where's her card? What is her name?— Tubb—Grubb?" said Carrie. "Here it is," taking it up between two supercilious fingers, and reading,—

Lady Grubb,
Smithson Villas, Pimlico.

"Pimlico! *So* i should have imagined," for, of course, any one who lived in that region was in the Miss Platts' opinion socially extinct.

"You certainly cannot do yourself the pleasure of spending a long and happy day at Smithson Villas," said Carrie with decision. "Goodness knows whom you might meet; and she would be bragging to her cronies that you were *our* cousin."

"I shall go if she asks me," replied Helen quietly. "It is no matter who *I* meet, and I will guarantee that your name does not transpire."

Was the girl trying to be sarcastic? Carrie looked at her sharply, but Helen's face was immovable.

"Well, I do most devoutly trust that she will not see fit to wait upon you again, or that if she does she will come in the laundry-cart!"

"I wonder what the Courtney-Howards thought of her. I'm sure I saw Evelyn at the window," remarked Clara. "Oh!" she added with great animation, "here is the Jenkins' carriage—Flo and her mother. What a mercy that they did not come five minutes ago!"

Now ensued general arranging of hair, of chairs, and of blinds; evidently the Jenkins were people worth cultivating, and indisputably of "good style."

"Fly away, Helen, at once," cried Carrie, "and tell Price to bring up tea in about ten minutes; and if there is time, you might just run round the corner and get half-a-dozen of those nice little Scotch cakes. I know Price hates being sent on messages in the afternoon, and you don't mind."

CHAPTER XXVII
IN WHICH EVERYTHING IS SETTLED
TO MRS. PLATT'S SATISFACTION

"When true hearts lie withered,

And fond ones are flown,

Oh! who would inhabit

This bleak world alone?"

Moore.

Lady Grubb's visit was succeeded by one from Mrs. Home—a kind, well-meaning little lady, as we know, but as yet attired in what had been a very nice Dirzee-made garment at Port Blair, and even passed muster for best on board ship, but which stamped her at once in the eyes of the Miss Platts as "bad style."

Her boys, too, so eager was she to see Helen, were not yet equipped in their new suits, and were anomalous spectacles in Highland kilts and sailor hats.

Clara and Carrie did not condescend to appear on this occasion, they saw amply sufficient of Mrs. Home and family over the dining-room blind.

Helen felt a sense of burning humiliation and shame to think that now, when she was at home among her own people, they would not even take the trouble to come upstairs and thank Mrs. Home for her great kindness to her, nor even so much as send her a cup of tea. She hoped in her heart that her friend would think they were *out*! But they went audibly up and down stairs and laughed and shut doors, and Mrs. Home was neither deaf nor stupid.

She stayed an hour, and Helen enjoyed her visit greatly (despite her disappointment at the non-appearance of her relations or, failing them, the tea-tray). It was one little oasis in the desert of her now dreary life; they conversed eagerly together and talked the shibboleth of people who have the same friends, in the same country; they kissed and cried a little, and parted with mutual promises of many letters, for Mrs. Home was going to Jersey, and thence to the Continent.

"Your friends are not our friends, and our friends are not your friends," said Carrie forcibly, and Helen felt that indeed, as far as appearance went, her visitors had not been a success, and for her own part never dreamt of being admitted within the sacred circle of her cousins' acquaintance.

Now and then she met people accidentally in the hall, or in the street when walking with her cousins; and once she overheard Carrie saying to Clara, apropos of visitors, —

"Of course there is no occasion to introduce Helen to any one," and this amiable injunction was obeyed to the letter. However, the omission sat very lightly on the once admired of all admirers at Port Blair.

One morning it happened that Helen was in the drawing-room when a bosom friend of Carrie's came to call—a Miss Fowler Sharpe, a fashionable acquaintance whom the Misses Platt toadied, for she had the *entrée* to circles barred to them, and they hoped to use her as a pass key.

They made a great deal of the lady, flattered her, caressed her, and ran after her, all of which was agreeable to Miss Sharpe. She was a very elegantly dressed London girl, who spoke with a drawl, and gave one the idea that her eyelids were too heavy for her eyes. She had come over to Cream Street to make some arrangements about an opera-box, and to have a little genteel gossip.

Helen was busily engaged in sewing Madras muslin and coloured bows on the backs of some of the chairs, where she was "discovered" by her cousins and their friend, to whom she was presented in a hasty, off-hand manner, which plainly said, "You need not notice her!"

Miss Sharpe stared for a second, vouchsafed her a little nod, then sat down with her back to Helen and speedily forgot her existence.

The three friends were soon deep in conversation, whilst she worked steadily on, kneeling at the chair she was dressing with her face turned away from the company.

Their principal topics were dress and weddings, weddings and dress, and who was flirting with whom, and what was likely to be a match, and what was not, and who looked lovely in such a gown, and what men were in town.

At length Helen, who had not been attending, caught one syllable that made her start and pause, and then listen with a heightened colour and a beating heart.

"Yes, I hear that Gilbert Lisle is actually coming back; he has been away among savages this last time, positively fraternizing with cannibals."

"Gilbert Lisle coming home!" cried Carrie. "Then Kate Calderwood will be happy at last. I suppose it will be all arranged this season?"

"Yes, his father is most anxious that he should settle; indeed, I believe he wrote him out a furious letter, and said that if he did not come home without delay he would marry again *himself!*" At this threat all three ladies laughed immoderately.

"Imagine any sane woman marrying such an old Turk as Lord Lingard!" drawled Miss Sharpe. "He is seventy if he is a day, bald and beaky, and with a temper that has a European notoriety; the very idea of his supposing that he would get *any one* to take him!"

"Yes, hideous old creature," chimed in Clara; "he always reminds me of a white cockatoo with a pink bill."

(Nevertheless, any one of these young ladies would have said "Yes" with pleasure had Lord Lingard asked them to be his.)

"I cannot imagine how any one ever married him originally," pursued Miss Sharpe; "and yet they say that Lady Lingard was one of the handsomest women of her day."

"Oh, but," put in Clara, delighted to impart this class of information, "you know, they say that she married him out of pique, and she did not live long. I suppose he worried her into her grave."

"No," rejoined Miss Sharpe; "though he *may* have helped to kill her, she died of consumption."

"Did she? and her eldest son is following her. He is in a rapid decline," added Carrie. "And you say that Gilbert Lisle is really coming home?" suddenly falling back on the original topic.

"So I'm told. Mother is going to send him a card for our dance. But I never believe in him till I see him."

"How I wish we knew him," ejaculated Clara, looking at her visitor wistfully.

"Oh, you know he is not a society man, only goes to a few houses and some country places where there is good shooting; now and then you see him at a ball, or in a squash in some staircase; but he has a very fair idea of his own value, and never makes himself *cheap*," and Miss Sharpe smiled rather disagreeably.

"That's the way with all these rich bachelors," exclaimed Carrie. "They are so spoilt, and so abominably conceited."

"I wonder how he got on among the savages?" said Miss Sharpe.

Little did she guess that the girl who was sitting in the background, with bent head and burning face, could have answered her question then and there.

"I wonder if it will come off with Katie, after all?" exclaimed Carrie. "She is the girl he used to ride with in the park last year, is she not?—very freckled, with high shoulders. She comes to our church. I wonder what he sees in her?" she added.

"It is his father, my dear, who sees *everything* in her: her property 'march,' as they call it, with the Lingard estates."

"And so she is to be Mrs. Gilbert Lisle?"

"I believe so." And with this remark the subject dropped.

Helen had listened to this conversation with crimson face and throbbing heart. Everything was accounted for now; he had been simply amusing himself with her. This man, who was accustomed to be made much of by London beauties, who was eagerly sought for by house parties in country houses—was it likely that he would be really serious in making love to an obscure girl like herself, a girl whom he had come across in his wanderings among savage islands? "No," she told herself, "not at all likely; his actions spoke for him. He had been simply seeing how much she would believe, repeating a *rôle* that he had doubtless played dozens of times previously. And during his wanderings his wealthy destined bride, Miss Calderwood, was all the time awaiting him in England. *She* was to be Mrs. Gilbert Lisle."

"I do declare you have stitched that on the wrong side out! What can you *have* been thinking of?" demanded Clara very sharply, when her fashionable friend had departed. "You will have to rip it, and put it on properly. Your wits must have been wool-gathering!"

If Clara had known where her cousin's thoughts had been, she would have been very much surprised for once in her life, and ejaculated her favourite exclamation, "Fancy, just fancy!" with unusual animation.

The day after this visit Helen was asked to accompany her cousin Carrie on foot to Bond Street, not an unusual honour. She was useful for carrying small parcels; true, her mourning was shabby, but none of the Platts' acquaintances knew who she was, and, if the worst came to the worst, she might pass as a superior-looking lady's-maid. On their way back from the shops Carrie took it into her head to take a turn in the park. It was about twelve o'clock, and the Row was gay with a fashionable throng of pedestrians. Carrie met several friends, to whom she gave a bow here and a nod there, and Helen, to her great amazement, recognized one while yet afar off, and, although garbed in a frock coat and tall hat—yes, she actually beheld Mr. Quentin coming towards her, walking with a very well-dressed woman, and followed by two red dachshunds. She was positive that the recognition was mutual, and was pleased in her present barren life to hail any acquaintance from Port Blair—even him! When they came almost face to face she bowed and smiled, and would have stopped, but he merely glanced at her as if she were some most casual acquaintance, swept off his hat, and passed on. Evidently Port Blair and Rotten Row were two very different places.

A flood of scarlet rushed over her face, which her quick-eyed companion did not fail to notice, and said—

"Who is that gentleman?"

"A Mr. Quentin. I knew him at Port Blair."

"Fancy! I have heard of him. He is quite in society; he is a friend of the Sharpes. I believe he is rather fascinating—but frightfully in debt."

Helen made no reply, but walked on in silence, and Miss Platt put two and two together with much satisfaction to herself. Helen's undoubted confusion signified of course that she cherished an unrequited attachment for this good-looking, faithless man who had just now gone by with a cool ceremonious bow. So much for her cousin's admirers in the Andamans!

It was now the end of May, and Helen had been six weeks in London, but so far not a word had been mooted to her about her future plans. She made herself useful, working, shopping, going messages; her aunt admitted to herself that she was quite as good as another servant in the house (though she did not actually use the word servant, even in her thoughts); she was a handy, useful, industrious girl, and did not put herself forward; so the matter of getting her a situation had been allowed to remain somewhat in abeyance.

Helen knew that she must eventually "move on," but had a nervous dread of broaching the subject to her relations. Day after day she failed to bring her courage to the sticking-point; but the question, ever trembling on her lips, at last found utterance, and finding herself alone with Mrs. Platt one morning, she said timidly—

"Have you made any plans about *me*, Aunt Julia?"

"Yes, my dear," was the surprisingly prompt answer, "it is all quite settled; I had intended speaking to you before, but something put it out of my head. I have an important letter to write just now, but when the girls go out this evening you and I will have a talk together."

In due time the Miss Platts departed in the brougham, bound for a little dinner and the play.

Helen, who had assisted to adorn them, partook of a meat tea with her aunt, and then they both adjourned to the little den upon the stairs. There, by the light of a crimson-shaded lamp, Mrs. Platt read the day's news, and Helen sewed and waited—waited for a very long time, and, needless to say, she was most impatient to learn her fate.

Her aunt was a lady who never worked, and rarely opened a book, but devoted her whole time to writing, talking, organizing, eating, sleeping and dressing. She perused the paper as a daily duty, just to see what was going on; and after she had now read every word of it, including advertisements, she folded it up with a crackling noise, and said rather suddenly,—

"This is a capital opportunity for us to have a nice little chat. I have been intending to speak to you for some time. Of course you know, dear, that your father left his affairs in a terrible state. I was not the least surprised to hear it, and all that can be scraped together for you is fourteen pounds a year—less than a kitchen-maid's wages," shrugging her shoulders. "There is no use in saying anything about the dead; what is done is done; nor that, to satisfy his ridiculous ideas of honour, he left his only child——"

"No, no use, Aunt Julia, for I would not listen to you," interrupted Helen with sudden fire. Mrs. Platt was astounded; this outbreak recalled old days, she positively recoiled before the expression of her niece's eyes, the imperious gesture of her hand. She leant back in her chair with folded arms, and sat for some moments in indignant silence, when she reached out two fingers and pulled the lamp-shade down, so that her face was completely in the shadow. She had reason to do so, for she was going to say things of which she might unquestionably be ashamed; and once more she commenced, as if repeating something she had previously rehearsed:

"Ours is the oddest family, we have so few relations on the Denis side, no nice connections, no influential friends; when your grandfather (why could she not say my father?) came to such a fearful smash all his old associates abandoned him, as rats leave a sinking ship. I married, and made new ties, your father married too; but, as far as I know, your mother had no respectable belongings. My sister Christina also made a wretched match; she married a half-crazy Irish professor she picked up at Bonn, he afterwards came in for some miserable Irish property, on which he lives, but *he* could do nothing, he can hardly keep the wolf and bailiffs from the door as it is. Christina, as I suppose you know, died last Christmas."

"No, Aunt Julia, I never heard of it."

"Oh, well, of course it does not affect you." (Nor did it apparently much affect Mrs. Platt.) "She and I had not met for many years. Then there is my aunt Sophia—your grand-aunt. She is an invalid, and lives at Bournemouth, scarcely ever leaving her room. She is very wealthy, and we correspond constantly, but most of her money goes to charities, in which she takes an interest, and unfortunately she takes no interest in *you*. She has got it into her head that you are worldly!"

Helen stared round the lamp-shade, to see if her aunt was joking.

"It's quite true," responded Mrs. Platt, meeting her gaze, "and once she gets an idea into her head,—there it stays. So it is rather unfortunate; but, at any rate, all her thoughts are at present centred on a mission to the Laps. Then," with a perceptible pause, "we come to myself. I am not a rich woman" (though she strained every nerve to appear so, and had upwards of three thousand a year), "I spend every penny of my income, and am often pressed for money. Of course, in the country or at the seaside we would have a margin, but the girls would not hear of living anywhere but in town—and naturally I have to study them, and their interests."

"Of course, Aunt Julia," acquiesced her listener.

"This is a ruinous neighbourhood, and this house, though so tiny, costs four hundred a year; no doubt for half that sum, I would get a mansion in Bayswater; but, as the girls say, there is no use in being in town at all if you don't live in the best part of it, and here we are! Then we require to keep up a certain style to correspond with the situation—a man-servant is indispensable, and a carriage; the horses, of course, are jobbed. Again, we have to entertain, to go to the seaside, to dress—and this last, even with Plunket making half the things, costs a small fortune! The long and the short of it is that, out of my very tolerable income, I never have a single sixpence at the end of the year. This being the case, you will readily understand, my dear Helen, that, much as I should *wish* to do so—I cannot offer you a home here."

"No, of course, Aunt Julia, I never expected you to do so," replied her niece in a low voice.

"You are a sensible girl, wonderfully so for your age, and I talk to you, you see, as openly and as frankly as if you were my own contemporary. I could not afford to dress you as you would require to be dressed, and take you out; besides, the brougham is a crush for three as it is, and three girls at a dance would be out of the question. I must say, I should have *liked* to have given you a season, but, as Clara points out, my taking you into society would entail leaving one of them behind, and charity begins at home; and, candidly, I am very anxious to see them settled."

"Yes, aunt, of course I understand that your own daughters should come first."

"And besides all this, my love," waxing more affectionate as she proceeded, "I really have no room to give you. Plunket requires one to herself; there is mine, and the girls', and the spare room, and, you see——"

"I see, Aunt Julia," interrupted her niece, "don't say another word. And now what are your plans for me?"

"Well, I had hoped to have got you a very happy, comfortable home, with a very rich old lady in the country, who required a nice cheerful young girl to talk to her, and read to her, and be with her constantly. She was rather astray mentally—a little weak, you know; but you would have got two hundred a year. However——" and she stopped.

"However, aunt——?"

"Well, I heard indirectly that she was liable to rather *violent* paroxysms occasionally, and came to the conclusion that it would not do! I have been making inquiries among my friends—of course, it's rather a delicate business, and I don't mention that you are my own niece; it would be so very awkward, you know; but I hope to hear of something suitable ere long. Meanwhile, dear, I'm sure you won't be offended at my telling you that we shall want your room next week!"

Helen's hands shook, her lips trembled, so that for the moment she was unable to speak. Was she to be turned out of doors? She had exactly four pounds in her purse upstairs!

"Clara's rich godmother always comes to us for June," continued Mrs. Platt, "and we have to study her, and to make the house bright and pleasant; it is then we always give our little dinner-parties. We do our best to please her; she is very liberal to the girls, and we could not possibly put her off. She will have the spare room, as usual,—and her maid always occupies *yours*."

"Yes, Aunt Julia."

"I have made a very nice, temporary arrangement for you, dearest! A lady I know, who keeps a large school at Kensington, has most kindly offered to take you gratis for a month or two,—till we can look about us. You are to teach the younger classes French and music."

"In short, go to her as governess?"

"Oh, dear me, no," irritably; "it is a mere friendly offer. She obliges you, you oblige her, as one of her staff has gone home ill, and she is rather short-handed just now."

"And will she pay me?" inquired Helen as bluntly as Mrs. Creery herself.

"Oh, no, I don't think there was any reference to that! Perhaps your laundress may be included; but you scarcely seem to understand that she is going to give you board and lodging for *nothing*. You are not sufficiently experienced for a governess!"

"But——" began Helen, thinking of her superior musical talents and fluent French.

"But," interrupted her aunt tartly, "if you can think of any other expedient for a couple of months, or have a better suggestion to make, let us have it, by all means!"

Her hearer pondered. There was Miss Twigg, Miss Twigg no longer; she was married, and had gone out to Canada. Mrs. Home was in Germany, her former schoolfellows were scattered,—to whom could she turn?

"Of course this is a mere temporary step, as I said before," urged her aunt. "I shall do much better for you in the autumn; I have great hopes of getting you a comfortable home through some of my friends, and as a favour to *me*. So, meanwhile, will you go to Mrs. Kane's or not?"

"Yes, aunt; I will do whatever you please."

"Very well, then, that is settled. I must get your things done up a little first. Your aunt Sophia sent ten pounds for you, and I was thinking that as the girls were going out of mourning—three months, you know, is ample for an uncle—that you might help Plunket to remodel one or two of their dresses for yourself."

Helen felt a lump in her throat, that nearly choked her. She would wear a cast-off garment of Mrs. Home's with pleasure, and accept it as it was meant; but Clara's and Carrie's!—never! And she managed to stammer out,—

"No, thank you, Aunt Julia; I shall do very well."

"But that black every-day dress is not fit to be seen."

"It will do in the school-room,—and I shall get another."

"Now I consider that wanton extravagance, when you can have Clara's for nothing. Perhaps your dignity is offended?" and she laughed at the mere idea of such a possibility, and then added, "By the way, *are* you proud?"

Helen made no reply, but bent her eyes on her work.

"Then, my dear child, the sooner you get rid of that folly the better,—for poverty, and pride, are no match for one another."

"How soon did you say I was to go to Mrs. Kane's, aunt?"

"On Monday next. You can leave your big box here still, and if you like to come over to lunch every second Sunday, you may do so. But I doubt if you will care for the long walk across the park,—or if Mrs. Kane could spare a servant to walk home with you."

"Then, thank you, I won't mind."

"Well, dear," rising as if a load had been removed from her mind, "I believe we have settled everything satisfactorily. It is so much pleasanter to talk over these matters face to face. And now, love, I'll say good-night. I daresay you would like to finish Carrie's handkerchief before you go upstairs." Then, stooping and kissing her, she added, "Be sure you put the lamp out carefully," and with this parting injunction, Aunt Julia opened the door, and departed, leaving her orphan niece alone with her own thoughts.

Helen stitched away mechanically for nearly ten minutes, then she laid down her work, and sat with her hands lying idly in her lap, and her eyes riveted upon the rose-coloured lamp-shade, but her thoughts did not take any reflection from that brilliant hue. The life that had begun so brightly now stretched out before her mental vision as grey and dreary as a winter's day. She was imperiously summoned to work for herself, to take up her post in the battle of existence, to toil for her daily bread for the future,—her only aim being to lay by some provision for her old age; she saw before her years of drudgery, with but this end in view. She had no friends, no relations, no money. A cold, dull despair settled down upon her soul, as she sat in the same attitude for fully an hour. At last she rose, folded up her work, carefully extinguished the lamp, and then made her way noiselessly up to her own apartment under the slates.

CHAPTER XXVIII
MALVERN HOUSE

"Come what, come may—

Time and the hour runs through the roughest day."

Macbeth.

A few days after her aunt had thus frankly unfolded her plans, Helen was out shopping,—officiating as companion and carrier to her cousin Clara—and again encountered Mr. Quentin. He was strolling down Piccadilly, looking like a drawing from a tailor's fashion plate, and evidently in a superbly contented frame of mind. On this occasion (being alone) he condescended to accost Miss Denis, entirely ignoring their previous meeting in the park.

"Delighted to see you,"—shaking her vigorously by the hand. "And how long have you been in town?"

"Nearly two months."

"I need not ask you how you are?"—Yes, to himself, she was getting back her looks—"And where are you staying?"

"With my aunt—in Upper Cream Street."

"Upper Cream Street!" he echoed, with increased respect in his tone, and a look of faint surprise in his dreamy blue eyes. "Then I shall certainly make a point of coming to see you.—What is your number?"

"Thank you, very much; but I am leaving on Monday—(this was Saturday)—and," looking him bravely in the face, she added, "I am going to a situation. I am going out as a governess."

Mr. Quentin was somewhat disconcerted by this rather blunt announcement, but he did not lose his presence of mind, and said in his most airy manner,—

"Oh, really!—well, then, on another occasion I may hope to be more fortunate—during the holidays, perhaps?" glancing interrogatively at

Clara Platt, who returned his gaze with a stare of dull phlegmatic hauteur, implying an utter repudiation of her cousin, and all her concerns.

Turning once more to Helen, he said,—

"Heard any news from Port Blair?"

"No, not lately."

"Awful hole, wasn't it? I wonder we did not all hang ourselves, or go mad!"

"I liked it very much, I must confess," she replied, rather shyly.

"Oh!" shrugging his shoulders, "every one to their taste, of course. No doubt it seemed an earthly Paradise to a young lady just out from school; and you had it all your own way, you know. By-the-by, I wonder what has become of Lisle? Some one said he was in California,—I suppose *you* have not heard?"

There was a half-ironic, half-bantering look in his eyes, and the same amiable impulse that impelled him to pull the legs off flies when he was a pretty little boy, was actuating him now.

"I," she stammered, considerably taken aback by this unexpected question, and meeting his glance with a faint flush,—"Oh, no."

"Well, I see that I am detaining you now,"—with another glance at Clara—"I hope we shall meet again before long; good-bye," and with a smile and sweep of his hat, he walked away in a highly effective manner. He was scarcely out of earshot, ere Miss Platt burst forth, as if no longer able to restrain herself,—

"Helen, how could you! How *could* you tell him all our private affairs. I never was so disgusted in my life. What was the good of informing him that you were going to be a governess, and, as it were, thrusting the news down his throat?"

"What was the harm? For the future, of course, he will drop my acquaintance. Though there is nothing degrading in the post, I am quite certain that he, as he would call it, 'draws the line at governesses,' and, indeed,—from what I have heard you say—so do you."

"Don't be impertinent to me, if you please, Helen. I think you totally forget yourself sometimes, and all you owe to mother and to us."

"You need not be afraid, that I shall *ever* allow such a heavy obligation to escape my memory," returned Helen, with complete equanimity.

Was she likely to forget these months of making, and mending, parcel carrying, and general slavery to her cousins Clara and Carrie? Her companion was conscious that there was a hidden sting in this speech, but contented herself with gobbling some incoherent remark, lost in her throat, about "ingratitude" and "insolence." After this little skirmish the two ladies did not exchange another syllable, and they reached their own hall door in dead silence.

"Odious, detestable girl!" cried Clara to her sister, as she flung off her hat, and tore off her gloves in their mutual bower. "What do you think? When we were coming home we met that Mr. Quentin, and he stopped and talked to her for ever so long, and she never *introduced* me!"

"Well, I'm sure! However, it was no loss, you know he has not sixpence."

"No; but listen. He asked her where she was staying, and said he was coming to call, and she actually told him, with the utmost composure, that he need not mind, as she was going to a situation on Monday as governess—I was crimson! I'm sure she did it out of pure spite, just to make me feel uncomfortable."

"Not a doubt of it," acquiesced her sister. "How excessively annoying! That man knows the Sharpes, and Talbots, and Jenkins', and the whole thing will come out now; after all the trouble we have taken to keep it quiet, and telling every one she was going to friends in the suburbs."

"Yes," chimed in Clara, wrathfully. "What possesses people to persecute us with questions about our cousin—our *pretty* cousin, forsooth! Such a sweet-looking, interesting girl. Pah! I'm perfectly sick of her name, and the prying and pushing of one's acquaintance, is really shameless. Old Mrs. Parsons has returned to the charge again and again. She has no more tact or delicacy than a cook. Do we ever worry her, about *her* poor relations, and 'how they have been *left*,' as she calls it?"

"No, thank goodness," replied Carrie, emphatically; now addressing herself to her own plain reflection in the looking-glass. "There is no coarse, vulgar curiosity about *us*, I am happy to say. *We* are ladies."

And with this sustaining conviction in their bosoms, these two sweet sisters descended affectionately arm in arm to luncheon.

On Monday morning, Mrs. Platt herself carried her niece to her future abode in the family brougham. Their destination was a square, detached, red brick mansion, remarkable for long rows of windows with brown wire blinds, an outward air of primness bordering on severity, and a brass plate on the gate the size of a tea-tray, which bore the following address: "Malvern House.—Mrs. Kane's establishment for young ladies."

As Helen and her aunt ascended the spotless steps, and rang the dazzling bell, the sound of many pianos, all discoursing different tunes, scales, songs, and exercises, was absolutely deafening.

Mrs. Kane received her new governess very graciously, and when Mrs. Platt had taken her departure, she personally introduced her to the scene of her future labours without any unnecessary delay, sweeping down upon the classes with Miss Denis in her train, and launching her into school-life with a neat little speech, which had done worthy service on similar occasions.

The school-room was a long apartment, lighted by five windows and lined with narrow black desks, at which were seated about fifty girls; and although silence was the rule, a little low buzz, a kind of intangible humming of the human voice, was distinctly audible to the new arrival, as she stood in the midst of what, to a timid young woman, would have seemed a kind of social lion's den.

Mrs. Kane had twenty boarders and thirty day scholars; and between the two parties an internecine war was quietly but fiercely carried on from term to term, and from year to year, and handed down from one generation to another, as faithfully as the feud between the Guelphs and Ghibellines. It was rumoured in both factions that Bogey's successor ("Bogey" was their flattering sobriquet for their late governess) "had come in a carriage and pair; Annie Jones had seen it out of the music-room window;" and the young ladies were inclined to treat her with more tolerance, than if she had merely arrived in an ordinary "growler." Of course, all the hundred eyes were instantly unwinkingly fixed on the new-comer as she walked up the room in the wake of her employer. They beheld a young lady in deep mourning, slight and fair, and—yes—positively pretty! quite as good-looking, and not much older than Rosalie Gay, the belle of the school. They noticed that she did not appear the least bit shy or nervous (twelve years in a similar establishment stood to Helen now); she was not a whit abashed by the gaze of all these tall, staring girls, who were subsequently surprised to discover that she was perfectly conversant with school rules and routine; and more than this, that despite her youth, and fair sad face, she could be both determined and firm.

A large staff of masters, who taught music, singing, drawing, dancing, and literature, came and went all day long at Malvern House; but the only resident teachers besides Helen, were a Mrs. Lane, a widow, who looked after the housekeeping, poured out tea, and taught needlework, and Mademoiselle Clémence Torchon, a Parisienne, with whom Helen found herself thrown into the closest companionship. They occupied the same room, sat side by side at table, and walked together daily behind the long line of chattering boarders. Clémence was a young woman of about eight-and-twenty, who had come to England more with a view of learning that language, than of imparting her own tongue. She was square, and stout, and sallow; was better conversant with French poetry, than verbs, maintaining her personal dignity by a stolid impassive demeanour; boasted a noble appetite, and was unblushingly selfish, and surprisingly mean. She honoured her new companion with a large share of her confidence, and during their daily airings, poured into her unwilling ears, the praises of a certain adorable "Jules," and even compelled her, when half asleep at night, to sit up and listen to his letters! letters written on many sheets of pink paper, and crammed with vaguely sentimental stilted sentences, signifying nothing tangible, nothing matrimonial, but nevertheless affording the keenest pleasure to Mademoiselle Torchon. The young English teacher could not afford to quarrel with so close an associate, and feigned a respectable amount of civility and interest; but how often did she wish "*ce cher Jules,*" not to speak of his effusions,—at the bottom of the deep blue sea! Once or twice mademoiselle had hinted, that she was good-naturedly prepared to receive a return of confidences in kind; and had even gone so far as to say, "Have *you* ever had a lover?"

Her listener's thoughts turned promptly to a certain moonlight night, the scent of orange-flowers, the shade of palms, and all the appropriate accessories of a love-tale, not forgetting Gilbert Lisle's eloquent dark eyes, and low-whispered, broken vows. Nevertheless, Miss Denis cleverly parried this embarrassing question, and mademoiselle, having but little interest to spare from her own affairs, dismissed the subject with an encouraging assurance "that, perhaps some day or other she might also have a Jules," as she was, though rather *triste* and frightfully thin, "*pas mal pour une Anglaise!*"

Mrs. Kane withdrew into private life the moment that school hours were over. When the bell rang at four o'clock for the departure of the day scholars, she disappeared and left the burden of surveillance to Miss Denis and mademoiselle—the latter, like the unselfish darling that she was, shuffled off her share of the load upon her companion's shoulders, and generally ascended to her own room, where she lay upon her bed, devouring chocolate-creams and French novels for the remainder of the day.

Helen's duties commenced at seven o'clock in the morning, at which hour she was obliged to be in the school-room, to keep order, and they were not at an end till she had turned off the gas in the dormitories at half-past nine at night; after that, her time was her own,—and she was then at liberty to listen to Clémence's maunderings, and Jules' last letter.

Mrs. Kane soon discovered that her new governess was a clever girl, with stability and force of character beyond her years, moreover, that she had unusual influence with the pupils, and was popular in the school-room; so she engaged her permanently at a salary of forty pounds a year— and washing. This offer was accepted with alacrity, for Mrs. Platt seemed to have wholly forgotten her niece, and the comfortable home that she had promised to secure for her, and Helen gladly settled herself down, as a permanent member of the Malvern House staff. Weeks rolled into months, months into quarters, and nothing came to break the dull monotony of her existence, beyond occasional letters from Mrs. Home and Mrs. Durand, and a visit to Smithson Villa; she actually hailed the arrival of the yellow brougham, with unalloyed delight, and had not shrunk from sharing it,— not merely with her hostess, and the dogs, and the weekly groceries, but with a leg of New Zealand mutton, that was to furnish forth the family dinner. She liked Lady Grubb, despite her little eccentricities. She even enjoyed (so low had she fallen!) the perusal of Mrs. Creery's latest effusions from Port Blair. In Lady Grubb's back drawing-room, with one of these in her hand, she seemed to hold in her grasp the last feeble link that bound her to her former happy life among those distant tropical seas.

She did her utmost to live altogether in the present, to invest all her thoughts and energies in her daily tasks, and to shut her eyes to the future— and still more difficult feat—to close them to the past. Month after month, she toiled on with busy, unabated zeal (Mrs. Kane warmly congratulating herself on the possession of such a *rara avis*, and giving her mentally, a considerable increase of salary). She rose early, and went to rest late, her mind was at its fullest tension all day long; she was working at too high pressure, the strain was beyond her physical powers, and the consequence was, she broke down. Gradually she lost sleep, and appetite, became pale, and thin, and haggard.

"My dear," said Mrs. Kane with some concern, "we must get you away for a change. The doctor says you ought to go home, and have a good long rest."

"But I have no home, Mrs. Kane.—I am an orphan," she returned, gravely. "I'm not nearly as ill as I seem, in fact I'm not ill at all! There is nothing the matter with me, I'm as strong as a horse. You must not mind my *looks!*"

"Would you not like to go to your aunt's for a week or two? I see she has returned from abroad."

"No, thank you, I would ten times rather go to the poor-house," she answered, unguardedly. "Excuse me, perhaps I'm a little hasty, but I'm proud, and I, if I must come to beggary, prefer public charity, to the private benevolence of—relations."

But in spite of Helen's repudiation of the hospitality of her kindred, Mrs. Kane wrote a polite little note to 15, Upper Cream Street, that brought Mrs. Platt to Malvern House, the very next day,—in a peevish, not to say injured, frame of mind.

"Well, Helen," she exclaimed, as her niece entered the drawing-room, "so I hear you are in the doctor's hands;"—making a peck at her as she spoke. "Let me see! there's not much the matter with you, I fancy.—For goodness' sake, don't get the idea into your head that you are *delicate!*"

"You may be sure that that is the last thing I shall do, Aunt Julia."

"I must talk to Mrs. Kane, and tell her you should take extract of malt. She will have to fatten you up.—Yes, certainly, you want fattening;"—speaking exactly as if she were alluding to a young Christmas turkey. "And so, I hear, you are giving satisfaction, and that you are a very good musician, and linguist! I am glad your poor father's extravagant education, has not been entirely thrown away! Mrs. Kane speaks very highly of you. But, dear me, child, why did you not take equal advantage of other opportunities; why did you not make hay in the Andamans?"

"Hay! aunt. There was none to make, beyond a very small crop in the General's compound."

"You know very well what *I* mean, you provoking girl! I'm certain you had offers of marriage. Now had you not?"

Helen made no disclaimer to this, beyond a slight shrug of her shoulders.

"Come, come! Silence gives consent. How many?"

"What does it signify, aunt? All girls out there——"

"That is no answer," persisted Mrs. Platt, tapping her foot on the floor.

"Well, I do not think it is fair to tell."

"But you could have married?"

"Yes, I suppose I may admit as much as that."

"And instead of being comfortably settled in your own house, here you are, slaving away all your best years, and best looks in a school. I'm sure you are sorry enough *now*, that you did not say 'yes!'"

"On the contrary, I have never regretted saying 'no,'—and never will."

"Perhaps there was some one who did *not* come forward?" inquired the elder lady, with a rather sour smile.

"Perhaps there was, aunt!" she rejoined, with a laugh, that entirely baffled Mrs. Platt, who, after surveying her for some seconds in searching silence, exclaimed,—

"Well, you are a queer girl! I can't make you out! I certainly could not imagine *you* caring a straw for any man! Your face entirely belies your real disposition; it gives people the idea that you are capable of deep feelings— perhaps of what is called '*une grande passion*'—whereas, in reality, you are cold and as unresponsive as the typical iceberg. However, considering your present circumstances, and youth, and good looks,—perhaps it is just as well!"

Having delivered herself of this opinion, as though it were an oracle, Mrs. Platt sank into a tone of easy confidential discourse, and imparted to her listener, that her recent campaign on the Continent, had not been entirely barren of results. A certain elderly widower, had been "greatly attracted" by Clara, and had paid her considerable attention, and that it was not unlikely, that they would have a wedding before very long. And after a good deal more in this strain, and yet more, on the subject of the frightful expenses she had incurred abroad, and the paralyzing prices of some of the French hotels, Mrs. Platt, with a final recommendation of extract of malt, went her way, and drove home alone, in her comfortable, plush-lined brougham.

Helen continued to struggle on from day to day, and conscientiously fulfilled her allotted duties. She indignantly refused to accept the *rôle* of invalid; she told herself that, could she but tide over the next six weeks, she would contrive a trip to some cheap seaside resort, and there recruit her shattered health—her health that was her only capital! What was to become of her if she broke down? she would have no resource but charity! She shivered at the very thought. Each day her round of tasks became more of an effort; she felt as if some dreadful, unknown illness was lying in wait, and dogging her steps hour after hour. Sometimes the room swam round, and figures and words in exercise-books seemed to mix and run about before her aching eyes. But so far, by sheer force of will she fought off the enemy, and fiercely refused to surrender.

When ten days had elapsed, Mrs. Platt was once more in Mrs. Kane's drawing-room, the bearer of a letter in her pocket, that she flattered herself would remove her poor relation entirely out of her own orbit.

"My dear, I declare you look really ill—very ill!" she exclaimed, as her niece entered. "Don't come near me,"—moving suddenly across the room, and making a gesture of repudiation with both hands,—"keep away, there's a good girl! I'm certain you are sickening for something,—diphtheria or small-pox! Small-pox is raging. You must see a doctor immediately, and take precautions. If it is anything, you will have to be sent to a hospital at *once!*"

"You need not be the least alarmed, Aunt Julia; there is nothing the matter with me. My head aches, and I'm tired sometimes; that is all, I assure you."

"Oh, well,"—rather relieved—"I'm sure I *hope* so, otherwise it would be most awkward! I understand now, that you really require a change, and it is principally about that, I have come over to see you. I have had a letter I wish to show you,"—sinking into an easy chair, and commencing to fumble in her pocket. "Yes, here it is,"—handing it to her niece, who unfolded it, and ran her eyes over the following effusion:—

> "Dearest Mother,—Carrie and I cannot possibly go home
> this week, there is so much coming off; and *Mr. Jones is here*!
> Please send down our black lace dresses, our new opera
> cloaks, and some flowers from that man in the Bayswater
> Road. We shall be rather short of money, so you might
> enclose some—say, a five pound note—in an envelope in
> my dress pocket. So sorry you are having all this worry
> about Helen. What a tiresome creature she is! Of course
> it is quite out of the question, that we should take her in;
> be *sure* you impress that very firmly on her mind, mother
> dear. Is there not a convalescent home for broken-down
> governesses? Some charitable institution that she could go
> to?—"

"Charitable institution!" echoed Helen, aloud.

"Oh, dear me! I believe I've given you the wrong letter," exclaimed Mrs. Platt, in great confusion. "Here! this must be your uncle's,"—extending her hand as she spoke. "I'm getting so blind, and this room is so dark, I really can't see what I'm doing," she added, in a rather apologetic tone, her eyes sinking before her niece's,—for she saw in them that she had read what Carrie had written; as for Helen, her heart beat unusually fast, her nerves were on edge, her wrath was kindled.

"Quite out of the question that we should take her in!" She had never dreamt of being lodged again under her aunt's roof, but somehow, seeing the fact so plainly stated in black and white, stung her to revolt.

What had her aunt and cousins done for her, that she should be sent hither or thither at their bidding? She had toiled for them, as an upper servant, a lady help, in return for food and lodging, and she was now wholly independent, and earning her own living by incessant hard work. These thoughts flew through her mind as she opened letter No. 2, which was written in a small cramped hand on a large sheet of paper, and ran as follows:—

"Crowmore,

"Terryscreen, May 8th.

"Dear Madam,—I am this day in receipt of your communication, informing me that my late wife's niece, Helen Denis, is in England, an orphan, and entirely dependent on her friends."—"Dependent on her friends!" re-read Helen, quivering with indignation and self-restraint—"I shall be glad to give her a home under my roof, and if you will favour me with her address I shall correspond with her personally, and make all needful arrangements for her journey to this place.

"I am, Madam,

"Your obedient servant,

"Malachi Sheridan."

"A very kind letter," said his niece, gratefully.

"Yes, poor crazy creature," acquiesced Mrs. Platt, "I suppose he *has* lucid intervals,"—then, after a pause, she added—"Of course you will go, Helen?"

"I am not sure; I must think it over."

"Think it over! what nonsense. What more do you want? At any rate, Helen, bear in mind, that *I* have done all I can."

"Yes, Aunt Julia; pray do not trouble yourself any more about me; I release you of all responsibility on my behalf. Indeed, in future, you may as well forget my existence!"

She had risen as she spoke, and leant her elbow on the chimney-piece, and her head on her hand. She looked unusually tall, and unexpectedly dignified. For a moment Mrs. Platt felt almost in awe of her penniless niece, but she soon recovered her ordinary mental attitude, and said rather sharply,—

"Don't talk nonsense! I see your nerves and temper are completely unstrung! I hope you will be all the better for your trip to Ireland, but I'm *afraid* you will find Mr. Sheridan's girls, a pair of uncouth, ill-bred savages, and, of course, the place is quite in the wilds, and——"

"So much the better, aunt; I like the wilds, as you call them, and you know I'm accustomed to savages."

"Then I'm sure if *you* are satisfied,—I am," said Mrs. Platt, huffily. "And now I really must be going, for we have some people coming to dinner,"— and with a polite message for Mrs. Kane, and a request that Helen "would write if anything turned up," a vague sentence, meaning perhaps a good situation, perhaps an offer of marriage,—Mrs. Platt embraced her niece, and took her departure.

Helen remained shivering over the drawing-room fire, re-reading her uncle's letter, and pondering on her future plans. After all, disappointing as had been her experience of cousins, she might yet draw a prize in the lottery of fate, and she determined to brave these Irish Sheridans. She had thirty pounds in her desk, quite a small fortune, and if the worst came to the worst, she could always beat a retreat. With this prudent reservation in her mind, and a burning impatience to escape *anywhere*, from her present surroundings, she sat down that very hour, and wrote a grateful acceptance of her uncle's invitation, and announced her intention of starting for Crowmore, within a week.

CHAPTER XXIX
"YOU REMEMBER MISS DENIS?"

"I say to thee, though free from care,

A lonely lot, an aimless life,

The crowning comfort is not there—

Son, take a wife."

Jean Ingelow.

Scene: a splendidly furnished dining-room in the most fashionable square in London; season, end of July; hour, nine p.m.; *dramatis personæ*, a father and son; the former, an old gentleman with a red face, beaky nose, and bristling white hair, is holding a glass of venerable port between his goggle eye and the light, and admonishing his companion, a sunburnt young man, who is leaning back in his chair and carelessly rolling a cigarette between his fingers. A young man so dark, and tanned, that his visage would not look out of place beneath a Spanish sombrero; nevertheless, we have no difficulty in recognizing our former friend, Gilbert Lisle.

"It's positively indecent for a man of your position to go roaming the world, like some ne'er-do-well, or family black sheep. FitzCurzon told me he met you on the stairs of some hotel in San Francisco, in a flannel shirt, butcher boots, and a coat that would have been dear at fourpence! He declared, that you looked for all the world like a digger."

"Curzon—is—a—puppy, who trots round the globe because he says it's 'the thing to do,'" (imitating a drawl), "and never is seen without kid gloves, and if asked to dine on bear steaks in the Rockies, would arrive in evening dress and white tie,—or perish in the attempt; not that he ever ventures off the beaten track of ocean steamers and express trains; he could not live without his dressing case, and a hard day's ride would kill him. He was in the finest country in the world for sport, and he never fired a cartridge!" It was evident from the speaker's face, that this latter enormity crowned all.

"Well, you shot enough for *six*! I should think you have killed every animal, from a mosquito to an elephant; this house is a cross between a menagerie and a museum. You have been away two years this time, Gil.

A Bird Of Passage | 229

'Pon my word, you are as bad as the prodigal son." Here he swallowed the port at a gulp.

"I admit that I have been to a far country, but you can scarcely accuse me of wasting my substance in riotous living," remonstrated his offspring.

"I accuse you of wasting your time, sir! which in a man in your position is worse. Why can you not content yourself at home, as I do, instead of roaming about like a play actor, or the agent for some patent medicine! Where's this you were last? a cattle ranche in Texas,—before that, California,—before that, Japan, dining on boa-constrictors, and puppy dogs; before that,—the deuce only knows; you are as fond of walking up and down the earth, and going to and fro—as—as—the devil in the Psalms, or where was it?"

"My dear father," replied Gilbert, with the utmost goodhumour. "You have compared me to a black sheep, a digger,—and I suppose, because it happens to be Sunday evening,—to the prodigal son; and finally, the devil! None of your illustrations fit me, and the last I repudiate altogether; *his* wanderings, if I remember rightly, were in search of mischief. Mine were merely in quest of amusement."

"Amusement and mischief are generally the same thing," grunted Lord Lingard. "Why, the deuce,—you are over thirty, and getting as grey as a badger.—Why can't you marry and settle?"

"Some people marry and never settle, others marry, and are settled with a vengeance," rejoined his son, now proceeding to light his cigarette.

"Bah! you are talking nonsense, sir, and you know it; a man in your position must marry—heir to me, heir to your uncle, heir to yourself."

"Heir to myself," muttered Gilbert, "well, I shall let myself off cheap. I must marry, must I? *Je n'en vois pas la nécessité. Après moi le déluge.*"

"Oh, hang your French lingo!" growled his father. "If I had not wanted you to marry, I suppose you'd have brought me home a daughter-in-law years ago—some barmaid, no doubt."

"Barmaids may be very agreeable young women; but somehow, I don't think they are just in my line, sir."

"Line, sir, line! I'll tell you what *is* in your line! confounded obstinacy. You had the same strong will when you were a little chap in white frocks,—no higher than the poker. Once you took a thing into your head, nothing would move you."

"In that respect I believe I take after you," returned his son, with the deepest respect. "A strong determination to have your own way, helps a man to shove through life—so I have understood you to say."

"Had me there, neatly, Gilbert! Yes, you score one. Well—well—but seriously,—I want to have a little rational talk with you. There is that fine place of yours in Berkshire, shut up all the year round—think——"

"Don't say, of my *position* again, sir, I implore you," interrupted his son, with a mock tragic gesture.

"Well, your stake in the country—think of your tenants."

"I have remembered them to the tune of a reduction of thirty per cent.— What more do they want?"

"They would like you to marry some nice-looking girl, and go down, and live among them."

"If I did, and kept up a large establishment, took the hounds, and kept tribes of servants, and had a wife who dressed in hundred-guinea gowns, and went in for private theatricals, balls, races,—and probably betting,—I should not be able to make such a pleasant little abatement in the rent! How would that be?"

"You would never marry a minx like that, I should hope! Listen to me, Gilbert," now waxing pathetic, "I am getting to be an old man, and you are all I have belonging to me. I am lost here alone in this great big mansion. Marry, and make your home with me; my bark is worse than my bite, as you know, I would like to see a woman about the house again—they are cheerful, and brighten up a place, especially if they are young and pretty. Just look at the two of us sitting on here over our coffee till nearly eleven o'clock, simply because the big drawing-room above is empty.—I am not nearly as keen about the club as I used to be, and these attacks of gout play the very devil with me."

And here, to his son's blank amazement, he suddenly dropped into poetry, and quavered out,—

"Oh woman! in our hours of ease,

Uncertain, coy, and hard to please;

When pain and sickness wring the brow,

A ministering angel thou."

"You speak in the plural, sir," rejoined Gilbert gravely. "You say, you like to see women about the house, that they are cheerful, they brighten up a place. Do you suppose—granting that I am a follower of Mormon—that six would be sufficient?"

"I'm not in the humour for jokes! I'm serious, Gilbert, whatever you may be. I want to see a pretty young face in the carriage, and opera box, and the family diamonds on a pretty neck and arms—they have not been worn for years—the very sight of them would make any girl jump at you," he concluded in a cajoling voice.

"Then, for heaven's sake, don't display them."

"Gilbert, you are enough to drive me mad. I begin to think—'pon my word, I begin to suspect—that you have a reason for all this fencing," glancing at him suspiciously beneath his frost-white eyebrows—"you are married already, sir; some low-born adventuress, some disreputable——"

"I am *not*," interrupted his son with a gesture of impatience.

"Then you are in love with a married woman!"

"You seem to have a very exalted idea of my character, sir, but again you are mistaken."

"Ha! humph!" tossing off a beaker of port; "then it just comes to this, you don't think any woman good enough to be the wife of Mr. Lisle! Now honestly, Gilbert, have you ever seen a girl you would have married?"

Dead silence succeeded this question.

"Come, Gilbert," pursued the old gentleman remorselessly.

"Well, yes—such a person has existed," at length admitted his victim most reluctantly.

"And where is she? Why did you not marry her? Where did you meet her?"

"I met her in the Andamans."

"The Andamans! Those cannibal islands! This is another of your confounded jokes!" Now looking alarmingly angry.—"I know as well as you do, that there are only savages there. Do you take me for a fool, sir?"

"There was a large European community at Port Blair. As to taking you for a fool, it would be the last thing to occur to me—on the contrary, the young lady took *me* for one."

"Then she never made a greater mistake in her life,—never. And why did it not come off?"

"She preferred another fellow, that was all."

"*Preferred!* humph—good matches must have been growing on the trees out there. Well, well, well," looking fixedly at his son, "there's as good fish in the sea as ever were caught—why not fall back on Katie?"

"It has not come to that *yet*, sir—and I would sooner, if it was all the same to you, fall back on a loaded revolver."

"She has the mischief's own temper, I allow—but what a property! However, you need not look for money—a pretty, lively English girl, that wears her own hair and complexion, and that can sing a song or two, and get out of a carriage like a gentlewoman—that's the style! Eh, Gilbert?"

"I suppose so, sir," rejoined his son gloomily; "but as the Irishman said, 'You must give me a long day—a long day, your honour.'"

"And the old savage replied—I remember it perfectly—'I'll give you till to-morrow, the twenty-first of June, the longest day in the year!' And your shrift shall be a short one, my boy! What are you going to do with yourself to-morrow?"

"Do you mean that you would marry me off within the next twelve hours?"

"No, you young stupid."

"Oh, well, I want to look in at the Academy and a couple of clubs, and in the evening I'm going to dine with the Durands senior, and do a theatre afterwards with the Durands junior."

"Oh!—Mary and her husband. Mary is a sensible woman. I want to talk to her. Ask her to dine—say Thursday? Mary has her head screwed on the right way. I shall consult her about you, Master Gilbert. I'll see what she advises about you. She shall help me to put the noose round your neck."

"The *noose*, indeed," repeated his son in a tone of melancholy sarcasm.

"Yes, yes, I'll settle it all with Mary." So saying, the old gentleman went chuckling from the room in a high state of jubilation.

The next afternoon Gilbert Lisle formed one of a crowd who were collected before a certain popular picture at the Royal Academy; but so far his view had been entirely obscured by the broad back of a gentleman in front of him; it vaguely occurred to him that there was something rather familiar in the shape of those broad, selfish-looking shoulders, when their owner suddenly turned round, and he found himself face to face with James Quentin.

"By Jove, old fellow!" exclaimed the latter, shaking his hand vigorously, "this *is* a pleasant surprise; and so you have returned from your travels—where do you hail from last?"

"Only New York; I arrived two days ago, and feel as if I had been away for ten years, I'm so out of everything and behind the times,—a second Rip Van Winkle."

"Then I suppose you have not heard *my* little bit of news?"

"No—o—but I fancy I can guess it, it's not a very difficult riddle—you are married!"

"Right you are! a second Daniel! Come away and speak to Mrs. Q., she will be delighted to see you."

Gilbert had not bargained for this—he would much rather never meet Helen Denis again; however, there was no resisting Apollo's summons, and in another moment he was standing before a velvet settee, and ere he was aware of it, his companion was saying, "Jane, my love, let me present an old friend—Mr. Lisle, Mrs. Quentin."

He glanced down, and saw a magnificently-attired, massive-looking dame, over whose head fully forty summers had flown; she was smiling up at him most graciously, and holding out a well-gloved hand—this lady was indisputably Mrs. Quentin—but where was Helen Denis?

Her new acquaintance made a gallant struggle to master his amazement, and to utter a few bald, commonplace remarks about the heat and the pictures; and presently suffered himself to be borne onward by the crowd. But Jim Quentin was not going to lose sight of him thus. He had married a wife considerably beneath him in birth, and it behoved him to keep a fast hold of his well-born friends, and a secure footing on the social ladder.

Lisle was a popular man; he had discovered this fact on his return to England, and had made considerable capital out of his name in various ways. It had proved to be an open sesame to a rather exclusive circle, who cordially welcomed Apollo when they heard that he and Gilbert Lisle were "like brothers," and had lived under the same roof for months. Lisle had been useful at Port Blair, and he would be useful in London.

"Well, were you surprised to find that there was a Mrs. Quentin?" he asked, as he came up with his quarry in a comparatively empty room, chiefly devoted to the display of etchings on large stands and easels.

"No, of course not—but," looking him steadily in the face, "she is not the lady I expected to see."

"What!" then all of a sudden he remembered Helen—Helen, who had been completely swept out of his mind by a twelvemonth of busy intrigues, and such exciting pursuits as fortune-hunting, tuft-hunting, and place-hunting. "Oh! to be sure, you were thinking of Miss Denis, but that did not come off, you see," he added with careless effrontery. "She was all very well—*pour passer le temps*—in an ungodly hole like the Andamans, but, by George! England is quite another affair."

"Is it—and why?" inquired his listener, rather grimly.

"Oh! my dear fellow, she has not a rap—she was literally penniless— when her father died, she was destitute."

"But you always understood that she had no fortune."

"Yes, but when I came to look at it, I saw that it would never do. I had next to nothing; she had nothing at all; one cannot live on love, and I don't think I was ever really serious. I did you a good turn though; *you* were rather inclined to make a fool of yourself in that quarter," administering a playful poke in the ribs, and grinning significantly.

But the grin on his face faded somewhat suddenly as he encountered a look in his companion's eyes that made him feel curiously uncomfortable.

"Where is she now?" inquired Lisle, speaking in a low, repressed sort of tone.

"'Pon my honour, I can't tell you! I believe she has gone out as governess—best thing she could do, you know; better than marrying a poor devil like me," he added apologetically. "She was a nice enough little girl, and she had not half a bad time of it in the Andamans. I daresay she'll pick up some fellow at home. Look here, old chappie," button-holeing him as he spoke, "this is my card and address; now, what day will you come and dine? Got a tip-top cook,—not that you ever *were* particular,—my wife has pots of money, and we give rather swagger entertainments. Whatever day will suit you will suit me; you have only to say the word."

"I have only to say the word, have I!" cried Gilbert, suddenly blazing into passion; "then I say that you are a scoundrel, Mr. Quentin. I say that you have behaved like one to that girl, that's what I say."

Apollo recoiled precipitately. He did not like the angry light in his old friend's face, nor the manner in which he grasped his cane.

"You jilted her, on your own showing, in the most deliberate, cold-blooded manner. Jilted her because you were tired of a passing fancy, and she was left, as you say, penniless and destitute. She may thank her stars for a lucky escape! Better she should beg her bread than be the wife of a cur like you! There's your card," tearing it into pieces and scattering it on the floor. "In my opinion you should be kicked out of decent society, and turned out of every respectable club in London. I beg that, for the future, you will be good enough to give *me* a wide berth," and with a nod of unspeakable contempt he turned and walked away, leaving his foe absolutely speechless with rage and amazement.

Underneath these mixed feelings lay a smouldering conviction that Lisle, for all his customary *nonchalance*, could be as bitter and unsparing an enemy as he had been a generous and useful friend. Pleasant, stately houses would close—nay, slam their doors on him at a hint from Lisle, and if the story got about the clubs, and was looked at from Lisle's point of view,—it would be the very deuce! In his exaltation he had somewhat forgotten the *rôle* he formerly played with his fellow inmate,—and we know that to a liar a good memory is indispensable,—he had spoken rashly and foolishly with his lips, and had been thus summarily condemned out of his own mouth! Alas! alas! he already saw his circle of well-beloved, titled friends narrowing to vanishing point, as he now recalled a veiled threat uttered by the very man who had just denounced him! On the whole, Mr. Quentin thought that his little comedy with Miss Denis would prove an expensive performance, and he returned to his wealthy partner, feeling very much like a beaten hound.

That evening, as Gilbert Lisle drove up to the door of Mrs. Durand's mansion, he said to himself, "Here I come to the very house of all others where I am most likely to hear the sequel to that rascal's story. Mrs. Durand is safe to know all about Helen Denis,—and if she is the woman I take her to be, she won't be long before I know as much as she does herself! I shall say nothing—I shall not ask a single question about the young lady; not, indeed, that it personally concerns me whether she is on the parish or not. Still, I should like to hear what has become of her."

(He made these resolutions as he entered, and passed upstairs, and presented himself in the drawing-room.)

Strange to say, Mrs. Charles Durand had arrived at a precisely similar determination with regard to him. Hitherto they had only exchanged a few hasty words, had no opportunity of raking up "old days," but to-night it would be different; "At dinner he is sure to make some allusion to Port Blair, and her name will come on the *tapis*, and I can easily judge by his looks, if there was anything in my suspicions—and very strong suspicions they were! However, I won't be the first to break the ice; as far as Helen is concerned—I shall be dumb."

Thus Mrs. Durand to her own reflection in the mirror, as she attired herself for the evening.

Here were two people about to meet, each resolved to be silent, and each determined to hear the other's disclosures on an intensely interesting subject. As is usual in such cases, the lady yielded first; her opponent was habitually reserved, and it came as second nature to him to wait and to hold his peace. He had one false alarm during dinner, when his former playmate, addressing him across the table, said, with her brightest air,—

"I saw a particular friend of *yours* to-day; who do you think it was?"

"I have so many particular friends," he replied, "that's rather a large order."

"Well, a *lady* friend."

"A lady friend! They are not much in my way."

"A lady you knew in the Andamans," looking at him keenly.

He cast a quick, questioning glance at her, but remained otherwise dumb, and she, smiling at her own little *ruse*, said,—

"In short, our well-beloved Mrs. Creery! She was driving in the park, in a dreadful yellow affair, like an omnibus cut down, along with another remarkable old person. She was delighted to see me, and hailed me as if I had been a long-lost child!"

Mrs. Durand smiled to herself again. She was thinking of the battle royal she had fought with Mrs. Creery over the reputation of the very gentleman who was now her *vis-à-vis*.

"She asked me particularly for you, and sent you a message—I'm not sure that it was not her *love*—and told me to be sure and tell you that Monday is her day."

"I really don't see any connection between Mrs. Creery's Mondays and myself," coolly rejoined that lady's former *bête-noire*. And, with a few general remarks about Port Blair, the monsoon, the sharks, and the shells, the conversation drifted back to less out-of-the-way regions.

The younger members of the party set out after dinner for the Savoy, to see Gilbert and Sullivan's latest production. They consisted of Captain and Mrs. Durand, two young lady cousins, a guardsman, and Mr. Lisle. Mrs. Durand and the latter occupied the back seat in the box, and discoursed of the piece, mutual friends, and mutual aversions, with a scrupulous avoidance of the one topic nearest their hearts.

At last, the lady could stand it no longer; and, during the interval after the first act, she turned to her companion, and said rather sharply, "You remember Miss Denis?"

"Miss Denis—oh, yes! of course I do!"

"Those are her cousins in the box next the stage—those girls in pink."

"Is she living with them?"

"Oh dear no! She stayed a month or two on her first arrival, and, by all accounts, they led her the life of a modern Cinderella, and afterwards turned her off to earn her bread as a governess."

"Indeed!" he ejaculated, with such stoical indifference that Mrs. Durand felt that she could have shaken him. But, after a moment's silence, he added, "I always thought she had married Quentin—until to-day."

"Oh, nonsense! You are not really serious! Of course you are aware that your friend, Apollo, has espoused a widow with quantities of money in the oil trade."

"Pray do not call him *my* friend; I am not at all anxious to claim that honour," he rejoined stiffly.

"Then you have been quarrelling, I suppose. I wonder if it was about the usual thing—one of my sex?"

"It was. I may say as much to *you*. In fact it was about Miss Denis—he treated her shamefully."

"What makes you think so?"—opening her eyes very wide, and shutting up her fan.

"Because he was engaged to her at Port Blair. He told me so. And when she was left penniless, he jilted her for this rich widow."

"He told you that he was engaged to Helen? Oh," drawing a long breath, "never!"

"Yes, and showed me a ring she had given him."

"Again I say, never, never, *never*!"

"My dear Mrs. Durand, there is no good in saying, never, never, never, like that. The ring he exhibited, was one that I had given Miss Denis myself!"

"Oh, sets the wind in that quarter!" mentally exclaimed the matron; "I thought as much." But aloud she replied, "Was it a curious old ring, without any stones, that was stolen from her the night of the ball?"

"It was the ring you describe. But it was not stolen, for she gave it to Quentin when he went to the Nicobars as a '*gage d'amour.*' I expected that he would have married her as soon as possible after her father's death; indeed, I understood that he was returning from Camorta with that intention. But you see I have been so completely out of the world, that I heard nothing further till I met Quentin and his wife at the Academy to-day; and he calmly informed me that he had never seriously contemplated marrying Miss Denis, and that the Andamans and London are quite a different pair of shoes! Pray, do you call that honourable conduct?"

"You are quite, quite wrong!" cried Mrs. Durand, excitedly. "Now you have said your say, it is my turn to speak; and speak I will," she added with a gleam of determination in her eye.

"Oh, certainly!" returned her listener, with rather dry politeness.

"Helen was, and is, a particular friend of mine, and I happen to *know* that she could not endure Apollo Quentin! She did not even think him good-looking! and he bored her to death. He stuck to her like burr, and she could not shake him off. She would ten times rather have talked to Captain Rodney, or Mr. Green,—or even to *you!* She was no more engaged to him than I was. She never gave him that ring."—Here her listener stirred, and made a gesture of impatient protestation.—"That ring was *stolen*, and sold for twenty rupees," concluded Mrs. Durand, in her most forcible manner.

"Stolen—sold!" he echoed, turning towards her so suddenly that it made her start. "Is this true?"

"*True?*" she repeated indignantly.

"I do not mean to doubt you for one second; but you may have been deceived."

"At any rate, I had the benefit of my *own* eyes and ears. They do not often mislead me."

"Then how——"

"If you will only have patience you shall hear all. Helen stayed with me for the last week at Port Blair; and the night before she sailed, when I went into her room I discovered Fatima grovelling on the ground at her feet, and holding the hem of her dress, and whining,—'A—ma! A—ma!' in true native fashion. 'I very bad woman, Missy,' she was saying; 'and I very sorry *now*. I stealing jewels—why for I sent here? And now I done take, Missy's ring and sell for twenty rupees.'"

"Sold it! To whom?" interrupted Mr. Lisle, his dark face flushing to his temples.

"*That* she refused to divulge. All we could prevail on her to confess was, that she had taken it the night of the ball, and that she did not think it was of any value; but seeing how much trouble Missy was in,—and Missy going away to England, she was plenty sorry."

"Stolen the night of the ball—sold for twenty rupees, and Quentin showed it to me the next morning!" exclaimed Lisle.

After this summing up, he and Mrs. Durand looked at each other for about twenty seconds, in dead silence.

"Where is Miss Denis now?" he inquired in a kind of husky whisper.

"I wish I could tell you! I'm a miserable correspondent; I never answered her last letter, written from a school at Kensington. I would rather walk two miles than write two pages. It's very sad, and gets me into great disgrace. But though I do not write, I don't *forget* people. As soon as I arrived at home I went off to this school to see Helen, and to make my peace."

"Yes?"

"The house was all shut up, blinds down in every window, the cook in sole charge, every one else away for the holidays. The cook only showed half her face through the door, and was not at all inclined to be communicative; but I gave her something to help her memory, and then she recollected, that six weeks before the school broke up, the English governess had gone away sick, but she understood that she had not left for good.—School opens again on the 1st of September," added Mrs. Durand significantly.

"Meanwhile, where is she?"

"That is more than I can say."

"Perhaps her cousins would tell you," glancing over at the Miss Platts.

"Not they—if they did know, I doubt if they would inform you, as they are even more disagreeable than they look,—and that is saying much. However, I shall get a friend to sound them about their cousin. I believe they treated her like a servant, and made her carry parcels, run messages, mend their clothes, and button their boots!"

"How did you hear this? from Miss Denis?"

"She never named them. I'm afraid to tell you, lest you should think me a second Mrs. Creery."

"No fear—there could be but *one* Mrs. Creery—she is matchless."

"Well, my sister's maid, Plunket—now really this is downright gossip— came to her from the Platts, and one day we were talking about fine heads of hair, and she described the beautiful hair of a poor young lady in her last place,—Mrs. Platt's niece, Miss Denis; and so it all came out, for of course I pricked up my ears when I heard her name."

During this conversation the curtain had risen on the second act, and the entire audience was convulsed with delight at one of Grossmith's songs, and yet these two talked on, and never once cast their eyes to the stage. Indeed, Mrs. Durand had almost turned her back on the actors, and was wholly engrossed in an interesting little drama in private life. The other occupants of the box were in ecstasies with the performers, and Captain Durand, after gasping and wiping his eyes, turned to his wife impatiently, and said,—

"Well, really, Mary, you might just as well have stayed at home, and talked there; you have done nothing but gossip. I thought you were wild to see this piece. If you are so bored yourself, you might at least give Lisle a chance of enjoying it!"

"Charley says I must not go on chattering any longer, distracting your attention from the play. We can finish our conversation another time."—So saying, she took up her opera glass, and addressed herself seriously to the performance.

As for Gilbert Lisle, he leant back in his chair, and also fixed his eyes on the stage, but he saw absolutely nothing. If he had been asked to describe a character, a scene, or a song, he could not have done so to save his life. His mind was in a state of extraordinary confusion; he was dazed, overwhelmed, at the situation in which he found himself.

So he had been the dupe, and tool, of Quentin from first to last! It seemed incredible, that Quentin, to gain a momentary empty triumph, had stooped to theft, in order to bolster up a lie, and maintain his reputation as a lady-killer. Then as for Miss Denis,—if she had not been engaged to Quentin, and had never parted with the ring, what must she think of him? He held his breath at this poignant reflection. If any one had jilted her,—if any one had behaved vilely, if any one was a dishonoured traitor, it was he—Gilbert Lisle—sitting there staring stupidly before him, surrounded by ignorant and confiding friends, who believed him to be a gentleman, and a man of honour! As he cast his eyes over a mental picture, and saw himself, as he must appear to Helen, he was consumed by a fever of shame, that seemed to devour him. To live under the imputation of such conduct, was torture of the most exquisite description to a man of his temperament;— who had such a delicate sense of personal honour, and such chivalrous reverence for other people's veracity, that he had fallen an easy prey to an unscrupulous brazen-tongued adventurer, like James Quentin. Fury against Quentin, restored faith in his lost *fiancée*, were all secondary to one scorching thought, that seemed to burn his very brain—the thought of the disgrace that lay upon his hitherto unblemished name. To have sworn to return to a girl,—to have vowed to make her his wife,—and to have miserably deserted her, without message, or excuse,—left her to bear the buffets of adversity as best she could,—to earn her own living, or to eat the bread of charity, was maddening—maddening. He must get out of the theatre into the open air; but first he leant over Mrs. Durand's chair, and spoke to her in a few broken and imperfect sentences.

"What you have told me to-night, has a significance that you cannot guess" (oh, could she not?) "It alters—it may alter—the whole course of my life. Mrs. Durand—Mary! you were always my friend, be my friend now. When you get her address, and you will get it—you *must* get it,—to-night, to-morrow—you will give it to me in the same hour—promise."

"Why should I promise?" she asked playfully, delighted to see the immovable Gilbert for once a prey to some powerful emotion.

He was pale—his very lips were trembling, big beads of perspiration stood upon his temples.

"Why should I tell you especially?"—she repeated, but looking in his face, she saw that he was too terribly in earnest to be in the mood for light badinage. Looking in his face, she read the answer.

"I *see*,—yes, you may depend on me."

Reassured by this pledge, he grasped her hand in silence, and rose to leave the box. But ere he departed, she turned her head over her shoulder, and murmured behind her fan, "I believe it is all going to come right at last.—And, Gilbert," lowering her voice to a whisper, "I always suspected that it was *you*."

"What's the matter? What has become of Lisle?" inquired her husband, looking sharply round as he heard the door close. "Where is he? Why has he gone away?"

"He was not in the mood for light comedy, my dear. He has just heard something of far more powerful interest than 'The Silver Churn,'" nodding her head impressively. "You remember a bet you made about him and Helen Denis, one evening in the Andamans?"

"I don't remember any bet—but I know you had some impossible idea in your head."

"Then *I* recollect the wager—distinctly—a new bonnet. And my idea may seem impossible, but it is true. It was *not* that odious puppy, Apollo Quentin, who was in love with Helen, it was,—as I repeatedly told you,— Gilbert Lisle. So to-morrow, my good Charles, I shall go to Louise's and invest—at your expense—in the smartest bonnet in London."

CHAPTER XXX
FINNIGAN'S MARE

"I do not set my life at a pin's fee." —*Hamlet.*

Helen's preparations for departure were rapidly accomplished; she had no voluminous wardrobe to pack, no circle of farewell visits to pay. Moreover, she was possessed by a feverish desire to escape, as far as possible, from maddening pianos, piles of uncorrected exercise books, and the summons of the inexorable school bell. She set out for Crowmore on the appointed date, with a delightful sense of recovered freedom, but—as far as her unknown relatives were concerned—strictly moderate expectations. Precisely a week after she had received her uncle's invitation, behold her rumbling across dear, dirty Dublin, in a dilapidated four-wheeler, drawn by a lame horse—her tender heart would not suffer her to expostulate with the driver on their snail's pace, and as the result of her benevolence, she missed her train by five minutes, and had the satisfaction of spending a long morning, in contemplating the advertisements in the Broadstone terminus! At length, after four hours' leisurely travelling, she was deposited at a shed labelled "Bansha," the nearest station to Crowmore. Bag in hand, she stepped down on the platform and looked about her; she was apparently the only passenger for that part of the world, and there was no one to be seen, except a few countrymen lounging round the entrance—the invariable policeman, and one porter. She gazed about anxiously, as the train steamed slowly away, and discovered that she was the cynosure of every eye, save the porter's, and he was engrossed in spelling out the address on her trunk.

"You'll be for the Castle, miss?" he remarked at last, straightening his back as he spoke.

"No, for Crowmore, Mr. Sheridan's," she replied, walking out through the station-house over into the station entrance, in the vague hopes of finding some conveyance awaiting her, and her baggage—but all that met her anxious eyes was a little knot of countrymen, who were gossiping round a rough rider, on a heavy-looking brown colt.

"Shure, Mr. Sheridan's and the Castle is all wan, miss," said the porter, who accompanied her, carrying her bag. "The young ladies wor here this morning, in a machine from Terryscreen, they expected you on the twelve,—and when you were not on that, they made sure you were coming to-morrow—they'll be here thin."

This was but cold comfort to Helen. "How far is it to Crowmore?" she asked.

"Well, it's a matter of in or about six mile."

"And how am I to get there?"

"Faix, I don't rightly know! unless Larry Flood gives you a lift on the mail; ayther that, or you could get an asses' car up the street," indicating a double row of thatched cottages in the distance.

"And when do you think Larry Flood will be here?" inquired the young stranger—ignoring his other humiliating suggestion.

"Troth, an' it would be hard to say!—it entirely depends on the humour he's in—he calls for the letters," pointing to a bag in the doorway, "just as he takes the notion, sometimes he is here at five o'clock, and betimes I've known him call at one in the morning!"

A sudden interruption made him turn his head, and he added, with a triumphant slap of his corduroy leg, "Begorra, you are in luck, Miss,—for here he is now!"

As he spoke, a red outside car, drawn by a wild-looking chestnut, wearing a white canvas collar, and little or no harness, came tearing into the station, amidst a cloud of dust. The driver was a wiry little man, with twinkling eyes, that looked as if they were never closed, a protruding under-lip, and an extravagantly wide mouth. He was dressed in a good suit of dark tweed, and wore a green tie, and a white caubeen.

"What's this ye have with ye, the day, Larry?" demanded one of the idlers, as he narrowly examined the animal between the shafts. "May I never," he added, recoiling a step backwards, and speaking in an awe-struck tone; "if it isn't Finnigan's mare!"

"The divil a less!" rejoined Larry, complacently. "Finnigan could get no good of her, and the old brown was nearly bet up. I'll go bail she'll travel for *me*," he added, getting off the car as he spoke, and giving the collar a hitch.

But this proud boast was received in ominous silence, and all eyes were now riveted on Mr. Flood's recent purchase—a white-legged, malicious-looking, thorough-bred—that was seemingly not unknown to fame.

"Well," said a man in a blue-tail coat, after a significantly long pause; "it's not that she won't travel for ye, there's no fear of *that*, I hope you may get some good of her, for she's a great mare entirely—but she takes a power of humouring."

"Shure she knocked Finnigan's new spring car to smithereens ere last week," put in the rider of the coarse-looking brown colt, "not a bit of it was together, but the wheels, and left Finnigan himself for dead on the road. Humouring, how are ye?" he concluded, with a kind of scornful snort.

"You got her chape, I'll engage, Larry, me darlin'," remarked another of the idlers.

"Faix, and I paid enough for her," returned her owner stoutly. "It isent every wan that would sit over her! she does be a bit unaisy in herself betimes" (a delicate allusion to her well-known habits of kicking and bolting). "Howd-somever, she's a grand goer, and I bought her designedly on purpose for the post.—'Tis *she* can knock fire out of the road."

"Oh! them sprigs of shellelagh can all do that," acquiesced a bystander, who had hitherto observed a benevolent neutrality; "but they does be dangerous bastes."

"What's that you have there, Tom?" inquired Larry, looking at the rough rider.

"Oh! a terrible fine colt of Mr. Murphy's—I'm just handling him a bit, before the next cub-hunting."

"He is a great plan of a horse," said the man in the blue coat, speaking with an air of authority, and his hands tucked under his long swallow-tails.

"Look at the shoulder on him!" exclaimed a third connoisseur.

All this was by no means agreeable to Mr. Flood, considering the tepid praise bestowed on his own purchase.

"What do you think of her, Larry?" inquired the rider. "Come now, give us your opinion?" he added in a bantering tone.

"Well, I think," said Larry, gladly seizing this opportunity to pay off Tom, the horsebreaker, and eyeing the animal with an air of solemn scrutiny. "Well, now, I'll just tell ye exactly what I think—I thinks he looks *lonely*."

"Arrah, will ye spake English!" cried his rider indignantly; "shure, lonely has no meaning at all—nor no sinse."

"I just mane what I say—he has a lonely look," and with a perceptible pause, and a wink to the audience, he added, "for the want of a plough behind him!"

At this joke there was a roar of laughter from all, save Tom, the horse-trainer, who glared at Larry in a ferocious manner that was really fearful to witness, but Larry, nothing daunted, turned to the porter with an off-hand air, and said,—

"Anything for me, Pat?"

"Nothing at all—barrin' the mails—and this young lady! I'm after telling her, you'll lave her at the gate. She's going to the Castle, only"— approaching nearer, and whispering behind his hand, with a significant glance at Finnigan's mare.

"Oh, the sorra a fear!" rejoined Larry, loudly, and then addressing Helen, he said,—

"Up ye git, miss, and I'll rowl ye there as safe as if ye were in a sate in church."

It was all very well to say "Up ye git," but, in the first place, there was no step to the car, and in the second, it is by no means an easy feat, to climb on any vehicle when in motion, and Larry's rampant investment kept giving sudden bounds and playful little prancings, that showed her impatience to be once more on the road. However, by dint of being held forcibly down by the united strength of two men, she consented to give the lady passenger an opportunity of scrambling up on the jarvey, and Larry, having produced a horse-sheet (with a strong bouquet of the stable), wrapped it carefully about her knees—then mounting on the other side of the vehicle himself, he laid hold of the reins, and with a screech to his friends to "give her her head,"— they were off, as if starting for a flat race—accompanied by a shout of "Mind yourself, miss," from the friendly porter, and "Safe home, Larry," from the little knot of spectators, who were gathered round the station door.

At first, all the "So-hoing" and "Easy now, my girl," might just as well have been addressed to the hard flint road, along which they were rattling. The "girl" kept up what is known as "a strong canter" for the best part of a mile, and Helen's whole energies were devoted to clinging on with both hands, as the light post-car swung from side to side with alarming velocity.

"You need not be the laste taste unaisy, she's only a bit fresh in herself," said Larry, soothingly, "and after a while when she settles down, you'll be delighted with the way she takes hould of the road."

A very stiff hill moderated the pace, and Finnigan's mare, subsided perforce into a slashing trot, and "took hold of the road" as if she were in a passion with it, and would like to hammer it to pieces with her hoofs. And now at last Helen ventured to release one hand, and look about her; she was struck with the bright, rich verdure of the surrounding scenery—Ireland was well named "The Emerald Isle," she said to herself, as her eyes travelled over a wide expanse of grass, thick hedges powdered with hawthorn, and neighbouring green hills, seemingly patched with golden gorse. Very few houses were visible, no sign of towns or smoky chimneys were to be descried—this was the real unadulterated country, and she drew a long breath of satisfaction, due to a sense of refreshment, and relief. Now and then they passed a big empty place, with shuttered windows; now a prosperous-looking farm, with ricks and slated out-buildings, and now a roadside mud cabin. Finnigan's mare, dashing madly through poultry, pigs, goats, and such sleeping creatures as might be imprudently taking forty winks, in the middle of the little-used highway—which highway, with its overhanging ash-trees, tangled hedges, and wide grass borders, was the prettiest and greenest that Larry's passenger had ever beheld—this much she imparted to him, and he being ripe for conversation, immediately launched forth with the following extraordinary announcement:—

"Och, but if ye had seen these roads before they were made! 'tis then ye *might* be talkin'! There was no ways of getting about in ould times—no play for a free-going one like this," nodding exultingly at the chestnut, who was flying down hill at a pace that made the post-car literally bound off the ground. "She's going illigant now—these chestnuts does mostly be a bit 'hot'—but where would ye see a better traveller on all the walls of the worruld?"

"She is not quite trained, is she?"

"Well, not to say all *out*," he admitted reluctantly; "she's had the harness on her about a dozen times, and she never did no harm—beyond the day she ran away at Dan Clancy's funeral, and broke up a couple of cars; and 'twas Finnigan himself was in fault—he'd had a drop. Shure, she's going now like a ladies' pony! Maybe you'd like to take the reins in your hands yourself, miss, and just *feel* her mouth?"

But Helen, casting her eyes over the long, raking animal in front of her, and observing her starting eyes, quivering ears, and tightly tucked-in tail, had no difficulty in resisting Larry's alluring offer. Little did she know the vast honour she was rejecting. Larry (like most Irishmen) was not insensible to a pretty face, and rating this young lady's courage beyond its deserts— owing to her equanimity during their recent gallop, and the tenacity of her hold upon the jaunting car—paid her the greatest compliment in his power, when he offered her the office of Jehu. Helen having politely but firmly, declined the reins, breathed an inward wish that the animal who had behaved so mischievously at Dan Clancy's funeral, would continue her present sober frame of mind until she was deposited at the gates of Crowmore. And now Larry began to play the cicerone, and commenced to point out various objects of interest, with the end of his whip, and the zest of a native.

"That's Nancy's Cover," he said, indicating a patch of gorse. "There does be a brace of foxes in it every season—that ditch beyond,—running along in company with the cover, as far as your eye will carry you,—goes by the name of 'Gilbert's Gripe,' because it was there—a nephew of Mr. Redmond's I think he was, in the horse soldiers—pounded every other mother's son in the field! Be jabers, I never saw such a lep! and the harse— the very same breed of this mare here—he never laid an iron to it! That's Mr. Redmond's place, in the trees beyond, and beyant again is the Castle. What relation did ye say ye wor to Mr. Sheridan?"

Helen was not aware that she had mentioned Mr. Sheridan at all, but she replied,—

"His niece—his wife's niece."

"You never saw him, I'll go bail?"

"No, never; but why do you think so?"

"Troth, and 'tis easy known, if you *had*, you would not be wanting to see him twice."

Larry grinned from ear to ear, but Helen's heart sank like lead, at this depressing piece of intelligence.

"He is greatly failed since he buried the mistress," continued Mr. Flood. "He is a poor innocent creature now, and harmless; he does be always inventing weathercocks, and kites, and such-like trash, when he ought to be looking after the place. Miss Dido does that; oh, she's a clever wan. Just a raal trate of a young lady!"

"Do you mean that she manages the farm?"

"Troth, and who else? 'tisen't the poor simple ould gentleman—the Lord spare him what senses he *has*—for he would make a very ugly madman! Miss Dido minds the books, and the business, and the garden, and the money—not that there's much of that to trouble her—and Darby Chute, a man that lives at the 'Cross,' buys and sells a few little bastes for her, and sees to the turf-cutting and the grazing. The shootin's all let—a power of the land too. What the ould man does with the rent of it, bates all."

"I suppose Darby Chute is a faithful old family servant?" said Helen, her mind recurring to the ancient retainers of fiction.

"Bedad, he is *ould* enough! but I would not answer for more than that; he is Chute by name, and 'cute by nature, *I'm* thinking! Mr. Sheridan has a warm side to him, and laves him great freedom.—The ould steward that died a few years back, was a desperate loss. Now *he* was a really valuable man; 'tis since then they have Darby, who was only a ploughman before. I'm sorry for the two young ladies; they go about among the people, so humble and so nice, as if they had not a shilling in the world—and more betoken they haven't many.—I wish to the Lord they were married! but they are out of the way of providence here,—there's no quality at all, this side. They do say, young Barry Sheridan does be entirely taken up with Miss Kate; but he's the only wan that's in it, and no great shakes ayther; and in *my* opinion— —"

"Is there no one living over there?" interrupted his listener, averse to such disclosures, and pointing to a long line of woods on the horizon.

"Shure, didn't I tell you that it was all Mr. Redmond's, of Ballyredmond?—The old people does be there, and an English young lady betimes, she is mighty plain about the head. I never heard them put a name on her," then in quite an altered tone, he added, excitedly, "By the powers of Moll Kelly, but I see the Corelish post-car, there ahead of us in the straight bit of road. Do you notice him, miss? the weenchie little speck. I do mostly race him to the Cross of Cara Chapel, where our roads part, and I'm thinking I've the legs of him this time! Altho' he has the old piebald, and a big start; we will just slip down by the short cut through the bog, and nail him neatly at the corner!"

At first this announcement was Greek to his fare,—but she began to comprehend what he meant, as he turned sharply into a bye-way, or boreen, and started his only *too* willing steed at a brisk canter!

"There's Cara Chapel," he said, indicating a slated building on the edge of a vast expanse of bog. "You'll see how illegantly we will disappoint him; he is on the upper road, and that puts a good mile on him. It will be worth your while to watch his face, as we give him the go-by, and finds we have bested him after all!!! Do you get the smell of them hawthorns, miss? they are coming out beautiful," (as they careered along a narrow, grassy, boreen, between a forest of may-bushes, white with flower.) "And now here's the bog," he added, proudly, as the boreen suddenly turned into a cart track, running like a causeway through a wide extent of peat and heath, that lay far beneath on either side, without the smallest fence, or protection. It was an exceedingly awkward, dangerous-looking place, and they were entirely at the mercy of Finnigan's mare, who rattled joyously along, pricking her dainty ears to and fro, as if she was on the *qui vive* for the smallest excuse to shy, and bolt—and the pretext was not wanting! An idle jackass, in the bog below, suddenly lifted up his voice, and brayed a bray so startlingly near, and so piercingly shrill, that even Helen was appalled; how much more the sensitive creature between the shafts, who stopped for one second, thrust her head well down between her fore-legs, wrenched the reins out of Larry's hands,—and ran away!

"Begorra, we are in for it now," he shouted. "Hould on by your eyelashes, miss; we will just slip off quietly at the first corner. Kape yourself calm! Bad scram to you for a red-haired divil" (to the mare). "Bad luck to them for rotten ould reins," reins now represented by two strips of leather, trailing in the dust.

"Oh! murder, we are done!" he cried, as he beheld a heavily laden turf-cart, drawn up right across the track.

"Oh, holy Mary! she'll put us in the bog."

The owner of the turf-cart was toiling up the bank with a final creel on his back, when he beheld the runaways racing down upon his devoted horse and kish. His loud execrations were idle as the little evening breeze that was playing with the tops of the rushes and the gorse—Finnigan's mare was already into them! With a loud crash and a sound of splintering shafts a thousand sods of turf were sent flying in every direction. Helen was shot off the car and landed neatly and safely in a heap of bog-mould that luckily received her at the side of the road; Larry also made a swift involuntary descent, but in a twinkling had sprung to his feet and seized his horse's head, calling out to his companion as she picked herself up,—

"'Tis yourself that is the fine souple young lady, and not a hair the worse; nayther is the mare, barrin' a couple of small cuts, and one of the shafts is broke—faix, it *might* have been sarious!"

"Arrah, what sort of a driver are ye, at all?" shouted the owner of the turf-cart, breathless with rage, and haste. "Oh, 'tis Larry Flood—an' I might have known!"

"And what call have you to be taking up the whole road?" retorted Larry loudly. "The divil sweep you and your old turf kish, that was nearly being the death of us!"

"Ah! and sure wasen't she running away as hard as she could lay leg to groun'?"

"Well, and if she *was*; diden't she see you below in the bog, and take you for a scarecrow? and small blame. Here, don't be botherin' me, Tim Mooney, but lend a hand to rig up the machine, and the tackling."

Thanks to the turf-cutter's generous assistance, in a very short time Mr. Larry Flood was enabled to come forward and announce to his fare, who had dusted her dress from bog-mould and taken a seat on a piece of wood, that "he was ready, if *she* was."

The young lady accordingly rose, and followed him, and gravely inspected the turn-out. The car was all down on one side still—the result of a spring broken in the late collision—but the reins had been knotted together, and the shaft was tied up with a piece of twine.

"It will hould all right," said Larry, following her eyes. "Any way, it will carry *your* distance, I'll go bail."

"Thank you; but I'm not going to try the experiment. I'm stiff enough as it is; and one fall in the day is ample for the present."

"Fall! What fall? Sure ye only jumped off the car. Diden't I see you with me own two eyes? And 'tis yourself that has them nice and tight under yow! and in elegant proportion!—Meaning your ankles, Miss,—and no offence."

"All the same I shall walk, fall or no fall," returned his late passenger, with a scarlet face.

"You are a good mile off it yet," expostulated Larry. "How will you get there?"

"On foot."

"And your bag; is that going on foot as well?"

"Perhaps you would leave it as you pass?"

"Indeed, and I will! Of course you are only English, and what could ye *expect*; but at the first go off you were as stout as any lady that ever sat on a car."

"Stout?" she echoed in supreme amazement. But perhaps in Ireland things had different names.

"I mane stout-hearted! and now, after all, you are going to walk. To *walk*!" he reiterated with indescribable scorn.

"Yes, and you will take the bag—it has no neck to break."

"To be sure, I'll lave it with pleasure; but——" and here he paused rather significantly.

"Of course I'll pay you," she said, fumbling for her purse. "How much?"

"Oh, well, sure—nothing at all! I would not be charging the likes of you. 'Twas an honour to drive such a beautiful young lady."

"How much?" she repeated, with a little stamp of her foot.

"Well, thin, miss, since you are so *detarmined*, we won't quarrel over two half-crowns; and if you would like me to drink your health in the *best* that was going," rubbing his mouth expressively with the back of his hand, "we will say six shillings."

Helen immediately placed six shillings in his greedy palm.

"Thank you kindly, my lady! and may you live seven years longer than was intended for you. It's not *my* fault that I did not lave you at your journey's end, as Tim Moony will allow. There's the mare," waving his hand towards the wicked-looking chestnut; "there's the machine," indicating the battered car and twine-tied shaft; "and they are both altogether and entirely at your service."

Helen shook her head resolutely, and made no other reply.

"Well, then, miss, as I see I can't *tempt* ye, I suppose I may as well be going; and I'll lave the bag inside the lodge. Keep on straight after the Cross till you come to a pair of big gates—and there you are."

Having given these directions and ascended to the driving-seat, so as to have what he called "a better purchase on the baste," Larry muttered a parting benediction, lifted his caubeen, and drove furiously away.

CHAPTER XXXI
"CROWMORE CASTLE"

"We have seen better days."

Larry and Finnigan's mare were not long in dwindling into a little speck in the distance; and when they had completely vanished Helen set out to walk to Cara Cross, the goal of the post-car races. Once there she had no difficulty in discovering the road to the left; and a quarter of a mile brought two massive pillars into view, each surmounted by a battered, wingless griffin. But there were no gates—unless a stone wall and a gate were synonymous terms in Ireland. Three feet of solid masonry completely barred the former entrance, and said "no admittance" in the plainest language. Helen leant her elbows on the coping-stones and gazed in amazement at the scene before her. She saw a grassy track that had once been an avenue lined by a dense thicket of straggling, neglected shrubs. To her right and left stood the roofless shells of two gate lodges. On the step of one of them she descried her bag; and only for this undeniable clue she would certainly have walked on and sought the entrance to Crowmore elsewhere. Being (as Larry had not failed to remark) an active, "souple" young lady, she lost no time in getting over the wall and rejoining her property. As she picked it up, she cast a somewhat timid glance into the interior of the ruin and beheld a most dismal, melancholy-looking kitchen, with the remains of ashes on the hearth; the roof and rugged rafters partly open to the skies; hideous green stains disfiguring the walls, and the floor carpeted with nettles and dockleaves. A bat came flickering out of an inner chamber, which warned her that time was advancing and she was *not*. So she hurriedly turned about and pursued the grass-grown avenue, which presently became almost lost in the wide, surrounding pasture. At first it ascended a gentle incline, over which numbers of sheep were scattered; some, who were reposing in her very track, rose reluctantly, and stared stolidly as she approached. On the top of the hill she came upon a full view of the Castle, and was filled with a sense of injury and disappointment at having been deceived by such a high-sounding title. Certainly there *was* a kind of square, old keep, out of whose ivy-covered walls half-a-dozen large modern windows stared with unabashed effrontery. But a great, vulgar, yellow house, with long ears of chimneys, and a mean little porch, had evidently married the venerable pile, and impudently appropriated its name. "Yes," murmured Helen to herself, as she descended the hill, "uncle showed his sense in calling it simply 'Crowmore;' a far more suitable name, judging by the rookeries in the trees behind it and the flocks of crows—more crows—who are returning home."

An iron fence presently barred her further progress along the almost obliterated avenue, and, keeping by the railings, she arrived at a rusty gate leading into what might once have been a pleasure-ground,—but was now a wilderness. Traces of walks were still visible, and outlines of flower-beds could be distinguished—with a little assistance from one's imagination— flower-beds, in which roses, and fuchsias, and thistles, and ferns, were all alike strangled in the cruel bonds of "Robin round the hedge." She passed a tumble-down summer-house—a fitting pendant to the gate lodges—and some rustic seats, literally on their last legs. Everywhere she looked, neglect and decay stared her in the face.

As she pushed her way through a thicket of shrubs, that nearly choked a narrow foot-path, she observed a tall man, like a gamekeeper, approaching from the opposite direction. He wore a peaked cap, drawn far over his eyes, and a very long black beard, so that his face was almost entirely concealed; he was dressed in a shabby shooting-coat, and gaiters, and carried a bundle of netting on his back, and a stick in his hand. As he stood aside, so as to permit her to pass, she had a conviction—though she could not see his eyes—that he was scrutinizing her closely; nay, more, that he halted to look after her,—as she ceased to hear the onward tramp of his heavy, clumsy boots. Another two minutes brought her to a little wicket, which opened on a well-kept gravel drive, a complete contrast to the overgrown jungle which she had just quitted. There was no one to be seen, not even a dog, though a clean plate and a well-picked bone testified to a dog's recent dinner. The hall door stood wide open (Irish fashion), but no knocker was visible,— neither could she discover a bell. She waited on the steps for some minutes in great perplexity, and gazed into a large, cool, stone-paved hall, crossed here and there with paths of cocoa-nut matting, lined with strange ancient sporting prints, and apparently opening into half-a-dozen rooms. Not a sound was audible save the bleating of the sheep, the cawing of the rooks, and the loud ticking of a brazen-faced grandfather's clock, that immediately faced the stranger. Suddenly a fresh young voice came through an open door, so near that Helen gave a little nervous start; a fresh young voice with an undeniable Irish accent, and this was what it said,—

"Dido, Dido! do you want to *boil* the mignonette, and all the unfortunate flowers?"

Emboldened by this sound, the new arrival rapped loudly on the door with her knuckles, and the same melodious brogue called out,—

"If that's you, Judy, no eggs to-day!"

"'Deed then, Miss Katie," expostulated a somewhat aged and cracked organ, "I'm not so sure of *that*.—We are rather tight in eggs, and you were talking of a cake, when the young lady comes — —"

By this time the young lady had advanced to the threshold and looked in. She beheld a large, shabby dining-room, with three long windows, heavy old furniture, and faded hangings; a stout girl with fair curly hair, sitting with her back to the door, knitting a sock; her slender sister—presumably that Dido, who was working such destruction among the flowers—was stooping over a green stand covered with plants, which she was busily watering, with the contents of a small copper tea-urn; and a little trim old woman, in a large frilled cap, was in the act of removing the tea things. Helen's light footfall on the matting was inaudible, and she had ample time to contemplate the scene, ere the servant, who was just lifting the tray, laid it down and ejaculated,—

"The Lord presarve us!"

The girl with the tea-urn turned quickly round, and dropping her impromptu watering-pot, cried,—

"It's Helen, it must be cousin Helen!" running to her, and embracing her. "You are as welcome as the flowers in May. This is Katie,—I'm Dido.— We went to meet you in the morning by the twelve o'clock train; how in the world did you get here?"

All this poured out without stop, or comma, in a rich and rapid brogue.

"I missed the early train and came on by the next. I got a seat on the post-car, but the horse ran away and upset us, so I preferred to walk to the end of my journey. I told the man, Larry — —, Larry — —"

"Larry Flood, Miss," prompted the old woman eagerly. "A little ugly sleveen of a fellow—with a lip on him, would trip a goat!"

"Now, Biddy, how can you be so spiteful," remonstrated Katie, with a laugh, "and all just because he wants to marry Sally."

"That's the name—Larry Flood," continued Helen. "I told him I would walk, and he left my bag at the—the gate."

"Oh! so you came by the old avenue! and a nice way Larry treated you! Just wait till I see him," said Dido. "How long were you at the door, Helen?"

"About five minutes."

"And why on earth did you not come in?"

"I was looking for the bell or the knocker," she answered rather diffidently.

"And you might have been looking for a week, my dear! They are conspicuous by their absence. We don't stand on ceremony here; you either hammer with a stone—there is one left on the steps for that express purpose, only, of course, *you* never guessed its use—or you dispense with the stone, and walk in—the door stands open all day long,—precisely as you see it."

"But, of course, you shut it after dark?"

"Yes, in a fashion; we put a chair against it just to keep the sheep from coming in! The lock is broken—it was taken off weeks ago by Micky the smith, and he has never brought it back yet. Now, I see you are horrified, Helen!—but this is not London—there are no thieves or housebreakers about, and we are as safe as if we had twenty locks and bolts. Here, Biddy," to the old servant, "Miss Denis is starving; bring up the cold fowl, and some more of those hot cakes, as fast as ever you can. Helen, give me your hat and jacket, and sit down in this arm-chair this minute, and relate every one of your adventures without delay."

It was impossible to be shy with Dido and Katie; in a few moments their cousin felt perfectly at home, and they were all holding animated eager conversation, and talking together as if they had known each other for weeks. Katie was an incessant chatter-box; no matter who was speaking, her voice was sure to chime in also, and to keep up a running accompaniment similar to the variations on a popular air! She was fair, very plump, and rather pretty,—with the beauty of rosy cheeks, bright eyes, and curly locks. Dido, the eldest, was tall, and graceful, with a head and throat that would have served for a sculptor's model; she had quantities of brown hair, and greenish-grey eyes. Without being exactly handsome, she had a look of remarkable distinction, and as she stood at the table busily carving a fowl for the delectation of her hungry guest, that guest said to herself, that her cousin Dido, for all her threadbare dress and washed-out red cotton pinafore, aye, and her brogue,—had the air—of—yes—of a princess!

"When shall I see uncle?" inquired his niece, with dutiful politeness.

"Oh, the Padré never appears in the daytime," replied Katie, "and he only goes out with the owls; but he will come down and welcome you, of course. He is very much occupied just now,—and grudges every moment, his time is *so* precious."

A grunt of scornful dissent from the old woman here attracted Katie's notice, and once more resuming her knitting, and her chair, she said,—

"Well, what's the matter now, Biddy, eh? Tell me, what do you think of Miss Denis?" speaking precisely as if Miss Denis were a hundred miles away.

Biddy thus adjured, immediately laid down a plate, and resting her hands on her hips, surveyed the new-comer as coolly and deliberately as if she was a picture.

"Shure, I'm no great judge, Miss Katie! but since you ax me,—I'll just give ye me mind. I think she's a teetotally beautiful young lady,—and that it would be no harm if there was twins of her!"

Helen coloured and laughed, and Dido exclaimed, "Well, that's more than you ever said of *me*, Biddy, and I'm your own nurse-child that you reared ever since I was six months old—you never wished for twins of *me*!"

"Troth, and why would I? Many and many's the night that I lost me rest along of you. Aye, but you wor the peevish little scaltheen! Wan of *you* was plenty!"

"And you never called *me* a teetotally beautiful young lady! I'm offended."

"Arrah, Miss Dido, sure you would not be askin' me to parjure myself!" retorted Biddy, with some warmth. "Ye can see with your own two eyes, that your cousin is a sight better-looking than ayther of yees; but you are a lady all out! The Queen herself need not be ashamed to be seen walkin' with ye! Sure, and aren't you cliver! and isn't that enough for you? They don't go together, I'm thinking—great wit, and great looks!"

"Biddy MacGravy," replied Dido, with great solemnity, "you started off very nicely,—wishing Miss Helen was a twin—but now you have spoiled everything! I really think you had better go before you say something worse,—I really do."

"And sure, and what did I say but what was the pure truth?" folding her arms over her white apron, and evidently preparing to discuss the subject exhaustively.

"You have merely told her, that it was doubtful if she was a lady, and that it was very certain that she was a fool."

"Ah, now, Miss Dido!" in a tone of mournful reproach, "see, now, I declare to goodness—Whist! here's the masther." And seizing the tray, the nimble old woman vanished like a flash.

"She is quite one of the family," explained Dido, "and says just what she pleases. You would never imagine that she had been for years on the Continent! She acquired nothing there, but the art of making cakes and coffee——"

"And paying compliments," amended Katie, with a giggle.

At that moment the door opened slowly, and a tall, but bent, white-headed gentleman entered the room. He had a noble head, a cream-coloured beard, reaching almost to his waist, and sunken, dark eyes, that looked out on the world abstractedly, from beneath a penthouse of shaggy brows. His hands were long and thin, with singularly claw-like fingers, through which he had a habit of drawing the end of his beard, as he conversed. He was attired in an easy, grey dressing-gown, a black skull-cap, and red list slippers.

Helen rose as he approached and extended one of his long hands. His dreamy eyes flashed into momentary life, as he said, in a curiously slow, nasal voice,—

"And this is my English niece! Niece, I am glad to see you, for your own sake,—and for your father's.—He was a worthy brother to my wife. I hope you will be happy here. By-the-way, how did you come?"

Before Helen could open her lips, Katie, the irrepressible, had begun to relate her recent experiences, as volubly as if she herself had been a passenger by the Irish mail; not to mention the Terryscreen post-car!

But long ere her recital had come to an end, her parent's thoughts were miles away—presumably in the clouds. At length the sudden cessation of the narrative, recalled him to the present once more, and speaking very deliberately, he said, —

"You must take us as you find us, niece. We live far beyond any sordid, worldly circle, enjoying simple, domestic retirement, and a purely rural life. Our wealth is that of the mind. In mundane substance we are poor, but at any rate we can offer you *one* thing, without stint — accept a welcome." And with a wave of his hand, implying that he had endowed Helen with some priceless treasure, and a bow signifying that the interview was at an end, Mr. Sheridan glided noiselessly away, leaving, as was his invariable wont, the door wide open behind him.

CHAPTER XXXII
BARRY'S GUESS

"O many a shaft at random sent,

Finds mark the archer little meant." —*Scott.*

The following morning Helen was formally conducted round the premises by her cousins. They explored the tangled shrubbery, the garden, and the yard; the latter was empty—save for a clutch of chickens, and a flock of voracious ducks,—and at least half the offices were minus roofs and windows.

"The whole place was tumbling down," explained Dido; "and as the Padré could do nothing, Darby Chute said he might just as well make the best of a bad job, and he took off the doors and rafters for fire-wood."

"Yes, and Barry was *raging*," supplemented Katie. "Barry is papa's heir.—He is our cousin, and lives a mile away on the Terryscreen road. He says there won't be a stick or a stone left together before long. He often comes over here. He declares the place is going to rack and ruin."

Helen glanced at the range of yawning, roofless stables, and could not help sharing in Mr. Barry's rueful anticipations; and Katie, interpreting her glance, added hastily,—

"But papa will restore it all some day. He always says his brain is his Golconda, and he will be a Crœsus yet. He says——"

"This is the dairy," interrupted Dido, suddenly turning a big key. "Mind the step."

It struck Helen that she frequently broke in upon the current of her sister's narratives, especially when she was attempting to give detailed descriptions of the sayings and doings of their gifted parent.

"This is the dairy," she repeated, ushering them into a white-washed, red-tiled room, filled with big, brown pans of wrinkled cream, tubs of milk, and golden pats of butter.

"We have five fine cows," she said, twirling the key round her thumb. "We sell the milk about the place, and the butter in Terryscreen market; Sally MacGravy takes it in every Thursday. She is cook, laundress, and dairy-maid. The 'Master' churns. By-the-way, I wonder where he is?"

"Where he ought not to be, you may be perfectly certain," responded Katie. "Yes, I see him, he is over in the turf-house." And sure enough, just above the half-door of a great shed, the ill-tempered face of an old brown mule was visible.

"And that's the 'Master,'" exclaimed Helen, rather relieved in her own mind; for visions of her eccentric uncle wielding the churn-dash had somewhat disturbed her.

"Yes," said Dido. "We call him the 'Master' because the name suits him so beautifully. He goes and comes exactly as he pleases, opens doors and gates, and walks in and out at pleasure. He was here when we came, eight years ago, and is consequently the oldest inhabitant. Some people say he is forty years of age; but at any rate he is older than any of us! Now let us go to the garden."

The garden was of vast extent, surrounded by high grey walls, and wholly devoted to fruit and vegetables. Grass pathways, lined with currant and gooseberry bushes, divided it into immense plots of potatoes, peas, and cabbages. In some places, so dense was the jungle of unwieldy bushes that these walks were quite impassable.

"What quantities of fruit you will have!" remarked Helen, to whom this huge garden was a novel sight.

"Yes, there will be a fine crop of strawberries—at least I hope so, for nothing pays so well," rejoined the distinguished-looking, but practical Dido. "We make a good deal out of the fruit; and we work hard ourselves; not in fancy aprons and with little trowels, but in real sober earnest; we plant, and prune, and weed, and water; and on the whole the garden is a financial success. And 'All Right' helps us. That's him there in the next plot—the man without the hat. He minds the cows, and goes to the post, and makes himself useful. He is called 'All Right' just because he is *not* quite all there! Here he is now," as an individual with a spade over his shoulder, and minus hat and boots, came shuffling down a neighbouring walk.

Andy was a middle-aged man, who looked quite juvenile; partly on account of his very light and abundant hair, and almost white eyebrows, and partly because of a certain childish expression,—relieved by occasional flashes of very mature cunning.

"Well, Andy," said Dido pleasantly, "you have a fine day for the young plants; how are you getting on?"

"Oh, finely, Miss, finely."

"Here is our cousin.—Another young lady to help you in the garden, you see."

Andy, in answer to this introduction, half closed his eyes and scanned her critically. After a long pause he scornfully replied,—

"Faix I expect she'll only be good for weeding, Miss Dido! And see here, Miss Dido, not to be losing all our day.—Will ye just tell me what's to be done with them ash-leaved praties and the skerry-blues? for sorra a know I know!"

"I'll go this very instant, Andy. Katie, just show Helen round the garden; but keep clear of the bees whatever you do."

"I'll tell you all about Andy now," said Katie confidentially, taking her companion's arm as they walked away. "You see what he is like! He was never very strong in the head at the best of times; but a mistake that happened a good many years ago, quite settled him.—A mistake about a murder."

"A murder!" echoed Helen, looking with startled eyes at the slouching figure that was carrying off her graceful cousin.

"Yes. You must know," continued Katie, now dropping into a tone of glib narration, "that Crowmore belonged to papa's uncle, an old miser, who lived in Dublin and let the house, and garden, and a few acres, to a man of the name of Dillon. The rest of the land was managed by the old steward, who was a first-rate farmer, and as honest as the sun. But to return to Dillon. He had a good-for-nothing son, called John, who never did anything but loaf and poach. In those days Andy was a handy-man, or boy, about the yard, and he and this John were always quarrelling. One day John beat him cruelly, and Andy was heard to declare that he would certainly have his life! Anyway, a short time afterwards, Dillon was found shot dead up at the black gate, between this and Ballyredmond, and Andy was taken up and lodged in jail. However, he was soon discharged, as it was proved at the inquest that Dillon's gun must have gone off accidentally, though some people say it did *not* to this day.—But some people will say anything.—At any rate, the whole affair gave Andy such a terrible fright, that he has never been the same since."

"And how is he affected?"

"Chiefly by the sight of a policeman—a 'peeler,' as he calls him. At the first glimpse, he takes to his heels and runs for his life. He never ventures beyond the cross-roads, and would not go within a mile of the black gate, by day or night, for millions; indeed, *no* one goes round that way after sundown," she added impressively.

"And pray why not?"

"Because they say John Dillon walks."

"Walks?" echoed Helen, with a look of puzzled curiosity.

"*Haunts* it, then. Dozens have seen him leaning over the gate, just about dusk, and it is quite certain that he shoots the coverts as regularly as ever he did; I've often heard the shots myself."

"Poachers, my dear simple little Katie."

"Poachers, *real* poachers, would not venture on the Crowmore or Ballyredmond estates for all the game in Ireland! I'll tell you something more extraordinary. Dillon had a brace of splendid red setters. I remember them when we first came, very old, and nearly blind. They say for a fact, that when these dogs would be lying by the kitchen fire at night, they would suddenly hear Dillon's whistle, and jump up and rush to the door, and whine and scratch until they were let out; and then they would be away for hours, and come home all muddy, and tired, and draggled, as if they had been working hard. Several people have told me they have seen this themselves."

"No doubt they have. Some one imitated John's whistle; I could do it myself, if I heard it once. Some clever poacher was sharp enough to make use of the late Mr. Dillon's excellent sporting dogs."

"I never thought of that," said Katie reflectively. "But every one here believes in Dillon's ghost. Darby Chute would not go up the woods after dark for all you could offer him; *he* believes in him, so does Barry. Barry met him once in the dusk; he was carrying game, and he looked so desperately wicked, and shook his gun in such a threatening way, that Barry confesses that he turned, as he expresses it, and 'ran like a hare.'"

"And what is this sporting ghost like?"

"He is very tall, with a long black beard, leather gaiters, and a peaked cap pulled over his eyes."

"My dear Katie, he was the first person to welcome me yesterday! We met each other in the shrubbery, face to face."

"Oh, Helen, *no!*" gasped her cousin, suddenly stopping and releasing her arm. "Were you not frightened to death?"

"Not I! I felt no qualms, no cold thrills; I received no hint that I was in the presence of the supernatural.—He looked alive, and in the best of health."

"But he was *not,*" rejoined Katie in a quavering voice; "that was just John, the terror of the whole country. Oh, Helen, dear, I hope he has not come to you as a *warning,*" her voice now sinking to an awe-struck whisper.

"A fiddlestick! it was undoubtedly a human being going out to snare rabbits. There are no such things as ghosts; at any rate, if this was one, he smelt very strongly of bad tobacco! Come now, to change the subject, do tell me something more about your bold cousin Barry,—who runs like a hare?"

"Oh, Helen! please, now really, you must not laugh at Barry. He can't bear being chaffed," remonstrated Katie, in some dismay. "He is as brave as any one in reality."

"Oh, indeed! and what are his other virtues?"

"Perhaps you may think him coarse and countrified, and too fond of contradicting every word you say, and laying down the law; but he is a very good fellow in the main, if you take him the right way."

"And what is the right way? Please instruct me, in order that *I* may find him a very good fellow!"

"Well; pretend that you think he is conferring a great, great favour, and he will do anything for you. He can stand any amount of blarney, but no contradiction!"

"Strictly between ourselves, my little Katie, I don't think I shall like this cousin of yours."

"Exactly what he said of *you,*" she exclaimed, clapping her hands in great glee. "He declared you would be a stuck-up English girl, with a grand accent, and a great opinion of yourself. He said you were sure to have had your head turned by all the attention you had received in those islands."

"Well, if it was,—which I do not admit,—it has had ample time to go back again. Governesses are not often the spoiled darlings of society."

"But you are not a bit like a governess."

"Am I not? You should see me at Mrs. Kane's."

"Barry wondered very much that you came home unmarried," continued Katie, who knew not the meaning of the words reticence and discretion, and delighted in the sound of her own voice. "He said it was either of two things— —" pausing meditatively.

"Did he, really! How kind of him to give his mind to my humble affairs," exclaimed Helen, with an irony entirely lost upon her cousin, who was now fighting her way through a small forest of currant bushes, and discoursing as fluently as if she was sitting in an arm-chair.

"Yes; he said it was either of two things—Helen, mind your eyes with that branch! Either—I'll give you his own words—either you were mortal ugly, or you had had a love affair, and the pigs ran through it—meaning a disappointment, you know."

Helen winced as though she had been struck, and if her companion had happened to glance round, she would have been astonished at the colour of her face;—a sudden deep blush suffused it from chin to brow. She told herself passionately that dislike was far too weak a term to apply to this country clown, whose clumsy curiosity had probed her secret to the very core. This to herself; but aloud she merely said,—

"Your cousin Barry must be blessed with a rich imagination?"

"Oh, no! he is not a bit clever; but he is uncommonly sharp. He rather prides himself— —"

Whatever he prided himself upon was not to be disclosed at present, for a sudden turn brought them close to Dido, who called out,—

"I thought I saw your heads above that thicket! I have to go to the Cross, to speak to Darby: would you care to come, Helen? You may as well learn all the geography of the place at once."

To this suggestion she promptly assented, and in a few minutes was walking down the neatly-kept front avenue, whose gates opened on the Cross (or cross-road); the middle of which amply testified to the indefatigable dancing that took place on Sundays (for "Crowmore Cross" was what the assembly-rooms would be in some populous, fashionable neighbourhood). A dozen cottages were scattered about, and the windows of one of them exhibited two long clay pipes, some red and white candy, and a ball of worsted, and on the strength of this rich display was called "the shop." Dido halted at the door of a comfortable slated house, and called out over the half-door,—

"Is Darby within, Mrs. Chute?"

"No, me lady, he is not," replied a little, withered old woman, dropping a curtsey; then, as her eye fell upon Katie and Helen, she said, "An' this is your cousin from England? The Lord spare you your health, Miss."

"And how are you yourself, Mrs. Chute?" inquired Dido sympathetically.

"Oh, I got a very heavy turn that last time, me lady; but that stuff you sent me and the jam did me a power of good. I'm finely now."

"Well, I'm very glad to hear it. Tell Darby I want to see him this evening, please—it's about the pigs; you won't forget?" said Dido, turning her face homewards as she spoke.

"Isn't it a funny thing, that of all the years we have been here we have never been inside Chute's house!" exclaimed Katie. "Mrs. Chute comes and stands at the door, but she never asks us further. This in Ireland, where the first word is, 'Won't you walk in and take a sate?' is *odd*."

"Is that his wife?" inquired Helen.

"Oh, no; his mother. He was nearly being married once to the daughter of a well-to-do farmer, but they fell out about her dowry. They 'split,' as they call it, over a chest of drawers. I don't think he will ever marry now. Somehow the neighbours don't like him; they say he is very distant and dark in himself."

"I heard you were wanting me, Miss Dido," said a squeaky voice, which made them all turn round with quite a guilty start.

Standing on the grass behind them (why could he not walk on the road?) Helen beheld a tall, elderly man, with sharp features and a pair of keen, grey eyes, set close together in his head. He had a coat over his shoulder, a stick in his hand, and a most deceitful-looking lurcher at his heels.

"Yes, Darby, I left a message," replied Dido, quickly recovering herself. "It's only to ask you about selling the store pigs."

"Av they are fit,—and with all the feeding they are getting they bid to be as fat as snails—ye might sell them on the fifteenth; but mind you," shaking his head solemnly, "pigs is down—terribly down! And so this is your cousin, Miss Denis?" putting his finger to his hat.

"Yes; and you would never know she was any relation, would you?" said Katie. "Would you guess we were cousins?"

"'Deed I would *not*. And I never thought them English ladies were so handsome till now," he rejoined, resting his hands on the top of his stick, and speaking in a deliberate, confidential squeak. "I declare that wan up at Ballyredmond has a face that sour on her, she gives me the cramps every time I look at her; an' her walk!" raising his stick and his eyes simultaneously, "for all the world like a turkey among stubbles. Now, av I was asked——"

"Darby, what *do* you think? Only fancy! she met John Dillon face to face last evening!" interrupted Katie with extraordinary irrelevance.

A very curious look flashed into Darby's eyes. It came and went in the space of half a second, and he rejoined, in a peevish, argumentative tone,—

"And sure, and how would Miss Denis know him?"

"She describes him exactly; cap and all."

"Yes, but all the same, I'm positive that it was no *ghost*," supplemented Helen stoutly.

"Holy St. Patrick, do ye hear her!" ejaculated Darby, in a tone of pious horror. "Well, well, well; poor young lady; it's easy seen she is a stranger! Don't ye be for letting her out about the place alone after dark just now," he added in a sort of husky aside.

"It's rather early for him *yet*," grumbled Katie. "From August to February is his usual time."

"Yes, the shooting season!" rejoined Helen, with a merry laugh. "Nothing more is needed to persuade *me* that the notorious John is anything worse than a common poacher!"

"Have your own way,—have your own way, Miss," wheezed Darby, irritably. And it struck her that there was the *soupçon* of a threat in his narrow little eyes as he added,—

"Maybe you won't get off so *aisy* next time he meets you! If ye will be said and led by me, ye will not be going about alone afther dusk. And mind, if anything happens, and ye are found with the print of five black fingers on your neck"—spreading out his own horny digits by way of illustration—

"and stretched as dead as a doornail, don't go and say afterwards that ye waren't warned."

With this remarkable caution, Darby hitched his coat over his shoulder, nodded his head impressively, and then turning to Dido, said,—

"I'll be up about them pigs this evening, Miss; but you need not be laying out to get a heavy price for them! I'm for my dinner now," and with an abrupt nod, Mr. Chute plodded off.

"I'm sure you are shocked at his free-and-easy ways, Helen—at all their free-and-easy ways!" exclaimed Dido. "But they mean no incivility, and they take an interest in the——"

"Yes, Darby, I can see, is very anxious that I should not put myself in the way of being strangled by John Dillon. Really, it will be quite exciting to go out after dark."

"And the *only* excitement we can offer you. You have no idea what a quiet place you have come to," said Katie; "we have no society at all. Papa never returned people's visits, or answered their invitations. He never goes out, excepting about the place, in the dusk; he is entirely buried in his experiments. People have all sorts of ideas about us; they think that the Padré practises the black art, and that Dido and I keep pigs in the parlour, and a threshing-machine in the back hall!"

Helen laughed aloud at this description. If Crowmore was shabby, it was beautifully clean; and if her cousins occasionally used the first thing to hand instead of a regulation implement, the interior of the house was not merely neat, but tasteful.

"Of course, that's an exaggeration," said Dido. "But no one calls here, excepting the rector, Barry, and old Mr. Redmond. He comes from mere idle curiosity, to see if we are all alive and the house not burnt down—he *said* so! He and papa fought frantically about a Greek word the only time they ever met. We tried to cut him, he was so awfully rude to the Padré; but he would not see it, and he comes here, and sends us books, and baskets of hot-house fruit and flowers, and fish and game. We call it Mr. Redmond's out-door relief. He is a kind-hearted old man!"

"And does he live alone?"

"No, there is Miss Redmond, his sister, a cripple from rheumatism, and his ward, a horrid, supercilious creature; and in the shooting season, he always has a house full. He rents the shooting of Crowmore as well. Papa lets it—he lets everything."

Her cousin's eyes travelled reflectively along the extensive demesne wall, and she said,—

"Crowmore is a large estate, is it not?"

"Yes; but you need not run away with the notion that it is a fine property. We are as poor as rats. On the other hand, Mr. Redmond is as rich as a Jew."

"Dido, do tell me who is the unfortunate English girl who has such a painful effect on Mr. Chute," inquired Helen, as she and her relatives strolled up the avenue arm-in-arm.

"Oh, she is not nearly as bad as he makes out, though personally I do not like her," replied Dido frankly. "She is the girl we were speaking of just now; a Miss Calderwood—Kate Calderwood—a great heiress."

"Has she freckles and high shoulders?"—halting as she asked the question.

"How on earth did *you* know?" cried Dido in amazement. "Her shoulders are up to her ears, and she is as freckled as a turkey's egg! But for all that they say she is engaged to be married,—and to such a good-looking man, to Mr. Redmond's favourite nephew, Gilbert Lisle."

CHAPTER XXXIII
"THE FANCY"

"All impediments in fancy's course

Are motives of more fancy."

Judy the Fancy was one of the most prominent characters about Crowmore. She lived at the Cross, and haunted that well-beaten thoroughfare from early morn till dewy eve. Despite her name, "The Fancy" was certainly no beauty; she had a yellow, wrinkled face, a pair of greedy little black eyes, and features which bore a ludicrous resemblance to a turnip ghost. Although she went bare-footed, she wore good, warm clothes, and a respectable white cap; and no stranger could have guessed at her profession until she struck up her habitual whine of—"Give the poor ould woman the price of a cup of tay, your honour, the price of a cup of tay, and I'll pray for ye; andeed ye might do worse than have the prayers of the poor!"

Sitting basking at her post, she taxed all comers, and taxed them most successfully; for the little world of Crowmore were mortally afraid to draw down the "Fancy's" tongue, and she received propitiatory offerings of sods of turf, and "locks of male" from her own class, and numerous sixpences, and coppers, from well-to-do neighbours.

She was the mother of Andy All Right, and looked to the Castle with confidence for the supply of her wardrobe, and praties, and sweet milk. She would sorely vex the spirits of those who figuratively buttoned up their pockets, by loud, uncomplimentary remarks on their personal appearance, painful allusions to family secrets, and dismal prophetic warnings of their future downfall. Many a stout-hearted man would rather (if he had no small change), go a round of two miles, than run the gauntlet of the "Fancy's" corner.

She had also other means of levying tribute that rarely failed; not begging with gross directness, or angry importunity, as I regret to say was her occasional wont, but merely exclaiming aloud, as if talking to herself,—

"Musha! and it's Mrs. Megaw! and 'tis herself has the finest young family in the whole side of the country; faix, no one denies that, not wan; and signs on it, 'tis the mother they takes afther!"

Or to a victim of the sterner sex (who are equally vulnerable in such matters),—

"And so that's Tim Duffy!"—in a tone of intense surprise—"sure, an' I hardly know him. Troth, and it's a *trate* to sit here and see the likes of him going by. It's an officer in the army he should be, instead of trailing there, afther a cart of turf!"

These little speeches, had an excellent effect, and generally bore a rich harvest. She had also an unfailing method of raising a spirit of emulation among her benefactors. As for instance, having received, we will say sixpence, from some charitable hand, she would turn it over rather contemptuously in her palm, and exclaim, in a tone more of sorrow than of anger,—

"Well, I always thought ye were as free-handed as Mrs. Ryan; and *she* never asks me to look at less than a shilling! But maybe ye can't so well afford it, dear; and God bless ye all the same."

As Helen and her cousins returned from church on Sunday, they descried the "Fancy" sitting on the hall door-steps; a clean cap on her head, and a pipe in her mouth.

"Your servant, ladies," she said, without rising, and gazing over their heads in a rather abstracted (not to say embarrassing) fashion.

"Well, Judy, and what is it to-day?" inquired Dido.

"Oh, it's only Mr. Barry. He is inside"—with a wave of her pipe. "He is a Justice of the Pace now, and I want him to do a small turn for me. Just go in and don't trouble yourself about me, dearie."

"So Barry is here!" cried Katie, visibly delighted. "What brings him? Sunday is never his day?"

"No," admitted her sister, as she followed her into the hall; "but he has come to see Helen; and it gives him an excuse for his best clothes."

Two large pointers with swaggering bodies, animated tails, and muddy paws, now rushed out of the drawing-room to meet them; and in the drawing-room, extended full length on the sofa, in an easy, negligent attitude, they discovered the pointers' master. Turning his face towards the door, he said,—

"So you are back at last," then rising slowly, and putting his boots on the ground, he raised himself to his full height, shot his cuffs, and stared fixedly at Helen, and she at him (it must be confessed); he was far, far worse than she had expected. She beheld a middle-sized man, with bandy legs, a red face, and beaming countenance,—lit up by an inward sun of self-complacency—dressed in a short cutaway coat, a white waistcoat, and brilliant tie,—the sleeves of his coat and the legs of his trousers revealed an unusual margin of red wrist and grey stocking; but these discrepancies did not occasion the smallest embarrassment to their wearer.

"I hope you have been pretty comfortable, Barry?" inquired Dido, with a rueful glance at the tumbled cushions and antimacassars.

"No; that old bench of yours is as hard as a board! This is Miss Denis, isn't it? Miss Denis," laying his hand on his heart, and making a low bow, "your most humble."

Which salute the young lady acknowledged by sweeping him a somewhat disdainful curtsey.

"Many in church?"—now looking at Katie.

"Oh, the usual set, Reids and Redmonds. Mr. Redmond walked down the avenue with Helen. Helen, you have certainly made a conquest *there*."

"Of course she has," quoth Barry, seating himself; "it is not every day he sees a pretty girl in these parts." Thus administering a compliment to her, and a backhander to his cousins in the same breath.

"What was Miss Calderwood saying to you, Dido?" inquired Katie,— totally ignoring the foregoing agreeable speech!

"Oh, she talked of the weather, and about Helen. She wanted to know when she came, how long she was going to stay, and if it was true she was a governess?"

"Odious girl!" cried Katie, "she has a knack of asking nasty questions. I can't endure her—nor the glare of her cold grey eyes."

"Oh, she is not a bad sort of young woman," protested Barry, sticking his thumbs in the arm-holes of his waistcoat, and leaning back in his chair. "She and I get on first-class; but all the same, and quite between ourselves, girls, I would never think of marrying her!"

Helen stared in astonishment. Unquestionably here was a creature who pressingly invited the most inflexible snubbings! He on his part had been gazing at her with untrammelled amazement and admiration, and now that these feelings had slightly subsided, began to engage her in conversation.

"And how do you like this part of the world?"

"Very much indeed."

"Humph! I would not have thought you were so easily pleased; it will seem uncommonly dull after all your fine times in the East; there you had balls, and parties, and admirers by the score."

Helen drew up her neck, and looked dignified, and he said to himself, "Ha, ha, my fine madam, I'll have to take you down a peg, if that's your style."

"Had you a comfortable situation in London at that school?"

"Yes, thank you," she replied haughtily.

"Well, we shall not allow you to go back this long time! Dido, we must take Helen (could she believe her ears?) over to the band at Terryscreen next week. I'LL treat you all at the hotel. You don't mind me calling you Helen, do you? You know we are all cousins here!" concluded Barry, with a discriminating readiness to claim kinship with a pretty girl.

"Yes," he said to himself, "Katie and Dido were not bad in their way, but this new connection was really splendid!"

In his mind's eye he already saw himself proudly parading her at the band, and driving his intimates, and maybe the officers (who were *not* his intimates) simply mad with envy.

She was a little bit stiff now, but that would soon wear off.

"And how is the great inventor?" he inquired facetiously.

"As usual," responded Dido, "quite well and very busy."

"Is luncheon ready? for I'm as hungry as a hawk," he said. "I hope you have got something decent to-day. None of your bacon and eggs! Mind, Helen, you don't let them starve you, they are by no means liberal with their butcher's meat," and he laughed uproariously, and evidently considered that he had said something exquisitely witty.

"We always have meat on *Sundays*," said Dido sarcastically, as she led the way to an excellent repast in the dining-room.

When Barry had taken the edge off his appetite, which he compassed in a manner that excited Helen's disgust, he looked across at her, and said abruptly,—

"What's the name of those islands you were at?"

"The Andamans."

"You had fine times; twenty men to one girl, and no end of tennis and parties; it's the other way about here," grinning complacently, "twenty girls to one man, and no parties, balls, or fun of any kind."

"I was only at one dance all the time I was at Port Blair."

"Port Blair! *now* i have it!" suddenly laying down his knife and fork, and speaking in a loud, exultant tone, "I *thought* i had heard of the place somewhere. Girls, I'll tell you who was at those islands for months, old Redmond's nephew! I say, Helen, did you ever come across a fellow, of the name of Lisle?"

"Yes, I knew him," returning his gaze with calm, untroubled eyes.

"He was there for a long time. What was the attraction, eh?"

"How can I tell you? Sport, I believe."

"Oh!" with a palpable wink at Katie. "Sport! There are a good many different kinds of *sport*. And now tell me what you think of him."

"I'm not prepared with an opinion at such short notice."

"Which means that you don't like him! Neither do I. Come, that's one bond of union—give us your hand on it," jumping up and stretching an eager red member across the table,—where it remained alone, and unsought!

"I never said that I did not like Mr. Lisle," returned Helen, with freezing politeness.

"Oh!" drawing back, visibly affronted. "So that's the way with you, is it? Well, he is not a bad-looking chap, and you know he is a great catch! Plenty of *other* girls would give their ears to marry him."

"Pray explain yourself, Mr. Sheridan," said Helen, fiercely. "Do you mean me to understand that *I* would have given my ears to marry him?" Her eyes were flashing and her colour rising, and there was every indication of a domestic storm.

"Don't mind him! Don't mind him!" cried Katie, gallantly turning the tide of battle, "it's only his chaff; he *loves* to put people in a passion. Barry, you must really remember that Helen is not used to your jokes *yet*."

"Nor ever would be," thought that young lady, wrathfully.

"Oh, well, no offence, no offence; I did not know you were so *touchy* about him! He is a great favourite with the old boy—I mean his uncle,—but he is hardly ever here, always rambling about the world. I think myself, he is by no means the saint his fond relations imagine, and that he has a screw loose somewhere."

"And I'm sure he has not," rejoined Dido, hotly. "I like him, though I've only met him once or twice. He is a gentleman, which is more than I can say for other people in this part of the world. He is delightful to talk to, very good-looking, never gives himself airs, never brags——"

"One would think you were his hired trumpeter," interrupted Barry, angrily. "What do *you* know, a girl like *you*! Believe me, still waters run deep. Give me a jolly, above-board chap that will light a pipe, and mix a tumbler of whisky punch, and open his mind to you! None of your cool, deliberate fellows, who smoke cigarettes, drink claret, and look as if you have seven heads when you make a little joke."

"I wonder if he is coming for the shooting," said Katie, amiably anxious to smooth matters. "He is fond of it, I know."

"Yes, and a fair shot, but jealous, as I found the only day I was out with him; *twice* he took my bird."

"Perhaps because you missed it," retorted Dido, coolly. "Sometimes he comes for a month's hunting in winter,"—turning to Helen. "He's a splendid rider, the best in the county."

"Well, I don't know about that, Dido! Ahem! I don't wish to praise myself, but I'll be glad to hear of a more forward man with the Bag Fox pack, than Barry Sheridan, Esq., J.P. Why, the very last time I was out I jumped a gate—a five-barred gate!" addressing himself specially to Helen.

"Then if you did, Barry," said Dido, rising and pushing back her chair, "it must have been on the *ground*! You know very well that you can't ride a yard. Your shooting I don't deny; but when you boast of jumping five-barred gates, you know you are talking nonsense." So saying, she walked out of the room, followed by the two girls and Barry—who brought up the rear after a considerable interval, muttering wrathfully to himself.

As he passed into the hall, he came in full view of the "Fancy," seated on the steps. On beholding him, she called out in her most dulcet coaxing key,—

"Oh, my own darling young gentleman, you are a sight for sore eyes; your 'Fancy' has been waiting on you these two hours!"

"Then she *must* wait," he growled, nevertheless approaching, with his hands in his pockets and a rather important strut.

"Oh, then, I know ye don't mane *that*. An' sure now, Miss," appealing to Helen, and languishing at her with her head on one side, "and isn't he an ornament to any country?"

Helen became crimson with suppressed laughter, and was totally unable to utter any reply. However, her levity was not lost on Barry, who made a note of it against some future occasion, when she should be repaid in kind.

"Well, Judy, what is it?" impatiently.

"Only a whisper, darlin'. 'Tis just this," suddenly rising to her feet, "ever since I lost me health, come Christmas twenty years, and manny and manny a time before that, I washed for your mother——"

"Just cut all that part, will you?"

"Well thin, I'm here at the Cross, a poor, lone widder, that has buried all belonging to me but Andy, and living on the charity of the public, as ye know, this blessed nineteen years! And now, a thief of a black stranger from beyant Terryscreen, has come and set himself down alongside of me. A *blind* man itself—any way it's what he lets on—and every one knows I'm *not*; and they are all for giving to the poor dark creature. And sure, he has me ruined and destroyed entirely!" now raising her voice a full octave, and commencing to cry with alarming energy.

"You know if I did right I'd give you six weeks of Terryscreen jail for begging in the public highway," said Barry, magisterially.

"An' if ye did that same," drying her eyes, and stretching out her hands, "I take these beautiful angels as mee witnesses, I'd rather have six weeks from your honour, than six days from another; and that's as sure as I'm standing here!"

Barry was palpably flattered, and grinned, and looked at Helen out of the corner of his left eye to see if she was impressed, as much as to say, "What do you think of *that*?"—But, unfortunately, she was grinning also.

"Indeed, it's bitterly cold in winter," put in Dido, "and I'm not a bit sorry that some one has taken your corner. With Andy in constant work, and milk, and potatoes, and a pinch of tea from us, you know you will *never* miss it."

"Arrah, Miss Dido! sure ye don't know what you are talking about. And how would ye? If that rapscallion gets a footing in my holding, it's ruin and destruction that's in it; just that, and no more! Why," lowering her voice mysteriously, "sure it's as good as a *farm* to me, darlin'! Aye, and betther; it's all in-comings, and no stock, and no rint."

A Bird Of Passage | 277

This amazing confidence threw an entirely new light on the subject. Her three listeners stared at the old woman in respectful astonishment. They would have stared still more, could they have seen the comfortably-filled stocking that was hidden away under the thatch of Judy's cabin.

"Well, I can't stay here all day. I'll see what I can do for you," said Barry, abruptly. "I've important papers to sign at home, and I must be off."

The truth was, that the good gentleman was ruffled at Helen's attitude of repressed amusement, and at Dido's courageous candour; and he felt that he could not punish the offending couple more simply, or more effectually, than by removing himself, and leaving them to their own devices all through the long Sunday afternoon. He flattered himself that Miss Denis would *soon* learn his value.

Now Barry was the only eligible bachelor, in a neighbourhood where there were legions of girls,—and was fully sensible of his own importance. In his secret heart, he believed that he had only to ask any young woman within a radius of say twenty miles, and, in his own homely parlance, "she would be thankful to jump at him." And he felt conscious that he was dealing a cruel blow to the little circle at Crowmore when, seizing his hat and stick, and calling his dogs, he bade them a general farewell, and hurried down the steps.

His departure was the signal for the "Fancy" to take leave. Willy nilly, she escorted him to the gate,—to the intense delight of the spectators in the doorway. Vainly he tried to shake her off; vainly he increased his pace; his manœuvres were totally unavailing, his companion still trotted bare-footed beside him, gesticulating as she went with both head and hands. Her eloquence undoubtedly had its reward, for within a week "the dark man from beyond Terryscreen" had mysteriously disappeared, and she reigned in undisputed possession of her own warm corner.

CHAPTER XXXIV
"THE SLAVE OF BEAUTY"

"A 'strange coincidence,' to use a phrase

By which such things are settled now-a-days."

Byron.

"Here's the comrade of your glove, Miss Dido," said Biddy, descending into the hall, where the three girls, attired in their best summer dresses (being about to set forth for a tennis party at Ballyredmond), were impatiently awaiting her.

"Will I do?" inquired Dido, as she received her property. "Or is my hat too shabby? This is its third summer, you know!"

"An' deed, an' you'll do finely; 'tis only too grand you are! What call is there to be dressing just for the ould gentleman and Miss Calderwood, and maybe Misther Barry, that ye can see any day of the week without putting yourselves to any rounds at all?" demanded Biddy in an acrimonious key.

"Oh, but this is to be quite a grand affair," protested her younger nursling. "We have had three days' invitation. It's my opinion," glancing at her pretty cousin, "that this 'at home' is given for *you*, Helen. Mr. Redmond has been here twice this week; you have bewitched him."

"I would not put it past him! for nothing grows old with a man but his clothes," cried Biddy scornfully. "And shure he might give something dacent when he went about it; I've no opinion of these grass parties and chape entertainments. God be with the good ould times, when no one was axed to cross the door, under a dinner or a ball; indade, Redmond's own father used to give the height of high feedin' and kep' a butt of claret standing in the hall, just ready to your hand. But now, when you go out, no one even so much as axes, if you have a mouth on you?—for—by a drink of tay, that wake, that ye can see the bottom of the cup!"

Notwithstanding this gloomy sketch, the three young ladies (to whom this "chape entertainment" was a delightful novelty) were not the least disheartened, and set off to walk across the demesne in the highest possible spirits, leaving Biddy and her apple-cheeked niece filling up the doorway, and gazing after them with the affectionate complacency of people who were surveying a creditable personal possession.

"There's not their like in the county!" exclaimed Sally, as she folded her massive arms across her apron strings.

"No, nor in ten counties! and what's the good of it all; will ye tell me that?" inquired her aunt peevishly. "There's Miss Dido, with the walk of a duchess and the voice of a thrush, and Miss Helen, a real beauty, and Katie not too bad entirely,—and not a sign of any one, watching wan of them!"

"I think Misther Barry has an eye on Miss Denis," insinuated Sally timidly.

"Is it that spalpeen? An' much good may it do him! She would not look at the same side of the road as him," returned Biddy fiercely. "He would not dar' to ax her. Shure she's the only one of them all knows how to talk to him, and that quenches him rightly."

"That's true for you," assented Sally, nodding her head in grave acknowledgment of this indisputable fact.

"It's just killing me," continued the old woman, "to see them young ladies wasting their looks and their years here, slaving in the house, and garden, like blacks. What's to be the end of it, at all, at all?"

"The end will be that the masther will burn us all in our beds yet," replied Sally with angry promptitude. "What is he up to now?" glancing at one of the tower windows, out of which vast volumes of dense black smoke were curling in lazy clouds.

"Oh, the Lord only knows!" retorted her aunt impatiently, as she turned and walked into the hall with an unusually sour expression on her jovial old countenance.

"There's no daling with the likes of him," she muttered as she descended to the lower regions, "for he will nayther do wan thing, or the other; he won't go properly out of his mind, and he won't lave it alone; and he has me fairly bothered, and me heart is broke, with his mischeevous contrivances."

Meanwhile, the three girls walked over the hill, and passed through Dillon's gate into the precincts of Ballyredmond, a fine park of seemingly endless extent, through which a beautifully-kept avenue wound like a white ribbon, by clumps of beeches, rows of lime trees, and great solitary oaks. Nearer the house beds of brilliant flowers broke the monotony of the turf, and a long gravelled terrace was crowned by an ugly but dignified-looking mansion, that seemed an appropriate centre for the surrounding scene.

The Misses Sheridan and Miss Denis were the last arrivals, and were received by Miss Redmond in the pleasure-ground. They found her sitting under a tree in her bath chair, arrayed in her best white shawl and a picturesque garden bonnet. She was a pretty old lady, with white hair, an ivory skin, and soft, caressing manners, and she greeted the three chaperoneless (to coin a word) girls with evident pleasure. Not so Miss Calderwood, the deputy hostess; her welcome was by no means so gracious or so genial. She gave the two Sheridans a limp shake-hands, and bestowed a curt bow and a long stare upon their cousin, the governess (who was looking remarkably pretty and well-dressed in one of the costumes upon which Mrs. Creery had once fixed her elderly affections). Evidently she did not think that Miss Denis was entitled to participate in the advantages of her acquaintance and patronage. However, Mr. Redmond more than atoned for his ward's deficiencies. He led Helen to a seat, introduced her to several of the county people, fussed about her rather too assiduously with tea and cakes and other light refreshments, and finally took share of the same rustic bench, and engaged her entire attention.

Biddy's dismal forebodings had been brilliantly refuted. We notice the party from the Rectory (a considerable contingent), several remote families, half-a-dozen officers from a garrison town, and last, but by no means least, our friend Barry, standing beside Miss Calderwood, with his hands behind his back, and such an air of serious criticism in his port, that one would imagine he was in an African slave-market, and contemplated the purchase of one or two of Mr. Redmond's guests.

Mr. Redmond himself never left Helen's side, and coolly (and I consider selfishly) dismissed all overtures respecting a game of tennis, with a bland wave of his hand. His beautiful young *protégée*, the desired partner of several eligible tennis players, was simply not allowed to have a voice in the matter.

"We are very happy here! Just go away, my good fellow, and leave us alone," was his complacent reply to each eager suitor. "You and I," to Helen, "will do better than that! we will stroll round the grounds together by-and-by, when all these energetic idiots have settled down to what they consider the business of life."

It never seemed to occur to him that Helen would have preferred to join the said band of energetic idiots, or to have liked the company of a younger swain—and presently he marched her off—to make a grand tour of the greenhouses and gardens.

Although Mr. Redmond was a little, round, old gentleman, who had white eyebrows, and wore an ostentatious brown wig—his heart was as young, as susceptible, and as fickle as if he was three-and-twenty; he delighted in a pretty face, and especially in the company of a lovely, smiling girl, like his present companion, who, besides all her other charms, proved to be a most accomplished listener. As they walked, he talked, talked incessantly; indeed, the garrulous old personage became most gratuitously confidential about his property, his neighbours, and his nephew. "My nephew" was dragged headlong into every other sentence,—conversationally you came face to face with "my nephew" at each corner; his opinion was quoted on all conceivable subjects, from politics down to black currant jam. Another listener might have been a little bored, and even irritated, but the pretty tall girl in white listened with a greedy attention, of which she angrily told herself she ought to be heartily ashamed.—The world was but a small place after all! Here, in what her aunt Julia called the "wilds," she was strolling along, *tête-à-tête* with Gilbert Lisle's uncle, undoubtedly the very identical old gentleman whom he had mentioned as carrying on an ink feud with his father, but who was somewhat partial to *him*. Partial was no word for it! infatuation was nearer to the mark.

"I'm sure all those young fellows are mad with me for carrying you off," and he chuckled delightedly. "But, after all, it's no reason that because I'm an old fogey I'm not to have a pleasant afternoon, too, eh? From the time I could walk alone, I was always the slave of Beauty!" Here he doffed his hat, and made Helen a most courtly bow, at which she blushed and laughed.

"Yes, the slave of Beauty; all the same," resuming his hat with a flourish; "I never married, you see! The fact was, I butterflied about too long, and then it was winter before I knew where I was! We are not a marrying family; there's my sister and myself, and my nephew, I'm always preaching to him, but he laughs when I talk to him, and tells me to go and marry myself— impudent rascal, that's a nice way to speak to his uncle, eh? All the same, he is a fine fellow, as true as steel, and a more honourable, upright gentleman never drew breath; whoever gets him for a husband will be a lucky girl."

The corners of his companion's pretty lips curved somewhat scornfully, and she said to herself, "Shall I explode a social torpedo under this innocent old gentleman's feet, and say I know your illustrious nephew, he asked *me* to marry him, and instantly took ship and left me; although he swore that he would return, as surely as the sun rose in the heavens! Would it be agreeable to her companion to learn that his paragon's idea of honour was more elastic than he imagined?"

"Two or three times," continued Mr. Redmond, "I've tried to marry my nephew to some nice girl, and it has always been a dead failure, I've picked out a beauty, had her to stay, got up riding parties, driving parties, and even moonlight picnics (as if moonlight picnics were irresistible), and it was all no go. Just as I thought everything was arranged, he would slip through my fingers like a piece of soap!" (precisely Helen's own experience). "Well, now I want to ask your advice. What do you think of those two yew-trees?" he demanded with rather bewildering suddenness.

"I—candidly, I don't admire them; they remind one of a church-yard."

"Exactly, and as I don't want to be reminded of anything so deuced unpleasant: down they shall come! And, now, what's your opinion of these new flower-beds they have just cut out in this ribbon garden?"

"I think they are not sharp enough at the corners; they are too much the shape of biscuits,—the 'People's mixed.'"

"So they are! and shall we have them filled with pink verbenas, or crimson geraniums?"

"Crimson—that lovely new, deep shade."

"And crimson it shall be! Allow me to give you this rose!" suddenly plucking one as he spoke. "My dear Miss Denis, I see that our tastes are identical.—I only wish I was a young man for your sake."

His companion made no response, but on the whole she thought she preferred him as he was.

By this time they had encountered various other promenading couples, and in a shady walk they came face to face with Barry and Miss Calderwood, and the latter, instead of passing by on the other side, with her nose in the air, halted directly in front of Helen, and said most abruptly,—

"Miss Denis, Mr. Sheridan tells me that you were in the Andamans with Gilbert Lisle,—and knew him *intimately*!"

Helen coloured vividly, partly at this sudden accost and partly because of that sting in the tail of the sentence, that thrice underlined word "intimately;" and Mr. Redmond, wheeling swiftly round so as to face her, ejaculated, "God bless my soul! you don't tell me so."

A Bird Of Passage | 283

"Yes, I knew a Mr. Lisle in the Andamans," admitted Helen reluctantly.

"Only fancy! How immensely funny!" drawled Miss Calderwood.

To Helen there had been nothing specially amusing in the acquaintance, so she closed her lips firmly and held her peace.

"Why—why—I've been talking to you about him for the last hour, and you never told me this!" cried Mr. Redmond, eyeing her with an air of angry suspicion. "Eh, what?"

"You mentioned no name," faltered the young lady, feeling that verily this quibbling with the truth was as bad as any downright lie; but confronted by three curious faces, with the eyes of Barry—of Gilbert Lisle's uncle—and Gilbert Lisle's betrothed, fixed imperatively on hers—was she to appease their greedy curiosity and boldly confess the painful reason of her silence? was she to proclaim the humiliating fact that they were all staring at the girl who had been jilted by that honourable gentleman?

"Mentioned no name—neither I did! And how were you to know? Eh, what? Well, and what did you think of my nephew?" inquired the loquacious old relative.

At this point-blank query Miss Calderwood flashed a satirical look at Miss Denis, as much as to say, "What a silly unnecessary question!" But Helen met her eyes with proud steadiness.

"I think most people liked Mr. Lisle," she answered with well-assumed carelessness.

"And how long was he at the Andamans?" continued Mr. Redmond.

"About six months."

"Six months! And what was he doing there all that time? Any little entanglement—eh?" rather anxiously.

"I cannot tell you."

"Ah!—I see that you know more about Gilbert than you will admit!" exclaimed Miss Calderwood with a sharp accusing glance. "I believe girls in India are odious creatures. I have no doubt he got into some scrape out there." Helen blushed scarlet. "Yes," with an unpleasant little laugh, "your face tells tales. I suppose he was drawn into some silly flirtation— men *are* such fools! Well, it is very good of you to keep his secret; it's more than others would have done!" and with this insolent hint and a patronizing nod the heiress walked on.

Helen felt almost breathless with anger. "She had the passions of her kind;" her eyes sparkled, her nostrils quivered as she gazed after her receding rival. What had she done that she should be insulted and flouted by this supercilious heiress?

"Scrape!—stuff! Flirtation!—rubbish! It's all jealousy, every bit of it!" cried Mr. Redmond, as he removed his hat and cautiously passed his bandana across his forehead. "Gilbert is not a ladies' man—I only wish he was! And so you knew him very well? Eh, what?"

"As well as most people," turning away to break off a bit of syringa.

"Well, now let me hear all about him," very eagerly. "He hardly ever writes, and when he does there's nothing in his letters. Come, now, what did he do? How did he pass his time?"

"I really cannot tell you much—he lived a long way off on the mainland. I believe he spent his days in fishing and sailing. He liked the Andamans because they were a lazy, out-of-the-world region."

"I hope to goodness he liked them for nothing *else*. Eh, what? Six months' sailing and fishing was the deuce of a time, you know! You don't—just between you and me, you know—you don't think he had any *other* attraction? Eh, what—what?"

"Honestly, I don't believe he cared a straw for any one in the place," raising her eyes gravely to his, and speaking with unusual emphasis.

"Oh, well, I fancy *you* would be likely to know," rejoined the old gentleman innocently. "We must have some nice long talks about Gilbert; but just now I'm afraid we will have to go back to the tennis-ground; I want to have a chat with old Mrs. Morony. I need not tell you I'd much rather stay here walking about with you," he added gallantly. "But I must not be too selfish; and I'll give the young fellows a chance!"

So Helen was at last released from this purgatorial *tête-à-tête*, and permitted to join the rest of the company.

When she took leave of Miss Calderwood (which I must say she did very stiffly), she read more than a mere contemptuous dismissal in that lady's eyes; she saw suspicion, ay, and dislike, lurking in those shallow grey orbs; but Mr. Redmond wrung her hand affectionately at parting and said in his heartiest manner,—

"And to think of your knowing Gilbert! Eh, what? Well, I have dozens of questions to ask you about him; I shall be over to-morrow or next day."

"Poor Helen, I pitied you," said Katie as they walked home. "It was too bad of Mr. Redmond to carry you off."

"*Il faut souffrir pour être belle*," added Dido, with a laugh. "What a dose you must have had of 'my nephew!—my nephew'!"

As far as the Misses Sheridan were concerned "the chape entertainment" had been a prodigious success. They had enjoyed themselves immensely; had played tennis, sipped tea, and strolled about the grounds under military escort. Katie's tongue as she tripped along went like the clapper of the proverbial mill; but Helen was preoccupied and unusually silent. To return *viâ* dillon's Gate at the hour of seven p.m. was a feat quite beyond the Misses Sheridan's courage, and in spite of their cousin's protestations and remonstrances they insisted on going round by the road and entered Crowmore by the old avenue. As they turned a corner they noticed Sally's portly figure speeding towards the Castle with somewhat guilty haste, and a man approaching in their direction with his hands in his pockets and a straw in his mouth. To Helen's amazement it was Larry Flood.

"More power, ladies," was his brief but novel greeting.

"A fine evening, Larry," returned Dido. "So you have been walking with Sally?"

"'Tis only wance in a way, your ladyship."

"Is Biddy still against it?"

"She's that much again it, that if I wor to go next or near the house she'd just pick mee eyes out! Maybe you'll put in a word for me, Miss?"

"I don't see why Sally should not please herself. She's old enough."

"Well, for that matter we are both of us pretty long in the tooth! But I'll have her before the priest in spite of the old wan yet, though she *is* trying to draw down a match with Darby Chute!"

"Oh, *that* would never do!" exclaimed Helen with involuntary emphasis.

"I'm entirely of your opinion, Miss," said Larry, turning towards her. "I see you're none the worse for that little tip off the car! An' you are looking just as beautiful as a harvest moon!"

"And how is Finnigan's mare?" she inquired, not to be outdone in politeness.

"Oh, faix!" scratching his head, "shure she nearly drowned herself and me about a month ago. Coming out of Terryscreen fair and aisy, we met a band of music all of a sudden on the bridge, and without the least provocation she just turned about and leapt over the parapet, car and all!"

"And did YOU go over, Larry?" asked Helen with benevolent solicitude.

"Troth, and I did not. *I* stayed on land. We had terrible work to get her out, though she swam like an otter, and there was no great harm done, barrin' to the shafts again; but the mails was soaking wet—just in a sort of pulp; and the postmaster was raging and spoke very bitter. The end of it was I had to get shut of the mare! A horse on the road is well enough; but when they show a taste for the water it's a different kind of driving is required. So I sold her to a canal boatman—and maybe she's aisy now. She'll be hard set to run away with the boat! Well, she was a fine traveller!" he concluded regretfully.

"And what have you now?"

"Only the blind brown, till the fair of Banagher. He's a hape of work in him yet, and there's no fear of *him* shying. Well, Miss Dido, I'll not be detaining you. You'll mind and put in a word for me with the ould 'fostooke,'—I mane Biddy Macgravy. Tell her I'm a warm man, and an honest man, and a dacent man. Sure all the world knows that! She's taking her pigs to the wrong market," he added significantly, as he abruptly touched his caubeen, and departed.

"Modesty, thy name is Larry Flood!" ejaculated Helen. "Every one know's he's an honest man, and a dacent man!"

"Well, yes, he is in his way," acquiesced Dido, "but HE knows who is the heiress of these parts, and that Sally is a splendid dairy woman, and has a fortune of forty pounds! not to speak of a second-hand gold watch!"

CHAPTER XXXV
"THE APPARITION"

"And having once turned round, walks on,

And turns no more his head,

Because he knows a frightful fiend

Doth close behind him tread."

Ancient Mariner.

However highly Mr. Sheridan's intellectual faculties might be rated by foreign philosophers, and corresponding *savants*, yet, like the typical prophet, he had no honour in his own country, and was credited by the most lenient, with wanting at least one day in the week! Even Andy All Right (who was dimly conscious of his own deficiencies), had more than once been heard to draw comparisons between himself and his master, which were by no means to the latter's advantage.

Helen saw but little of her uncle; indeed, only on those rare occasions, when he joined his family at dinner, and during that meal, he rarely opened his lips, save for the purpose of swallowing food, his attention was wholly absorbed by some object not present, that monopolized all his thoughts. Now and then he would pause, lay down his knife and fork, lean back in his chair, and meditatively comb his beard with somewhat inky fingers, sometimes he would suddenly catch fire at a passing remark, and use it as a text for an unexpected and eloquent lecture on astronomy, biology, philosophy, or even hydrophobia; he had an excellent and intelligent listener in his niece, who followed him patiently through all the mazes of his varied subjects, anxiously endeavouring to glean information for the benefit of herself and her pupils; (and what she could not comprehend, from its being enclosed in a labyrinth of words, she modestly attributed to her own mental density). As Mr. Sheridan proceeded with his discourse, his voice gradually gained such force, his words came so rapidly and so opportunely, that he seemed to be completely transformed. As he warmed to his subject, he would start from his seat, his dark eyes flashing, his weird hands waving, he looked more like an impassioned Druid, invoking his countrymen to war, and human sacrifices, than a modern paterfamilias, presiding at a frugal domestic meal. Then, as suddenly as it had kindled, the fire would expire, he would pause abruptly, sigh, and presently push back his chair, and steal noiselessly from the room.

He lived altogether in the tower, behind barred and bolted doors, and through which Dido and Biddy had the sole *entrée*, and there,— secure against interruption, or indiscreet investigation,—he carried on some mysterious undertaking, to which he gave the rather vague name of "scientific research." But loud explosive sounds, odours (not of Araby), and dense volumes of smoke, were the only outward symptoms of his industry.

During all the summer months every one at Crowmore pursued the even tenour of their way, with uneventful regularity. Larry drove the red car, and made surreptitious love to Sally, the "Fancy" clamoured at the Cross, Darby continued to plunder his master, and that master remained shut up in his fastness, throwing away time, and money, with both hands.

Helen was an adaptable girl, and was now as much at home at the Castle, as if she had lived there for years: she had completely regained her health, and spirits, and was as full of life and energy as the indefatigable Dido. She toiled in the garden with unremitting industry, and took as profound an interest in the weekly "cart," and the result of Sally's "day," as did her cousins themselves. She had learnt how to make butter, to bandy blarney with her relatives, to baffle Barry's compliments, and, the greatest feat of all,—elude Mr. Redmond's cross-examinations.

By the middle of August, the bushes in the garden were bent down with fruit, and many and many an hour, the three girls spent picking strawberries, currants, and gooseberries for the public market, or for private sale. Time passed merrily enough in songs, stories, jokes, and riddles, but no story, song, or riddle, had half as much interest for the Misses Sheridan as their cousin's experiences at Port Blair! This topic afforded inexhaustible entertainment to these two county mice; over and over again Helen was called upon to recount her arrival, her first impressions, to describe boating, shelling, and picnic parties. Indeed, after a time Dido and Katie said they were perfectly familiar with the appearance of every one in the settlement, and declared that they almost felt as if they had been in the islands themselves! Strange to say, that in the midst of all her glowing descriptions of people and places, Helen never once let fall the name of *Lisle*. It was— had her simple cousins but known—like the play of "Hamlet," without the Prince of Denmark. She gave spirited representations of Mrs. Creery, and mimicked Lizzie Caggett's screech, and Apollo's languid drawl. She had an extraordinary faculty (I will not say talent) for such imitations, a faculty that had been inflexibly nipped in the bud at school, an accomplishment that she doubtless inherited from her versatile Greek mother. Who would have guessed that, at a moment's notice, pretty Miss Denis, could take off the voice, laugh, and demure manner of any specified acquaintance? She had never practised this art till now, when she discovered that a few such illustrations, brightened up her narrative, and threw her audience into ecstasies of delight.—Helen was undoubtedly an unusually clever girl, when she could thus infuse interest, amusement, life and romance into a story—and yet omit the hero!

One evening, after early tea, the three girls were busy in the garden, sitting on little three-legged stools, among a thicket of bushes, picking raspberries into a huge tin can, when Helen—whose thoughts were sharpened by her cousins' grinding poverty, their unremitting endeavours to make both ends meet, and their father's apathetic seclusion—said suddenly,—

"Don't think me a Paul Pry, Dido; but do tell me what uncle is doing.— Is he writing a book?"

"No; not now.—He *has* written several splendid pamphlets on gravitation, and about a dozen on wind; there are thousands of them upstairs; they did not sell; they were above the average intellect; indeed, I could not understand them myself. But then, I'm not clever!"

"Yes, you are, Dido," said her cousin decidedly. "You are a first-rate musician, a capital German scholar. I wish I had half your brains!"

"That is nonsense, my dear——"

"Papa has invented no end of wonderful things," interrupted Katie proudly.

Helen looked up expectantly, and Dido answered,—

"Yes; little machines for measuring and weighing air; but, unfortunately, his most remarkable contrivances have all been discovered before!"

"And what is he doing now?"

"He is constructing an apparatus that is to be the marvel of the age. It is to be an overwhelming success. A surprise to humanity; but I do not know what it is!"

"Can you not guess?"

Dido shook her head gravely, and Katie burst out, "Poor papa is out of his element here. When we were children—indeed, till Dido was sixteen— we lived in Germany, as you know, at a cheap little place, called Kraut, and the Padré had plenty of congenial society, and made many literary friends, who profess a great interest in his work still. He takes them into his confidence. They know all about it.—They often write to him——"

"To ask for money," appended Dido bitterly. "They are not real *savants* and inventors, and great literary lights, as papa fancies—at least, I don't think they are. Certainly, some of our neighbours at Kraut were clever, intellectual people, but others, whom papa picked up in the train, or in the gardens, or the street, it's my opinion they were all impostors. You remember the man from Baden, Katie; you remember the Pole; you remember the Italian who——"

"Don't talk of them!" cried her sister impatiently. "They were all swindlers and thieves!"

"And still papa has faith in strangers!" continued Dido. "A man has only to claim him as a brother inventor, and say he is short of funds, and were he making an instrument to bray like an ass, the Padré would send him a cheque for fifty pounds.—And yet he grudges himself a pair of slippers, and says he can't afford a door-knocker! I've no patience with these hateful foreign harpies!" she concluded, tossing a handful of fruit into the general receptacle, and rising as she spoke. "This can is nearly full," she added; "you two can finish it without me, and I must go in and weigh the strawberries." So saying, she tucked her stool under her arm, pushed her way through the bushes, and vanished.

"Dido is vexed," exclaimed her sister, looking straight at Helen; "and indeed it is trying sometimes, to think that while she works so hard to earn a few shillings, the Padré sends away hundreds of pounds to any person who chooses to write him flattering begging letters! And he spends a fortune on books—expensive scientific works. He orders whole boxes full; and when they come he never even opens them! There are a dozen great cases, all mouldering, out in the coach-house. When mamma was alive she kept some of the money; and she and the old steward managed pretty well. After they died there was no one—for of course the Padré could not have his mind disturbed about pigs and grazing stock. After a time he took a great fancy to Darby; and Darby and Dido do their best—and very bad it is! Barry wanted to manage the property, but papa was furious at the bare notion! I myself, think it would have been a good plan, but Dido set her face against it; and when she does that you may give up your point. You have no idea how poor we are, Helen."

Helen thought she had some glimmering idea—they could not be poorer than she was!!! her uncle having borrowed all her earnings, (with the exception of a few shillings), shortly after her arrival.

"What becomes of the rent?" she asked.

"Oh, I don't know! It's paid to papa."

"And the money for the grazing?"

"Is paid to him also," admitted Katie reluctantly.

"And what has uncle done with his time all these years?" she asked impatiently.

"Rome was not built in a day," rejoined Katie rather confusedly. "I believe he is making something marvellous, and that it is nearly completed. Of course we are pinched now, but we shall be rich some day. I don't grumble, neither does Dido; for we believe the Padré will be the great man of the age, and that in years to come, we shall be known as the daughters of the celebrated Malachi Sheridan!"

Helen noticed, (not for the first time) that Katie generally talked fluently of her father in her sister's absence; indeed Dido rarely alluded to him; on the contrary, she would turn the subject rather abruptly, when it touched upon him or his pursuits.

"Dido is not quite so sanguine as she used to be," said Katie, slowly filtering a handful of fruit through her fingers. "She has never been the same, since the Padré sent away Mr. Halliday,—her lover."

"Her lover! Dido's lover!" ejaculated Helen.

"Yes! don't say I told you, but she had one once. She did not meet him *here*, so you need not stare."

"Perhaps she may not like you to tell me any more—so please *don't*," entreated Helen, with extraordinary self-denial.

"Oh, it's no matter!—it's no secret, the Reids and every one know all about it. It happened two years ago. After papa's long illness—Dido was completely worn out with nursing him, and the doctor said she must have a change to the seaside—and as the Rectory people were going to Portrush she went with them, and was away for two months—it was there she met him. He had some appointment in India, and was only on six months' leave.

She came home looking quite beautiful—even Barry remarked it—and she was engaged to Mr. Halliday—providing papa made no objection. He wrote to the Padré, a very nice letter I believe, and what do you think the Padré did? he tore it up into little bits, enclosed it in an envelope, and sent it back by the next post!"

"Oh!" groaned Helen, "how frightful! and was Mr. Halliday nice?"

"*Very* nice.—Of course I don't go by Dido,—but the Reids were enchanted with him. He came here, nothing daunted, and insisted on papa giving him an audience. I was out—just my luck—but Biddy told me they were shut up in the drawing-room for an hour, and that she heard the Padré roaring and raving like all the bulls of Bashan. At last Mr. Halliday came out, looking very white and queer; he had a long interview with Dido,—and then he went away. Poor Dido, how she used to cry at night! She told me that Mr. Halliday wanted her to marry him right off, without papa's consent; as there was nothing against him, and he was ready to take her out to India then and there and give her a happy home, and she said she would have gone—only for one reason——"

"And what was that?"

"I've been trying to find out for two years, and never discovered it yet."

"I wonder what it could have been?" said Helen, musingly—"want of money?"

"No! I'm sure it was not that, Mr. Halliday is rich. I've tried to guess it, and I've given it up at last as a bad job."

"And so," said Helen to herself, "her merry, lively cousin Dido—whose wit and spirits rarely failed her—had had what Katie would call 'a disappointment,' too!"

"This can is quite full, so come along," said that young lady, rising with joyous activity. "Thank goodness, these are the last of these odious raspberries for this year."

The two girls had locked the garden gate, and were crossing the yard, carrying the can of fruit between them, when they were nearly knocked down, by Sally and Andy, who came running frantically in an opposite direction, and without the smallest apology dashed through the back door, which they slammed loudly after them. Prompted by very excusable curiosity, the spectators followed by the same entrance, and discovered Andy in the middle of the kitchen, looking as if his wits had entirely departed, and Sally wiping the perspiration from her face with the corner of her apron, and loudly expounding some terrible experience to Dido and her aunt.

"Oh, save us and send us, Miss Katie!" she exclaimed as she entered, "I'm after seeing the frightfullest thing that walks above ground! It was ayther an evil sperrit or the ould wan himself! Oh, musha, musha, I never get such a turn in mee life! Oh, Andy, darlin', what did we ever do to bring such a thing about us?"

But Andy was utterly incapable of making any reply, and stood trembling, and open-mouthed, in the middle of the floor.

"But what *was* it?" demanded Helen, approaching the table and laying down the can.

"Well then, miss, I'll just describe it, and I'll lave it to yourself to put a name on it. Andy and me was down at the far croft, looking at a sick cow, and were coming home, thinking of nothing in the world, when all at wanst, I saw within two perch of me, what I thought was a tree walkin'. I nudged Andy, and we both looked, and sure enough, there it was, as plain as plain, with big wings reaching down each side, and a long tail trailing after it;" here she was so overcome by the bare recollection, that she was obliged to stop and gasp for breath, and once more apply her apron to her countenance.

"Well, miss, it went by quietly, within about the length of this kitchen of us,—and never passed no remark, so we just took to our heels, and ran for the dear life, and small blame to us. And now, Miss Dido, av I was to be hung in diamonds, I will never set foot outside the yard after dark!" she concluded with a whimper.

"Sally, I wonder at you!" exclaimed Helen, "*I'll* put a name to it, fast enough—it was the mule you saw! In the dark he looked larger than usual, his ears were the wings—they are big enough for anything—his tail—was just his tail!"

"Ah now, Miss Helen, get out with your jokes! Is it the mule I'm driving these eight year, and me not know him? Any way, I saw him in the harness room as I went out—it was never the mule, it was ayther Dillon in another form—or——" here she paused significantly, and left her listeners to complete the sentence for themselves.

The next evening, Helen was sitting out under a hay-cock, after tea, reading a venerable magazine. She had had a very fatiguing day, and overcome by the sultry, drowsy air, she fell fast asleep.—After a pleasant little doze, she awoke with a guilty start, and discovered that the stars were out, and the midges had gone in, that the air had become chill,—and that she had been asleep. Somewhat ashamed of herself, she rose, picked up her book, replaced her hat, and was turning towards the house, when a curious trailing, whirring noise on the grass, arrested her attention. Glancing behind her, she beheld what seemed to be a colossal, winged figure, pacing the sward within ten yards of her recent nest. A figure somewhat resembling old Father Time, with pinions which rose and fell, expanded, or collapsed at will. She stood and stared, in blank bewilderment. The creature, like a gorged vulture, appeared to be making futile efforts to rise from the ground and fly! but, in spite of its exertions, and violent, almost passionate flapping of its wings, it still remained a prisoner to mother earth. *What* was it? Was it as Sally had suggested? Her heart stood still, for she now beheld it moving towards her! she felt her knees giving way beneath her,—her hair rising on her forehead; she leant against the hay-cock for support, and tightly closed her eyes. Hearing no sound for the space of a minute, she ventured to open them once more, and it was nowhere to be seen. Seizing this opportunity, she flew across the lawn, and darted into the candle-lit, ever-open hall, from thence into the dining room, where she sank into the nearest chair, gasping for breath. She had barely recovered the power of speech, and was about to explain her condition to her astonished cousins, when the door opened gently, and her uncle came into the room; he stood near the table, and looking at her fixedly with his coal-black eyes, said, in his usual slow way,—

"I'm afraid I alarmed you somewhat, niece—you saw me just now trying the apparatus."

Helen gazed at him blankly, unable to utter a word.

"You look quite foolishly startled; but come with me, and you shall be completely reassured. Dido and Katie," addressing his daughters, "rise and follow me, my children, and behold with your own eyes the fruit of my labours!"

CHAPTER XXXVI
"THE APPARATUS"

"The flighty purpose never is o'ertook."

Macbeth.

The three girls lost no time in responding to this invitation; they crossed the hall, passed through the door connecting it with the Castle, and ascended a rugged, spiral stone staircase in the wake of Mr. Sheridan, who preceded them at a swift pace,—carrying a light in his hand. Halting on the first landing, he threw open a door, and said to his niece,—

"This is my library. Here I think, calculate, and write. This room has been the birth-place of many a glorious inspiration."

By the glimmer of one candle, Helen made out a large apartment that seemed to contain nothing but books. They lined the walls, loaded the tables, and covered the floor. Here and there they stood in untidy stacks, as if cart-loads of volumes had been shot about the room at random. The books were doubtless ancient, for a disagreeable odour of fusty paper and mouldy leather, impregnated the atmosphere, and Helen was glad to withdraw to the chill but less oppressive staircase, when her uncle, with a dangerous wave of his composite, said,—

"Now let us ascend to the '*Locus in quo*'—in short, to the laboratory."

When they reached their destination they found the same wild disorder reigned there as they had just witnessed below. A forge and bellows, a carpenter's bench and tools, a lathe, quantities of peculiar-looking bottles,— presumably containing chemicals; a furnace, steel tools, newspapers, lumps of coal, bits of whalebone, and the remains of Mr. Sheridan's dinner on a tray were all mixed up together in extraordinary confusion. In the middle of the room stood a large table, on which lay a mysterious object, concealed by a red cover. It was something long, something broad; but all further speculation was ended by Mr. Sheridan delicately raising the cloth, and solemnly displaying what looked like a pair of umbrellas blown inside out!

"I suppose you know nothing of aerostation?" he said gravely, addressing his niece.

She shook her head; shameful to state, the very name was new to her.

"It is the art—as yet in its infancy—of travelling through the air; an art that has ever baffled mankind. In me,"—pointing to his beard with a long forefinger,—"you see the fortunate inventor of a pair of wings, by means of which I hope shortly to make the first aerial voyage—and fly to Dublin."

To an ordinary listener, this announcement would have seemed the mere raving of a Bedlamite; but the three girls were profoundly impressed by the inventor's voice, and presence, and enthusiastic belief in himself, and they hung upon his words, with parted lips, and awe-struck eyes.

"It is quite true," he resumed, "that Borelli and Liebnitz, both denied the possibility of any man's flying. But Bacon and Wilkin, thought as *I* do," he added with a nod that implied,—"and so much the better for *them!*"

"Observe this," now tenderly holding up a wing. (It was of immense length, and seemed surprisingly light and flexible.) "Here it is annexed to the shoulders, by means of mechanical contrivances; these springs, and a certain amount of muscular exertion, waft a human body into the elements! *Once* fairly afloat, a very slight effort, similar to a bird's, will keep one going for hours! The first ascent is the principal,—and indeed, I may say,—only difficulty. Fairly poised in the air, the process is ludicrously simple. The main idea is, to attach to one's person some mass, which, by being lighter than air, raises itself, and the annexed incumbrance. But these details are rather beyond your mental grasp. To be brief, this little contrivance of mine blows into atoms all other modes of human locomotion—trains, steamers, carriages, bicycles,—their fate is sealed. We shall all be as the birds of the air in future. The boon to humanity will be incalculable; and, believe me, the day predicted by good Bishop Wilkin is not far distant, when every man who is going a journey, will call for his *wings*, just as he now calls for his boots!"

"I hope you will make us each a pair, papa," said Katie, "whenever your own are finished."

To this request her parent vouchsafed no notice, but continued to expound with increased animation with one hand, as he held up a pinion in the other.

"Roger Bacon, the greatest genius the world has seen since Archimedes, was confident that it was possible to make instruments for flying, and that a man with wings, sitting in the middle thereof and steering with a rudder, may pass through the air. I quote from his *Opus Magnus*, which he wrote in the form of a letter, to that enlightened prelate, Pope Clement the Fourth!"

If anything had been needed to convince Helen and her cousins of the practicability of the matter in question, the mention of Roger Bacon was sufficient; and Mr. Sheridan, noting the expression of reverent attention on their faces, was kindled to still greater enthusiasm.

"Bacon was a marvellous man! it is true that he indulged in chimerical notions with regard to prolonging life, and placed some confidence in astrology, yet the imputation on his character, of a leaning to magic was totally unfounded. He studied languages, logic, and mathematics; his information was exhaustive, his premises sound, as in the case in point," waving his hand dramatically towards the table. "And now, my children, I will attach these wings to my shoulders, in order that you may be convinced of their extraordinary value, and of the amazing dignity which they impart to the human body! Dido, light another candle. No,—no assistance is required,—I can adjust them myself."

Helen and her cousins, looked on with breathless interest, whilst Mr. Sheridan deftly arranged and strapped on the apparatus. Then he held himself erect before them, and commenced to pace up and down a cleared space at the end of the room, and as he paced to and fro, he continued to expound as volubly as ever, on the importance of his prodigious discovery.

If any cool-headed, matter-of-fact persons had happened to climb the ivy, and look in through the shutterless window, and "discovered" the room dimly lit by two candles (placed on the ground), the gray-robed figure with trailing wings, lecturing with outstretched hands to a group of eager-eyed girls,—they would have unhesitatingly declared, that they were witnessing the exploits of the inmates of some private lunatic asylum.

"My dear children," continued Malachi in an impressive tone, "in me you see, the instrument of introducing a discovery that will be of untold benefit to all mankind—wherever the wind blows, it will carry the name of Malachi Sheridan. Of course aerostation is as yet in its infancy," tenderly stroking one of his pinions as he spoke, "but everything must have a beginning. Look at railways; they had *their* origin in an ordinary domestic kettle, and behold they now cover the face of the globe; this invention has to do with air, and like that element, is—sublime! I have made an exhaustive study of air currents; there are certain places where there is a continual brisk movement in various directions! these will be the termini, the junctions of departure, the same as Waterloo or Euston—but again let me not take you out of your intellectual depth.—See how easily the apparatus works," he exclaimed, pulling a small cord; and it became evident, that he could extend or compress, his huge appendages at will. Now they towered above his head—now they spread out—and now they collapsed, with marvellous facility.

"Night is the only time, in which I can as yet venture abroad," he said regretfully, "and there is something unsympathetic in the chill atmosphere after dusk, that is discouraging to aerial attempts. Would that I could go forth in full daylight, and spread out my pinions to the sun!"

"If you came into the garden, when Andy was at his dinner, you might manage it easily, papa.—We will keep guard at the gate," said Katie, the ever practical.

"I'll—see—about it—yes, yes, it may be done! And you, Dido, my daughter, shall now have your heart's desire. These will bring you riches— money—money in millions. Do not deny, Dido, that money is your idol; you worship money," he added, gazing at her austerely.

"I, papa!" she cried. "Oh, no!"

"Then why do you annoy me with your prayers and tears, craving money, money, money? What is money? A few miserable pounds of yellow ore; and they tell me that it makes a man happy! Miserable, miserable, wretch!" he exclaimed with angry scorn.

"But, indeed, papa——"

"There, that is sufficient!" he shouted, with a fiery flash of his black eyes.

"Niece Helen," turning to her, after a somewhat awkward interval, and surveying her critically, "you will doubtless make a graceful aerial figure. Let me assure you that a happy day is coming, when you may wing your way back to tropical lands, and migrate at pleasure, like the swallows, and the wild geese."

Here he paused, and flapped his pinions so successfully, that both candles were instantly extinguished, and the company were left in outer darkness. Dead silence ensued, which lasted about a minute.

"Dido, you know your way," said her father at length in his ordinary tone, "never mind the lights, the matches are below.—Go; I will no longer detain you, my children. I have some important details to accomplish that will occupy me for hours. Go—good-night, good-night."

Thus imperiously dismissed by this voice from the gloom, the three girls groped their way slowly, and carefully, downstairs, and finally into the hall, where, sitting down on the first seats they could find, they sat and stared at one another, in solemn silence. Of course Katie was the first to speak.

"I wonder if this will come to anything?" she exclaimed. "It's very wonderful,—but then the Padré always thinks of things that never occur to other people!"

"It does seem to be a marvellous discovery," said Dido, in anything but a triumphant key. Was it the light, or what, that made her face look quite anxious and careworn? "Of course we won't mention what we have seen to a soul! eh, Helen?" glancing nervously at her cousin.

Helen nodded her head in impressive assent, but made no audible answer. Down among commonplace surroundings, and away from the spell of that imposing winged figure, with its sonorous quotations from Bacon and Wilkin—cold distrust came whispering into her ear. Could it be possible that she had discerned the mysterious reason, that held Dido to her duty? Could it be possible, that her uncle Malachi was *mad*?

CHAPTER XXXVII
"IN CONFIDENCE"

"No hinge, nor loop,

To hang a doubt on."

Othello.

This is Dido Sheridan's birthday.—She is twenty-four years old to-day. Her cousin Helen's offering is to take the shape of this hat, which she is engaged in trimming with somewhat anxious feelings. This straw hat, a bunch of daisies, and a few yards of cream-coloured lace, have swallowed up her very *last* shilling, and there she sits, pinning, and twisting, and unpinning and untwisting, in the greatest perplexity. Her thoughts are running upon charming constructions, that she had seen in milliners' windows in Bond Street, that looked so simple and yet were so effective (and so expensive). How were they put together? Certainly *not* by amateur fingers, my dear young lady! After a long struggle, sheer perseverance was rewarded by a result that would pass admirably in Terryscreen, if not in Tyburnia. "Yes, it really looks very nice," she said to herself aloud as she held it up critically. Then, of course, she went over to the glass and tried it on! The next thing was to see how it suited Dido? so she walked to the door, and called "Dido" in her clearest treble.

"She's out in the garden, miss," returned a voice from the dining-room, "with a parcel of hucksters from Terryscreen; they are after the apples and onions."

Helen reached her hat from its peg, and ran down the steps, and in another moment was at the garden gate. There, in the middle walk, beside the sun-dial, stood Dido, rake in hand, sun-bonnet on head, solemnly bargaining with two weather-beaten women, whilst Darby Chute sat on the side of a wheel-barrow, and listened, and looked on, with a cunning and diverted countenance. Properly speaking, this selling of fruit and vegetables "all standing" was Andy's legitimate business; but, unfortunately, Andy was not to be trusted with finance! He had been known to ask half-a-crown for a head of cabbage, and to sell a whole plot of cauliflowers for three half-pence!

"You are very stiff to-day, Miss Dido," expostulated one of her customers. "Shure, I bought all Mr. Reid's apples at a shillin' a hundred, and you are talking of two! I wish I was sellin' to you."

"*Our* apples are the best in the country, Mrs. Carmody. You get a penny a piece for them, I know, and I cannot let you have them for less than what I say."

"Here's your cousin Helen a-coming," wheezed Darby. "Sure she thinks she's sharper than the whole houseful put together. Maybe she'll drive a bargain for ye, Miss Dido! Avick!"

"Oh, indeed, the less *you* say about bargains, Darby, the better," retorted Helen severely. "I wonder you were not ashamed to bring home such a price for those calves!"

"Shure, I can't help the prices, miss; calves is down—all stock is down, and what does a beautiful young English lady like you know about farming?"

"Not much, indeed! but I used to go marketing in London, and I paid thirteen pence a pound for veal; and fancy a great big calf selling for twenty shillings! It's ridiculous!"

"I met Miss Katie and Misther Barry on the road there below," said Darby, clumsily turning the subject. "She was perched up on the back of his horse—on his saddle—and mighty unaisy she looked; faix, and so did the horse! All at wanst it gave a little lep, and down she came on the top of Misther Barry. Oh, she was not a happorth the worse—she fell into his arms! The horse tore off home, and Mr. Barry was left raging! I laughed, till I haden't an eye in me head!"

Helen looked at him indignantly, and turning to her cousin said, "Dido, your hat is ready, come and try it on!"

"Mrs. Carmody, you can take the beans and the cabbages at your own price—I'm going in now," said Miss Sheridan, taking her cousin's arm, and so departing.

"Mrs. Mooney and Mrs. Carmody expect to get the things for nothing. I don't know which of them is the greatest skinflint! And Darby just sat there grinning, and never helped me a bit. He was worse than useless!"

"Never mind Darby, but come into the drawing-room and put on your hat; you can see yourself beautifully in the glass over the chimney-piece!"

"It looks lovely,"—taking it up admiringly. "Yes,"—advancing to the mirror—"and it suits me too! What do *you* think?"

Helen ascended to the fender-stool, so as to have a good view, and to be enabled to give her cousin the benefit of her candid opinion.

"I had no idea you were so clever, with your fingers," continued Dido; "I won't know myself in a new hat. This will come in nicely for Mr. Redmond's tennis party next week. I should not be a bit surprised if we meet *my nephew* there!" and she laughed merrily.

Of course all this time she was contemplating herself in the glass—and lifting her eyes to her cousin's reflection, to her astonishment she noticed that she coloured to the roots of her hair! With a sudden flash of comprehension she wheeled right about and looked at her curiously! but Helen moved hastily away, and walking towards the window said,—

"Those daisies are too much at one side, they must come out."

"Never mind the daisies, Helen! I'm going to be very impertinent—I'm going to be as bad as Barry. I'm going to guess something about *you*."

"Guess what?" sitting down in the window seat, and turning as if at bay.

"Guess something about 'my nephew.' Why did you blush just now, and why is he the only person you met at Port Blair, whom you never mention? Well, well," in answer to the expression of her cousin's face, "I see you don't like it, so I won't say any more. If you don't wish to give me your confidence I won't try to steal it."

After a moment's hesitation she added, with averted face,—

"I suppose Katie has told you all about *me?*"

"Yes, poor Dido! it was a hard, hard case," replied Helen, gently taking her hand.

Dido sighed, and nodded her head, and then remarked, in quite a cheerful voice, "I try not to think of it—it could not be helped."

An unusually long silence succeeded this speech, and at last Helen said, "What I am going to tell you, Dido, I have never spoken of before, not even to papa. I have never put my—my—experience—into words—yet. I wonder very much how it will sound, both to you, and me. No! You must not gaze at me like that, or I shall never be able to tell it. Look out of the window and listen. Dido," lowering her voice to a whisper, "you were right about Mr. Lisle."

"Yes," nodding her head with quick assent.

"You know everything about my life out there, all excepting—*that*. He was at the Andamans when I arrived, but I did not meet him for a month or more. He lived far away on the mainland—he did not go into society; and because he was silent and shabby, people thought he was an impostor, or some needy adventurer, or that he was hiding from his creditors—if not worse—so he was a kind of social outlaw."

"What! Mr. Lisle, with his thousands a year!" cried her listener in a key of angry astonishment.

"Yes; and he never undeceived any one—I suppose he was laughing in his sleeve all the time. He told me once that he rather enjoyed living in the Palace of Truth, and being valued for his appearance alone,—and rated according to his wardrobe! especially his hat!"

"And when did you meet him?"

"We met one evening, on a kind of savage coast, where I was accidentally deserted by a picnic party. I was nearly mad with fright, and luckily for me, Mr. Lisle's boat was passing, and he saw me, and took me off. On our way home we came in for an awful storm; over and over again I thought we should have been drowned, but after the most dreadful hour I ever spent, he landed me safely on Ross pier."

"Yes!—well, that was certainly a romantic beginning. Go on."

"Then he came and called. Papa liked him. Yes, and so did I. He was so different to other people; he had a distinct personality of his own. He had read and travelled, and kept his eyes open. He put old things in a new light; in short, he was charming to talk to, and I was always glad whenever he came and spoke to me,—though it was not very often. At one time, he ventured over to the station tennis parties, and was quite callous to Mrs. Creery's snubs and Lizzie Caggett's scowls. Then for weeks he would disappear."

"And all this while had he ever said anything?" inquired Dido with the authority of a girl, who had had an authenticated proposal.

"He never paid me a single compliment in his life; but I believed he liked me."

"And you liked him?"

Helen made no direct answer, but continued her tale, and her cousin accepted her silence for the proverbial consent.

"At length we had a grand ball, my first and only dance. To every one's amazement, Mr. Lisle appeared in irreproachable evening dress, and danced nearly the whole evening."

"With *you*, of course?"

"No; with a married lady, a Mrs. Durand."

"Well, I must say, that I think that was rather peculiar."

"Oh! but I found out afterwards that they had known each other as children, and been old playmates and friends. I confess I was angry, and— very, well—I suppose jealous. Afterwards I danced the last waltz with him, almost in spite of myself, and when it was over we walked up the island in the moonlight. Dido," suddenly raising her eyes to her cousin's, "I shall never forget that night if I live to be a hundred! The look of the sea, the stillness, the fire-flies, and the moon, bright as day, casting sharp shadows of palms, and cactus plants, across our path. I shut my eyes, and I can see it *now*. Then we talked. He told me that he was going away the next day—a trip to the Nicobars. He also told me that he understood that I was going to be married to Mr. Quentin, whom you know I detest,—and offered me his congratulations! Of course I denied this indignantly, and he seemed positively not inclined to believe me at first, and then—and then—he asked me. He told me—I need not go on—Dido, *you* understand the rest!"

"And am I to understand that you said 'Yes'?"

"I believe so."

"You had no idea who he really was all the time?"

"I knew he was a gentleman, that he was well educated, and well bred; like every one else, I thought he was poor, but that made no difference to me."

"You never dreamt that he was the Honourable Gilbert Lisle, with about twelve thousand a year?"

"Never! He was commencing to tell me something, when Mrs. Creery swooped down upon us, and carried me off."

"Hateful old woman! And afterwards?"

"We never had an opportunity of speaking till the very last moment. He followed me towards our bungalow, and said he would come over and see papa early the next morning, before he sailed if possible. If not to look for him in six weeks time,—and to be sure not to forget him."

"Well?" ejaculated her listener breathlessly.

"That was nearly two years ago.—I have never seen him since."

"What?" cried Dido, jumping to her feet, and tossing her new hat passionately down on the sofa. "And you believe that *that* man was Gilbert Lisle. He was nothing of the kind! Mrs. Creery and Miss Caggett were perfectly right. He was an impostor. He and the real Mr. Lisle are as different as night from day!"

"But Mr. Lisle was in the Andamans at that time. Mrs. Durand, who was a great friend of mine, could not be mistaken—it was she, who really told us who he was, one night at the General's. He was travelling about in search of amusement. I was a school-girl, and an easy prey—and all the time he was engaged to Miss Calderwood."

"He was not, and he is not," retorted Dido, decidedly. "That is only old Mr. Redmond's pet project—and Katie has got some silly idea into her head because she saw them riding together once or twice; for that matter, so did I! She looked as cross as two sticks, and he looked bored to death; she told me once, in a burst of confidence, you know her style of being one's bosom friend one day and cutting you dead the next?"

"No, I don't" (shortly), "Miss Calderwood and I never coalesced."

"Well, she imparted to me that Mr. Lisle had a hateful temper and unsufferable manners, but that one could not expect everything! I said to myself, if *you* expect to be Mrs. Lisle, you will find yourself excessively mistaken. Mind you, *I* am speaking of Mr. Redmond's nephew."

"So am I."

"It is incredible that it should be him. Could there have been any misunderstanding? Did you flirt with any one when he was away?"

"I flirt? I never did such a thing in my life!"

"Excepting with poor old Mr. Redmond; his infatuation is really pitiable," interrupted her cousin with a laugh. "Well, Helen, believe me, Gilbert Lisle never voluntarily broke his word to man or woman. There is something in the background that will be explained *yet*. I have a presentiment about it, and my presentiments are infallible."

"Do you ever have them about yourself?"

"No; excepting that I shall live and die an old maid; of course, there ought to be one in every family."

"Yes, and I reserve that post for Helen Denis! Now, never mind my humiliating experience, please tell me something more about Mr. Halliday?"

"I fancy Katie has left me but little to tell! I met him at Portrush, and there was nothing romantic about *our* first meeting; no rescue from a jungle; no hairbreadth escape—he was simply taking tea at the Reids, in the most hum-drum fashion. We used to go for expeditions along the coast, and sit upon the rocks by the sea, and watch the waves, or the moon, and talk—*you* understand the rest!" (smiling significantly). "And one night, as we were walking home, he asked me to marry him—oh, Helen, I was so surprised, and so happy! but it did not last long—"

"Do you ever hear of him now?"

"Yes, occasionally, through the Reids; but it is all over.—We shall never meet again."

"Well, at least you have the consolation of knowing that he loved you, and wished to make you his wife; there is some poor satisfaction in *that*, whilst I," and here she broke down, and buried her face in her hands. But this emotion was merely momentary; presently she lifted her face to her cousin, and said, "So you see that I have had a lesson for life; I shall never, never marry."

"Neither will I," returned Dido, with much emphasis.

In the midst of their interesting confidences, and mutual assurances of celibacy, the door opened, and Biddy's befrilled face was thrust in, recalling them sharply from romance to reality.

"Miss Dido, will ye come out, av ye plase! Mrs. Carmody says she'll go to two shillin' a hundred for them apples, and the onions sixpence a stone!"

CHAPTER XXXVIII
"SALLY'S SUBSTITUTE"

"I stood

Among them, but not of them."

Childe Harold.

In a large flagged room on the basement story, Helen, Katie, and old Biddy, were seated round a well-scoured table, making busy preparations for the despatch of a creditable "cart" to Terryscreen Market; neat bunches of salads, bouquets of flowers, and bundles of asparagus, testify to their industry. As far as the young ladies are concerned, their labours have been lightened by the interchange of riddles, chiefly very poor ones, and the worse they were, the more they laughed, and the more Biddy sniggered.

"I give up that one, as to what makes more noise than a pig under a gate!" said Helen, holding an exquisite bouquet of roses towards her cousin. "There is no answer. The pig could not be beaten."

"I wish I had some more twine," she added, looking anxiously around.

"I wish you had, my dear," returned Katie, "but I can do nothing *but* wish! My hands are full. There is some in the cup on the chimney-piece in the office. No, that's *gum*; it's in Dido's desk."

The office was a little den behind the dining-room, consecrated to business, and the communings of Dido and Darby. The latter was in the act of leaving it, when Helen appeared; his face looked more foxy than usual, and there was a sly smile in his eyes as he said,—

"And what way are ye the day, Miss Denis?"

"Busy, Darby, terribly busy; I have half the asparagus to tie up yet, and not a plum picked."

"Shure 'tis nothing but divarshion for the like of yees," he rejoined contemptuously. "An I would not grudge to see you young ladies so entirely fond of flowers and gardening—'Tis a nice quiet taste."

"Divarshion, indeed? There's little divarshion in picking gallons of fruit in the blazing sun—and as to the wasps! but I'm in a hurry, Darby, I have not a moment to spare. Please let me pass," she said, now walking into the little office, where she discovered Dido seated at her brass-bound bureau, surrounded by papers, and dissolved in tears.

"What on earth is the matter?" she inquired, laying her hand on her cousin's shoulder.

"Nothing—nothing at all," hurriedly drying her eyes, and averting her face.

"Come, Dido, I am certain that you are the last girl to cry for nothing. What is it? Won't you tell me? Two heads are better than one. Is it these accounts?"

"It is just this, Helen," wheeling round with sudden energy, "I've come to the conclusion that it is hopeless to go on struggling any longer, and trying to make both ends meet; I strive, and strive, to keep out of debt—we spend next to nothing on ourselves, as you know, and when I think I am getting my head above water at last, down comes something and pushes me under, such as a big bill that I never expected, and that nearly breaks my heart. Look at this," holding out a rather dirty scrawl, "here is one now, and Darby says it must be paid at once. And I did not even know it was owing. It's for seed-potatoes, and guano, and wire to keep out the rabbits— altogether eleven pounds," she concluded with a little sob.

"Eleven pounds!" ejaculated her cousin, taking it up and examining it.

"I notice that it is made out by Darby—does not that strike you as rather peculiar?"

"Oh, no; he always does it," returned Dido, (the unsuspicious,) pulling out a little drawer as she spoke.

"See! I have only three shillings, till after to-morrow, and these Murphys declare they can't wait any longer than Monday—they are pressed themselves, and Darby says they *must* be paid. To hear him talk, one would think I had only to go out and pick up sovereigns on the gravel!"

"Then let uncle pay," said Helen sternly, "it's not more than the price of one of his old books. I do think, Dido, that it is rather hard that you should have to work for the support of the whole family, and that all the income from the place goes, I may say, on *air*! Barry told me that, even as it is, it brings in a thousand a year."

Dido made no immediate answer, but sat resting her chin on her hand, and gazing fixedly out of the window. At length she seemed to have come to some settled decision, for she rose and said, "I think I will try the Padré once more; it's rather a forlorn hope, but nothing venture, nothing have. Wait here till I come back, Helen," and with a melancholy little nod she quitted the room.

Helen sat down in her cousin's chair in front of the old bureau, with its inky baize desk, and numerous musty drawers; and noted with feelings of hot indignation, the traces of Dido's tears—tears that had splashed unchecked upon the leaves of an open account-book. Sitting here before these tear-stained columns, she asked herself dispassionately if a man who had brought forth nothing but second-hand inventions, after forty years of costly experiments, was likely to revolutionize the universe at last?

No, she had no patience with his concentrated selfishness, and *no* faith in the apparatus. As to Darby Chute, she had never trusted him, and although she had no solid grounds for her suspicions, yet she could not divest herself of the idea, that he was a rascal! She was aware that Darby did not eye *her* with any favour, and indeed he had more than once made craftily-veiled inquiries as to *when* she was going away?

"It was no use," said Dido, entering the room, and shaking her head hopelessly. "I knew it. He just held up empty hands. That is his invariable answer when I beg for a little money. It will just have to be, as Darby says," sitting down, and looking at her cousin despondently, "we must sell the white cow."

"Not the one I call *my* cow; not Daisy?" cried Helen in consternation.

"Yes; she is the best of them all. She will fetch the most money. Darby thinks we might get twenty pounds for her at the fair to-morrow. There is no use in putting off the evil day, and I hate to owe a penny. I cannot sleep if I am in debt."

"You should see what some girls owe, and how they sleep," said her cousin, thinking of the Miss Platts, and how very lightly their milliner's accounts lay on their minds. "Is there no resource but Daisy? Can you suggest nothing else?"

"Nothing, unless—" and she hesitated and coloured—"unless I borrowed the money from you, and I would not do that, for I might never be able to pay you. No; there is nothing for it but Daisy!"

"My dearest Dido," said Helen, putting her arm round her neck, "what a horribly mean wretch you must think me all this time. Don't you *know* very well, that every farthing I possess, would have been in the common purse months ago, only—only—uncle borrowed all my money the day after I came here."

"What do you say?" cried Dido, jumping to her feet. "Oh, no, Helen; oh, *surely* he did not! Oh!" in great distress, and her eyes filling with tears. "This is worse than all! This is *too* bad. Oh, my dear, foolish child, why did you let him know you had a farthing?"

"He asked me, and what could I say?"

"He has such odd ideas about money. He looks upon it as a kind of common property, and he has all kinds of queer, wild schemes about abolishing it altogether.—Was it much?" she asked anxiously.

"Never mind, Dido, how much. The loss is yours, dear; not mine. It would have been in your hands long ago, only for this."

"Helen," said her cousin, looking very pale, "I can speak to you, as I can to no one else—not even Katie. Papa is not like other people!"

"No," assented his niece with a very serious face.

"He was always eccentric; but latterly he has been getting more so. Sometimes," lowering her voice, and glancing nervously at the door, "he is——"

"Yes; I think I understand," nodding her head gravely.

"Biddy guesses it; so does Barry. Katie suspects nothing, poor child. I've kept this to myself ever since I've known it," leaning her face on her hand, and covering her eyes.

"And that was the reason that you would not listen to Mr. Halliday?"

"Yes;—mamma dreaded it, and not long before she died she—told me— and she made me solemnly promise, to guard him as closely as possible, to keep him near me as long as he had the faintest chance," her voice dying away to a whisper.

Helen took her cousin's hand in hers, and her face was full of sympathy.

"He was only a little strange at times," continued Dido, "especially about money. But during the last year I have seen it coming, and this is one reason I've always resisted having Barry to live here, and taking over the place; this is the reason that I struggle with all my might to keep him and the Padré apart, for if he and Barry were to meet constantly, Barry would *know*, and Barry would immediately insist upon what is only to be the last resource. I promised mamma," here Dido broke down, and leaning her head against her cousin's shoulder, wept miserably.

"My poor Dido!" said Helen, smoothing her hair tenderly. "What a burden you have had to bear all alone, and how noble, and unselfish, and patient you have been. When I think of you, and think of myself, I am bitterly ashamed! I have been latterly entirely wrapped up in myself, and my own affairs, I never seem to give a thought to other people, and you— you have renounced your own happiness for the benefit of others— —"

"I am not unhappy," interrupted Dido, drying her eyes; "or, at any rate, I would not be, if he was getting better; but he is getting *worse*, much worse—I see it coming nearer and nearer!" and she looked up at her companion with pallid lips and startled eyes. "For days, when you do not see him, he is sitting still in the workshop, and never opens his lips. I carry him up his meals, and he takes no notice. Other times he has delusions. Not long ago, when I went up to speak to him, I found him pacing up and down the room, shouting into a long tube; he would not answer when I spoke, but at last he went and wrote on a bit of paper, '*Leave me, mortal, I am the trumpet of Fame!*'

"See," searching in her bureau, "here it is! I brought it away unintentionally, and then I hid it here, I don't know why."

Helen gazed at this proof of her uncle's mental aberration with startled eyes, and then she said quietly, —

"I think the time has arrived when something ought to be done. Uncle should have an experienced person to look after him, and surely *you* might manage the money."

"Yes! Barry must know at last, and Katie, and every one," said Dido, tearing up the scrap of paper with a sigh; "but to-day he is as sane as I am, and as busy as possible over the apparatus, he may not have another attack for a long time. Let us put it out of our heads. Don't think of it, we will talk of something else. I must send word to Darby this evening about Daisy; twenty pounds is the least— —"

"Dido, Dido!" cried her sister, bursting into the room, "come down this moment; Sally has fallen over the step in the dairy and sprained her ankle, she is lying groaning on the settle in the kitchen, and she won't be able to stir to-morrow?"

"Oh, of course!" exclaimed Dido, starting up. "Do misfortunes ever come alone?"

Half an hour later, the three girls were standing together looking blankly at their preparation for the morrow's market. There lay golden butter, cream-cheeses, pounds of honey, bouquets of flowers, and last, but not least, their precious stock of grapes—grapes nursed through the winter, in a windy old vinery, with a tenderness they had but ill repaid.

"Is Sally's ankle very painful?" inquired Helen after a long pause.

"Yes; I've bathed it with arnica, but she won't be able to put her foot to the ground for a week."

"Could Andy go?"

"Andy, my dear girl, wouldn't set foot in Terryscreen to save his life; he was in jail there! It's just our luck, the best cart of the season! I'd take it myself, only I would be known. There would be no real disgrace in doing it—it's ten times more shameful to owe money."

"There's nothing for it but to put away what will keep, and to use the rest ourselves," said Katie, the ever practical.

After a moment's silence, Helen said suddenly, "Look here, Dido, why should not *I* take the cart?"

"You!" shrieked her cousin. "Are you mad?"

"Now, just please to listen quietly, both of you," she returned with decision.

"In the first place, I'm a stranger to all but the Reids and Redmonds—that's one point," reckoning on her fingers. "In the second, I can get myself up in character so that you would never know me. Thirdly, I flatter myself that my brogue is undeniable. Fourthly, I've plenty of confidence. Fifthly, I mean to go."

"Helen, you are not serious?" said Dido, gravely.

"Never more so, my dear.—I know the market prices as well as yourselves. I shall dress myself up in an old garden frock and sun-bonnet, and you will see if I don't pass off as a good-looking slip of a country girl. You know very well you can't tell my brogue from Sally's in the dark, so I will be your market woman, ladies, and come home to-morrow with my pocket full of money, 'an ye may make your minds quite aisy about me,'" suddenly adopting a brogue and dropping a curtsey. "No one will know a hate about it, barrin' the Masther and meeself."

At this her cousins burst out laughing, and finding that she was so sanguine, and so resolute, and that all their expostulations were uttered to deaf ears, they submitted to the scheme without further demur. Of course Sally was taken into the secret, and when the subject was very gently broken to her by her smiling, would-be deputy, at first she held up her hands dramatically, and invoked both the local and her own patron saints; but in the end she came round. Her thrifty soul revolted against the wanton waste of all her beautiful cheese and butter, and presently she was instructing Helen (who sat beside the settle, gravely attentive), with immense animation, and impressive authority.

"You'll find the Masther very tough to drive, miss, but he knows every stone of the road, and is acquainted with all the shops, so ye may just lave it to himself; there does be no use in prodding him, or striving to drive him, for his mouth is as hard as the heart of Pharaoh, — and he is that determined in his own way, that nations would not hould him! First and foremost, ye go to Clancy's with the butter and the eggs, an' you'll not take less than a shilling a pound, dear, and sevenpence the dozen. She'll bate you down, seeing you are strange, and it's not Sally MacGravy she has to dale with! but just you say, 'Divil a copper less you'll take,' and let on you are going to Dooley's across the street. Afther that I'm thinking you will never be able to stand forenint the fruit and vegetables in the square, so ye might go over to Dooley's in *earnest* and offer him the vegetables and fruit chape; that's in raison, do ye mind. Then there's the grapes and flowers, I don't know what to say about them at all! They must just take their chance; it's the butter that's lying so heavy on me! With regard to the cowcumbers, and honey, and cream-cheeses, a messman does be in from barracks, a fellow with an eye like a needle in his head, and the deuce for bating you down. Then, wance in a way, ye have the officers' ladies; them's the wans for the flowers, and you'll mind to charge them double, darlin'! that's about all," concluded Sally, coming to the end of her instructions, and her breath, simultaneously.

Next morning, at grey dawn, Helen was astir and dressed; her cousins, who had hardly been able to sleep a wink with excitement, attended her at her early breakfast, poured out her tea, buttered her toast, and surveyed her appearance with subdued giggles and expressions of astonished delight. They assured her repeatedly that they would pass her on the road and never recognize her. She was arrayed in a clean but faded cotton, turned up over a striped dark petticoat, a pink sun-bonnet, a white apron, and a little checked shawl. Certainly she was not quite as *like* sally as her relations could have wished—which, considering that Sally was bordering on forty, and weighed fourteen stone, was not surprising—but they both emphatically declared that she would readily pass for what she professed to be—"a good-looking slip of a country girl who had taken Sally's place."

"Too good-looking, Helen, dear," said Dido, kissing her as she mounted the cart. "Keep your bonnet pulled well over your eyes, and try and do not show your teeth when you laugh; and above all stick to the brogue!"

These were Dido's final injunctions; and she escorted the cart half-way down the avenue, and then took off her shoe, and threw it after it for luck. The last glimpse Helen caught of her favourite cousin, she was hopping along the damp drive, in quest of the said slipper.

The Master was not to be hurried. Two hours for the five miles was his *own* time, lounging along in a leisurely way, in a series of zig-zags from ditch to ditch.

It was a lovely August morning; the dew lay heavy on the grass, and silvery, gossamer cobwebs hung about the hedges. Helen felt her pulses beating with excitement entirely untouched by fear. A bold adventurous spirit possessed her; there was something so utterly novel, so deliciously strange, in her present undertaking; as if she had left Helen Denis behind, and had embodied herself in a new identity!

Presently the Master was overtaken and passed by various carts, and even by pedestrians—who had each, and all, a word for Sally. But this was not Sally! this was a black stranger, who was not disposed to waste her time in idle badinage, and who took no more notice of them than the stick in her hand, and seemed an "impident, stuck-up piece!" However, it was the Crowmore mule; there was no mistake about *him*—once seen—never forgotten!

"Mind that mule," cried one, "or he'll break everything that's on him, and run away with you!"

"Faix, and no loss if he does!" retorted another.

"Musha, an' will ye look at the nate foot and ankle we have, hanging so aisy and so careless over the side of the shaft! 'Tis a lady we are, all out! Do ye mind the gloves on her!"

A Bird Of Passage | 315

"Bedad, an' if she is, she looks mighty at home on an ass's car," shouted a fourth.

The subject of these and other delicate witticisms, was not sorry to find herself jogging over the cobble stones of the High Street of Terryscreen. Greatly to her astonishment, the Master, of his own accord, rose a beautiful trot for the town, and rattled up in gallant style to Clancy's, the butter shop. His new driver's heart beat unusually fast as she alighted, made the reins secure, and taking a heavy basket on her arm, proceeded to air her brogue in real earnest.

Early as it was, the place was crowded, and she had some difficulty in edging her way to the counter, where she was at once confronted by a big, stout woman, with a merry face, and her hands on her hips, who, staring at her hard, said, —

"An' where is Sally the day?"

"She's hurt her foot," replied her substitute, in a voice that was scarcely above a whisper.

"And so you are doing her work?"

"Just for the time, Mrs. Clancy."

"From this part of the country, dear?"

"No; a good bit beyant."

"Oh, well,"—tasting the butter with her finger and glancing at her sharply—"butter is down, ye know. Elevenpence."

"Is it?" innocently. "I am not to go home with less than the shilling."

"Is that the way with you? Well, we'll say elevenpence halfpenny, honey!"

"No, Mrs. Clancy, mam, I really *dar* not do it!"

"Well, I see she has ye well schooled, and I suppose you'll just have to get it! Eighteen pounds did ye say?" now going towards the till—but being waylaid by a customer, Helen was left to wait among the crowd for a considerable time.

Far from every eye being centred on her, as she had tremblingly feared, no one noticed her by word or glance; and her courage, which had ebbed as she entered the shop, now came back in full tide.

The Clancys were driving a roaring trade, if one might judge by appearances. Their establishment was thronged by men in corduroy and frieze, and women in long blue cloaks, or plaid shawls, all bargaining, buying, or gossiping. She was wedged in between the counter and two stalwart matrons, who were holding forth to one another with great animation. And oh, how their garments did smell of turf!

"And what way is Mary the day, Mrs. Daly?" inquired one.

"'Deed, an' I'm thinking, she is just dying on her feet; first she had a slight sketch of a cold, now 'tis a melancholy that ails her. John took her up to Rafferty's funeral, thinking to cheer her out of it, but she got a wakness standin' in the berryin'-ground, an' 'tis worse she is, instead of better."

"That's bad! An' how is Dan?"

"Oh, finely. Shure he has the pledge! Glory be to God!"

"Musha, an' I wish Pat had! When he comes into the town here, he gits into that much company there's no daling with him at all. Ye can't be up to them men! I thought this morning he was getting very good entirely, when I was in Fagan's store, and saw him and a couple of chaps drinking coffee. Shure, wasent it that Moody and Sanky they were at—an' wasent it half whiskey?"

"Ah! now ye don't tell me that?"

"An' 'deed, an' I do! I don't say as a needleful of sperrits ever did any wan any harm—but there does be *some* would drink the Shannon!"

"Purviding it was potheen," supplemented her listener, dryly.

"There's your change, Alannah," called out Mrs. Clancy across the counter, "and mind ye, it will be elevenpence next week."

Helen smiled agreeably, nodded her head, and pocketed the silver. Sally would surely be able to do battle for herself by the following market day! After a considerable struggle she made her way out of the crowd, and once more ascended the market-cart. So far so good—the butter and eggs were off her mind—now for Dooley's, and the vegetables. But, unluckily, the Master—who was, as we know, an animal of great strength of character— had determined to trot off to his usual station, near the Courthouse. Of course Helen could please herself about Dooley's, but he and the cart went to their accustomed post. The habits of years were not to be thus trifled with! This clause had not been in the bond. Helen had meant to have got rid of the fruit and vegetables (even at a sacrifice) and to have immediately afterwards set her face towards home—but to stand and sell her wares from the cart in the open market, was an ordeal that she had never anticipated. However, as she and the Master came together, together they were bound to return, and her arrangements were solely dependent on his good pleasure (a somewhat humbling reflection). For years he had been accustomed to stand for three hours per week in Terryscreen Market Square, just behind the Courthouse, and to vary the programme to-day was an idea that never once entered his grizzled head. His lady driver, who had discovered that his mouth was all that Sally had prophesied (and more), meekly abandoned herself to her fate, and having loosened her tyrant's bit, and administered a "lock of hay," set to work to lay out her wares, and arrange her stall to the best of her ability. As she gazed around upon the crowd, and listened to the confused buzz of many brogues, her head failed her, her boasted confidence seemed to be oozing away at the tips of her fingers. Supposing she lost her head, supposing she was discovered? But who was to discover her? argued common sense; and if she had passed in Clancy's shop, surely she would pass here. She was doing no harm, quite the reverse; and when she thought of Dido's difficulties, and Dido's tears, and those three shillings lying in her desk, and looked round on her fine stock of garden produce, capable of being turned into silver coin of the realm, she recovered herself, and by the time she had sold her first head of cabbage, her courage and *sang-froid* were completely restored!

CHAPTER XXXIX
"THE MARKET GIRL"

"We met—'twas in a crowd." —*Haynes Bayley.*

Helen soon discovered that the Crowmore cart had quite an established reputation; her peas, and beans, strawberries and asparagus commanded a brisk sale. Customers came flocking round her, and she actually ventured to retort to some of their sallies with mild replies in kind.

"Shure, we are all fighting and killing one another to dale with you!" said a sturdy old farmer, vigorously elbowing his way to the front. "Aren't we for all the world like flies round a pot of honey! 'Tis yourself has the jewels of eyes, avick! But why do ye wear gloves?"

"To keep me hands like a lady's, to be sure," she retorted, promptly.

"Oh! well, as long as ye don't cover up your face, I don't care a thraneen! And what are ye asking for the white cabbage?" making an abrupt descent from blarney to business.

Who shall depict the emotions of Larry Flood, when, lounging up to have a little idle dalliance with his sweetheart, he found himself confronted by the young English lady? Yes, the young English lady! She was busily engaged in selling three cauliflowers and a bunch of parsley to the priest's housekeeper, and seemed just as much at home at the trade as Sally herself. She looked up and gave him a sign of warning, and when the press of business had somewhat abated, he sidled over to her and made the following cautious inquiry in a husky whisper, —

"In the name of goodness, miss, will ye tell me if I'm in me seven sinses?"

"I believe so, Larry," she answered with a merry smile.—"Don't betray me, for your life! Sally hurt her foot, and I offered to take her place just for to-day. I'm getting on beautifully you see; and no one is a bit the wiser."

"I could not make out what was up!" exclaimed Larry, "there's been a crowd round the cart as if it was an execution! 'Tis only now I got next or nigh it. And signs on it! they had raison, for such a sight as yourself has never before stood on Terryscreen Street. But I don't like it, miss, no, not for you—you are too venturesome; and if you'll allow me, miss, I'll try my hand at selling. I'm not for the road till five o'clock. I'll do my best for ye, and tell as many lies as a horse-daler, and you might just slip over into the hotel, and they'll wait on you hand and foot."

"No, thank you, Larry, though I'm very much obliged to you all the same. That would never do—never!"

"Well, I'm not aisy in me mind. It's the fair day, and supposing some of them young Bostogues come round ye, and gives ye some of their lip?"

At this disagreeable suggestion the young lady blanched visibly.

"I shall go home early,—that is to say, as soon as the mule will go," was her rather enigmatic reply.

"Early or late, do you see that window over beyant?" pointing to a ledge in a neighbouring store. "Well, I'll just take me sate there, wid this whip, an' if I see any one offer to as much as look crooked at ye, by me sowl! I'll bate him to a *jelly*; and that's as sure as my name is Flood. So at any rate, miss, ye need not be anxious!" and having made this alarming announcement, her self-elected protector stalked away and actually established himself in the said window-sill, where he sat sentry, with his whip in hand, and his eyes on Helen's stall, looking daggers at her customers.

The messman duly came, and purchased lavishly from the new market-girl, and did not attempt to "bate her down," as had been predicted; on the contrary, he paid her some very ornate compliments, and lingered so long that Helen literally trembled lest Larry should misconstrue his civilities.

As the morning wore on, it brought some fashionable patrons, among them several ladies, who, after turning over and sniffing every separate bouquet, purchased half-a-dozen of the best. During her dealings with these Helen kept her sun-bonnet well pulled over her eyes, and commanded her countenance to the best of her ability, whilst they discussed her appearance in French, and declared that she was the prettiest Irish girl they had ever seen. The fame of the beautiful market-girl must have been noised abroad, for several young men came crowding around the cart, and eagerly demanded "button holes." For these she charged double prices without the slightest compunction. (Meanwhile Larry stood in the background armed with his whip!)

"A shilling!" exclaimed one of the customers, "oh, I say, come, you must not be getting these extravagant notions into your head, Kathleen Mavourneen, Eileen Aroon! One would think you had been in Covent Garden! I suppose you fancy that a pretty girl may charge what she pleases.

Here's two shillings; one for the flowers, and the other for a good look in your charming face."

"'Deed," scornfully tossing back a shilling, "An' it's more than any one will ever ask to lay out on your honour's."

As the unhappy gentleman was unusually plain, his companions seemed to experience the keenest delight at this sally, and one of them, pressing forward, and taking up a bouquet, said, —

"How much for this, my prickly wild rose?"

"Two shillings, your honour."

"Too dear! say eighteen-pence, Acushla ma cree."

"Sure the times is bad, your honour, and we must live."

"And where *do* you live, when you are at home—where do you come from?"

"Where I'm going back to," she returned, carelessly jingling her silver in her pockets.

She was making a fortune; her career so far had been one unbroken triumph, and her heart beat exultantly as she rattled her shillings and half-crowns, and complacently surveyed her almost empty cart. Carrying her glance a little above it, she met point-blank the eyes of a gentleman on horseback, who was looking over the heads of her customers. He wore his hat tilted far over his brows, and was gazing at her with grave, concentrated scrutiny—the man was Gilbert Lisle. For a moment she stood as if turned to stone, then suddenly wheeling about and kneeling down, she pretended to tie her shoe-string, but her fingers trembled so ridiculously, that this was indeed a farce. She felt a sense of choking panic; nevertheless, she was called upon to exercise all her self-command, for an officious old crone, who presided at the next stall, came over and shouted to her, saying, —

"The gentleman on the horse is spaking to you, Alannah; see here!" displaying a sovereign that had been thrown among the cabbage-leaves. "He wants a flower."

"Tell him they are all gone," she replied, still fiddling with her shoe-string. However, it was impossible that she could carry on this pretence much longer—and when with beating heart she at last ventured to raise her head, he was nowhere to be seen. Was it a dream? no, for there lay the piece of gold.

"It's ould Redmond's heir," volunteered her neighbour, eyeing the money with greedy eyes. "He's a great traveller, he has been away round by India, where me son is. I've never known him notice the likes of *you* before, and I know him man and boy. What ails ye? ye seem to have got a turn—ye look so white and wake."

"What would ail me? nothing at all—I'm a bit tired standing so long, and I'll just sit down on this creel till I see me way to getting out of the throng."

"Well, you are easily bet up, I'll say that for you," muttered the other, moving back to her own stall. "One would think ye wor a lady!"

It was eleven o'clock, all Helen's stock was disposed of, but for the present she saw no prospect of making her way through the crowd, and was compelled to sit, and wait, and listen to the surrounding gabble, which she did half unconsciously, for her thoughts were centred in her last customer; from which subject two tall countrymen were the first to attract her attention. They were standing so close to her that she made a kind of third party in the conversation, which proved unexpectedly interesting.

"What are you doing here, Tim?" inquired one; "sure you have nothing to sell."

"An' it's at home I ought to be! with all me barley standing; but sure I'm drawn for the jury, and bad luck to it."

"Troth, and so am I! an' I'm due in there," jerking his thumb at the Courthouse, "at twelve o'clock."

"Me hands is that full at home, I don't know what to be at first. However," as if it was some small satisfaction, he added, "the devil a wan I'll bring in guilty."

"Nayther will I," agreed his companion, in solemn tones. "I seen Darby Chute in the day, with a few little bastes and a fine cow," (the name possessed a spell for Helen, and bound her attention at once). "I met him coming out of the bank, ere now; 'tis him has feathered his nest."

"Faix, ye may well say *feathered*," retorted the other, with a loud laugh; "he does not give the gun much time to cool!"

"Begorra, it's a shame! an old mad man and a couple of girls—well, if poor Pat Connor was to rise out of his grave, and see the way things is going."

Just as the conversation was becoming most exciting, these two tall countrymen moved away. Not five minutes afterwards, Darby's own well-known husky squeak fell upon Helen's ear. Little did he guess who it was that was sitting with her back to him, in the pink sun-bonnet. He was accompanied by a companion, and they were evidently about to clinch some bargain.

"I'm not very swate on that Scotch whiskey," said the latter, "it has not the right sort of bite in it to plase *me*! An' now Darby, me boy, what's the lowest you are going to say for the ould lady?"

"Ould lady! Holy Saint Patrick, do ye hear him? is it the young, white, short-horn cow, on her second calf?"

"I just mane the big bony cow you are striving to stick me with, for twenty-three pounds."

Helen pricked up her ears—twenty-*three* pounds!

"See here, James Casey, av I was to drop down dead this blessed minute, I won't take a halfpenny less than the twenty pounds, and only I'm hard pressed for money, and times is bad, I would drive her home afore me. She'd be chape at five-and-twenty: a pedigree cow. An' ye know it! so ye need not be playing with me, as if I was trying to sell you an ould Kerry Stripper. Take her or lave her, you are keeping others off, and the fair is getting thin."

After ten minutes of the fiercest chaffering, and many loud invocations and denunciations on both sides, the bargain was closed, and to Helen's great joy, she saw twenty dirty one-pound notes counted into Darby's horny hand, the price of Daisy. The fair was getting "thin," as he had said, and as the clock was striking twelve, she and her empty cart emerged from the *melée* of pigs, sheep, and turf kishes, and waving a friendly farewell to Larry, she proceeded homewards at a brisk trot. Naturally, most of her thoughts were occupied by Gilbert Lisle, and she was consumed by a burning desire to know if he had recognized her? Had it been only amazement at a curious likeness that she had read in that glance?—a glance that revived a spirit that she thought was laid; it stirred—it recalled days of painful endurance, nights of tears. "However, that is all at an end now," she assured herself, half aloud. "Thank goodness I have lived it down."

She cast one or two apologetic thoughts to Darby Chute; yes, her conscience smote her with regard to him. Darby, after all, was an honest, upright man! Hearing is believing, he had done as much to sell Daisy to good advantage,—as if she had been his own property.

CHAPTER XL
"BARRY'S CHALLENGE"

"The place is haunted." —*Hood.*

The Master's trot proved to be a mere flash in the pan, and after a mile the aged animal subsided into his normal pace,—namely, a desultory and erratic stroll. His driver, wearied by this monotonous crawl, alighted, and accompanied the cart on foot, walking at the mule's head, with her sun-bonnet tilted over her face, and her thoughts miles away—say as far as Ballyredmond. Proceeding in this somewhat absent fashion, it came to pass, that in turning a corner she nearly fell into the arms of Barry Sheridan, who, taking her for what she represented at the first glance, exclaimed, "Hullo, my Beauty, 'tis yourself;" but, "The deuce!" "The devil!" were his concluding ejaculations, as he recognized the Crowmore mule, and something familiar in the cut of the market-girl's pink sun-bonnet—not to mention the face that was under it. Finding herself fairly caught, and that escape was out of the question, Helen resolved to make a virtue of necessity, and to brazen it out to the best of her ability.

"What the mischief does this mean?" he blustered, authoritatively.

"It means that Sally has hurt her foot," she returned, with complete composure, and speaking in her natural voice, "and I have been her most successful substitute."

"Bother your long words! Do you mean to tell me you have been selling vegetables and butter in Terryscreen?"

"I do," she answered gaily.

"Then, not alone old Malachi, but every mother's son in Crowmore is mad. I'm blest if I ever saw anything to beat *this*," surveying Helen, and her costume, and her flatteringly empty cart, with wrathful amazement.

"You need not be alarmed, no one recognized me, excepting Larry Flood—the cat is *still* in the bag, unless you let it out."

"What put it into your head to go play-acting about the country, along with the market-cart? What did you do it for?"

"Merely to make money; an article that is rather scarce at the Castle. You hardly suppose that I did it for a joke, do you, or for pleasure?"

"Well, all I can say is, that if I had anything to say to you——"

"Which you have not," she interrupted quickly.

"There you go, as usual—snapping the nose off my face. I was only saying if I *had*. However, I'm glad enough to meet you in any shape—alone."

Helen glanced at him nervously, and waited to hear the sequel to this rather significant remark.

"You see, up at the Castle, you have Dido pinned to your elbow all day, and I never get a word with you."

"It seems to me that you get a good many, all the same."

"Well, not *the* word. Look here, Helen. Of course I know that you are only a teacher in a school, and have not a shilling to bless yourself with, and never will have—worse luck; but you are a thundering pretty girl, and I am very spoony on you, so here goes. Will you marry me?"

"I?" she ejaculated with a gasp of incredulity.

"Yes; you to be sure! Who else?" approaching his arm affectionately to her waist. But a very sharp rap on the knuckles from the stick she carried in her hand caused him to change his mind.

"Come now, you don't mean *that*, I know?"

"Yes, indeed I do! please keep to your own side of the road."

"And is it to be yes? Am I not speaking to the future Mrs. Sheridan?" he inquired with an air of jaunty confidence.

"No, indeed you are not!"

"Oh, I say! you are not in earnest!" in a bantering tone. "Think it over. I'm not a bad sort of fellow. I've a snug little place. I'm old Malachi's heir. I'm quite a catch, I can tell you—you might do worse."

"Impossible!" she exclaimed scornfully.

"Do you mean to tell me you are serious; do you mean me to take no in earnest? For, mind you, I'll not ask you *again*," speaking with angry vehemence.

"I really mean no! You may consider that the honour is declined."

"And pray, why did you encourage me, and pretend you were fond of me, eh?"

"You must be out of your senses to say so."

"Not a bit of it! You did encourage me, flirting and arguing, and making sharp speeches just to attract my notice and draw me on; why any one could see it with half an eye!"

At this amazing statement the little remnant of the lady's temper completely gave way, and halting in the road, and turning to him with blazing eyes, she said,—

"Mr. Barry Sheridan, a few plain truths shall be spoken to you for once in your life. I would not marry you if you were a king. You are rude; you are ignorant."

"No, I'm not," he interrupted furiously.

"Yes, you are," she continued inflexibly. "Only last night I heard you pointing out the constellation of O'Brien's belt! and you cannot spell two words; you are ignorant and boorish. This may be your misfortune, not your fault; but it *is* your fault that you are selfish and overbearing, and as vain as the frog in the fable. You imagine, you poor blind ostrich," mixing her metaphors in the heat of her irritation, "that any one of the girls in the county would marry you! If you asked them, they would laugh in your face.—If you do not believe me, you can make the experiment, that's all.— You will have to improve very much indeed, before you may aspire to the hand of any *lady*, however penniless." So saying, she lightly hitched herself up on the cart, gave the mule a bang with her stick, and rattled noisily away.

Helen's return was hailed with acclamation; her cousins, who had long been on the look out, met her at the gate, and escorted her to the kitchen, where she poured out her earnings and rendered a faithful account of her dealings to Sally—Sally, who cross-examined her sharply, and was transparently jealous of her success. Indeed, the only poor consolation left Miss MacGravy was, that her deputy had failed with the "sparrow-grass."

"One and sixpence, miss, I tould ye, and ye took the shilling! however, ye were clever with the cauliflowers, and on the whole, ye done well!"

"I should rather think she *had* done well!" said Dido, sweeping up the silver. "What are you going to say to them next week, Sally, when they all come asking for the smart new girl?"

"Oh, faix, it's not many will do that, they are mostly too earnest after bargains—but if they do, I'll just tell a good one when I go about it, and face them all down, that there was ne'er a one in it, but myself!"

"You won't find it easy to make them believe that," said Dido emphatically; "that would be a *good* one with a vengeance!" taking her cousin by the arm and leading her affectionately to the upper regions, where a delicate little repast awaited her.

Helen having given her relatives a modified account of her adventures (in which she dwelt on Larry's ferocious guardianship, but skipped all mention of the two most thrilling incidents of the day, *i.e.*, Gilbert Lisle's unexpected appearance, and Barry's unwelcome proposal), was considered to have richly earned the right to enjoy an afternoon of pure and unalloyed idleness. The white blinds in the drawing-room were pulled down to keep out the sun, the sashes were up to admit a little breeze, and she lay back in a comfortable chair, watching Dido's busy fingers at work.

Presently her cousin looked up, and said, "I don't know whether it's the colour of the blinds, or what, Helen, but you look completely done up. I'm afraid that adventure this morning was too much for you!"

"Oh, no, not the least—my arms are a little stiff from driving the mule, that's all, *tough* is no name for him!"

"Only fancy your making nearly five pounds!" laying down her work as she spoke.

"I made more than that—something which I have not shown you," putting her hand in her pocket, and holding it out, with a sovereign in her palm.

"Gold!"

"Yes. Who do you think rode up and tossed it down among the cabbage-leaves, and asked for a flower?"

"Not—*not* Mr. Lisle?"

"Yes, but it was Mr. Lisle."

"And you—did you faint?"

"Not I. I stooped and pretended to be tying my shoe the moment after I recognized him. Of course he may have been staring at me for five minutes, for all I know. No doubt he thought the market-girl had a look of his former sweetheart, and he threw her a sovereign, as a kind of little salve to his conscience," contemptuously balancing the said coin on her middle finger.

For quite two minutes Dido did not answer. There was not a sound in the room, excepting the lazy flapping of the window blind. At length she said rather reproachfully,—

"Helen, I think if I had once cared for a person, as you certainly did for Mr. Lisle, I could not speak of him so bitterly."

"I am sure you could not! But you are naturally far more amiable than I am, and your illusions have never been shattered. The last two years have hardened me. I seem to stand alone in the world. I have no protector but Helen Denis. I use my natural weapon, my tongue, rather mercilessly sharp, cutting speeches seem to slip out of my mouth unawares, and they hurt no one half as much as they do me, afterwards,—when I am sorry!"

"I never heard you say anything sharp, until that speech about Mr. Lisle. Now that he is in the country, how will you meet him?"

"Certainly not 'in silence and tears,' like the individual in the song; most probably with a smiling allusion to our former delightful acquaintance."

"Now, Helen, you know you won't."

"No! Well then we shall probably shake hands, and say—'How do you do? What lovely weather we are having.' That will be all."

At this moment the door was thrown open with a violence that shook its ancient hinges, and Katie, who had been absent ever since dinner-time, burst into the room. She was breathless with excitement, her cheeks were crimson, and there was certainly a spark of triumph in her eye.

"Girls!" she gasped, "what do you think has happened? No, I'm not going to let you guess, because I can't keep it another second—Barry has asked me to marry him!"

An awful pause ensued, and then Dido said, in a sharp voice, "And of course you said no!"

"And of course I said yes! Only imagine my having a proposal before *you*, Helen!" darting an exultant look at her pretty, pale cousin, who now suddenly unclasped her hands from behind her head, and sat up erect, and looked at her with eyes wide with horrified surprise.

Vanity is one of those curious elements in human nature which defy every rule, and impel the victim into the most unexpected courses. Barry had been put upon his mettle, and he was resolved to show Miss Denis her mistake at any cost. Accordingly he offered himself to the very first young lady he met, who happened to be her cousin, Katie, and here, within four hours of Helen's scornful rejection of his hand, he was engaged to a girl under the same roof as herself! The long exciting day, the unexpected encounter with Gilbert, Barry's proposal, and Barry's revenge, were too much for her over-wrought nerves; to the horror of Dido, and the amazement of Katie, their cousin received the news—and she, who had always been so *down* on Barry—in a storm of hysterical tears!

The next day brought the successful suitor to Crowmore to receive the congratulations of his friends; his attitude was one of sulky triumph as he nodded his acknowledgements of Dido's tepid felicitations, and Biddy's brief greeting—Biddy, who had more than once imparted to the bride elect that "she would not grudge Mr. Barry a good bating, to take the concate out of him!" For once he obtained an interview with his uncle, and then he sought Helen,—but at first she was nowhere to be seen! All the afternoon she had been digging dandelion roots out of the gravel, with a kitchen knife, a weary, exasperating performance, and now, with an aching back, she was enjoying well-earned repose under a beech-tree on the lawn. She had scarcely begun to realize the delight of this exquisite August evening, scarcely turned a page of her book, when, to her great disgust, she heard a loud "ahem," and, looking up, beheld Barry—Barry, gazing at her with angry, vindictive eyes! His recent penchant had been speedily replaced by a good, sound, substantial hatred, which he was at no pains to keep out of his countenance. Helen raised her head and looked at him, and beheld defiance in his port, and triumph in his glance. No rebuff, no rejection, could quench the unquenchable.

"So you see you were wrong!" he sneered; "who is the ostrich now—who is the frog, eh? I wonder you are not above calling people names!"

"Go away, and don't dare to speak to me, sir!"

"But I will speak to you!" he retorted defiantly. "You see, with *all* your fine talk, the very first girl I asked took me, and was glad of the chance!"

Helen merely lifted her eyes again and looked at him with frank disgust.

"I'm going to live here; the old fellow agrees. Katie is his favourite daughter, and any way, it is high time to take the money out of his hands, and that there was some sane person over the property! I shall give Darby Chute the sack," he grinned at Helen, and she read in his eyes that she would undoubtedly "get the sack" also.

"Of course you'll say nothing to them about yesterday," dropping his tone of authority for one of querulous entreaty, as his eyes fell on Dido and Katie, hurrying across the lawn. "You keep what I said to you to yourself?"

"Need you ask?" she returned scornfully.

"Come away from under the tree, and sit upon these shawls!" cried Katie. "That bench is so unsociable. Here," spreading it as she spoke, "is one for you and me, Barry, and you may smoke, to keep away the midges."

"I don't want *your* leave to do that," was the gallant reply as he flung himself heavily at the feet of his lady-love, and commenced to blow clouds of tobacco into the air. Presently he said, "How much did the cow fetch, Dido?"

"Only sixteen pounds—I'm *so* disappointed; but Darby said he was glad to get it, as there were no buyers of dairy stock—only shippers——"

"Sixteen pounds!" echoed Helen. "Are you sure?"

"As sure as any one *can* be, who has the money in their pocket. Darby brought it up this afternoon."

"Then, Dido, Darby has robbed you—robbed you shamefully! I overheard him sell the cow yesterday, and I meant to have told you, but other things put it out of my head; he sold her for twenty pounds—no wonder people say he has feathered his nest!"

"Oh, Helen," cried Dido, in dismay, "what is this you are telling me?"

"Just what I've been telling you for the last year, and you would not listen to me," said Barry in a loud voice. "I always knew he robbed you out of the face!"

It does not often happen that twice within twenty-four hours, a man's predictions are fulfilled to the letter—Barry's star was undoubtedly in the ascendant, he literally swelled with triumph.

"I saw the money counted into his hand," continued Darby's accuser; "twenty one-pound notes, and I thought how pleased you would be, and— he kept back four!"

"I've a great mind to go down to him this very evening, and impeach him to his face. I suppose he has been doing this all along. No *wonder* i can't make both ends meet!"

"Don't go to-night," said Katie gravely, "wait till to-morrow. I hear John Dillon is about again—he shot the Crowmore grouse bog yesterday."

"I always knew that he was nothing but a poacher. Why don't some of the people try and catch him!" inquired Helen calmly.

"But it *is* john Dillon—exactly as he was in the flesh—he has been seen scores of times! Why, you saw him yourself, Barry, *you* have met him?" said Katie, appealing to her lover with judicious docility.

"Yes! and I would not meet him again for a million of money. Catch him, indeed! that's a good joke! You know the man that was found last winter drowned in a bog hole; they say he was seen struggling with a big black figure on the brink, and that it was John Dillon put him in, and no less!"

"I don't believe in Dillon's ghost—a ghost that shoots and smokes!" retorted Helen scornfully.

"I tell you what, Miss Helen Denis, it is all very fine for you to say, you don't believe this, and you don't believe that—talking is easy. I'd have some respect for your opinion, if you will start off now, alone, and walk to the black gate and back—this," glancing up to the sky, "is just about his time."

"Do leave her alone, Barry," exclaimed Dido, irritably; "why are you two always wrangling with each other? Helen, you are not to think of going."

"Yes!" returned her cousin, rising, "I should like a walk. I'll go, if it is only to prove to you and Katie, that I have more courage in my little finger, than other people have in their whole body."

"Do you mean that for me?" demanded Barry fiercely, rising on his elbow as he spoke.

"If the cap fits, wear it, by all means! You said a moment ago, that you would not face Dillon for a million. I don't care a fig for Dillon,—and I am going to meet him now!"

More than this, she was eager to seize the excuse to have a nice long stroll through the woods by herself, in order that she might arrange her ideas, and meditate at leisure—for thanks to her affectionate cousins, she rarely had a moment alone.

"Do you think you will catch him, or will he catch you?" inquired Barry rudely.

To this she made no reply, and, resisting Katie's eager, almost tearful entreaties, she snatched up a shawl, and sped away across the grass; and, as she did so, Barry shouted after her,—

"Mind you carve your name on the gate, to prove you go there *at all*!"

CHAPTER XLI
"THE POACHER'S GHOST"

"But I am constant as the Northern Star."

It was not dark, it was not even dusk, when Helen, having fought her way through the laurustinus and syringa of the pleasure-grounds, mounted the hill which lay between Crowmore and Ballyredmond. Here she paused on the summit, and looked back. What a change even two days can make in one's whole existence! Two evenings previously she had been picking mushrooms on this very hill in her ordinary, tranquil frame of mind; now, glancing down on the old Castle, Crowmore was to have a new master, and she must leave its shelter! Her annual pittance would soon be due, and she would thus be enabled to return to her duties, at Malvern House. Well, she had never intended to quarter herself altogether on her cousins! With a half-stifled sigh she turned her face towards Ballyredmond, whose gables and chimneys peeped above the trees. And so Gilbert Lisle was under that roof—probably at dinner at that moment, sitting opposite to Miss Calderwood! "Of *course* he is engaged to her," she said aloud; "Dido only denied it because the wish was father to the thought! I dare say they will be married soon; perhaps before I leave. Well, I think I shall be able to decorate the church, and even to accept an invitation to the wedding—if I get one!"

These thoughts brought her to the notorious gate, which separated the two estates. It led from the hill-side pasture of Crowmore straight into the dense woods of Ballyredmond and was at present fastened by a stout padlock. There was no sign of John Dillon; no sound to be heard, save the cawing of rooks and the cooing of wood-pigeons; and, without a moment's delay, Helen dived into her pocket, produced a small penknife, and commenced to carve her initials with somewhat suspicious haste. She was not the least afraid of ghosts; her solution of the great "apparatus" scare had effectually banished all such fears; but it was a silent, lonely place, where she had no desire to linger.

The wood she was operating upon was hard, the penknife brittle, and the process slow. She had only achieved the letter H, when her ears, being quickened by an almost unconscious apprehension, caught the tread of a footstep coming through the plantation. Nearer and nearer it approached;

now it was walking over leaves, which deadened the sound; now it stepped upon a rotten twig, which snapped. Her heart, despite her bravery, commenced to flutter wildly. Was this the poacher's ghost? she would know in another second; in another second the branches were thrust aside by a grey tweed arm, and she beheld, not John Dillon,—but Gilbert Lisle! and she felt that the sharpest crisis of her life, was at hand.

He stopped for an instant, as though to collect himself, then came straight up to the gate and doffed his cap. He looked grave, and extremely pale; and after a perceptible pause, he said,—

"Miss Denis, I am very glad to meet you again."

In answer to this she merely inclined her head. At this supreme moment she could not have spoken to save her life.

"I see that the pleasure is entirely on my side; and, naturally, you believe me to be the most faithless, perfidious—"

"The past is past," she interrupted in a low hurried voice. "Let us agree to forget that we have ever met before. I was a silly school-girl; you were a traveller—a man of the world, seeking to enlarge your experience of places and people. You experimented on *me*. It was rather cruel, you know, but it does not matter now. We do not live in the age of broken hearts!"

"Miss Denis!" he returned passionately, "I'd rather a man had struck me across the mouth than be obliged to stand and listen to such words from a woman! And the worst of it all is, that your taunts seem well-deserved. You do not know the *truth*. Look here," hastily producing a letter addressed to herself, "I was on my way to leave this for you with my own hands. I did not venture to expect that you would see me; but since I have so happily met you, will you listen to me?"

"No, Mr. Lisle," she answered coldly, "I am not a school-girl *now*."

"Pardon me, but you must—you shall—hear me," suddenly closing his hand on her wrist with a vice-like grasp, and speaking with unusual vehemence.

"Of course I must hear you, if you choose to detain me against my will! Would you keep me here by such means?" she asked, her voice trembling with indignation.

"I would! Yes, brutal as it sounds, I *would*. Every criminal has a right to be heard; and from you, in whose eyes I appear a miserable traitor, I claim that privilege. I will no longer suffer you to think me a base, false-hearted cur! There," suddenly liberating her hand as he spoke, "There, I release you, but I appeal to your sense of honour, and justice, to give me a hearing!"

Helen made no reply, but, as she did not move, he naturally took silence for consent, and, without a moment's delay, began to plead his cause in rapid, broken sentences.

"Do you know, that for the last ten days I have been searching for you everywhere, and that I have been half distracted!—At first I addressed myself to your aunt, who curtly refused your address, and made some sceptical remarks on my motives in seeking you; then I travelled down to Tenby, and interviewed Mrs. Kane,—unfortunately, she had lost your last letter, and could only remember that your post town began with a T,—which was rather vague. Next I telegraphed out to Mrs. Holmes—who replied with 'Malvern House.' Finally Mrs. Platt was induced to believe that I was in *earnest!* she sent a line to Mrs. Durand; Mrs. Durand forwarded it to me instantly. I started for Ireland within half an hour, and here I am!"

"But why?" inquired the young lady frigidly.

"Simply because, until the last fortnight, I believed you to be the wife of James Quentin! Yes, you may well look indignant and scornful; I richly deserve such looks. You shall judge me, you alone—Here," suddenly removing his cap, and laying his hand on the gate. "I stand as it were at the bar before you. Be patient with me for a few minutes; hear my defence, and then you shall say if I am guilty or not guilty.—I leave my cause, my fate, my future life in your hands!"

Helen listened to his appeal in profound silence; poignant memories, maidenly pride, trembling expectation, struggled fiercely in her breast. In the end her heart proved to be her suitor's most eloquent advocate, and with a hasty gesture of assent, she motioned him to go on.

"You remember that night at Port Blair, when we parted, as I hoped but for a few hours? Well, I went home and waited up for Quentin, and talked to him in a way that astonished him. Nevertheless, he stuck to his point, and blustered, and stormed, and swore that you *were* engaged to him."

"And you believed him?" she exclaimed, with repressed emphasis.

"I did not believe his words. What converted me was his facts—the fact that he possessed the wreck ring, and placed it in my hand. That was sufficient. I thought, when you could give *him* that,—you could not care for *me*."

"And from first to last you were Mr. Quentin's cat's-paw?"

"His cat's-paw, his tool, his fool; whatever you like!" vehemently. "I was an infatuated idiot. I mistook him for a gentleman, and measured him by a wrong standard. He told me lies by the dozen, and when I left the Nicobars I was under the impression that he was about to return to Port Blair, and to marry you at once. I went to Singapore, to Japan, to California; I rambled about the world, quite beyond reach of news from the Andamans. Indeed, news from the Andamans I never sought—*that* page in my life was closed. I came to London about three weeks ago, and almost the first people I met were Quentin and his wife! After that, Mrs. Durand cleared up the whole business.—She told me how your ring had been stolen, and she it was, who succeeded in wringing your address from your aunt, and that's about the whole story!"

"What did Mr. Quentin mean?" inquired Helen gravely.

"It's hard to say. He is a notorious lady-killer. He did not like to be cut out. He was going away, and was utterly reckless. I believe he had a comfortable conviction that he could commit any social enormity in those out-of-the-way islands with the utmost impunity. He believed that when he sailed away, he put himself beyond the reach of all reprisals. And now, Helen, what do *you* say? If you only knew what I have felt the last fortnight, you would think that I've been pretty well punished for being Quentin's dupe! Am I guilty or not guilty? Can you ever forgive me?"

"Yes; I do forgive you," she replied at length, with a little catch in her breath.

"And we will go back to where we left off that evening at Port Blair," suddenly leaning his arms on the gate, and looking at her earnestly.

To this she shook her head in silence.

"There is some one else?" he said, in a low voice.

"No, there is no one else," she answered, without looking up.

"Then you are really implacable; and, indeed, I cannot wonder."

"I am not implacable," and she laughed a little nervous laugh; "but I am a governess!"

"And what in the world has that to do with it?"

"Everything. I am not a suitable wife for a great landed proprietor like you. You took us all in at Port Blair; but now I know who you really are, it would never do. I am a lady, certainly—your wife can be no more than that—but I have no money, no connections."

"I don't understand you," he said, rather stiffly.

"Ask your friends, ask your father, your uncle, *they* will explain it all very forcibly."

"That is a miserable excuse, and will not serve you. My father has been goading me towards the yoke of matrimony for years. My worthy uncle, little knowing, talked of you all lunch-time, to-day, and wished himself a young man for your sake—not that if he were—you would listen to him, I *hope!*"

"I am not going to listen to any one."

"Yes, you are, you are going to listen to ME. When I was a poor obscure nobody at Port Blair, you accepted me as your future husband—you know you did."

"Yes; and now that I'm a poor obscure nobody at Crowmore, you wish to return the compliment."

"Helen!" he exclaimed, in a tone of sharp reproach, "you don't believe in your heart that I set any value on my money, or my birth. I want you to take me for myself alone, as if you were a dairy-maid, and I was a blacksmith. Will you?" extending his hand.

"But if I say yes, what will become of Miss Calderwood?" she inquired, ignoring the proffered clasp.

"Miss Calderwood is nothing to me, I am nothing to her; our estates suit one another, that's all. You don't suppose that I care a straw for Miss Calderwood, or she for me?" coming as close to her as the gate would permit, and looking at her fixedly. "You know very well that I care for no one but *you*; don't you, Helen?"

Helen raised her eyes, and looked at him—and believed him.

"I'm afraid you have had a very rough time of it since we parted—both at Port Blair, and in London?—I hate to think of it."

"Yes. I was miserable at first, most miserable," her eyes filling. "Afterwards I got on better, and I've been very happy here."

"But, my dearest Helen—" (N.B. from Miss Denis to Helen, from Helen to my dearest Helen, had been a rapid transition)—"Is not your uncle very" mad, he was going to say, but changed it to the word "odd?"

"Very, very odd; indeed, more than odd, poor man, but he was very good to me. I am fond of my cousins, especially Dido. Katie is going to marry her cousin Barry."

"Unhappy Katie!" in a tone of profound commiseration. "Tell me, Helen, has that ill-conditioned Orson ever dared to make love to you?"

"Never mind—I detest him—in fact, it is to prove that he is a coward, that I am here now. He defied me to come up here, and cut my name on this gate. See, I have got as far as H."

"I see! and it is hardly worth your while to add the D," he added, significantly. "Before very long you will have another initial. And why did Mr. Barry Sheridan defy you to cut your monogram on this gate?"

"Because it is said to be haunted by Dillon's ghost! No one ventures here after dusk."

"Indeed! Do you know that I came across *your* ghost in Terryscreen yesterday; a market girl who is your double. When I saw her I felt that it was a good omen, that you and I would be face to face ere long."

"Yes, and you were kind enough to toss her a sovereign—here it is," now producing it; "it has been burning a hole in my pocket ever since. Yes," in answer to his stare of incredulity, "I may as well confess to you at once, that it was not my double that you saw, but myself. You may well look amazed. Did I not play my part to perfection?"

"Inimitably—but why?"

"We," with a backward wave of her hand, "are miserably poor! Uncle's inventions absorb all the money. Darby, the steward, is a thief, and Dido has nothing to look to but the garden; every week she sends a cart to market, and it is the mainstay of the housekeeping. Sally, the dairy-maid, was laid up—I took her place."

"And when did you pick up the brogue and the blarney?"

"Oh, that was the easiest part of the matter! I can take off anything."

"*You* can?" rather startled.

"Yes, ever since I could speak; but I never attempted it in earnest till yesterday. Please take back your sovereign," holding it out.

"What am I to do with it? Fasten it to my watch-chain as a memento of the day my wife sold vegetables in the market square at Terryscreen?"

"If I were you, I would not talk of your wife before you have one," returned the young lady, blushing crimson. "I think you might give it in charity."

"So be it!" obediently placing it in his waistcoat pocket. "After all, I'm glad that you and the flower-seller were identical. I always thought you were the prettiest girl in the world and it gave me quite an unpleasant shock to see your counterpart."

(After this speech it was no longer in Helen's power to say that Mr. Lisle had never paid her a compliment.)

"And who have we here, coming down the hill with a brace of rabbits over his shoulders, and a gun under his arm?" he asked abruptly.

Helen glanced behind her, and beheld a man approaching with a black beard and peaked cap, and shrank closer to her companion instinctively, as she answered,—

"It must be John Dillon!"

And it was. The seemingly solitary white figure offered a peculiarly tempting opportunity to the ghost, and he advanced with long and rapid strides (not being aware of the presence of a third party, who was at the other side of the gate and somewhat in the shade). He was within three yards of Helen, and had already stretched out a threatening arm, when,—

"Hullo, John!" in a masculine voice, caused him to pause and recoil a step or two. "I say, you seem to have had good sport?"

John glowered, backed, and would have fled, but Gilbert was too quick for him. He vaulted over the gate, and said,—

"Come here, my friend, and give an account of yourself. It's not every day that I see a ghost! Let me have a look at you!"

Very slowly and reluctantly the spectre slouched back, and stood within a few feet of his questioner. Flight was useless; he had to deal with a man of half his age, and thrice his activity. Moreover, his gun was not loaded.

"And so I hear that you made a capital bag on our bog on the eleventh, John; what do you do with your game? You know you have no game licence and are a terrible poacher; woodcock, pheasants, hares, all come handy to you. My uncle tells me that three hundred head of his long tails were sent away to Dublin and sold last winter, and this in spite of watchers at night, and every precaution; you won't leave a head of game in the county! Now, I don't mind betting a sovereign that you have a brace of grouse in one of your pockets."

Here John, who had hitherto simply stood and glowered, showed signs of moving off, but his captor took him firmly by the arm, and leading him out beyond the shadow of the trees, said,—

"Mr. Darby Chute, if I'm not greatly mistaken! I've suspected you for years. Just take off your cap, will you? Now your beard, if you please?" And, sure enough, there stood Darby.

For some seconds there was an eloquent silence, broken at last by Helen who, notwithstanding her scepticism of Mr. Chute, was unprepared for *this* *dénouement*.

"Oh, Darby, how COULD you?" she exclaimed with horror.

"Mr. Gilbert," he stammered in a tremulous voice, "I've known ye, man and boy, and ever since ye wor a terror with the catapult. 'Twas I first taught you to handle ferrets, and sure you would not go and expose me now?"

"Why should I not? You have poached this estate for the last ten years; not modestly now and then, like your neighbours, but as systematically as if you had leased the shooting. You must have made your fortune."

"Fortune, indeed! an' how would I make a fortune?" indignantly.

"Easily, Darby! what about the white cow you sold for Miss Dido for twenty pounds, and you only gave her sixteen?" demanded Helen authoritatively.

"Arrah! what are you talking about, miss?" he asked with an air of virtuous repudiation. "Do ye want to destroy mee character?"

"It is all right, Darby, *I* was there. I heard you sell it to a man named James Casey. We will send for him to-morrow if you like."

"Faix, I see I may as well make a clean breast of it—I see that it's all over," remarked Darby with sullen self-possession.

"If you mean the shooting of the best covers in the county, and robbing old Mr. Sheridan, I think you are about right, and that it *is* all over," returned Gilbert emphatically.

"Well, sure, if *I* did not take from him, some one else would," was the cool rejoinder. "'Tis a shame for the likes of him, to be tempting poor people!"

"I suppose it was your shots that we used to hear in the woods?"

"I expect it was, Mr. Gilbert."

"And it was you who terrified the wits out of every one after dark— more especially other poachers. That was a clever dodge."

"It was not too bad, Mr. Gilbert.—Some people does be very wake in themselves, and shy at night."

"And there are not half enough knaves in the world, for the fools that are in it! You are a most infernal rascal."

"Maybe I am, Mr. Gilbert; but I never went again me conscience."

"You could not well go against what you have not got."

"And, sure, what is game but wild birds?"

"And the cow, was she a wild bird?—I suppose you sent all your bags to Dublin?"

"Faix, an' I did, Mr. Gilbert!" returned Darby with perfect equanimity.

"And who bought your spoil?"

"Oh, a spalpeen in William Street, a rale chate! he never gave me more ner two shillings a brace. Don't *you* have no dalings with him," said the culprit with heroic impudence.

"And now, what am I to do with you, Mr. Chute? You are convicted here as a thief and poacher, on your own confession."

"Well, now, since you *ax* me, I think ye might as well let me off, Mr. Gilbert! Sure, it won't be no pleasure, or relief, to you to prosecute me, and me old mother would think bad of me going to jail. Won't you spake a word for me, Miss Helen? Sure, there's no one but yourself can say a hate against me, and ye would not like to be put up in the witness box at Terryscreen."

"You need not be distressed about Miss Denis, Darby," said Gilbert sternly. "I could prove enough without her. If I do let you off, it will be on account of your old mother, and because I've known you ever since I could walk, and because the harm is done now, and to publish your knavery, would make half the county look like fools."

"Look here, Mr. Gilbert, I'll never offer to fire a shot in anyone's ground again, nor to set foot in Crowmore. And I'll make restitution on the cow, an' wan or two small matters beside, in all twinty pounds. There now! I'm laying me sins bare before you—and what more can I do?"

"You can leave the country! You must clear out within twenty-four hours, and never show your face again in these parts, either as John Dillon or Darby Chute. And, as to the restitution, I shall have a word with Father Fagan, *he* will see to that."

"Very well, Mr. Gilbert," he rejoined quietly, "as you plase. But I warn you that there will be nations of poachers in it, when I go."

"Nations or not, go you must. I wonder what my uncle would say if he knew I let you off so cheap."

"'Deed then, Mr. Gilbert, I'm thinking he would just destroy both you and me! Howd-somever, I've a brother in America, and I've long laid out to go there. So it's not putting me much about!"

"And is less inconvenient than jail! Well, I daresay you will be smart enough even for some of them."

"Shure, how would I be smart, that never had no book learning?" protested Darby scornfully. "Look here, Mr. Gilbert, if that's your young lady—and, faix, it *looks* like it—I never saw any one make a worse hand of coortin' than yourself. Raally, I'm surprised at ye! You at one side of the gate, and her at the other. Miss Helen," now turning to her, "I suppose ye may as well have this brace of grouse," producing the birds from his pocket. "And with regard to that little account you were spakin' of, and the *other* change, I'll send it up the first thing in the morning, and may be you won't let on, but it was a mistake."

"Indeed, Darby, I shall tell the whole truth," cried Helen indignantly. "You need not expect *me* to keep such a thing secret."

"Well, I'll be out of it to-morrow! so it's no great matter. Good-bye, Mr. Gilbert; good-bye, Miss Helen. You and I were never very thick, still I wish you both luck and grace, and that you may live long and die happy," and picking up his cap and gun, Mr. Darby Chute walked away with considerable dignity.

"There's a nice ruffian for you!" exclaimed Gilbert emphatically.

"Yes; and to think how he must have robbed uncle, and poor Dido!"

"And to think of the years he has been poaching the country. However, never mind him now, we have something else to talk about."

"But there's the stable clock striking eight, and I must go. And it's your dinner-hour at Ballyredmond."

"Not to-night.—To-night I don't want any dinner. (Could manly devotion go further?) I am going to walk back with you. Thank goodness, there is no Mrs. Creery to hustle me away *this* time."

To his proposal the young lady made no demur, no protestations; not even when he insisted on taking her home by the longest way, up the hill, out by the road, and in by the new avenue! The whole distance was about three-quarters of a mile; the time occupied three-quarters of an hour; the moon, a full harvest moon, had risen, and the twilight had given place to a light almost as clear as day. Seated on her own door-step, smoking her little dhudeen, they descried the "Fancy,"—and she saw them! The unexpected appearance of an interesting-looking young couple strolling down the road, was a welcome windfall to this active old woman, who instantly sprang up, and darted out, to waylay them with her invariable whine of,—

"Give the poor old woman the price of a cup of tay, your honour. Oh!" recognizing him, "and 'tis yourself is welcome home, me own darling Mr. Gilbert. Give me the price of a new petticoat, and that you may *gain the lady!*"

In answer to this romantic appeal, he promptly threw her the sovereign that Helen had returned, and Judy (having made herself acquainted with the value of the coin) accompanied the lovers to the gates overpowering them the while with shrill benedictions.

From the following few words it would appear as if the "Fancy's" good wishes were wholly superfluous, and that the lady had already surrendered.

"Good-night," she said as she paused half-way up the avenue. "You really must not come any further."

"And pray why not?"

"Because they know nothing, and it will look so strange," she stammered. "I should like to tell them first," she added rather shyly.

"Then I shall come over at cock-crow, to-morrow. May I come to breakfast?"

"Yes, you may. Good-night," holding out her hand.

"Good-night! and is that all? I am not going to let you run off like that, *this* time!" detaining her. "You have forgotten something."

"Oh, of course! how stupid of me—the grouse to be sure!"

"No—NOT the grouse!" replied Gilbert—who was far bolder than Darby imagined!

Two minutes later Helen's cousins,—who had been sitting with the drawing-room door open, and the hall door as usual, eagerly listening to every sound,—heard her running up the gravel, and then up the steps. Her cheeks were scarlet, but on the whole, she did not look as if she was flying from a ghost!

"What a fright you have given us!" cried Dido, rushing at her. "Katie and I have been almost distracted.—You have been away nearly two hours."

"Have I really!" she exclaimed apologetically. "I did not think I had been half that time."

The anxieties of her relatives had evidently not been shared by Barry, who sat with his feet upon a chair, a paper in his hand, and a look of stolid indifference on his face.

"Well, did you see Dillon?" he demanded, as she entered the drawing-room.

"Oh, yes! I saw him," she returned carelessly; "and here," exhibiting the birds, "are a brace of grouse he gave me!"

"I don't believe you!" bringing down his boots with a loud bang.

"And there's his beard!" tossing a black object into Katie's lap,—who immediately rose with a loud shriek, and shook it off as if it had been a rattlesnake.

"I'll tell you something else,"—addressing herself specially to her cousins. "What do you think? We made a grand discovery this evening. John Dillon, the notorious ghost poacher, is your esteemed friend, Darby Chute!"

When the ensuing storm of exclamations and questions had somewhat subsided, Dido said suddenly, "But surely he never confessed all this to you alone? Who was with you? What do you mean by *we*?"

Helen's sole answer was a brilliant blush; and, strange to say, this reply was sufficient for her cousin.

A year has elapsed since Gilbert Lisle stood on his trial at the black gate. He has now quite settled down in the *rôle* of a married man, and spends most of his time between Berkshire and Ballyredmond. However, his wings have not been *too* closely clipped, for people who bore a striking resemblance to him and his wife were met in Tangiers last winter; and they are meditating a trip to the East, and paying a flying visit to Dido (Dido who is now residing on the plains of Hindostan and learning the practical use of punkahs and mosquito nets).

Thanks to Helen's good offices, the course of Miss Sheridan's true love ran smoothly after all, and she was married with considerable *éclat* from the Lisles' house in London. Between that mansion and 15, Upper Cream Street—there is a cloud. Helen and her relatives exchange dignified salutes when they meet in public, but there their intimacy ceases. Mr. Lisle has forbidden his wife to cross her aunt's threshold (an embargo that is by no means irksome to that young lady), and the Misses Platt tell all their acquaintance what an odious, ungrateful creature she is, and how once upon a time they took her in, and kept her out of charity. And *this* is their reward!

Nevertheless, the Honourable Mrs. Gilbert Lisle does not forget old friends. She is not ashamed to see the Smithson Villa vehicle standing before her door; and she has more than once visited at Malvern House, and entertained Mrs. Kane, and some of her former pupils. Lord Lingard has been altogether captivated by his daughter-in-law. She is everything his heart desires; young, pretty, and pleasant. He has invested her with the family diamonds!

Barry and Katie reign at Crowmore. The place is much altered, for the better; the old lodges have been swept away, the wall is gone, the gates restored; the garden is pruned, the yard is reclaimed, and the out-offices are roofed, and filled. Katie is happy in her own way. She rather enjoys being bullied by Barry, is lenient to his little foibles, and she listens to his vainglorious personal reminiscences with deep interest, and implicit faith. On one point alone she is somewhat sceptical, viz., that Barry could have married her cousin, had he chosen;—her pretty cousin Helen, who occasionally drives over from Ballyredmond in a smart Stanhope phaeton, and seems perfectly satisfied with her own husband, and who snubs Barry, as mercilessly as ever!

Mr. Sheridan, poor gentleman, has now but few lucid intervals. He is at present engaged in an absorbing search for the elixir of life, and lives in his tower along with a companion, whom he treats with the most reverent respect and calls "Archimedes," but to the outer world he is known as James Karney—a keeper from a lunatic asylum.

Biddy, thanks to Helen's good offices, has relented at last, and permitted her niece Sally to bestow her capable hand upon "that little sleveen, Larry Flood." The market-cart has consequently been abolished, and the Master's occupation (like Othello's), is gone. He is now a pensioner at Ballyredmond, where, to quote his late charioteer, Mrs. Flood, "he never does a hand's turn, barrin' thievin' in the haggard, and chasing the cows."

The "Fancy" continues to flourish, to levy tribute, and to make a comfortable income out of her holding at the Cross. And, according to the last accounts from America, Darby Chute reported himself to be doing *well*.